Who's Lovin' You?

STEAMY EDITION

METAMORPHOSIS SERIES
BOOK ONE

LULA WHITE

First Edition 2025

www.lulawhitebooks.com

ISBN: 978-1-959784-12-8

Content Warning

<u>*STEAMY EDITION</u> There are two editions of this book. The steamy edition contains graphic sexual depictions. The clean edition "fades to black," and contains kissing and flirting, but is safe for sixteen-year-old plus readers, or those with moral inhibitions.

**This book contains offensive language and references reflective of 1976 and the social dynamics of that time that are not acceptable today.

This is a work of fiction referencing real events to lend authenticity and meaning to the story's themes and messages, but many plotlines and figures have been dramatized and reimagined for entertainment. Harlem, Bronx, and many of the restaurants and locations mentioned actually exist. However, all of the characters and plot are fictionalized as products of the author's creation. Concerning historical figures that have been long deceased (i.e., Maria Theresa, Marie Antoinette, and Emperor Joseph II), the incidents are complete fiction.

Welcome back to another dance in these pages, Loves. I've missed doing this and I'm so glad to be back.

As always, *of course*, there's a playlist for this yummy love story.

This playlist is not set in stone, and it'll likely grow and evolve the first few weeks after release, as I expect some of you gems to suggest songs of your own that resonate in a scene or a moment in the story. That's kind of the point of this novel—coming together for nostalgia, feel-good, and our young, audacious dreams.

You won't see Grandmaster Flash and Sugar Hill Gang on the playlist because the first hip hop records weren't produced until 1979 and 1980, and this book is set in 1976, when disco was still very popular. I almost put them on here anyway just for vibes and nostalgia, but those songs will be on the *Circa 1979* (Lionel & Roberta) playlist. Unfortunately, DJ Kool Herc never recorded his genius. It was live in the club, house party, or block party only. So I've included Kool Herc's inspirations that he played often per my research, such as James Brown and Jimmy Castor.

On Spotify it's free to set up an account and listen. If you're reading the paperback version of this, you can just go to Spotify and search my name. You'll see my playlists.

But I'm also placing the full link here:

https://open.spotify.com/playlist/6qgHP5taQAuYmte WD4f3lD

I hope you love A'Lelia and Emeric as much as I do.

A'LELIA (AH-LEEL-YAH)

Papa = Father
Pépé = Grandfather
Mamman = Mother
Meme = Grandmother

DECEMBER 2, 1976

"WHY DIDN'T the Black people have to do the draft and go fight in the Civil War like everybody else?" a curious seventh grader asked, her blue eyes alight. Her shoulders tilted all the way forward from her position on the floor, legs folded, she waited for a valid justification. "Wasn't the whole point of the war to free Blacks in the first place?"

"Because in 1863 when the New York Draft Riots occurred…" Al began to explain, but the giant door at the entrance of New York's oldest museum pulled her attention away from the tour group of students.

From Central Park West, in walked a deliveryman carrying giant boxes that stacked high over his head. They were here! The angels flapping their wings in Al's chest almost flew her down the marble stairs to grab them and tear them open.

"Because in 1863, what?" An eager middle-schooler returned Al back to the second-floor lobby area.

"Most Black men were not considered citizens." She finished her response while her mind still skipped down the list of all the tasks needing her attention over the next two weeks. "To be considered a citizen, Black men had to own a certain amount of property and meet many requirements. Citizenship was not automatic for everyone back then. So they were not eligible for the draft."

"Not even here in Yankee New York, where nig... I mean... *Af...ro...Americans...* got everything handed to 'em?" another student inquired among the school crowd from Kansas. She'd said the "Afro-Americans" syllable by syllable, as if someone had had to remind her many times.

Just beyond the students, the museum assistant director quietly waved for Al's attention and tapped her watch, for which Al was grateful.

For these next sixty seconds, she deployed her serene smile that, unfortunately, she had to roll out too often, and which never saw a day of rest. "No. Not even here in New York. Where Black Americans ride atop the clouds in chariots of gold. No, not even here in Black folks' Heaven were Black men considered citizens."

Al glanced at her own watch. As always, the clock had flown and she had no time to spare, but there was one additional point she would make sure these students from Kansas understood before they left. "However, although America did not recognize them as citizens, many Black men went to the battle lines and fought anyway. Even the Black men who were already free."

"That's a bunch of baloney!" a student insisted. "This is New York! Black people get all kinds of special stuff here they don't get anywhere else. It served New York right if the Irish got mad and burned this town to hell. My mom says Yankees do too much for too many niggers and that's why your city is broke and President Ford told you all to 'Drop Dead' last year!"

"Tommy!" his teacher snapped. "You apologize right this moment!"

"It's true!" he sputtered, fuming, his eyes targeting Al. "Say it ain't!"

"Isn't," another student corrected him. "Say it *isn't* so."

"Say it idn't so," the first kid attempted again, not getting it right that time, either.

"Apologize," the teacher repeated, her face turning Christmas-ornament red.

Al wasn't interested. As if she'd summoned him, the delivery man walked into the bottom floor again with another stack of boxes and she let out a subtle, overjoyed sigh.

"Everyone, the question-and-answer part of this tour is concluded," Al informed them. Her tone may have been a bit too happy. "I'm afraid visiting hours are over. Our usher will be happy to escort you back to your school bus. Thank you so much for visiting the New York Historical Society. Do come back again."

"Just one more question!" somebody called. "The usher downstairs said your grandfather is a famous scientist? Who invented a neat device in World War One. Is he around here? Can we meet him before we leave? Please?"

Al knew precisely which usher had set the stage ahead of her tour. Hal always warmed them up first with a story or two about Al to reduce the likelihood of heckling during her presentation.

"Yes, it's true, but since my pépé is older than this building, he doesn't get around so much anymore," Al lied behind her well-trained smile. Her grandparents' calendar was busier than hers, especially during the holidays when New York's Black social scene fired on all cylinders.

"What is a pépé?" one of the youth asked, his face wrinkling in confusion as his teacher gathered them to leave.

"That's French for grandpa."

"Why are you calling him a French name?" another student noted. "Black people can't be French! They're African!"

"Byron, quiet down now. That's enough," the teacher chastised, without correction that Blacks were capable of multiple languages and identities.

Sometimes, Al did call up Theodore Césaire to see if he was around, since he didn't teach at Columbia on Fridays. If he needed a distraction, he would stroll over from their family's building a few blocks up Central Park West, to the Historical Society's delight. But alas, she refused to call him for this group today.

"Everybody, down the stairs *now*," the teacher ordered.

Thank God. "You all, take care. Enjoy your travels back to Kansas."

Al flew down the stairs, hardly able to contain herself, her wing-tipped patent shoes taking her straight toward the boxes, where she counted that she'd received every one of them. She would wait until she arrived at the hotel and open them in front of her most eager recipients.

"You need help with them boxes, baby?" Myra, the evening cleaning woman, taking a pause from her dusting. "Them for the Annual Children's Presents program, huh? I've heard so much about that. My grandfather used to be a bellman at the Murray Hill, and he would just go on and on about how y'all really do it big for them babies."

"Yes, ma'am, they are! But don't bother with me, Miss Myra. I'll be just fine!" Al called out, already headed up the stairs to her tiny office in the very back. Squeezing between piles of folders of historical clippings and donations from families around the city, she began wrapping up for New York's famously angry winds.

"Dr. Césaire?" a gentleman's voice spoke behind her.

That title, music to Al's ears, spun her around. "Dr. Abrams, you know I've got a whole two more years before my dissertation is finished."

"It's already a done deal, and you're just walking toward it now." The Society's director was only a few years shy of her grandparents, and she enjoyed his company, even if it was just to debate the finer points of Georgian history during the eighteenth century.

"You're too kind, and I'll remember that when I'm combing through all those suffrage pamphlets this weekend."

"Not a chore for you at all. I do need a word with you before you go, I'm afraid." Hands in his pockets, today he didn't lean against the doorframe cavalierly the way he so often did for an afternoon tête-à-tête.

Afraid?

"Sure, everything all right?" Her instincts picked up the trench between his bushy eyebrows and the uncomfortable sag of his mouth.

"Things have been rough these past three or four years with the city, as you're well aware," he started.

He didn't have to say the rest. She had feared this.

"So it's finally happening."

Head hanging, he brought his eyes up from scanning the floor. "Afraid so. First of the year. We won't be closing fully. The facility will still be open to professional researchers. Of course, that includes you. But we'll no longer give tours or admit the public until we can find the cash to keep the lights on. We'll keep a skeleton staff of just four, and all of us will have our hours cut." The pain sank his shoulders. "If there's anything the Society can do to support you, we're always a call away. You know, I'll probably draw my last breath roughing up your grandfather at chess, so you'll always know where to find me."

"We'll reopen sooner than you think," she reassured him in a light hug. This museum had been her second home for years when she hadn't been away studying.

It had been her idea to bring her family's memorabilia and collectibles here to New York's first museum. Now, on her way out, she toted her resource books past the display cases holding her great-great-great grandmother's shoes, breeches, and saber.

Myra held the door open. "You'll find something else in no time, Ms. Césaire. We sho is mighty proud o' you and your family, with everythang y'all do in this city. God is gonna shine His light on y'all real bright," she said, with a kiss on the younger woman's cheek.

"Thank you so much, Ms. Myra. I'll keep you and Mr. Earl and the grandbabies, in my prayers."

Sucking in, Al inhaled the warmth a final time and threw open the door.

Her breath was instantly devoured in bone-chilling cold. She needed two more trips back inside for cups of hot water to unfreeze the metal door on her mother's car. For several more minutes, Al shivered on cold leather seats. With numb fingers and toes, she steered away from the Upper West Side.

Arriving at the Murray Hill Hotel, where some of the children already exited their cars and spotted her. Their eyes grew at the sight of boxes on her backseat. Their parents scolded them to stay back, to no avail. Like excited bells ringing, they hung off the edge of the curb, itching to throw open her car doors, their joy squelching Al's earlier frustrations and uncertainty.

Despite the down times across the city, it was still Christmas. The Black families of New York would come together for one of its most sacred traditions, what had sustained them for more than a hundred years. Nothing could shut down the Annual Christmas Children's Presents.

~

The bellman barely had time to open Al's back car door. One of the youth beat him to it.

"Be careful, and hold it tight!" Al warned while dropping a few dollars inside the Salvation Army red bucket. The hotel's massive steel doors were flanked with cypress trees and a stunning wreath, all twinkling in Christmas lights. Inside the lobby, a wonderland of life-sized ornaments welcomed them. More parents and grandparents eased up, ready to crack into the boxes at last.

"There's our beautiful A'Lelia!" Miss Clara did a dance, shaking her hips from side to side. "Come on in and let's see what we've got!"

For the last four years that she'd directed the Presents, Al didn't allow them to pick their own uniforms, and they were a surprise. Annoyed the first year when they didn't know what to expect from Al, the parents now viewed the Presents box-opening right up there with opening their Christmas presents.

But more important than what was in those boxes, were the long, tight hugs.

"How you doin', baby?" Miss Clara murmured.

"Better now, Miss Clara," Al replied, her eyes closed, grateful to finally be among those she'd known her entire life.

"All right, all right! It's time! I've been waiting since August!" newly minted Senator John Hayes said over all the heads. "As many daughters as I've put through this program, I should get the first look!"

"No jumping the line, Senator Hayes!" Miss Clara called with a proud grin on her way to hug him. "You may have won the vote in November, but in here, you'll wait, right along with the rest of us."

"My new status is supposed to get me free donuts, good vittles, and the first look at these Presents costumes."

"No, but it'll get you school pick-up duty next week," another parent replied.

"Everybody, are we ready?" Al held up a pair of scissors. "Who wants to help me do the honors?"

Younger kids' hands shot up.

"Tarvis, why don't you come over?" She picked the smallest one. Covering his hand with hers, Al guided him, and they sliced through the tape.

More parents streamed in, unwrapping their kids, their attention on the boxes even as they greeted one another.

He held up one of the boys' tuxedos, this one crimson and embellished with gold, to a round of applause from the parents.

"Let us see the girl costumes!" One of the children rushed to pull out a rich cranberry ballerina tutu. The floodgates opened, and they all combed the packing list for their names and sizes, fawning over the organza, skirts with crystal rhinestones glittering in the light. Pressing the satin bodices to their chests and spinning around, girls pretended to be on the stage already.

This year's theme was "Christmas All Over the World," a celebration of Blacks who'd come to New York, bringing their stories from many parts of Earth. So the tutus for the younger girls, tuxedos for the gents, and gowns for the older girls, consisted of colors from rich green to festive orange to celebratory yellow to royal blue.

"Al, you're always outdoing yourself," Gloria, one of her Madames sorority sisters said. "Your mama and grandma will be proud. Or should I say, your mère and Grand-mère?"

"G, oh, my God." Al beamed at the sight of her old Fieldston classmate's burgeoning belly. "Look at you. When are you due?"

Al hadn't seen much of her friends this year so she had missed the burst of pregnancies since all their weddings last year.

"February, but I wish he was coming tomorrow." Behind her pregnancy fatigue, Gloria still beamed from inside. "Carl and I are so ready."

"Girl, that is going to be one pretty baby. You two will be so in love."

Al and Gloria had moved in the same circles their entire lives, vacationing in the same communities and attending the same dances and school programs, until Gloria headed off to Yale six years ago.

"I could say the same to you!" Gloria gushed. "Mama keeps talking about this amazing exhibit you put on for the mayor's party a few months ago, your fundraising over the summer, and all your work teaching about what Black women did in this city. Before we know it, you'll be Historian to the Governor or something."

A wave of melancholy rose in Al that she pushed back down.

"I love seeing your mother around town. Tell her 'hello' for me."

Once Gloria rejoined her younger brothers, Al took a moment to massage her knotted muscles. Then, she put her brave face back on.

"All right, friends," Al said, "It's time to grease the wheel and get work done. Rehearsal starts in five. Everybody, grab your lines. If you forgot your scripts, I have extras in my bag."

Children took their places while others recited their lines. Parents and older siblings who were running late shepherded in children at the back of the room.

Al tried her best to focus, correcting them when somebody slouched, mumbled, or forgot their part. But over the next few minutes, one realization set in. Ten years ago this month, she and Luke had attended their first ball together.

"Was that good, Miss Césaire?" Little Tarvis asked.

"Y-yes, that was good. Better," she lied while preoccupied.

Memories took her back to late January of this year, one memory now clutching her.

Sometimes, it's like you're a pretty prude, too stiff to shag your way out of a book...

That day, Luke had sat across from her, his face clear as an afternoon day, handsome and clean-shaven under the skylight at the Yacht Club, the scent of his cologne, The Inimitable Mr. Penhaligon, floating across the table. She'd just bought him a fresh bottle for Christmas. Until that day, she'd been sure for years that she and Luke would be married with a family by age thirty.

"A bit more to the right, Danielle," Al instructed now, so the parents wouldn't wonder where her head had gone.

"Like this, Ms. Césaire?" another child asked.

"Stronger. Head up, shoulders back, and project more. You're proudly proclaiming your Saint-Domingue heritage to the world, Ernest," she instructed.

Then, Al moved behind a giant column where no one could see her. Her hand cupping her face, she pretended to study their movements in deep thought, while she slyly rubbed away a tear.

"Ms. Césaire?"

The hotel manager was standing behind her. Swiping at her face a final time, she hoped no evidence remained.

"Mr. Granger, you came to see how it's going? The parents will be glad to say 'hi.'"

"Actually," he said, his face tense, "I was hoping we could speak." He stepped back to allow her to walk ahead. "Outside."

"I can only manage for a moment. These Broadway stars are working pretty hard here."

After motioning for Miss Clara to take over, Al headed out of the ballroom and scanned for whichever admirer wanted to speak about the youth. She prepared to politely decline any invites for the children to perform at some church or nonprofit event. Outsiders often inquired, but the Presents had always been private, reserved for New York's tight-knit families. It would stay that way. But no one was standing in the corridor.

"What can we do for you, Mr. Granger?"

"Ms. Césaire, you'll have to forgive me." The hotel manager had all the joy of a man who'd just buried his pet. "I hate to be the bearer of bad news, but the current owners are selling the hotel. The new owners have asked me to inform you that they are unable to accommodate your event here." He lowered his voice. "I'm so terribly sorry."

Now Al paid attention. "Did we miss something in the paperwork somewhere? A mistake we overlooked?"

Pained, he replied, "Absolutely not."

"Then what's the meaning of this?" Al attempted sweetness in her tone as best she could. "I can meet these new owners and explain to them how important this event is, how long we've been coming here, so long we're one of the fixtures."

"Yes, madam, however—"

"Al, everything all right out here?" Gloria exited the doors and wobbled to her side.

Al maintained her poise, but her worry was multiplying over what this meant for a program that had run for more than a century. "Do these new owners know who our families are? Why couldn't they come tell us this themselves?"

Mr. Granger's Adam's apple danced up and down. "They left delivering the news to me, and they've instructed me to return your deposit." His shaky hand pulled an envelope out of his pocket and offered it to her.

"What's that for?" Miss Clara walked out to join them. "What's going on?"

Al let the check linger between the two of them. "You can't just cancel a signed contract. There is nowhere else we can go this close to Christmas."

"Cancel?" Senator Hayes repeated on his way toward them. "Cancel what?"

"Apparently, the Murray Hill Hotel has new owners who don't want our money." An astonished Al couldn't believe she was saying the words.

The Black cliques of New York kept an unwritten list of establishments around the city that never "had anything available," or were always "remodeling." Even though this was the seventies, the acceptance of Blacks had only improved somewhat since the fifties and sixties. Since the Black community knew those "unavailable" hotels, they only operated within a safe list of venues. The Murray Hill had always been on it, just as happy to take Black money as they were anybody else's.

Mr. Granger's face now matched the crimson holly berries in the decorations. "It's most unfortunate, but this was not my decision, and it's out of my hands. The hotel staff will help you all out with your things."

Al's sweetness sleighed out the door. "Help us out? You mean, we can't stay another hour and finish rehearsing?"

"We don't need you to help us out." Gloria glared at the manager, her tone sharper than Al's. "We need you to bring our children some of those hot apple cider cups and then leave us to what we were doing. You have no basis to cancel the contract, and until you do, we're not going anywhere."

A squirming Mr. Granger faced the group and set the envelope on a nearby table. "And as I said before, madam, they are not available. I'll just leave this here and you can grab it on your way out."

Miss Clara plopped her indignation onto her hips. "On our way out? Now, you wait just one durn minute! We've been here for over ten years. We want to see legal documentation that you've got a basis."

"How many lawyers have we got? A few of them patronize this place," Senator Hayes added. "I'll call Adam and some of our friends to file an injunction. This will be over by tomorrow afternoon, tops."

While he went to a rotary phone and spun the numbers on the dial, Al watched in disbelief as the hotel staff, the same workers who had greeted Al and the children at every rehearsal, now marched into the ballroom, shoving the decorations and props back in the boxes as if manhandling trash.

"*Don't* touch those!" Gloria snapped.

"Ma'am, we're just doing our jobs," one of the staff replied.

A small group of service workers watched from the hallway, their hands covering the horror in their dropped jaws.

Where else would they find another venue three weeks before the event? Al would not cancel. She didn't care if they held it in the middle of Fifth Avenue.

"Don't worry, honey." Miss Clara rubbed Al's back. "We'll

handle this. Like Hayes said, this will be over by tomorrow evening."

The teenagers packed up their homework they'd brought to study during down time. Some of the younger children froze, their gazes glued to the scene unfolding in front of them.

"Miss Césaire." Little Tarvis patted Al's hip, his finger pointing at the hotel workers. "They didn't say 'excuse me.'"

"Tarvis, it's…they just…" How did she ease the sting? "They forgot. They're so busy doing their important work of helping you that it slipped their minds. I'll make sure and remind them so they remember next time." No other solution had come to mind besides flat-out lying.

On the outside, she maintained her composure. Yet, beneath her bones, Al was fuming.

"Are we getting kicked out?" a nine-year-old asked more bluntly, not quite old enough to fully understand, but old enough to suspect more than Al was telling them.

"No," Miss Clara lied. "An emergency came up; we asked for help, and they're assisting us, is all." She flashed a quick glance at Al. "You just focus on memorizing your lines. We'll be back in a day or two."

The coldness of hotel workers toting out their things underneath lovely Christmas decorations was a vicious kind of irony.

Scraping her mind for a plan, Al spun around to go make some calls of her own. She would ask her meme and mamman to call up friendly news reporters and writers around the city.

"That load must be a lot. Let me get some of it, ma'am."

"We already said not to touch our stuff," an upset Al snapped, despite how she was barely juggling two boxes stuffed with Christmas scripts, chorus books, fake candles, and robes. "We've got it."

Mostly White hotel patrons stood around the lobby gawking at her and the children. Al hurried to remove the youth from this embarrassment as soon as possible.

Somewhere in the corner of her eye hovered a white-jacketed hotel worker. "Seems you're having trouble with all that. At least let me get one of them."

Distracted, Al scanned the lobby for another phone. "My trouble is not the boxes. My trouble is your new boss. If you can't bring him to me so I can speak to him, get out of our way." The moment she said it, she tripped over somebody's scarf, and her entire box of contents spilled across the marble floor.

They both dropped to start picking up items at the same time.

"Ow!" She'd bumped heads with this hotel worker, and now her forehead blared.

"Mmph. Sorry about that."

"Sorry doesn't cut it. I had already told you I've got it." Fuming the hotel had sent this guy to try and work her, Al shot out her arms to block him from touching anything else. Still not bothering to lift her gaze while fussing, she duck-walked across the floor, shoving things back in her box. "If you really want to help, go tell your boss to make this right or we will sue him."

"What?" he asked.

When Al shot up from the floor, her eyes finally met his.

On the other side of the box stood a worker in a uniform slightly different from all the others. The hotel had even sent one of the cooks to help put them out? But he smelled like they'd just pulled him from an antiseptic closet. Despite Al's upset, he was calm. The autumn foliage in his eyes was soothing, though hidden under long lashes that almost kissed when he squinted. A tiny mole at the corner of his top lip, bony nose jutting slightly left, held her a second longer than she intended. Al could see why the hotel had sent him. He would have been attractive if he hadn't been kicking her out.

"Listen, ma'am, I'm sorry you're not having a good night—"

"Not as sorry as you *will* be once we send the newspapers."

"Ms. Césaire," one of the others called to her. "Can you do a meeting at your house tomorrow?"

"I sure can." She switched back to the task at hand.

The gaze of nosy, wealthy onlookers burned brighter than Christmas lights. Some of them sympathetic, others smug, the hotel's White patrons filled the lobby with whispers and snickers.

Fighting off tears she refused to let them see, her head up high, she marched back through those doors.

Of one thing, she was certain. One of New York's oldest Christmas celebrations was not over. Whoever these new owners were, *they* would fall long before the Presents ever did.

Two

EMERIC (EMM-RIC)

"ME AND MY COWORKERS…?"

Tonight, of all nights, Emeric couldn't be late.

After the shift he'd just worked, he couldn't have been happier to see Black people in this "fine" hotel in Mid-City. He'd assumed they were all headed to the same event—the Swordsmen fraternity's interest meeting. What were the odds of *two* Black groups holding a meeting in this "upscale" establishment on the same night?

In a hurry to find the correct ballroom before the meeting started, he'd run into her.

She was some kind of mad. But he did not sense ass-whooping-in-the-street anger. This woman was on a mission, a meteor carrying so much force it rocketed through her mind's eye and pushed Em out of her way.

Then, he stumbled at her silken sands of skin that curved into perfectly rounded, fluffy lips, framed by feathered curls, all designed with elegance God could not have rushed, requiring several moments for Emeric's senses to fully process her.

Em immediately assumed that, surely, some blessed man

had snapped her up and that she already wore a Swordsman's ring. Still, *just* in case, despite being hella late *and* not knowing where he was going, he'd checked. Good Lord.

He'd wondered if those perfect curls were a wig. Late or not, he was hellbent on finding out. So he'd bumped her head with his to see if the hairline shifted back. He might have done it a little too hard, though. When she rubbed her forehead, he'd gotten his answer.

Now, he roamed the corridors for Ballroom B with her fragrant honeysuckle and magnolia lingering in his nostrils, the best thing he'd smelled in the few months since he'd moved to New York.

In a hurry for the meeting, he approached somebody for directions.

"Oh, perfect!" the hotel guest said. "My wife and I need extra arms. Can you carry these out to the valet?" The man held out his boxes and large shopping bag, staring at Em with expectation to take them.

On the other side of those items stood Emeric, not wishing to be labeled as "rude," not even in this circumstance where someone had been rude to him by assuming.

"Uh…I…I can grab an employee who'll do that for you."

"Oh," the White man stated, shocked, "that's why I grabbed you. Are you going to get these, or should I get your boss?"

Em bit his tongue to avoid asking how the man was certain Emeric wasn't the boss. "I'm late for a meeting. Do you know where Ballroom B is?"

Em entered the Swordsmen's interest meeting thirteen minutes after it started.

"Young brother, you're late." The sign-in Swordsman tapped his pen on his wristwatch with that chastising expression Black elders had down pat.

"I ran into another event and thought that was this one."

"Whatever the case, we don't accept tardiness in our ranks. Don't make that a habit. I'll excuse it this one time. Straighten your tie." The older gentleman next aimed his pen at Emeric's chest. "You planning on somebody having a medical situation tonight, brotha? Where's your black bag?"

Emeric dropped his gaze to his chest. He was still wearing his doctor's jacket. He'd rushed out of the hospital in a hurry to get here on time. Now, he understood why people thought he worked here.

"Thanks," he mumbled. So damn embarrassing when he was trying to make a first impression with one of the most exclusive men's clubs in New York. But more important than that, he needed one of these men to help him.

For the next two hours, he listened to the speeches, songs, history, membership list over the last forty years since their creation, and the list of the rigorous qualifying activities during several weeks of initiation. All while struggling not to fall asleep. Em had only attended this meeting because his aunt had insisted. He wasn't sure he'd even stay in New York, let alone go through some intense pledging process.

After the meeting, one of the older brothers approached him.

"You the new cat coming out of Meharry?" He passed Emeric the Swordsmen fraternity's application packet and materials. "Your family is the Shipmans, right? Used to be up in Sugar Hill? Your aunt is Dee Shipman, but her last name is Perry now?"

"Yessir, that's her. The one and only."

"I'm Dr. Franklin, the new Chief of Surgery at Harlem. She told me to look out for you. I hear you're over at Hillside."

"Dr. Franklin! Man!" Ecstatic, Em nearly shook the man's hand off. "I applied for my residency there, but you guys turned me down." A lot of these northern hospitals had rejected him, despite his high board scores and graduating from medical school ranked third in his class.

The older man shook his head in a tacit apology. "Your packet was impressive. Fraternity president, Fulbright scholar, your Southern community healthcare initiative and all that, I enjoyed reviewing you. We actually had a surprise couple of openings on our team."

After what had been a brutal first five months, Em was bursting at the seams to leave his assignment. As impossible as that might have been, he *had* to try. He'd had no idea when he applied that Hillside Hospital was the literal back alley of New York hospitals, stuck in the Lower East Side, home to an insane asylum from the 1700s. He could not stay there another two years.

The elder surgeon continued. "But I wasn't the only one on the selection committee, and it came down to five people. It was a tough call, and you know the song and dance. You're not from around here, didn't go to any of the schools, didn't personally know any higher-ups. We couldn't accept you ahead of kids who were born here, or who either came from Yale, or Harvard, and damn sure not ahead of kids from Columbia right up the street."

Dr. Franklin placed a hand on Em's shoulder. "Plus, you know how hard it is to leave an assignment. You would be breaking your legal contract you signed."

"I'm well aware, but I'm sure *you* must know how *we* are treated at Hillside." Emeric bucked his eyes to hint at what he didn't say. Rather than performing surgical operations, he was scraping dead skin from patients for surgery prep.

The senior surgeon's silence, several seconds long, confirmed he did know what Black residents endured.

"Hang tight, pay your dues while we keep an eye on you. Get your name out there these next two years. I'll have you on your next go 'round."

Colder than New York frost, that letdown blew through Em. "You gotta be kidding me."

He shouldn't have said that out loud, but he'd hoped his aunt's connections around the city could get him out of this assignment and into something better.

"Chin up, man, it's not all bad," Dr. Franklin said. "That's why you're here tonight, right? For some brothas to help you through. What are you doing with yourself after hours?"

"Uh…shh…" He was too crushed by the bad news to think straight. "I'm into books." But he hadn't touched any since he'd been in New York. "Plus, I collect model trains. But these days, sleeping is mostly it."

He also missed his mama's cooking, inside jokes with his sisters, the skating rink with his classmates, backyard barbecues, and playing with his nieces and nephews.

The older man chuckled. "Sounds about right for those first two or three years on the rounds. You made a good call coming to New York. Go meet the fellas and get to know the players. Your Aunt Dee attends church at Mount Bethel, right?"

"Yeh, yeh. Uptown. That's it."

"They hold a health clinic on Saturday mornings. The Swordsmen and some other guys volunteer there a few hours some weekends. It's a good way to meet doctors working their way up the ranks like yourself. You'll make some solid connections." With a slick side grin, the chief rocked back on his heels. "Might even be some stone foxes in there, if you're interested in that."

Only as necessary. Em loved women, but he was the youngest boy in a house full of sisters. He didn't have the headspace for a woman, or constantly reassuring her he wasn't out cheating after every late shift.

"I guess a honey here and there keeps that blood pumping strong, right?" He stared around the ballroom at all the bright-eyed Swordsmen hopefuls, shaking hands and laughing while Em fished his hopes out of the gutter.

"That's the spirit, Doctor…what is it?"

"McPherson," Em answered.

The senior doctor nodded. "I'll be expecting your application come January, Dr. McPherson. I know your aunt is taking good care of you, but if you need anything else—advice, a strong drink, to shoot a little pool—give me a ring. Let me introduce you to one of our frat. He got here a year ago. Harold!" He waved over another guy. "Come over here, man. This is Emeric McPherson out of Memphis. He's only been in town for a minute. Why don't you fellas take him out for drinks. See that he gets his bearings."

Crestfallen, Em declined. "Thanks for that, but I should get home."

In his head, a lone voice was already declaring victory. She would say she had been right.

Harold extended his hand. "We'll hook you up. A few of us are headed to the West side for grub and drinks. You want in?"

For a split second, "no" sat on the tip of Em's tongue. After the disappointing news Dr. Franklin had just given him, he only wanted to be alone with the Jack Daniels he kept hidden in his suitcase. He needed to figure out this New York thing.

On the other hand, he was stuck in this city. He needed to start making friends, or at the very least, some valuable connections.

"Yeh, where at?"

On the car ride up Lexington Avenue, he passed beggars on the street and people his age singing in the cold, warming their hands over dumpster fires. Golden flickers of light in boarded-up buildings and broken windows told a story far different than the vibrant New York in *The Godfather* and *The*

Jeffersons. He'd found himself wondering where was the "up" that George and Weezy were movin' on to.

Emeric knew crime and deterioration existed in every city, especially his home town. He simply had not expected this much of it. Even some of the "nicer" streets had been left to the wild.

A street guy popped out of thin air, leaning against Em's car window in an oversized wool coat. The man threw open one of his jacket flaps.

A surprised Emeric jumped backward, over his center console, expecting the dude to whip out a gun. Instead, the red stoplight reflected on rows of shiny gold rings and necklaces along the man's inner coat.

Checking right and left, as if for cops, the man shook the coat flap so all the jewelry jingled. "I got every size, mane— twelve-inch, sixteen-inch, eighteen-inch, twenty-two inch, twenty-fo...you name it, I got it. Rangs, bracelets, earrangs, too. Gon' 'head an' gitcha pretty lady sump'm nice fo' da halidays."

"Nah, my man, thanks but I'm kosher," Em said through his window, rolled all the way up. Gripping the doorframe, he subtly pressed his silver door lock to make sure it was all the way down.

Condensation clouds escaped the man's mouth and collected on Em's window. "You sho? Ya mama don't need nuttin'? Grandma straight? You got a uncle?" The man eyed Em's new Cadillac, a gift from his parents when he'd graduated the year before. "That sho is a nice car ya got yaself. I know some place you can take it, get it waxed up real clean. They'll hook you right on up. You be da shiniest thang in New Yawk. Whatcha say, pimpin'?"

"Naw, naw, I'm copacetic. My mama straight, Daddy, everybody, man, they don't need nothin'. I appreciate it, though. You have a nice night. Stay warm out there."

And Em thought Memphis held the undisputed record for street hustlers.

His heart rate coming back down, he proceeded toward Harlem with thoughts of who he could call back home to help him fix his terrible mistake.

Twenty minutes later, he crossed One Hundred Tenth to the Blacker side of the city and East Harlem. The farther North he journeyed beyond the Upper East Side of Manhattan, the more dilapidated, crumbling, and abandoned buildings that greeted him. Hanging a left turn from Lexington onto One Hundred Twenty-Fourth Street, he drove over some of the most famous cross streets in the world—Park Avenue, Madison Avenue, and Fifth Avenue.

Finally, he hit the popular Lenox Avenue, the North-South route through Harlem, or "Harlem's Heartbeat," what Langston Hughes had called it in "Juke Box Love Song." Before spinning that right turn, Em waited for the preacher on the street to finish screaming his damnation and step back off the curb. In the never-ending paradox of New York, the Jackson Five's "Santa Claus Is Coming to Town" blasted from a lightless building covered in graffiti, plagued with busted windows. Santa might have bypassed it his last few trips.

Em rode up in front of the Art Deco neon sign that trumpeted the legendary Lenox Lounge. His Aunt Dee and Uncle Ike had already brought him here, told him stories of how it once brimmed with the likes of Count Basie, Duke Ellington, James Baldwin, Dizzie Gillespie, Miles Davis, Billie Holliday, and Malcolm X. But those were not the folks in here tonight.

Concerned about his car, he parked as close as he could to the front window so he could occasionally peek out and check.

"Man, get on in here!" Harold called to him from the door. "That car's not goin' nowhere!"

Once he was inside the zebra-print walls and velvet booths, the introductions started.

A loudly dressed guy stuck out a hand. "Lionel, man. Born and raised right here in New York, never leaving. What you eatin'? I'm hungry as hell. I heard about you showin' up to do surgery at the check-in desk," Lionel cracked.

"Damn, already?" Em put in his order and included a Scotch. "How much time y'all spend on business and how much y'all spend gossipin'?"

"I got enough dough to waste time on both, youngblood. Don't worry, one day, you'll get there." Lionel's smile was cocky. Decked out in a copper velvet blazer, accentuated with a butterfly collar on a silk satin shirt, this dude had an ego louder than his voice. "What kind of doctoring you do?"

"General surgery," Em answered, "and what do you do that's got you so moneyed? I might want a piece of that."

"He does his daddy and his granddaddy," another guy, Brent, piped up.

The others fell out guffawing over their drinks.

"And his great-granddaddy!" Harold chimed in.

Lionel flipped them all his middle finger. "Real estate, bruh."

"He turns a profit…every now and then," Brent interrupted, clearly the prankster of the bunch. "The man's question was what do you do, not what do you *try* to do."

Brent and the others busted up again. Though Em was exhausted, the familiar sound of brothers acting up was the shot he didn't know he'd needed.

The waitress finally brought out their plates, and Em was more than ready. Once she set down chili-grilled shrimp prepared in garlic oyster sauce over rice and string beans, stuffed catfish loaded with crab meat and shrimp in wine garlic sauce, Harlem Southern-fried chicken wings with waffles, collard greens, and mac and cheese, they all tucked in their ties and swapped plates to share it family-style.

For Emeric, the taste didn't quite land where it needed to in his soul, but it was far better than what his aunt would cook.

"So what you got goin' for the holidays, man?" Harold asked, between fork-loads. "Who you poundin' on? Found you some beaver yet?"

"Chilling with my aunt and the family. As for…a woman…" This was his first night out with people who weren't family or fellow residents. Too tired from his new schedule, shagging had been the furthest thing from his mind.

Until earlier that evening.

Magnolias and honeysuckle and turquoise eyes sang Christmas carols in his head now.

"Oh, damn." Harold observed him. "He over there thinkin' 'bout *some*body."

"Nah, man, I just…can't even remember the last time I…" He shouldn't have been admitting this to a table full of guys. "I've just been real busy since I moved here, is all."

"Hell, no man is ever *that* damn busy." Lionel scooted out of the booth. "There's no amount of business in the world that's gonna keep me out the nappy nap. Ya hear me? Excuse me. I need to make a call."

Curious, Em asked the others, "Do y'all know who that other Black group was at the hotel tonight? They were a bunch of Black kids and their parents. They might have been rehearsing for a play or something."

"Yeh, the Children's Presents." Brent switched to his dessert, sweet potato pie. "For the kids. It's a Black New York thing, since White folks act like we're invisible."

Em took a chance with his next question. "You wouldn't happen to know who the girl is in charge?" Or at least, she made threats like she was in charge. He snapped his fingers to help him remember. "Blue-green eyes, redbone, about five-seven, maybe five-eight. I think I heard somebody call her Miss…Ce…Caesar?"

He wanted to know who she was, but now he also hesitated to share too much info. Describing her felt like he was exposing a gem he wanted to keep a secret in the vault of his chest.

"Damn. Where she at? She sound fine as hell," Filer cracked.

"Really gorgeous?" Brent dug into his pie. "Almost too damn gorgeous to be human? Nice lips, pretty neck, kind of a porcelain complexion? In the real cold months, she might even pass for White?"

"Yeah, maybe. What?" Em grew slightly agitated. "She your girl or somethin', man?"

Brent scraped the last of his pie off his plate. "So you're talkin' about one of the Césaire girls."

"Oh, it's more than one of 'em?" Filer asked. "She got sisters? Don't dillydally, brotha."

Brent shook his head. "Keep truckin', man. That family does not fool with folks lacking the proper Whiteness credentials."

"Who are you talking about?" Lionel returned to the booth.

"He's asking about the Césaire girls," Brent answered.

"What about 'em?" Em asked, confused. "What's wrong with 'em?"

Lionel resumed with his own dessert. "The Césaires have been in New York since before New York was *New York*. Just like we have."

Em's curiosity kept pushing him. "And who are you?"

"The Middletons. My people have been here a long time, since before the Revolution. The Césaires came here during the French Revolution. They were servants in the courts of France or something like that. I don't know too much more about them. But it's no secret they don't marry or date outside a certain pedigree. Light-skinned only." Lionel stared Em up and down. "But you check that box. You can close those puppy eyes you makin' now, though, if your money and status don't reach back at least three generations."

"Dude," Brent replied to Lionel, "your *brown*-skinned family is the same way while you talkin'."

Lionel shrugged and took a long sip. "I didn't say I was judging. I'm just telling how it is."

As far as Em was concerned, what difference did all that make? He refused to qualify himself as worthy enough for somebody he didn't know, whose character was as familiar to him as the atmosphere on Mars.

"Anyway, Casanova, we've got some get-downs comin' up if you diggin' it. You ever hear of breakin' music, my guy? I'm not talkin' 'bout that disco static they playin' on the radio neither. I'm talkin' about that *smoke*, cooked in these New York streets, a sound you haven't heard of down South. They don't even play it on the radio."

Em was glad he'd come out tonight. "The way you talk, that sounds off the hook. You got my attention."

"DJ Kool Herc, Sparkle Club, Hevalo, Twilight Zone… those boys work that turntable." Brent closed his eyes and nodded like the beats already played in his head.

Lionel's eyes lit up. "I'm opening spots in my investment club. Next week, we can discuss these it over lunch at a new spot downtown, Windows on the World. It's at the top of the World Trade Center. That's where the big boys play. Your bread needs to be big, too, partna."

Lionel waited, as if expecting Em to blink at a financial requirement.

This didn't sound bad at all. Even if he didn't remain in

New York, he could still have investments here. "Sounds good, just don't sell me one of your *unprofitable* assets." Em finished his drink. "Put me in a good one."

Harold and the others chuckled.

"Brotha, you're blessed I'm about to share with you where this city is headed, once these White boys resurrect it from the dead." Lionel lowered his voice and stared at Em. "If you want in, the time is now. My train won't be stopping for passengers later."

"I'm listening," Em said. "When is this dinner you speak of?"

"Right on." Lionel held up his glass for a toast. "Welcome to New York then, Doc. You just might have found yourself the right crew."

On his way home, Em passed the turn for Aunt Dee's house and drove farther down Lenox Avenue.

The flower shops had already closed at this hour. Slowing his car, he rolled up to the abandoned apartment building he'd driven past many times since arriving in New York. Behind boarded-up windows burned a few flickering lights. As always, he pictured it the way it would have appeared in 1936, back when it pulsated with business, famous people, and money.

I wish you were here to tell me how to do this.

Too late at this hour to step out of the car as he normally did, Em touched three fingers to his lips and held them toward the building in an air kiss.

Then, he headed to his aunt's Mount Morris Park house.

"How did it go?" His mother's youngest sister, Deidre, came to meet Em in the foyer. Since one of her children was away at college and another had recently married and moved into her own home, she had bedrooms to spare. "Did Rodrick say he could bring you over to Harlem?"

"The guys were cool." He unpeeled his heavy outerwear. "But he can't help right now."

His aunt's face fell. "Oh, sugar, I'm sorry. These next two years will fly right on by. They'll be over before you know it. I set aside a plate for you. It's on the warmer. Come sit."

"Actually, Auntie Dee, I ate with the fellas, so I'm shot. I don't remember how I drove home with my eyes almost closed." He let out a tiny sigh of relief that he'd dodged her bland string-bean casserole. She definitely hadn't learned to cook from the same family he was in.

"You're finally getting out and meeting people. You know that clinic is going on this weekend. They'd love to have you come help. You might get something out of it." She stretched out her arms.

Twenty-four hours after he'd left for his last shift, he now hugged her goodnight. "I'm doing four sixteen-hour shifts already this week." And he was due to start another, first thing in the morning. "I'll think about the church, Auntie. Love you."

"Emeric?"

He dragged his haggard body around. "Yes, ma'am?"

"No matter what your mama and us went through, I still believe New York was a good call for *you*, baby."

From what he'd experienced so far, he doubted it. "I hope so."

Finally, the bed. At the edge of dreams, all his thoughts fell away but one.

The name of this meteoric force was Miss Césaire.

EM PUSHED through the doors of the city's worst hospital at seven thirty-three. Despite the fatigue from the week—particularly last night—still wearing on him, he was excited.

These first few months, he hadn't seen any action alongside the attending surgeon, and sitting in the wait-your-turn position was driving him nuts. Particularly when they'd prioritized newer residents ahead of him for big surgeries. But a couple of days ago, he'd looked at the resident schedule and saw that he was *finally* teaming up with Dr. Berger in the OR today.

After munching up two gingerbread cookies left in the break room that he never would have touched if he'd had time for breakfast, he pinned his badge on his surgical scrubs. Carefully, he placed the surgical cap over his Afro so it wouldn't be too jacked up when he took it off, and then headed to the central nurses' station to make sure he was going to the right operating room.

"Good morning, Ms. Essie, how we doin' today?" he asked one of the nurses.

"I'm doing all right, but my knees didn't get the memo. And yourself, Dr. McPherson?"

"I'm sure those knees have a lovely Christmas break on the way. As for me, I can't complain at all." He was sure to smile sweetly at her and let his eyes remain on hers for at least two seconds since she knew all the good gossip.

He caught an extra injection of gladness on his way to the OR. He wouldn't be stuck in pre-op, bored reviewing x-rays and exams, ordering labs, explaining the process repeatedly, and dressing wounds.

Back home, he was in the operating room with Doc Lew only months into his first year as a resident. Though Em had gotten impressive evaluations and plenty of experience, Southern rural hospitals were in dire need. Doc Lew had often put him in the OR more out of necessity than merit, especially as farming accidents increased during busy spring planting season and fall harvest. Yet, despite Emeric loving the hands-on experience, it still fell short.

Finally, for the first time, Emeric would be operating in New York. Today, he became more than a smalltime Southern practitioner. Once he reached the operating room, he went for a pair of latex gloves.

"Dr. McPherson, good morning," Dr. Merrill Cleveland, the chief resident, said.

"Dr. Cleveland, good to see you. It might be a long shot since this is my first op with you all, but I'd love to open her or either close her. I've performed three hundred and twenty-six surgeries, two hundred and five with no supervision. Like I said, I know I'm the new guy, but just reminding you all." He added a laugh at the end, an attempt to avoid triggering "Black man angst."

Cleveland looked up from the sink where he was scrubbing in thoroughly. At a table stood a circulating nurse waiting with regular gloves, and on the operating table lay the patient, still awake and waiting for identity confirmation and any final questions.

"Dr. McPherson, my apologies."

"Apologies?"

"Yes, I see they must have forgotten to give you the updated schedule for today at the desk."

"Updated schedule?"

Merrill swallowed. "It's changed. You're back on pre-op."

The other residents filtered in, heading for the sink to scrub in.

"How? I've been biding my time for five months now." Em's vocal cords failing him under the surge of emotions.

"Why don't we step outside a moment?" Merrill offered.

Em felt the collective gaze of residents around the room following him out.

"What's the issue, man?"

"Yesterday, you saw the patient for pre-op, went over the surgery with her?"

His mind racing, he flipped through the faces of everyone he'd attended to, wondering if he'd said or did something wrong, or whose shoe he'd stepped on. "Yeah, of course, I remember her. Everything went smoothly. She didn't have any questions. She understood it all." Now that he recalled this patient, he remembered they'd even shared a good joke about food she couldn't eat before the procedure.

Merrill squared his shoulders. "She asked that you not be in the OR. In the meantime, we've got a car accident with a pedestrian, a few wound washouts, and an ischemic bowel you can see to. Why don't you go and help them out?"

The wind seeped out of Emeric. She asked that he *not* be? On *what* grounds? It was a question he didn't need to ask.

But before he simply acquiesced, Em pushed back. There were surgeries happening all over the building, especially in these last three weeks of the year.

"Is there another operation somewhere I can go scrub in for?"

"Afraid not," Merrill said.

"You're a—"

Emeric dared not finish that thought. Speaking truth on a job while Black could lead to career suicide. Once Merrill went back inside, Em forced himself down the hall. He and that patient had laughed together easily. She hadn't seemed uncomfortable with him at all, such that today she wouldn't want him in her operation.

A New York residency was supposed to have been a step up. New York was supposed to have been "liberal." Friendly to Blacks. A haven of opportunity and money. His brothers at Meharry occasionally told of some inconveniences in the big city, but far more often, they bragged about the properties their families owned from the Hamptons to Westchester, of Martha's Vineyard, Sag Harbor, and the 'insider' affairs. They'd sold this town as a place he should definitely try out for just a year or two, and Em had listened. Stupidly.

"Dr. McPherson, back so soon?" Essie said at the nurses' station. "Oh!" She grabbed a slip of paper in front of her and handed it to him. "Looks like there's an updated schedule. Here ya go!"

He hesitated a moment, staring at her to see if she was mocking him, if she'd known the schedule had changed when he'd first come through but withheld it the first time so he'd be embarrassed. Coming out of Tennessee, he'd crossed too many people with an ax to grind, particularly medical assistants and clerks upset that he was performing a surgery and not cleaning it up.

She popped a wrapped Christmas cookie on top of the paper and snapped her gum with what might have been a genuine smile.

"Thank you."

So began his next sixteen hours. With winter now in full swing, he spent more time checking drains and replacing wound vacs.

He simply had not accounted for the likelihood that New York was, in fact, *not* liberal.

"Honey, how did the meeting last night go?" his mother asked during his collect call home over a break.

From the lunch his Aunt Dee had made him, he shoved as much cabbage as he could get in his mouth and explained, "Yeh, it was cool, Mama. The guys were all nice."

"Did that one doctor say he could help you with this situation on your job?"

"I can't really talk now, but he said it might take a little more time." He spit his cabbage back out in a few seconds. It tasted like Aunt Dee had seasoned it in the dirt at Marcus Garvey Park. Em drained his Coke bottle to wash out the bitter taste.

"You know I can tell when you're lying to me." His mother was getting started. "Your voice isn't all hyped up the way it is when you're excited."

"I know, Ma." Biting his tongue, he refrained from firing off his most natural response to her. Instead, he pulled up the hospital cafeteria menu and busied himself with what was on it today, if only to tune her out. He was already beating himself up enough.

"Several of the boys from your initiative have asked about you. They want to know how you're doing," she said in reference to the high school guys for whom he'd created a high-school-to-medical-school mentoring program that was still going. "Doc Lew asked about you, too, over at the clinic."

"I'll call the boys this weekend once I've had some sleep. Tell them I miss seeing them, too. Alvin tells me they're doing well. I'm proud of 'em."

Emeric's friend had taken over Em's community health program when he'd left.

"You don't have to miss them. You can come back and oversee your program yourself." Her worry ticked away in his ears, louder than on a timer. "You can be home by Christmas. You didn't take much up there with you. We can just send you a ticket."

"Mama, that's out of the question for me now." Like, Dr. Franklin had told him the night before, if he transferred again so soon, without an excuse or some exception, it would end his career. He was stuck here.

In the cramped office he shared with the other residents, he could not explain that.

Seeming to read his thoughts from hundreds of miles away, his mother murmured, "There's no shame in admitting you shouldn't have gone up there, like I told you."

Pushing Aunt Dee's food around the container, he considered his mama's words that bothered him.

"In the meantime, your aunt says there's a health clinic at the church where you can volunteer." Her tone counted down the seconds of makeshift peace they had remaining. "Emeric, you haven't gone to Lenox Avenue, have you?"

The timer went off, her ultimate question signaling the end of pretense.

"Mama, I have to work until midnight, and this is my fourth sixteen-hour shift this week. Let's talk about it later."

"So you *have* gone over there?" she insisted on knowing.

"Mama, look, I've got to run. Love you."

"There's nothing special about it. I wish you wouldn't. Promise me you won't." Her words rushed out hastily.

"Call you in a few days." He hated to do it, but before her next breath, he pressed down the switch hook.

This time, Emeric was beyond her reach.

With only five minutes left on his break now, he grabbed

a container of clam chowder in the cafeteria to eat on the way back upstairs.

"Hi, Dr. McPherson."

The nice nurse he'd seen around the building squeezed on the elevator alongside him, and the horde of after-lunch staff rushing back to their shifts. He glanced at her name tag, but it was flipped over.

"Pam," she reminded him.

"Right. I've been meeting a lot of new people these last few months. What it is, Pam? How ya been?"

"Good! Oooh, that's a nice Southern accent you got. You're from Tennessee, right?"

"Yes, ma'am. It snuck out of me just then. Sometimes I forget to hide it. I can't have you Northern folks judging me like I came out of the swamp."

Pam had a nice, throaty chuckle on the other side of that pretty smile. "I wish you wouldn't. The southern flair is comforting. We need more of that around here. Merry Christmas and all, by the way. How's the residency treating you?"

"It's...it's cool." Em wasn't a convincing liar. "Keeps a man on his toes. That's for sure."

"Hillside will definitely keep your blood circulating. While we're here, there's an, um..." Her deep dimples pulled back to reveal pristine white teeth. "My sorority is hosting a Christmas party next weekend, and if you're not doing anything..." She inhaled what might have been a gallon of nerves. "Do you...would you...be interested in going with me? If you have other plans, I understand. Or you might be too tired with all the hours you put in..."

"You know, I'm honored you thought to ask me. I sure do appreciate the warm welcome. But, I actually do have some other things goin' on." *Like what?* Maybe he should have started dating to preoccupy himself while he figured out this

New York situation. He hadn't found a cuddle buddy for those precious nights he wasn't toiling in these corridors. However, that buddy could *not* be a co-worker. "I hope you have a good time and enjoy yourself."

He was hit with bouts of loneliness, but he didn't have the bandwidth right now for a woman's expectations.

Driving home at twelve-thirty in the morning, he made a left turn off of Lexington Avenue and rode down Forty-Fifth Street to avoid the guy selling jewelry out of his coat jacket. A few blocks ahead sat Times Square, all its brilliant fluorescent lights casting a soft haze on the hard streets, almost promising Em there was a light for him in the dark. Or at least, that's what he wanted to believe.

Making the right turn onto Forty-Fifth Street, he passed the Rockefeller Center his mother had occasionally slipped up and gushed about. During those times, the lights of her childhood had flickered on her face, before she would catch herself and go dark again.

His car rolled past the burning trashcan fires, abandoned cars, and streetwalkers flanking the sidewalks. Beyond the street corner's brokenness stood a glorious wonder of a Christmas tree, tall and glimmering in the distance. The Rockefeller Center Christmas tree shined bright enough to be its own star in the night sky. Just beyond it, the New York City skyline touched the crescent moon, confirmation of its refusal to let go of the light.

At Aunt Dee's, everybody had gone to bed. On the fridge message board was a note:

> *Harold*
> *212-833-4964*
> *Hevalow Club tomorrow night at nine.*

Em didn't see why not. It just so happened, he would be in post-call, with some precious hours away from the hospital. He'd be dog tired but would manage it for a couple of hours. For now, he dropped into bed, intending to sleep until at least noon.

At seven-thirty the next morning, his eyes opened. With people chatting in the front room and a big truck humming somewhere out in Mount Morris Park, he could not force himself back to sleep, no matter how deep he buried himself under the covers. At eight-fifteen, the racket had only gotten louder. Apparently, he was awake for good.

"Baby, how was dinner?" Aunt Dee asked him in the living room.

"Hey, Em." His younger cousin, Donovan, came in right on time. "Dad and me are about to clean out the garage to get the house ready for the holidays. You want to come help?"

Aunt Dee waved off her youngest son. "Go on, Don, this man has put in a lot of late nights this week. Let him rest some." With her face wrestling concern, she turned to Em. "Your mother was worried about you after you and her talked yesterday. She told me to keep an eye on you. I'm headed out shopping. You want to come? Want coffee? I can whip you up some breakfast."

Emeric suspected he knew what his mother really wanted her sister to do. "Aunt Dee?"

"Yes, nephew." Her face confessed she was anticipating his next ask.

"Mama's not here now. So can we talk about it?" No sugar-coating it.

Her hands worked the drying towel around her cup for far too long, with Dee's eyes aiming everywhere except for on him. "Nephew, it's not my place. That's between you and your mother, when she feels she's ready for you to know that."

He wanted to press the issue more, but his Uncle Ike came in.

"Dr. McPherson! We haven't seen much of you around here. That doctor life is doing a number on you. What you say about taking out some beers, cleaning out the garage, and throwing some decorations on the house? We can put on the game while we work."

Em didn't mean to be standoffish, but despite his fatigue from the late work nights, he was restless. His spirit would not allow him to spend another off day sitting idle at the house.

"Actually, Uncle Ike, thanks for including me, but I've got some things lined up for today. I should probably jump in the shower."

He just might take up Dr. Franklin's offer. Also, if he planned to go out tonight, he could use a fresh haircut. First, though, he had some personal business.

Half an hour later, he steered from his aunt's Mount Morris neighborhood and headed for his first stop, a flower shop. Purchasing a small bouquet of light-blue carnations. Since he was still in Harlem, he didn't have to drive far to his next destination. Pulling his car over, he shut off the ignition.

Yet again, he'd arrived at the dilapidated housing complex, mostly empty, with a few squatters inside. But Emeric pictured this place, not for the destruction the world had brought down on it, but for what it was before then—one man's dream, realized.

Getting out, Emeric walked to the curb with his flowers and set them down. Placing three fingers on his lips, he sent an air kiss to the memory of the *true* 468 Lenox Avenue.

Four

A'LELIA

"I AM SORRY, Miss Césaire, but we don't have anything in such a short time this close to Christmas," yet another hotel manager reported over the phone the next day.

She had called managers at the Waldorf-Astoria, Park Hotel, the United Nations Plaza, the Roosevelt, Ritz-Carlton, St. Regis, the Biltmore. She had already dropped to the next tier of hotels around the city and had almost run the gamut on that second-tier list.

"Don't give up hope, baby." Al's grandmother, Suzanne Césaire, her meme, entered Al's apartment with an armload of boxes. "Adam will win us that injunction, and then this will go down the drain. Once we wrap the Presents this year, we can start hunting for a hotel that will show us some respect."

Al's best friend and mother had also showed up to help her search for an emergency venue.

"I'm calling my leads at the *Amsterdam News* and *The Times*, so they can put reporters on this," Al's mother, Catherine, or her mamman, said. *Amsterdam News* was the city's historic, Black-owned newspaper.

"Exactly. Black folks should know to stop patronizing the Murray Hill Hotel since they're no longer on our team," Jillian, her best friend, insisted.

Mamman Catherine and Meme Suzanne divided up the family's Rolodex of contacts around the city. Jillian took to the white pages of the telephone book, with her own family's Rolodex of contacts she'd brought along.

Sarai, their housekeeper, had been at work preparing a light working dinner for the meeting this evening. Now, she brought in a large platter of one of Al's favorites—Croque Madam—a French dressed-up version of the ham and cheese sandwich. Sarai set down béchamel-drenched crisp white bread, with layers of melted Gruyere cheese, smoked ham, and a poached egg on top.

"Cut all that out and come eat. Put some more meat on those bones."

"I've got enough meat on me as it is, Miss Sarai. Besides, I can't." Anxiety twisted her stomach and she doubted she could get any food in there. She hadn't slept a wink, tossing and turning while hotel patrons still stared at her like she didn't belong there. The scene repeated on the 8-track of her mind.

"Nonsense, child, there's no such thing as a woman—especially a Black woman—having too much meat on her." Sarai set down the napkins and cutlery on the coffee table.

"Al, eat something," Mamman coaxed. "You didn't have breakfast either."

Jillian didn't hesitate to plop sandwiches on her plate and fill her glass with ginger ale. "Miss Sarai, these Croque Madams of yours are the best!"

Instead of eating, Al snatched up the phone with a vengeance, determined for these new owners to read about the Annual Presents in *The New York Times* at a much nicer hotel and to feel shame for what they did. Before she could spin a single number on the rotary phone, her mother pressed down the switch hook.

A flood of anger pooled into tears her mother blinked back, before she caressed Al's face. "Baby, I'm proud of you for holding your head up in front of all those people. You know I've been there. If you want your papa and me to go over there, we will."

Al swung her head. "No, Mamman."

The time would come for her parents to show support, but Al refused to keep begging a hotel after it had disrespected their community this way.

Mamman continued, "Then, you're doing all you can. And you *will* prevail. At some point, you will have to trust God to do the rest. Eat."

Al finally forced down more food so the others would stop bothering her about it.

Meme looked around the room while setting down her porcelain china. "Al, why haven't you decorated this place yet? Christmas is in three weeks."

"When do I have time with school, teaching a class, my research, the Annual Presents, *and* Historical Society? Besides, when BB gets here, she'll do it. That's always been her thing," she said, thinking of her feisty younger sister, in college at UCLA, due to fly home on Sunday. That gave Al three more precious days of peace and quiet before BB arrived and shook up the place.

"Baby girl, you need some life in here." Her mamman strolled to the record player. "You love music and going places, Al, and you *really* love Christmas." Opening up the sideboard she'd passed on to Al, Mamman thumbed through the vinyl records. "You've had enough staying to yourself. It's time to come out of this building."

"Mamman, I'm not turning into anything. You know how demanding the PhD program is. And I *do* go out all the time."

Al stared at the others and waited for them to confirm they understood. Instead, they stared back. Uncomfortable silence amplified what they weren't saying.

Jill batted her eyes. "Using the microfiche room at the library doesn't count as going out."

"I have work to do!" Al shot back.

"The beach is way more fun than sniffing dust in a building older than World War One."

"Don't knock antiques older than World War One!" Eighty-five-year-old Meme Suzanne raised a hand, and the others laughed.

Sarai reentered the room with several cups of eggnog and passed them around. Al's mother slid out the vinyl and laid it on the turntable, moving the tonearm over until the needle touched the right song. The Jackson Five's "I Saw Mommy Kissing Santa Claus" fired up, and Mamman started off the drinking and dancing. The others sang it with her, and Sarai coaxed Al up, shoving a cup of eggnog in her hand.

"You spiked these!" Jill slurped down some more.

"I sure did!" Sarai said, pivoting to Al. "Your turn! Drink up, Miss Al!"

"IIIII saw Mommy kissssing Saaaanta Claus…" they all sang between slurps of rum-spiked eggnog. Sarai had poured in so much liquor, Al was certain the cups contained more alcohol than eggnog.

Al allowed them to distract her from her mission for a while. Each time she tried to sit down, one of the others pulled her back to her feet.

Next, Otis Redding serenaded them on "This Christmas," the song that was becoming the official kickoff of the holidays, and Al couldn't fight this one.

"Fireside blazin' briiiiight…" she finally sang, her voice veering off-key as the eggnog kicked in.

While she and her meme circled under one another's arms, the phone rang and Al leaped.

"It's Adam," her mother reported, out of breath and putting her earrings back on. "He and the others are on the way up."

They all broke out to put things back in order and straighten themselves up. The others had done a good job of keeping Al so preoccupied she'd almost forgotten the meeting.

Attorney Adam Payton, Miss Clara, and four other long-time organizers of the Children's Presents entered Al's apartment.

"What you ladies been in here sipping on?" Attorney Payton asked. "Don't be stingy with it now. Bring it on back out here, Miss Sarai. Don't hide it now that the holy folks are here."

"Brother man, please." Catherine Césaire teased in their hug. "We'll let you know when we see some holy folks."

"Well, Counselor, don't keep us in suspense," Meme said, her face expectant. "Did you kick their butts or what?"

Al folded her arms, eager for a solution, and for her vindication.

Attorney Payton opened his briefcase and held up the court papers. Spread across the top of it was a big red stamp, "DENIED."

"I am sorry, Miss Al," he said, "the judge refused our injunction. But he will entertain a full lawsuit if you'd like to file."

"They must've bought the judge," Mamman said.

"That's the only way they're doing this." Jill squeezed her friend.

Meme huffed. "Well, we can't just cancel an event we've been having for over a hundred years."

Jill raised her hand as if she were in school. "Now, don't chase me off with a stick. But would it be such a big deal if we just gave the kids a break and didn't have it this year? I used to dread my speeches at the Presents. All the other kids would be watching, *and* my mama and daddy, *and* our relatives visiting from out of town. It was so stressful."

Al followed her friend down memory lane. "She's not lying either. One year she was so nervous she drank a bunch of water and then vomited all that on my new shoes."

"I remember that!" Mamman laughed. "I had just bought you those shoes."

Her mind made up, Al leaned into her next words. "That's what the Presents is about—the memories, being nervous, gaining our confidence, learning how to stand up in a world trying to keep us small."

Al's meme curled her eighty-five-year-old hand into a firm fist she pumped in the air. "That's my girl. We are not quitters and we surely don't let racists keep us down."

One of the other Presents board members shifted in her seat with concern. "Maybe Jill is right. If we can't find a decent location, would it make sense to have it, only to be in a shoddy building or neighborhood? That would be a bigger embarrassment than not having it."

"Who said we would be in a bad neighborhood?" Al asked just as an idea sprang into her head. "Oh, my goodness! Why didn't I think of this earlier? The Historical Society! We could use the museum!"

"It would certainly be different," Mamman said. "I don't see why not."

"Unique. Fresh." The idea excited Al more, the longer she talked. "It would be a nice break from what we've always done."

"Yes, it would. Rather than some fancy hotel, we could go to a place holding history." Miss Clara was beaming. "Good job there, young lady."

The door to her apartment opened and closed. "What's all this racket in here? You folks are in here partying like I'm already in here," Al's pépé, Theodore Césaire, fussed on the way in.

"Dr. Césaire!" Adam bellowed over his eggnog. "The man himself!"

True to his flair for sarcasm, Al's grandfather backed up and peered in the hallway mirror, patting himself all over. "Well, I'll be damned. You're right. I *am* still me. Before you said that, I thought I had transformed back to young and good-lookin'. Like Billy Dee Williams. Well, you blew that one."

"You'll always be young and good-looking to me, baby." Meme walked over and laid one on his lips.

He grabbed her fingers from his chest and kissed the tips.

"Aww," Jill swooned. "I never get tired of those two. They are so cuuute!"

Al's heart also softened into warm custard. Not a day went by that she didn't feel blessed her grandparents were hers. Since Al had become a historian studying their family history and learning their hardships and challenges, her admiration had deepened.

"Guess who I found wandering around at JFK?" He wagged his thumb behind him.

"BB!" Meme cried.

"My baby!" their mother crowed. "I thought you weren't flying in until Sunday!"

Roberta, Al's younger sister by five years, walked in the door, with the bellman towing nearly a month of luggage behind her. There went Al's precious last three days of quiet.

"I switched my last stage performance with somebody

from LA and called Pépé to see if we could surprise you. Please, tell me dinner's ready! That layover was brutal. Siiiis-terrr!" BB sang in her I'm-about-to-make-you-sicker-than-sick voice. She wrapped her arms around Al's waist.

Al hugged her little sister back and sniffed the marijuana in her hair. "My closet is off limits. Other than that, I'm glad you made it in, precious. No smoking your trash anywhere near my room."

"Youuu won't beee here alllll the tiiiime," Bertie sang in her overly Hollywood way of doing everything.

Falling over herself with laughter, Jill ate BB right up. "Girl, let me live vicariously through you! Tell me all about sophomore year in Hollywood." She cast an eye at Al and cackled. "I mean, at UCLA."

Al wasn't ignorant. She knew her sister split her time on the West Coast between the beach and the discos, squeezing in just enough school to come home and milk checks out of their parents, with claims she was studying "film."

While the others ordered more food, and an impromptu Christmas party took form in her apartment, Theodore Césaire came to check in on his grandchild.

"Baby girl, I heard about what happened. You need me to do anything?"

It was certainly tempting, and Al fixed her lips to tell him 'yes.' What was the point of having an influential family if she couldn't put her last name to good use?

"Pépé, I'm just fine." With a heavy heart, she kissed his cheek. "I'll get it figured out. Not that any of us need to tell you, but you's a mighty fine man."

Something inside Al stopped her from asking her grand-father to step in, like seeing money on the ground and a tiny voice warning not to pick it up.

He pressed her to him, and in their embrace, Al waited for his next words of wisdom and encouragement.

"You're right. You don't have to tell me. I am a mighty fine man."

"Pépé!"

His dry humor was half the engine of their family. "I also don't have to tell you we support ya, however this turns out, right? So don't be hard on yourself. You've got enough to worry with."

"Sure, Grandpa."

While the others caught up with BB, Al went to call Mr. Abrams about using the museum, but she sank onto the chair upon hearing his answer.

"The building needs structural work," he explained. "It barely meets the Code. We primarily keep it open by reducing the number of groups we let in at a time. Your insurance will never take a risk on your event. Not to mention, some of those two-hundred-year-old artifacts—such as the ones on loan from your family—require higher security. With crime around the city as widespread as it is now, those display cases need replacing. Overall, it should have a much stronger surveillance system. I am sorry, Ms. Césaire. I wish I had a happier answer for you."

The Presents would be canceled on her watch.

Sadness silenced the apartment once she informed the others.

"You tried your best, sweetheart," Miss Clara said. "We should probably call the parents to let them know. In case they want to make other plans."

"This is not a reflection on you, baby." Meme came to hold her hand. "There's no way you could have foreseen this."

Al faced everyone in the room. "Even so, one hotel should not have the right to shutter more than a hundred years. The Presents is our legacy after the Riots."

"As the oldest person in here, whose uncles, aunt, and grandparents were in that riot, and who did my first Presents back in 1896, I can tell you the building didn't matter so much back then." On the other side of the room, Pépé stared back at her.

He thumbed his chin as if rewinding the music box of his memory.

"You see, even though the Césaire family had been here a hundred years at that point, and we were more accomplished than most White people around the city—homes, businesses, properties—in their eyes, we were still colored."

Not a single noise interrupted Teddy Césaire's words. Sarai dried her hands and leaned in the kitchen entryway. His face set in stone, Dr. Césaire's aged finger shot up.

"Even though we had the means, the ingenuity, and a *much* stronger pedigree and lineage than most of 'em, they would only let us go so far. Their acceptance was *never* truly acceptance. It was tolerance, so long as we offered something they needed. We were still limited in what we could build, who would design and build it, and where we could go." He emphasized every syllable now. "It burned my papa up somethin' awful."

He stared beyond them all to an era the others couldn't see, his mind still seeing those harrowing times clearly.

"The way my pépé told it, after the Irish went on their rampage, killing Black folk, setting the Colored Orphans Asylum on fire, killing a Black carriage driver over on West Twenty-Seventh, and drowning Black longshoremen and porters in the Hudson and East Rivers, a lot of Black people left the city. But for those of us who stayed, my aunt and her friends decided they weren't getting chased out, and their children would not be intimidated. They started the Presents to celebrate those who were still here. It was held wherever families felt the youth would be safest, at whatever respectable club or venue would give us a contract. That was normally a church, a civic club, or a dance hall."

His voice dropped with his shoulders, as if he now missed *his* elders who had long left him. Pépé wiped away a tear, and Meme approached to circle his shoulders.

Al's phone rang. Not a soul went for it.

"Back when I was born, it was still quite rare if Blacks could hold our Presents in some fancy hotel. If we did, it was a real magic trick. Likely, because somebody had booked it who could pass for White and the hotel hadn't sniffed them out. But the most important thing was that we were having it at all, under threat of our very lives."

Pépé's eyes now sharpened, focusing in on Al.

"Our families were grateful just to have us present. Which fancy hotel we had it at, what the colors were going to be and all that…"

His hand and head waved around at Al, her mother, and grandmother, in good-natured humor over their hand-wringing.

"We didn't have the luxury to care about that. It wasn't a competition. It was a celebration. We were still here. We had endured. The Presents was our promise—our *guarantee*—to the world that our children would endure. The fancy hotel is just a confirmation, so the rest of the world will not forget. Nor can they ignore. The heart and muscles of the Black body will always pump with fresh blood—the talent and ingenuity of our youth. No matter how outsiders try and kill us."

Hugs closed out his reminder. More rum and eggnog were poured—in some glasses, only rum—and for the next few minutes, the solemnity of Dr. Césaire's story held the apartment.

Though Al's heart hadn't lifted, it had been refueled.

"Why can't we have it at a church?" Of course, the person who would break the solace would be BB. "Like returning to our roots."

"It's been a mighty long time—not in sixty years—but it has been done before," Meme said.

"St. Philip's? Abyssinian?" Mamman suggested the Black churches of New York that had been around over a hundred and fifty years.

"How do we know we won't run into the same problem we've been having all day?" Miss Clara asked. "That they're booked with their own holiday festivities."

Al got up and passed out old phone books, dividing up the letters for the others to call. "Only one way to find out. We won't know until we've tried."

""Yes, sir, thank you." The next day, a despondent Al placed the phone back in the cradle and stared at the others. "We're down to eighteen churches that might be big enough to host the Presents. Seven Black, eleven White."

Sitting cross-legged on the floor, BB reached for the list and studied it. "Hm. Why isn't Mount Bethel on here?"

Al looked to their meme with a tired grin. "That church would have been on Meme's list. You missed one, Meme." She had never visited, but from her historical knowledge of New York, she knew that church had been one of the cornerstones of Black New York for over a century.

"That one should be on the list," BB said. "It's one of the oldest, prettiest churches in Harlem, if not the prettiest. I visited there a few times with my girlfriends from school."

"I can call them up now." Al had no time to waste at this point.

"Dearest." Her grandmother's arm shot out with surprising energy to halt Al. "I'm not so sure Mount Bethel would appreciate your call. Maybe you should skip that one. We've run into trouble with that bunch in the past." Meme's mouth twitched like her sentiments ran deep. "They aren't particularly fond of us. As you're learning for yourself, not everyone around the city is an admirer."

Al and BB swapped their silent understanding. Growing up, they'd always had to navigate the occasional disdain for their family, mostly due to Pépé's part in the Great War.

Al set the phone back down. "Well, Meme, anybody who doesn't admire you doesn't admire me. Cross Mount Bethel off the list." Checking her watch, she saw it was eleven forty-five. "If we leave now, we can visit the top churches on our list and be back home in time for *The Jeffersons*."

"I can come with you to scope out churches, and after that, we can head to a boutique for manicures," BB suggested.

Al rolled her eyes. "Sure, I'll treat the broke college girl to a manicure."

Jill perked up. "Since there's playtime involved, I'm coming, too."

Al stared them both down. "But when we're done, it's right back here to keep working."

"Speak for yourself." BB added more decorations to the Christmas tree. "Me and some of the girls are headed to the Bronx tonight. And since your wig is on too tight, you could use some loosening up, too."

"Some of the girls and *I*," Mamman corrected BB. "You know your sister doesn't wear a wig. And what will *you* be doing in the Bronx?" In full mama mode, their mother crossed her arms and waited.

"It's slang, Ma," the nineteen-year-old replied, her shoulders hunched while she feigned innocence. "And we're just dancing, is all. Having fun at somebody's house. Damn."

"Excuse your language, mademoiselle," Mamman chastised. "You just flew in last night anyway. Why don't you give *your* wig a break and stay here?"

"I'm surprised she lasted this long without hitting the

street." Al started straightening up. "My wig and I will be just fine in house shoes on the couch, with hot cocoa and good books."

BB let out a snore. "Al, when was the last time you went out—not to see some dinosaur bones having sex in a traveling exhibit either, but really let your hair down?"

"And she hasn't even been to any of those lately," Jill volunteered. "Ever since you and Luke broke it off earlier this year—"

Al shot her best friend a silencing stare. "That has nothing to do with anything." The nerve suddenly jumping in her neck said otherwise.

BB rocked a bit, like she was teetering on the cusp of her next words. "Yes, it does, Al. What she was about to say is you're hurt and embarrassed that Luke is the one who broke it off."

"BB, quiet. You don't know what you're talking about." Straightening her apartment, she gathered up phone books, vinyl records, stray Christmas ornaments, anything to avoid being still for this conversation.

A determined BB gently locked her arms around her older sister until Al could no longer move.

"All summer long, you were too scared to go back out there." From behind, the younger sister buried her face in her sister's neck. "I don't blame you for peacin' out on jive turkeys asking why a pretty girl couldn't get her man down the aisle. But you can't stay hidden forever, sissy."

Those words smoked up Al's airway.

"For the umpteenth time, I'm not hiding."

On her knees, Jill wobbled over and joined in the hug, gripping Al around her hips. Meme and Mamman both stared at Al, their agreement tacit.

Of course, BB would be the one to finally come out and say what the others had been side-stepping all year.

"You're the finest fox in the world after me, sissy. Show Luke and everybody else. After we see these churches, let's hit the Bronx tonight and celebrate *you*."

"I don't need to party as a testament of my value, BB. I'm fine."

"Girl, go be *better* than fine," Jill chimed in. "*Dance.* Soak in the music and sweat it back out again. Feel good for *you*."

"Right on." BB nodded her agreement on the back of Al's neck.

Surprisingly, their mother clicked her teeth. "I hate to say it, baby, but this time, the kid is right."

BB jumped up. "Give me five minutes to get cute before we hit the streets. I'm already cute, but I'm five minutes from perfection."

"You're five minutes from being left," Al threatened.

"I'll make you a bet, Al," BB called out from the bedroom where she was changing. "If I can get a church to commit to the Presents before you do, you have to come to the club with..." She stopped herself, apparently realizing her screwup. "The house party. You'll have to come to the house party."

Jill and Al busted up laughing.

"Too late, young lady, I heard that!" Mamman said, hanging another ornament. "And how exactly are you sneaking into clubs under twenty-one? Who's letting you in? What kind of people? *Where* in Bronx?"

"Mamman, stop bugging out, okay? Rachel's coming with me. And you trust her."

"*Rachel?*" their mother crowed.

Jill squeezed Al while just the two of them were in the kitchen. "It's time for you to be more than okay. Don't say 'no.' We don't have to stay out too late. I'll bring you back whenever you say the word."

"I'll think about it. That's not a yes, though. I'll just wait another couple of hours and say 'no' then." Al grinned on her way to the dining room to tidy up. Placing the generations-old ornaments inside carefully, she closed them up the boxes.

A lone, yellow slip of paper floated from one of the boxes and swirled to the floor. Her jaw dropped.

She struggled to hold the slip of paper in her shaking fingers.

International Registered Letter
September 8, 1914
Leopold Césaire
Château Cesaire
33630 St. Émilion, France

"Oh, my God." She moved to the kitchen, rummaging through the utensils. "Oh, my God."

While she pulled a pair of tongs from the drawer, BB popped in. "What's that?"

"Don't touch it! The oils from your fingers will rub off on it." Al came back with tongs to pick it up. "It's something from the Great War. It looks like a mail receipt. From Leopold Césaire! He must've mailed something to Pépé."

"You mean the Césaires in actual France? Didn't he die during the war?"

Now *this* was something Al could be excited about. "Yes, he's the one. Open up that scrapbook on the top shelf."

While they stored it, their mother also inspected it. "That's from Papa's close cousin, Leopold. September eighth? That was only weeks after the war started."

"Hey, Meme!" Al shrieked.

On the couch, Meme had slumped over and fallen into a nap.

"All the action these last couple of days has her tired,"

Mamman said. "You're taking this to the museum to find the letter that goes with it? Don't forget to show Papa. He'll have to tell us what this bit of business was about."

Al poked around the boxes, checking for any other papers tucked inside. "My God. Leopold must've been terrified. The Germans were already marching in France. What on Earth could Leopold want to tell Pépé right at the start of the war?"

BB STRUTTED out of their fourth church wearing the smile of a Cheshire Cat. "Welp! Now that I've saved your butt, it's time for my manicure." She'd received offers from two churches, albeit White ones, and now she did a little hip-bump on Al's side, pushing her sister over. "I've already got your club outfit planned. You're gonna show off that bootay."

Al sighed. "I never agreed to this bet of yours."

"But you didn't say 'no' either, and it's too late now. You're goin' out tonight."

Jill was clearly loving every minute of BB being home to tell her sister the unvarnished truth.

They loaded up in Al's car and started off.

"Before we quit for the day, I want to see just one more church." Al hadn't stopped thinking about it.

"Why?" Jill asked. "This is a weight off your shoulders. You have a venue, Al. Now you can start planning and the Presents will go on. What else do you want?"

Al shrugged. "Yeah, but the church is White."

Jill sucked her teeth. "So is the Murray Hill Hotel. That never stopped us from having it there."

"That's different." Al reasoned, "How many Black-owned hotels do you know of around here? We go to White hotels because we don't have much choice. But if we're using a church, that's different. I feel like we shouldn't settle for a White church until we've exhausted every comparable Black option."

"Word, Sissy." BB nodded. "I can't be mad at that."

"Which church are you exhausting?" Jill asked.

Already driving up Tenth Avenue, Al headed toward Harlem. Tenth Avenue turned onto Amsterdam Avenue. "Mount Bethel."

Jill's surprise took center stage. "Wait a minute. Isn't that the church your grandmother said was foul toward your family?"

Al's chest twitched with guilt when she thought of dismissing her beloved grandmother. "How do we know what that's about? When did it happen? How long ago? What if it was some misunderstanding or words got lost in transla-tion? Besides, it's a church, not a military camp. There are God-fearing people in there."

"I don't know, Al." Jill shook her head. "It's not like your meme to advise you *not* to go somewhere."

That stoked Al's curiosity even more. Al rarely ignored her parents' and grandparents' requests. But for some reason, today, her fascination outweighed her obedience. "It won't hurt anything to just stop in and see what it looks like inside. I've always wanted to."

In front of the massive church, lots of cars rolled in and out.

"Why are all these people out here on a Saturday?" BB noted while they hunted for a parking spot. "Is there a special program here today?"

Jill squirmed, clearly still uncomfortable. "They're not dressed for anything special."

In frigid thirty-degree cold, a long line of Black people stretched out of the church doors, down several tiers of steps, and around the block. Gospel music streamed from the large speakers outside, and people patiently chatted and laughed while they waited.

Already infatuated with the Gothic Revival windows she was now seeing up close, Al marveled on her way inside, a tentative Jill and BB behind her.

With a stern face, one of the church's workers stepped in front of Al and blocked entry to the building. "Ma'am, people attending the health clinic need to go to the back of the line."

"I-I'm not here for my health. I'm visiting to see the architecture." Al thought strategically. "And maybe to speak to your pastor about…a financial contribution we might make to your church."

"Do you have an appointment? What is your name?"

"No appointment. My name is A'Lelia… Anders." She decided to use her mother's maiden name.

"This way."

On her way inside, Al's focus instantly hit the ceiling. Or rather, ceilings.

"Righteous," BB murmured, her eyes scanning the cathedral.

"Sweet baby Jesus." Jill ran her hand along the heavy dark wood, mahogany pews, their finials intricately carved so each one formed a different biblical figure from one bench to the next.

"What an amazing flip-of-concept from the gargoyles used in Neo-Gothic art," Al gushed.

The finials topping the first bench end were carved into angels, their wings shaped upward to meet in a point over their heads. Al gasped at the sight. The angels' faces, their head shapes, and just as important, the kinky coils atop their heads were clearly Black.

"My God." Even BB was at a loss.

Nobody had yet blinked.

The next bench finial was carved into church bells. The next were shaped into praying hands. The finials on the bench after that were an open Bible, its pages meticulously cascading over one another.

Among the recessed wall niches and sculpted marble pillars was elaborate African biblical Al had never seen before, and in her historical studies of the Black diaspora and its artists—from Aaron Douglass to Jacob Lawrence—she'd seen a lot. Only rarely had she seen biblical storytelling depict Black bodies. For that, one had to travel to remote European and African towns. Yet, here, through stained window panels, Black angels danced, worshipped, and frolicked around the risen Christ, a Black man, all in multi-colored artwork that came alive to bless this Black version of Heaven.

The stone towered high and endless until the walls and windows met vaulted ceilings in a dance of beams, coffers, and gold-leaf woodwork of flying buttresses over their heads.

The potential for what Al could do with this place far exceeded the Murray Hill Hotel. She could arrange fake candles on the stairs from the pulpit, place track lights along the pew bases to cast soft shadows, and the children would file down the aisle in their white-and-gold robes.

"Put your tongue back in," Jill whispered.

The church member returned from an office in the back and waved them forward. "The pastor will see you. You can come in."

Jill and BB started trailing Al, and the church member held up a hand, no less serious than an air traffic controller.

"Just her."

"This shouldn't take long," Al reassured them. Thoughts

danced in her head of transforming this place into a Christmas wonderland. "Cool beans."

Al entered what turned out to be the office of the pastor. Embarrassed, she realized she did not know his name, having just wandered in off the street. "Hello, sir, I'm A'Lelia Anders."

Teddy Césaire's granddaughter was never unprepared when making an ask.

She offered her hand, expecting him to return the civility. The man didn't budge from behind his desk, still holding his pen upright as if merely pausing a beat to let her speak her piece and go.

"What may we do for you, Miss Anders?"

Al had not anticipated his flatness. "I've always admired your church from outside and I was hoping to speak about using it for our annual holiday program."

Confusion struck his run-down features. "My aide out there informed me you were looking to become a patron of Mount Bethel. She was incorrect?"

Though he was still seated and Al stood over him, his gaze somehow lowered her. As if his eyes were scales weighing the value of every word, which she now understood needed to carry heavy import.

"Yes, i-in a sense, that is what I'd like to do." Al remembered to straighten her shoulders and project. "There is an event I'd like to have here. We would pay good money, and it's for an important cause. For Black youth."

In just these few moments, his eyes—a leader's eyes—sifted out grains of fantasy or illusion that failed to add up to substance.

He waited. His face being unreadable, she wasn't sure if that had gone over or not, so she continued.

"Our children have an annual Christmas program; we've had an unexpected issue and we need a venue. We would prefer not to cancel. This has never been canceled in over a hundred years. Again, we're happy to pay you all a respectable amount if you have any openings."

The scales of his mind seemed to seesaw, weighing her words, his glance at her inquisitive. "And what such long-standing Christmas program would this be?"

"The Annual Christmas Children's Presents." Certainly, he would recognize that. There wasn't a single Black person breathing air in New York City who didn't.

His pen lowered. "It's been around since 1865, the end of the war."

He even knew the year.

Al's heart swelled with pride. "Yes."

"One hundred and eleven years," he stated. His fingertips crested one another.

"Precisely." A giddy Al let out a relieved sigh. "So can you accommodate us? Our timeline is tight, and our options limited. We have one offer from a church, but we would much prefer to be in a Black church, if we could."

The pastor's gaze held her.

"And in all the one hundred and eleven years you've put on your illustrious event, you've never once invited the children of this church, or even the children of this city. Rather, you come here, not to include our youth, but to have your event in our faces. You don't want us. You just want what we've got."

The tiny air balloons in Al's lungs aired out, leaving her little oxygen with which to speak. Hence, the pastor continued to do the honors.

"You bypassed our members outside waiting in frigid temperatures for hours to receive healthcare. It's what you and your kind have been doing in this community for decades—not including our members, not offering them options for advancement that they might experience a sliver of your opportunities, only welcoming them to your homes and elite enclaves to fill positions of servitude. Only now that you've encountered an inconvenience which you equate to a need, do you finally find it within you to come and find us. And in doing so, you add insult to injury by mocking our members' circumstance and station under the ruse of making a donation."

Al reeled.

From her dizzying thoughts, she attempted a response. "Thank you, Pastor, for such a frank assessment of 'my kind.' In some ways, y-you may be correct." Along the fault lines of her inner strength, she scrambled to lay down sandbags so her emotional dam did not break. "Like m-many communities, we congregate with those we know and with whom we are familiar." Her dam was giving way. "We may not be hu…"

She refused to simply accept him diminishing her family and friends.

"We may not hurt like your members do, but we do hurt, and we do bleed. No amount of money or 'slivers,' as you call it, changes that. Our children may not all suffer in the same manner, Pastor, yet they endure challenges of their own."

Her grandmother had warned her not to walk through that door.

"You mean, while they vacation in Sag Harbor and Martha's Vineyard? Attend their cotillions and private finishing schools, and take European trips with their White friends? Tell me, Sister Anders." His fingers tapped his desk, as if he'd performed this intellectual surgery so often it was effortless. "Which finishing school finished you?"

"I will not stand here and be judged because I'm not poor enough for you." No matter what he thought of her means or her background, her family had done a great deal for this town. "I'm sorry I came here. I apologize for troubling you and your members. No slight was intended. I appreciate your important time."

Before she could turn all the way around, behind her, his seat squeaked.

"Not so fast, Ms. Anders." He blew past her and down the other end of the corridor, in the opposite direction from which she came. "This way."

Intrigued by what he needed her to see that finally compelled him to get up, Al followed. The corridor opened to a dining hall filled with makeshift cots of people receiving medical care, separated by curtains. Volunteer nurses, doctors, and assistants milled about the place. Packed with monitors, health kits, bandages, gauze, and much more supplies, the dining hall was neatly divided into several rows of the sick. More sat in chairs along the corridor, with blisters, burns, coughs, wounds, swelling ankles, broken bones, slings, casts, and wheelchairs, all waiting their turn to be seen, the collective Black body of New York.

This makeshift operating room was a defibrillator shocking Al straight through the heart.

The pastor turned and stared at Al. "Do you mean to convince me your challenges are on this level, Ms. Anders, that they threaten your very ability to survive?"

"I don't mean to convince you of anything. I only ask not to be despised for not being one of the people sitting on those cots. I'm still human, and a caring one. You don't know me."

Several coughs and groans passed in the time he studied her.

"The problem is not that you have means, Ms. Anders. The problem is that yours and your friends' convenient compassion ends when it's time to embrace these brothers and sisters as *more* than your pets." He shoved his hands back in his pockets and allowed her to take in the weight of what she saw. "What is the amount you would 'contribute' in exchange for using our church?"

Convenient compassion.

To that, Al had no response.

"Four th...thousand dollars. Plus cleanup crews, food, service staff, and tech crews." In light of the suffering she surveyed, her quest for the Presents now tasted like castor oil on her tongue.

"Mm-hm. By chance, where is your Anders family located?" His eyes shifted from the clinic back to Al. "For some reason, you look familiar. I just can't place from where."

Al's knees weakened.

"The Anders are from Louisiana." It was true. Her mother's side of the family was indeed.

One of the scales behind his eyes dropped lower. "Your mother or your father?"

Why did he feel the need to ask? Why hadn't he simply accepted the answer she gave him? Any person would have assumed a woman's last name belonged to her father.

Al would not tell anymore lies in the Lord's house. "My mother's."

The pastor's knowing gleamed in his eye. "Can't say I'm familiar. And your father?"

Al swallowed.

Hands in his pockets, expectant, the pastor would not leave a stone unturned.

"Césaire." She released it and lifted her chin. She would never be ashamed of her grandfather's work in the Great War. "My father is Erwin Césaire."

If she'd thought his face could not be more stern, she'd been wrong.

"Erwin Césaire? Son of Dr. *Theodore* Césaire? Theodore and Suzanne?"

Did he have some personal connection beyond the casual gossip?

"Yes."

Al braced herself.

His short laugh lacked humor. "So your name's not A'Lelia Anders but A'Lelia Césaire."

Al had only offered it as a white lie. Now came the black side of a simple intention.

"That is correct."

"So you lied to get in here. Your deception makes sense. Daddy always said that's how your whole family is. You're just like them…heartless, conniving, liars."

Al no longer stared at a pastor but a man who had devolved into someone else.

"I made a mistake. You will *not* stand there and lie on us. I don't care if you're a pastor or Jesus himself."

Emotion—maybe even rage—welled into his eyes, into his throat that was suddenly hoarse. "There is no way—and I mean none—I would *ever* let a family of thieves and murderers walk in these doors and pose like you're good people."

His words turned Al upside down.

"Pastor, I understand you may disagree with war and my grandfather's contributions to keeping our country safe, or his inventions, but that doesn't give you the right to disrespect him in front of me."

He found Al laughable. "You think I'm talking about a war. That was bad enough, but no, I'm talking about your family's *private*," he said, finishing with his eyes, "evils."

What in God's name? Why was she entertaining this conversation? Why was she allowing this man she didn't even know to shake her at her core?

"I'm leaving now, sir." She turned to do just that.

"My granddaddy was a postman. He delivered the mail to your family a long time. So did his daddy before him."

This personal element stunned Al and nailed her down.

"They took the mail to your family during World War One," he continued, his voice thick. "When post office checkers had to open foreign mail."

World War One. Leopold Césaire.

Facing one another once again, he glared at Al like she should have known what he was talking about.

His voice fell to less than a whisper. "We know who you all are. Who you *really* are. What you did to your own kin." Snot ran down his nose. "On the blood of Christ, this congregation will not participate in the evil of your *German* house. Not even for four *million* dollars."

German?

"I'm French!" Al corrected him. It was terrible to be associated with German culture in America. Particularly, because of World Wars One *and* Two. "My family is West African and French. Césaire is a *French* name. You lie."

Unflinching, the pastor held firm.

"My grandmama and daddy swore me to secrecy, so I'll never tell. Only because of my love and loyalty to them. Now, I wish you well, young sister. Our business here is concluded."

He stormed off as if *he* were the one whose family was just called German.

Thieves and murderers? Private evils?

German?!

Of all Al had heard about her grandfather through the years, this was debilitating.

...a family of thieves and murderers...

What you did to your own kin.

Al placed a hand against the wall to steady herself and stumbled to search out her sister and best friend.

Even during World War One, when post office checkers had to open foreign mail.

It wasn't possible. She'd catalogued the family's letters, scrapbooked the memorabilia, preserved and stored their jewels and fabrics in vaults, and had reviewed ship manifests and business documents from the eighteen hundreds. She had lived and breathed their family history the way Einstein had lived physics, until the woman was inseparable from the history.

We know who you all are. Who you really *are. I'm talking about your family's* private *evils.*

"No, you don't," she muttered to him, though no one else was in the corridor.

"Ma'am," a voice spoke somewhere in another world.

Even during World War One, when post office checkers had to open foreign mail.

From what country? France? Africa? That's where they came from.

…the evil of your German *house.*

"Lies." If his grandfather had known the Césaires for a long time, there must've been a dispute and the pastor had inherited a grudge from his forefathers. "We're African and French. You're a liar."

"Ma'am."

But the disbelief in his eyes, the specifics of his memory, the way he'd lowered his voice, as if he didn't want anyone to know that he knew…

It was one thing to be enemies with a man, but who in their right mind would manufacture brazen lies? Her grandparents didn't deserve it. Those were fighting words he'd uttered.

Al's knees buckled, but the wall no longer held her up. Her mind spiraling to make sense of all she'd ever known, the pastor's insults still echoing between her ears, her heart racing, Al dropped.

On her way to the floor, firm arms caught her from behind.

"What's your name?" a man murmured in a steady, reassuring tone.

"I'm French…" Where on Earth did he get German from?

"What is today's date?"

Her boots were swept from under her. Lifted, she was carried in steady arms.

"I'm F…" she attempted to mumble. "World War One."

"Have you eaten today?"

She nodded while she felt herself being set down.

"I'm not clear what exactly you're doing with your head, but I'm going to check your vitals."

Where had she heard this purposeful, calm voice before?

"That's… I don't…" *Form a complete thought, Al.* "I don't need that."

"Your breathing is irregular."

Dizzy, lightheaded, Al stared directly into a man's Afro, lowered underneath her nose while he was immersed in his work. Soothing warmth slipped inside her palm, and a firm finger applied pressure under her wrist.

"How do you know? You haven't…" How *did* this stranger know?

"Because your breathing's not the way I remember it night before last." Finally, his gaze shifted from what he was doing, and his eyes checked into hers.

Comforting, autumn eyes. The slightly crooked, distinct nose.

"You work at the hotel. What are you do…"

Instant humor spread his lips into an easy, maybe even lazy, smile. "Right. I work at the hotel."

He withdrew from his neck a stethoscope Al hadn't

noticed, and started checking her heartbeat, pressing the metal along different points of her chest. Al gazed up the black cord connecting his ears to the most vulnerable part of her, for him to hear her rhythm.

Underneath the cord between them was his name tag, *Dr. Emeric McPherson.*

"Night before last at the hotel, your breaths were deeper, like you were upset but focused. Now, they're shallow, quick, and off rhythm. Like you've been jarred. Did you just get some bad news or something?"

Al couldn't believe these odds.

"I…you're a doctor."

He lifted her chin and continued his exam, his fingertips lightly pressing different points of her throat. "Aah. So that's why I haven't slept much this week. Thank you for enlightening me. Right on, then."

"What were you doing at the hotel carrying my things?" Still confused, she was trying to figure it out.

He was all seriousness while evaluating her. Taking out a pen light, he checked both her eyes. They must have been in good working order to observe his smooth, cornsilk skin. With long, elegant fingers, he moved from one eye to the other, his focus on his tasks giving him a vibe Al couldn't yet put her finger on.

"I'll need you to open your mouth and say 'ah'," he said in a soothing voice. He stood back and waited.

"My *mouth?* Y-you mean you want to look *in* there?"

Al was coming back to her senses. Taking her pulse, listening to her heart, feeling her throat, weren't what she'd had in mind when she'd entered the church.

Equally stunned, Dr. McPherson stared back. "Have you ever seen a doctor who didn't?"

"But I'm healthy. That's not necessary."

It wasn't clear if he was agitated or amused. "I just had to catch you and carry you in here."

"Thank you very much. I'll see if I can find a medal to give you, but I'm copacetic now."

"I like rewards, so I'm holdin' you to that medal. But you also claimed to be good while you were blackin' out." A Southern accent peeked through his words.

"Al?" Nineteen-year-old BB rushed in protectively, followed by Jill. "What are you doing to my sister? What's wrong?"

The doctor turned to them. "Your sister almost fainted in the hallway, and we brought her in for a quick check. I'm just making sure she's okay before sending her back out in that weather. As you can probably imagine, she's not the most cooperative."

BB drank up Dr. McPherson, scoping him from the top of his two-inch Afro to the tips of his polished leather loafers. BB's mouth snapped shut, a schemer's grin appearing and quickly disappearing. Scratching her head, she played dumb and spun back around to her older sister.

"Al, you know you got that one condition. The one on your scalp that makes you limp in your right leg. Let the man run his check."

"We've got things to do," Al insisted. Without this church as an option, they needed to choose another and start signing contracts fast, meaning the church BB found would have to suffice. "Right, Jill?"

She looked to her best friend for backup.

Jill suppressed a laugh. "I don't see why we couldn't do it later. The venue's waited all this time."

Wow.

"I *don't* have a condition. This was a small mishap. There's a lot going on right now." Her family legacy was under attack. She'd just been called an evil German. Al lowered her voice. "You will not believe me when I tell you how serious it is."

BB shook her head at the doctor. "You see what I'm saying? Her scalp condition also causes confusion. We'll be out in the hall. Sorry for interrupting." She pulled on Jill, and the two bumped into each other on the way out. "Continue."

Chuckling at the two sisters, the doctor motioned at Al. "I'm gonna need that arm."

Al gave in. Removing one arm from her coat, she raised her sweater sleeve so he could slide a pressure cuff around it. Their foreheads barely missed each other this time. Though they didn't clash physically, something between them connected.

"Are you and her twins?"

Al thought of a world where she and BB would have exited their mother at the same time, where they did everything together. Al would have lost her mind. "She wishes."

"She must be the younger one."

Al shot him a hairy eyeball. "What makes you say that?"

Clearly comfortable in his skin, he gazed back at her. "I'm the baby in my family, and my sisters all look at me like they're one breath from sending me to an early grave. I know a big sister when I see one."

Cocking her neck, she inquired. "Then why'd you ask if we were twins?"

"To distract you and you'd think about something other than me taking your blood pressure, your heart would slow down, and I could get an accurate reading." His eyes widened in a not-so-humble brag that he'd gotten an advantage.

Which tickled Al. Or maybe she was more tickled by his apparent love for his job, how easily he attended people—or perhaps, how easily he was attending her.

"I hope you got your situation worked out a couple nights

ago," he murmured while they waited for the cuff to measure his effect on her blood activity.

He had seen her in her moment of humiliation. The memory flickered in her mind's eye of being thrown out of a hotel and told she didn't belong there, having her contract canceled as if she were disposable. This doctor had witnessed it.

"I'm working it out."

"I fear for the fool who tries to stop you." The warmth in his autumn eyes told Al he'd meant it in good-natured jest.

The machine beeped, and the two jumped, brought back to the task at hand.

"It's one fifty-nine over ninety-three," he informed her. "That's high. I should hook you up to a monitor and confirm you're not having a more serious episode, but I already know you won't let me."

"How did you guess?"

"Call it a hunch after these two run-ins. But I'm not too worried about ya. You've relaxed, your vision has straightened out, and you're looking at me with both eyes now," he joked. "You still calling yourself French? That your name?"

Al bit back her laugh. "It's A'Lelia."

"Is today's date still World War One?" His open-mouthed smile warmed more than her heart.

She rolled her eyes. "No, that's not what I was... No." Unable to suppress her own amusement, she stared at him. "Today is December 4, 1976."

"Right on, right on. Then, I guess we can skip the heart monitor for today. Still, Ms. Césaire, you should go see your regular physician as soon as you can."

"Pump the brakes. How do you know my last name? You know me?"

"Somebody addressed you a couple of nights ago at the

hotel." While he removed the cuff from her arm, his lengthy eyelashes almost kissed hers.

An aroma of the outdoors engulfed her. Was he wearing Equipage by Hermes?

"No man could forget that name." He backed away, wrapping up the cuff, his gaze still cuffing Al. "Or the woman wearing it."

Al was arrested.

The good doctor was smooth, a high-quality vinyl press on the record player delivering an even rendition of O'Jays, no noise or static.

"Ms. Césaire?" somebody else interrupted.

Mesmerized, Al had no interest in seeing who it was. Jumping down from the cot, she was unsure if she could trust her knees.

He rushed to steady her. "You got it?"

Their heads almost bumped again.

Thankfully, Al's knees didn't embarrass her again. "Yes, I've got it."

"I suppose I'm releasin' you then." There went that sprinkle of Southern flavor on his conversation.

"Are you really now, Doctor?"

Where did *that* come from? Why didn't she just say *thank you?* She had intended to follow that remark with something clever and pithy about his giving her permission to leave. But she was a ball of nerves, with no remotely intelligent comeback.

He seemed curious while he may have been figuring her out. "You don't *want* to be released?"

Was it that obvious? They were in the church, and here she was, lusting. She was supposed to be seeing about children.

She backed into a rolling tray of metal tools, sending

them crashing to the floor. She started to pick them up. *Good God.*

"Don't worry, I'll... I'll get it," he offered, politely, patiently. Sympathetically.

"Thank...good day to you, Doctor." What color had her face turned?

"Miss A'Lelia."

He'd said her whole name. Perfectly. Most people got it wrong the first few times, calling her Lela or Cecilia instead. Who would stop staring at the other first?

"Ms. Césaire?" At Al's side stood a young woman her age, and right behind her was an older woman. "Your sister calls you Al, right?"

Dammit.

"Y-yes." A distracted Al attempted to recollect her... "That's me."

"I'm Pastor Freeman's daughter, Nadia Freeman, and I'm a reporter with the *Harlem News*. I was here today writing up a feature on some of these doctors at the clinic when I ran into your sister, Roberta. She told me what happened at the Murray Hill Hotel." She gestured at the woman next to her. "This is my mother, Daphne, First Lady of Mount Bethel."

The pastor's wife extended her hand. "Hello, Ms. Césaire, what a pleasure it is to meet one of the storied Césaires. You all are giants in this city, and it's my honor to shake your hand."

"I'm not the giant, First Lady," Al said, "my foremothers and forefathers are. I can only hope to fill shoes that big one day."

"Can we step out and speak privately?" First Lady Freeman asked.

"Of course." Why would these two talk to Al, considering the pastor's clear animus toward her?

"Listen, baby," First Lady Freeman began, "I apologize for

my husband's upset. He doesn't always mind the difference between his personal feelings and his work as a minister. How to keep his private sentiments just that—private. Tomorrow, after our day service, our board of directors will have a meeting. You can present your offer to the board and let them decide. What was it again? Four thousand dollars, you said?"

At this point, after the terrible lies Pastor Freeman had spewed about her family, this church was the last place Al dared to bring their money.

"First Lady, I can't come to where I'm not wanted, or where 'our kind' are resented. I appreciate your invitation, but we're not so desperate for a venue that we'll tolerate disrespect."

The First Lady placed a hand on Al's arm. "Miss Césaire, Pastor Freeman is too proud to say it, but our church could use the funds. It seems we could all help each other out here."

Her daughter added, "I've been wanting a write-up on the Césaire family for years, particularly your grandfather. He's got to be one of the most fascinating Black men in New York. Maybe even in the world. But he doesn't exactly return phone calls. And yours is one of the only Black families I know that can recount your history beyond America. Outside of chains. If our board helps you with your venue situation, would you give me a historical piece on the Césaires?" Her shoulders hugged her ears. "Plus, maybe an exclusive interview with Dr. Theodore Césaire?"

So that's why they'd had a change of heart. Within minutes of the pastor calling Al and her kin evil Germans, now his daughter wanted a feature?

Al was suspicious. She and her family were extremely protective of her pépé, and she would have to sniff this out for some covert motive.

On the other hand, this church was stunning.

Still, the children's parents would push back. Al would need to walk a razor-thin line here.

"I don't want to commit my grandfather without talking to him first. He rarely gives interviews anymore. Nor should he have to. He's given enough over his life. How about we stick with family history only? I can get you a couple of quotes from him."

The First Lady gushed. "Good. This is real good. This could work nicely for everybody. Tomorrow then? The board meeting is at three."

Al couldn't help a last glance over her shoulder.

But Dr. McPherson was gone. Should she go back and invite him to…tea? A French café? A show? A museum? *To do what, Al?* Look at the lives of dead people? For a stroll through a library to get lost in a world of books that would never read her back? Any of her favorite things? What was she going to do? Study him to death?

But he was a doctor. He could appreciate culture.

He was still a man, though. Men needed thrill. *Action.*

Al returned to the sanctuary. Somebody as smooth and creamy as he was likely had a girlfriend anyway.

"Siiissyyy!" BB sang, her entire face smug. "Ready to get foxy for tonight?"

"No. I'm not going to a breaking club on some seedy side of town," Al whispered. "You go without me and have fun."

Al had business to attend. Who was this Pastor Freeman, and what exactly did he *think* he knew about her family? She would do some digging, especially because his daughter wanted a full spread. Al couldn't ask Meme since she'd ignored Meme's warning. When Meme learned this was the possible location, Al would have some explaining to do.

Lost in thought, she ran smack into her little sister.

"A deal is a deal, Ally Cat. Didn't I just help you land, not one church but *two*? Your location problem is solved and it's time for you to relax. If I don't get you out of the house tonight, you'll have a stick up your crotch the entire month I'm here and we'll tear each other's eyes out."

"Roberta! Mind your mouth. You are in a church," Al said on her way around her sister and out of the gigantic front doorway.

This time, Al paid attention as she left. She made eye contact with the line of people, gazing at some of the tired faces standing and sitting in the line. She did not hurry over, around, or through them. A small act, but still action.

"Baby girl's got a point, Al." Jill ran ahead and barred Al from the car door. "Take a breath. Stop pushing so hard, A'Lelia." Jill pulled Al into a hug and the rest of the world fell away. "It's Christmas. For tonight, just go boogie down and be merry."

SHE WAS CLUMSY.

Two nights ago, she'd tripped over a scarf everybody else had seen and stepped over.

He didn't mind it. Actually, he liked it. She was so damn gorgeous—all that perfect skin, perfect hair, perfect makeup, perfect figure—she needed an imperfection *some*where. To see her tripping over herself enhanced her. Her relatable humanness didn't just define her beauty, it accentuated her. Like when a famous actress had a mole, or a gap between her teeth, or a unibrow, it gave her a badge of uniqueness that shifted her from pretty to surreal. If a woman owned her badge right, it even made her iconic.

A'Lelia's clumsiness took her from being a Dorothy Dandridge, a lovely portrait that was unreal, and hence untouchable, to a lovable, everyday woman ripe for touching. Her sister had called her Al. A simple name. Even better.

She seemed like one of those people who was all brain but turned uncomfortable for regular conversation. That moment when she'd gotten tongue-tied was adorable. He could untie it.

"Yo, man, thank you." One of the guys Em had just treated for eczema sores shook Em's hand. "I seriously appreciate this. A lot. And I'm gonna go check out that ointment you're talking about, too."

"Yeah, do that, brotha. It's too cold out there, and it'll get colder over the next couple of months. That ointment should help until you get your insurance back, man."

"Copacetic, my man. Merry Christmas to you and yours," the young brother said on his way out.

"Same to you! One more time, though, where did you say you got your hair cut again?" Em needed a shape-up before he met the fellas at this Hevalo joint tonight. For his first time going out in New York—off-the-hook kind of going out, not some sleepy church or work gathering—he needed to be spiffy.

"House's Barbershop, over on Seventh and One-Eighteenth. Tell 'em Abe sent you. They'll hook you right on up."

"All right then, man, thank you!" Em was sure to wash up before he switched out his doctor's jacket for the wool overcoat. His six hours of volunteer time complete, he started toward the exit.

Ahead of him, the pastor and First Lady of the church were personally thanking each volunteer on their way out.

"Son, we appreciate you giving your time today," the pastor said to him, gripping Em's hand doubly. "I'll be sure and tell your Aunt Dee how helpful you've been. She brags on you a lot. If you need a church home while you're in town, our doors are open."

"Thanks for that, Pastor. Actually, if you don't mind, I was wondering if you could, um, connect me with the young lady you were talking to earlier. A'Lelia Césaire, I believe?" He made up something on the fly. "Is she a member here? I met her a couple nights ago, and it looked like she was in charge of an event? I wanted to see how I could attend?"

The pastor's warmth iced. Were the two of them messing around?

First Lady Freeman overheard Em's question and stepped forward before her husband could speak. "Yes, baby, Ms. Césaire will be back here tomorrow afternoon at three. She's putting on an annual youth program. They're in a bit of a pinch, and she's looking to have it here."

"A youth program?" Kids. Was she a teacher or something?

"Yes, sweetheart, the Annual Christmas Children's Presents. It's been around since the end of the Civil War, to bring Blacks back together after the Draft Riots."

"Yeh, minus the Black folk."

Did Em really hear the pastor mutter those words?

First Lady Freeman instantly brushed aside her husband's slipup with a bigger smile and a pat on Em's shoulder. "If you're looking for a cause to support, young man, the Presents is definitely a worthy one."

"That's not a cause. It's a show." The pastor's words this time were unmistakable, especially his tone.

Something was definitely up between Pastor and Miss A'Lelia.

The Draft Riots? Em wondered, moving past the long line of people.

At House's Barbershop, while his Afro was shaped, he picked up restaurant suggestions that weren't in his mama's 1960's-era *Green Book* she'd given him. Now he had options for those hard work days when he couldn't handle Aunt Dee's cooking. After his head was in good order, he stopped through Adele's Kitchen on Seventh, or rather, Adam Clayton Powell Jr. Boulevard and One Eighteenth Street, where the owner, Geraldine Griffin, loaded his carton down with country-fried steak, collard greens, and yams, so full he could hardly close the container. Just in case, he ordered several more containers for the others at the house so this wouldn't look like what it was—him dodging Aunt Dee's cooking.

A few minutes after seven in the evening, he walked in.

"Oh, baby, what you got there?" Dee asked.

"Grub, Auntie. Why don't you take a load off tomorrow and relax? Enjoy ya some Adele's Kitchen. I got enough for everybody."

"Oh, that's sweet, but I already cooked up a lasagna."

Don popped out of his room. "You got any catfish in there?"

"I got you. Right here, man." He slid an arm around Aunt Dee's shoulders and kissed her cheek. "I had wanted to catch you before you started cooking, but the line at the barbershop was long. Just add these to the leftovers tomorrow, Auntie."

"Of course, baby. This was real sweet of you. Your friend called while you were gone. Wanting to know if you were still 'down' tonight." She waggled her head and tried to put a funny spin on it. But the trembling corners of her mouth gave away that she was worried. "Did he say you two are headed to some club? Where exactly? It's quite a few bad spots in this city."

Em kissed Aunt Dee's forehead. "I noticed, Auntie, but Memphis ain' no Santa's workshop either. Yes, it's a club over there, called Hevalo. They want to put me on this new music called breakin'. You ever heard of that?"

"Isn't Hevalo in Bronx? That area's awfully dangerous."

"You goin' to see DJ Kool Herc, man?" Don asked over his plate of catfish that was pretty full considering his mama had just fed him. "He is off the hook!"

Aunt Dee stared at her seventeen-year-old son. "And how would you know?"

"Um," Don stammered, "my friends told me."

The moment Dee turned her back, just over her shoulder, Don gave two thumbs-up and did a chef's kiss, eyes rolling up to his forehead in approval of this DJ Kool Herc's turntable skills.

"Don't worry, Auntie." Em guzzled the last of his grape Kool-Aid. "I'll be back early enough to rest up for church tomorrow." He knew that would make her happy.

"Say what? You're goin' where after all these months I've been asking?"

"You heard me. I'm coming to Mount Bethel's day service with you."

Em studied his Rand McNally map book so he'd know the streets to take before he left the house. Windows rolled up, his Smith & Wesson that his father bought him tucked under his seat, Em steered out of Harlem.

On the streets, every set of beautiful Christmas lights were offset by three or four burning trash cans, particularly once he crossed the Macombs Dam Bridge over the Harlem River, rode up Interstate 87, and switched to Interstate 95.

Em's heart shook in its chambers. On the other side of the river, before he exited at Jerome Avenue, what looked to be a ten-story apartment building lit up the night. Massive orange flames blanketed the rooftop and clawed at the sky in the heart of the Bronx. Placing his foot on the brakes, he slowed his car while he reconsidered Dee's worry back at the house. The sight reminded him of houses set on fire back in the South. But even if the White fire department didn't come, Black families would go get pails and do something. Here, people on the streets continued with business as usual. In the fifteen minutes he drove on the interstate watching it burn, never did a single fire truck roll up to put this one out.

Stepping out of his ride and into the cold, his pistol strapped to his ankle, Em strutted across the street. The fire still blazed several streets away. No one paid it the slightest mind as the line outside the Hevalo kept growing. People confabbed and shivered in their club attire like it was nothing. A Black Santa walked up the street, shaking his Santa hat in hand for the occasional dollar or a few coins.

"Ayo, Memphis! Memphis!" At the door, Harold waved him in. "I was wondering if you'd show, Brotha Docta. I'm waiting on Pretty Boy Lionel. Brent is already in there at the bar."

"Righteous, man."

"Prepare to have your mind blown tonight. You will never ride anything like this rocket ship ever in your life, Negro."

"We'll see about all that," Em riffed back while they exchanged a grip. "You better not be jivin', bro. It's colder than an Eskimo's behind out here. I coulda been at home under the heater drinking hot chocolate with my auntie."

"Boy, get on in there. Hot chocolate with your auntie…" Harold's gaze inspected the booties in spandex shorts, corduroy skirts, sparkly hot pants, and right above go-go boots. "You can call me Santa. I'm stuffin' somebody's chimney befo' the night is over."

Em's gaze followed Harold's, and he broke into his country twang. "They ain' Southern girls, but I'll see what y'all in here workin' with."

The next sounds almost kicked Emeric out of his body. He had to hold onto his heart. Ridiculously loud base pounded the air, blasting his eardrums and shattering his nerves. "What the hell?"

While he searched around him for signs of a raid or upheaval, the packed club had gone wild. Brent appeared at his side, jumping up and down, one hand fighting the air, the other hand unable to keep his drink in the cup. Over their heads, under spinning neon strobe lights, a new warm-up act came onto the stage and hit the turntables. Emeric's nerves settled once a familiar James Brown song spun on the vinyl. Relieved, he began inhaling normally.

Immediately, he was yanked from his comfort zone.

The first percussion break in the song dragged. And dragged. And dragged.

"What the…?"

James's vocals disappeared, but the song's beat marched on. An unprepared Emeric was snatched into a funk-music portal. He whipped his head up to check out who was doing this. A young DJ who may not have been old enough to enter the club was at the front creating an entirely new song with well-timed breaks.

Unlike any sound Em had ever heard in any club or on any radio, the disruption was hot grease clashing with everything Em understood to be music. These pauses, or "breaks," in sound gave space for dancing clubbers to groove to the underlying beats.

A few steps away, his hand in the air, Lionel stared at Emeric as if to say, *I told you, Negro.*

"What you think, Doc? They ain' slingin' this kinda sound in Memphis!" Brent screamed, still jabbing his hand to the rhythmic breaks, his drink spilling everywhere. "Cat's name is Afrika Bambaata. New cat. He got a couple moves on them tables, don't he?"

Lionel and Harold squeezed in next to them, all smiles, eyes shining.

"Look at this dude! Acting like he just felt an earthquake!" Harold laughed at Em. "Ya not in Tennessee anymore, Negro. These Bronx turntables gon' turn you upside down."

For the Memphis transplant born and raised in the birthplace of blues, who partied on Beale Street regularly, whose heart swelled with pride that he'd met BB King, Bobby Blue

Bland, and Ann Peebles, this "breakin'" sound broke Em's eardrums.

Gritty and disrespectful, the sound was broken windows, trashed cars, and burning buildings that now defined New York. This must have been Bronx's blues, unmusical and defiant, a form of protest that police couldn't arrest.

"Dr. McPherson?" a woman's voice said behind him, a hand tugging his arm.

"Nurse Pam! You into this, uh, breakin' music, too?" he yelled at the top of his lungs.

"I'm from Bronx!" she screamed back in his ear. The constant breaks were an abrasive soundtrack to the night. "I was going to Kool Herc's house parties over on Sedgwick before he got big. You're new, huh?"

"Yeh, I'm getting used to it!"

"I can tell! You're looking kind of lost." She was amused at how out of place he felt. "You want to dance?"

Em laughed. "Y'all can dance to this? I'll try anything."

She took his hand and guided him through the sweaty bodies, where she started jerking her shoulders and her neck like she was spasming. Em was a pretty good dancer and watched to figure out how to move to it. Em bobbed his head and became acquainted with the DJ's unpredictable delays. He pieced them into a rhythm. Pam found his efforts hilarious.

Several footsteps away, a girl and a guy yanked their arms and legs in the same spasmic jolts as the rough sound. Doing a pretty impressive job, they entered a dance-off, for who could damn near break their necks most persuasively. The girl was holding her own, her full Afro crown of loose, unruly curls swaying over her shoulders, dropping and dipping on her free-flowing body. No bra under her red sequin halter, her jugs thumped up and down right over her belly rippling and rolling, showing off bare skin just above her skin-tight, spandex bell bottoms, the foxy little mama was throwing down tonight. This girl owned the floor, and every brother watching her perform was wishing she'd own him. Lord help whoever was unwrapping that for Christmas.

"So, Dr. McPherson, what have you been...?" Pam attempted a question, but between the sound system, the crowd, and the occasional chords of the actual song, words were lost in the soul inferno.

"You come here a lot?"

"What'd you say?" she hollered.

"This one of your spots?" He almost hurt his throat trying to be heard. As he screamed in her ear, Em caught his first glance at the face on that hot breaking girl.

He missed Pam's response while figuring out where he'd seen that face. Em squinted. The answer materialized.

Snapping her arm out, whipping it up, pumping it round and round, dropping her booty all the way to the floor, and break by break, snatching herself back up, she was the little sister!

Baby Sister Césaire! The chick who'd teased her sister in the clinic a few hours ago!

"Oh, shit." *That's* what high society girls were learning these days?

Em's gaze automatically darted around for a sighting of the older sister. He couldn't picture the prim, proper Miss A'Lelia from the Murray Hill Hotel stepping into a joint like this. He wondered if A'Lelia even knew Baby Sis was here.

"Everything all right?" Pam yelled.

"Yeh, it's cool. This breakin' stuff is just dope, is all."

"You want to get a drink?" Pam asked.

He took another glance at the circular dance space. Baby Sis had disappeared.

Dammit. "Yeah, let's do it." He checked one more time but didn't see Baby Sister Césaire.

"Doc?" Behind him, somebody tapped his shoulder. When he turned around, there stood Baby Sis, appearing from among all the bodies. The kid's vivacious energy held its own party across her face that glistened with glitter and sweat. "You break?"

Emeric couldn't have been more overjoyed. Her electric vibe was a light show.

"Nah, this is my first time here!" Not caring about his great big grin, he screamed. "I dig it, tho."

"Come on," Baby Sis shouted and tugged him. "I'll show you some moves so you don't look like a nimrod." She was already taking off, apparently not seeing Pam in the crowd on the other side of him.

He pivoted to an irritated Pam. "Just let me catch up with this family friend real quick and I'll be back for that drink."

"All right then, pimpin', we see you!" Brent teased him.

"One on the grill and one on ice?" Harold bellowed. "Negro, you ain' been in New York ten minutes."

"Nah, it's not like that," he tried to explain.

Baby Sis pulled him to the small dance space and held out both her arms, waiting for Em to follow her lead. As foolish as he felt, he mimicked her, primarily because she was so sincere about it. Baby Sis's neck jerked from side to side along with her hand. Em repeated her move. Smiling with approval, she turned her waist left to right in robotic form, and waited. Em did the same, but accidentally threw an extra hand and arm snap in there.

To Jackson Five's Dancin' Machine, Em started letting loose, becoming a kid again. Before long, random movements were flying out of him. Baby Sister rolled her arms from left to right, across her shoulders, and she tapped Em's hand so that he imitated the roll across his upper body as well. He passed it on to Harold who had jumped in.

"Go, Memphis! It's ya birthday!" Brent screamed around him.

Em and Baby Sis did the robot around each other, having fun and goofing off. On the other side of the fellas, Em sighted somebody else, the friend. The second honey who'd been with A'Lelia at the clinic today also huddled up with a dude, her arms flung over his shoulders.

She was here. *Had* to be. He'd seen two out of three now.

Baby girl must have read his mind. With a side-smile, she threw her chin in the other direction and pulled Em down to yell in his ear.

"I had to make sure you were solid first. You can't be some space cadet going up to my sister!"

"Word? So I passed your test?"

"You passed this first one," Baby Sis answered.

Em held out his hand for a grip, and she shook it, raised it, brought it down, and then let go, snapping her fingers. He was digging her.

Staring across the club in the direction she'd gestured in, he scanned a lot of heads. Before he could ask where, Baby Sis had returned to her club business.

The friend scoped Em, and her eyes grew, her face a happy surprise. So he was right. She flicked her head over her shoulder, indicating A'Lelia's general direction. Bowing his head as thanks, he kept walking and searching.

All the noise fell silent.

Her perfect press n' curl was perfect no more. It napped up at the roots, the curls now puff balls and no longer recognizable. Perfect skin, shiny with sweat that crept down her silk top and wet the smooth fabric in splotches. But, yet again, she was on a mission. She looked pissed.

Em followed her gaze, past several heads, to a dude who seemed trapped in her line of sight. This man eyeballed her back. Unsmiling, tense, the two might have just spotted each other. The dude's hands were gripping some other honey's waist who circled her moneymaker round and round on his manhood. He was wearing that look every man wore at one point or another, of the idiot who'd been caught.

Did Em want to get in the middle of that? The way she'd fallen all over herself earlier that day, she hadn't acted like a woman attached to a man. But clearly, she was. Maybe Em should step off.

Then again, they stood in a club, not a wedding chapel. He wasn't asking for this chick's hand in marriage. Judging by the tension, she might have needed to boogie down herself.

Rolling that brain and attitude around on her lovely neck, she started walking away. Clearly irritated, she shoved past the clubbers, away from him.

Emeric pursued. Through throngs, bumping into drinks and blazed joints, past women's hands roving all over him, he thrust his whole body forward, to reach her.

The bird who'd flown the coop of the South and migrated north just in time for winter, still unsure what he flew in search of, closed in on his tree. Drawing near to her, a winter bird spread his wings.

A PRETTY PRUDE TOO STIFF TO *shag your way out of a book.*

Al was determined not to let Luke's words own her, but for months, they had played on repeat in her head. She had avoided a face-to-face with Luke all summer.

Tonight upon seeing Al, he'd frozen, his hands glued to another woman's butt pressed against him, lust dripping all over him.

The strobe-light flared across his face just as Al's gaze intersected with his. An atom of hope had floated through her, her electrons orbiting in search of a long-delayed connection, on a subatomic level. But yet again tonight, Al's electrons went unanswered. Luke had other ideas for his physics.

She didn't have the energy to pretend she didn't care. She had taken her first step and faced the public by coming here. There was no point in staying. In time, she would manage these run-ins with him better, but for tonight, she was peeling out. Guys tugged on her arms and her waist to dance.

"Baby girl, you too cute to look so mad."

"No, thank you. I'm cool." She couldn't yell loud enough over the music, not bothering with eye contact.

"Foxy lady, you want to groove?" Somebody else pulled on her.

"No, thank you."

The bathroom door was within sight. She could go and collect herself for a few minutes. Almost there, she prayed it was clean.

A hand gripped her wrist, firmly and assertively, as if the gesture itself was a statement. No voice followed. Al swung around, her refusal on the tip of her tongue.

"What it is, French?"

Surprise sucked out her remaining air.

His eyes crinkled with joy. Expressive and playful, they said 'hello' to her insides. Those eyes expected nothing, but their gaze absorbed everything. Artfully designed lips parted for his tongue to wet them up. Not trying, not forcing, he was just having a good time in his skin. He and his big, silly, disarming grin came toward her before his mouth nuzzled her ear. "You remember how you said you'd find me a medal for saving your life today?"

How did this happen three times in two days?

His smile activated hers. Every other angry thought about Luke fell to the wayside.

"Saving my life? Aren't you overstating it?"

"Nah." With one arm, he closed the inches between them. He eased the other around her waist and pressed Al to his chest. "I recall this knight in shining armor who was wearing a breastplate of fine steel, he had a sword, and one of them real big helmets so it didn't mess up his hair. And he scooped you up and put you on his hoase."

In his Southern accent, he pronounced horse as "hoase," as if there was no "r."

The music volume cranked up, so Al had to scream her next words into his ear.

"On his what?" she asked teasingly, even though she knew the answer.

"Hoase!" he hollered.

"Horse?" Al repeated, correcting him.

"Yeh, that's what I said," he yelled back over the blaring speakers, confident that he was saying it right. "Hoase."

Her face at his shoulder, she sniffed notes of Old Spice, blended with what she could have sworn was Hermes. "I didn't know you would be here, so I don't have a medal for you to put on and ride away with on your *hoase*." Al bellowed at the top of her lungs and swerved her head for emphasis, because his smart-aleck cockiness required a worthy response.

"But you still owe a brotha." He slid her arm around his neck, where his fingers tarried at her elbow, a casual touch exciting her senses to a nonsensical degree. "So how you plan on settlin' up?"

The Jimmy Castor Bunch's "It's Just Begun" fired up the place with its quick city drumbeat and horn spinning on the turntables. Clubbers suddenly lost their minds, and Al peeked at the front of the room.

DJ Kool Herc, popular far beyond these Bronx streets now, announced his presence on the sound system.

But Afrika Bambaata was still working his own turntables, almost as if he refused to leave. Suddenly, the two DJs were having a standoff. But Kool Herc had the loudest setup.

Al and BB swapped ecstatic glances for the rivalry that charged up the club.

"Bambaaaata! Bambaaaata!" Kool Herc sang into his system. "Turn. Your system. Down." The clubbers joined in the singing, and Kool Herc amped his music higher until Bambaata's was drowned out.

Al expected the doctor to look toward the turntables for a sighting of the iconic DJs. Instead, when she checked on Dr. Emeric McPherson, his focus remained on his main event.

"You know how to dance to this breakin' stuff?" he exclaimed straight into her ear. His grip around her tightened, and he nestled his bearded cheek alongside hers. Settling his hips next to hers and popped his pelvis to the beat.

"Not in a million years," she hollered back.

"I doubt that. Not judging by what I just saw." Easy. Except for their need to scream. "Ain' no way your baby sister can break it down like a mechanic and you don't know how to work a little something yourself."

Al loved to dance, every bit as much as she loved music, but she would never display that side of her in here. She didn't share BB's careless abandon.

"Can *you* break, Doctor?"

"Psssh. Can I break? I'm a pro now. Baby sister taught me everything I need to know. Check me out." He snapped his chest and then his arms, snaking across his upper body, twisting and flicking his hands.

Forgetting the most famous DJ in New York was on the ones and twos, Al chuckled at this country boy imitating Bronx culture. He had rhythm, and his moves were respectable, but something was missing. "You're a little off."

Dr. McPherson's jaw dropped, and he drew back. "Oh?"

"Yeah." That just flew out. Speaking in slang was not how she was raised, even if her sister purposely defied their upbringing. "I mean, yes."

The strobe light flashed past his eyes, illuminating their full focus on her. "No, you had it right the first time. *Yeah.* So tell me what I'm screwing up." The doctor waited. His fingertips waited, perched on her waist.

"You've gotta pop like you love this city," Al insisted. "Like

Bronx is *in* you, not like you're an outsider still flirting with it."

His astonishment was flattering. "Hahaha! Why don't you show this outsider what you talkin' 'bout?"

Al considered it a moment. Could she really reveal her most intimate dance moves she only performed alone in her bedroom? That kind of brazenness had always remained locked up only for A'Lelia.

Maybe tonight, Al would take a couple of plays from her little sister's playbook and let go.

"Y'all, give it up for Coke La Rock!" somebody declared into the microphone, introducing the breakin' master of ceremonies.

Kool Herc broke the beat and held it while Coke La Rock started the call-and-response, and the two musical geniuses spun out a funky new cut.

Tonight was Al's song. Closing her eyes, she gyrated her belly, popped it, and curled. The rhythm flowed across her shoulders, broke at her arms, and beat through her fingers. Her new song wasn't really new. But feeling her song *was* new. A'Lelia rolled her neck and jerked it around, her bedroom groove easing out of her.

The music slowed, and Kool Herc must've pulled his next song from Al's subconsciousness. Raw and sensual, neurotic, funky, electric guitar bassline streamed through the speakers and under Al's bones. In anticipation of her favorite singer serenading her, her atoms and electrons waited. Sultry Diana Ross kicked off "Love Hangover," the song Al had on vinyl and 8-track, not including her collector's copies signed by the diva herself. Attending three of Diana's concerts that year were the few actual legitimate outings Al had enjoyed. Now, the song's electric eroticism called a new grownup version of Al out of her.

She finally opened her eyes again.

Inches from hers, Dr. McPherson's long lashes were nearly closed, but not completely. They formed slits of blackness through which he had been studying her.

Al's cheeks began to burn from self-awareness. She'd forgotten herself.

"You must like this song."

Cooling herself down in this hot club would be impossible. "I must love this song."

His breath teased Al's temple. "The song surely loves you, too, honored to have you moving your head to it like that." His fingertips lightly tapped on her bare back.

No expectations, no girlhood fantasies tonight. "The honor is mine."

His hips to hers, her pelvis to his, her waist, her breasts, his chest, their breaths, all a dance of atoms and electrons shaping time.

"Dr. McPherson." Another voice interrupted their slow, circular, easy two-step. "You must've gotten lost on your way to the bar. So I brought you your drink."

Over his shoulder stood a woman about Al's age wearing irritation that signaled something was amiss here.

Al drew back. "I didn't kn…"

"Pam, hey." A befuddled Dr. McPherson left outer space in his head and returned to the club, where he'd apparently forgotten somebody.

The woman forced a smile that missed the pleasantry. "You have *two* old friends here tonight, Doctor? You sure are popular to be new in New York."

Several blinks of his eyes revealed he hadn't expected to be caught. His following laughs were nervous.

"I'm making friends kind of fast now." Out of sorts, Emeric attempted to assuage both women, but he turned to Al. "Look, you wanna…can I…"

"I need to go. Big day tomorrow." Al refused to ignore the

warning signs again, and she really did plan on waking up early. "Pam, nice to meet you! Thanks for the dance, Dr. McPherson!"

"A'Lelia." His hand closed around her wrist, his fingers sliding into her palm, lifting it. Easy. Natural. Atoms and electrons. "Can you gimme a minute? I'd like to drive you home."

"Al," another man's voice spoke. Luke stood behind her. He might have even appeared remorseful. Or was this lost expression actually shame? "Can we step outside and confab?"

She'd gotten what she came here for tonight. It had nothing to do with either of them. "No."

AL FINALLY THREW off the bedcovers. If sleep hadn't come to her these last four hours, it likely wasn't coming. There was no way this Pastor Freeman would cast aspersions on her lineage and her family's place in New York. If he'd said this to her face, he'd probably repeated it to other people, too. She only needed a few minutes of digging through family collectibles and Al would have the evidence she needed to shut him down.

Passing her club outfit that she'd tossed over a chair, she caught a whiff of Dr. McPherson's outdoorsy cologne. In her mind's eye, his long eyelashes still aimed at her while his arms hung on her hips.

There was no time to reminisce. She had two clear missions. First was the mail delivery receipt from 1914 she'd discovered. Second was disproving the pastor's accusation. Al would take her proof of her family's Afro-French heritage right to that pastor's face—*no* German ancestry anywhere in them—and once he read it with his own eyes, she would demand a full-throated public apology.

Taking out her catalogue she'd created listing the family's

collections, Al ran her finger down the "Letters" section. Pépé would have received one from his cousin, Leopold, in France. The location column would inform her where she'd placed the letter—the Historical Society, in the basement of this building, at her parents' home in Scarsdale, or at her grandparents' home also in Scarsdale. She scanned the dates of letters she'd logged.

June 29, 1914.

July 6, 1914.

July 14, 1914.

July 28, 1914.

August 7, 1914.

August 19, 1914.

August 31, 1914.

Hm.

May 4, 1915.

The letters had come faster once the fighting began, and then they had stopped for a time. Back when she was making this list at age fifteen, she'd only been listing what she'd found, with no more thought for the timeline than simply ordering her pépé's disheveled papers.

Now, Al rubbed her sleepy eyes to ensure they didn't fail her. She checked several more times, certain that repetition would reveal the letter and its location and make her eyesight a liar. Peering under the "Documents and Other Papers" in case she'd accidentally listed it with his diagrams or formulas. Yet, no other category indicated the letter either. Al stopped.

She had never made an entry for a letter on September 8, 1914.

Yet, the postal receipt on the table stared her in her face. A letter had surely been delivered to this very building.

Pépé probably didn't even know where he'd placed it. Science was his forte, not homemaking. Most scientists with ideas, calculations, and theories floating around in those big brains, were grossly disorganized. She often found the occasional note, photo, award, or commendation under his desk, shoved in an old briefcase, or used as a placeholder in a book.

Yet, what confounded her now, which hadn't crossed her mind at age sixteen, was the long period of time that no letters had arrived after August 31. Why did Pépé and Leo stop communicating so abruptly? Sickness? A hardship? Or worse, had there been a falling out? According to her list, this series of letters were at Pépé and Meme's home in Scarsdale. She'd have to drive out there.

But her grandparents' home couldn't be the only one she visited. Her pépé was not the oldest of his siblings. That would have been his sister, Aunt Jeanne.

For proof of their family's Afro-French origins, she would have to drive to Aunt Jeanne's home. The oldest sibling in each generation always received the oldest, rarest records, particularly the artifacts from France and Africa.

The sun still hadn't risen when she headed out of her apartment. The elevator dinged, and out stepped a hungover BB.

"Where are *you* going this early in the morning?" BB asked in her drunken bliss.

"I could ask where you're coming from this early in the morning, but I don't want to know. Take a shower before you get in bed. Just in case Mamman comes and checks if you're here. You'd better not be smelling like that if she does."

BB mockingly mouthed the same words and waggled her head. "You wanna know what happened after you blew off the doctor last night?"

Al's knee-jerk instinct wanted the answer, but she swatted away that thought. She refused needing to know a man's whereabouts any longer. "I didn't blow him off. Whatever he did, it's none of my business."

BB leaned lazily against their door. "You did blow him off. You don't want Luke to think you're taking up with somebody else."

"I don't care what Luke thinks."

"Now who's not telling the truth? You still want him to come back and say he's sorry. That he can't live without you."

"If that's the case, why didn't I go outside with him when he asked me to, so he could tell me that?"

Miss BB's lips stopped flapping. "Luke asked you to talk?"

"He did."

BB scowled. "So there's hope for you and him."

Al stepped on the elevator and pressed for the garage. "No. There's hope for me. And *maybe* for him without me."

An intoxicated BB grinned a lopsided grin of pride in her sister. "Righteous. I'm putting my chips in for Doctor Man. He danced with that other lady."

"Good for them."

The elevator doors slid closed. "He didn't dance with her the way he was dancing with you!"

"Wake yourself up in time to go with me to Mount Bethel today? And not a word to Mamman!" Al called out just as the doors shut.

The doctor had been a good time last night, but she wouldn't get stoked for a man she would probably never see again.

Still, on her way down Interstate 87 from Manhattan to the suburbs, Al stuck in the *Diana Ross* album 8-track released in March and forwarded it to number A3. Despite the morning freeze, she cracked the window half an inch so a little wind tickled her scalp. In her mind, she played on repeat how Dr. McPherson's eyelashes nearly stitched together, his pupils shining at her once she opened her eyes and realized he was watching.

He was clearly shagging with Pam, and that had put a

damper on the moment. But still, the vibe had been easy, and that was undeniable. Pam, or no Pam. If Al felt that temporary bliss with a random stranger she'd never met, she would feel it again with the right man one day.

Just after dawn, she pulled her car into the Scarsdale driveway at Aunt Jeanne's quaint, post-Depression-Era house. Al's sixty-five-year-old second cousin, Marian, waited at the side door and held it open.

"A'Lelia, girl, I'm happy to see you. It's been a while. What in Heaven's name could be so important you're here at dawn? Especially as cold as it is."

On the blood of Christ, this congregation will not participate in the evil of your German *house. Not even for four* million *dollars.*

"Marion, I only have documents of our family history until the 1850s. Before then, can you point me right to proof of our ancestry in France from the 1700s?"

Inside, Marion poured coffee. "You know I don't know anything about all that, girl. You're so much like your papa and pépé. Those big brains so full of information you can't even walk straight. Cream? Sugar?"

"Both. When will Aunt Jeanne wake up?"

"About an hour. She'll have her breakfast and coffee, watch a little Sunday morning news while I take out her hair curlers, and at ten, we'll head out."

"Would you have a problem if I stick around after you leave? It'll take time to go through those boxes. I can leave the key at Pépé's."

"You can keep the spare key for now. Start taking those boxes with ya as you please. My children and grandchildren will never bother with any of that junk. I need to finish writing out Mamman's Christmas cards. Hopefully, you'll find whatever you're looking for."

Rolling up her sleeves, Al started in on the boxes.

After much digging, she located a photo of her great-grandmother five times removed, Maria Josepha, in the only trip she'd ever made to New York from France. Called Josepha for short, born in 1768, she'd made the journey to see the success of her children and grandchildren in 1849, at the age of eighty-one. But this photo of the matriarch depicted no joy or motherly pride. Instead, she sat solemnly, appearing angry. In fact, her sons whom she visited looked distraught. Though she had seen this picture plenty of times, Al now noticed for the first time how her unsmiling ancestors appeared to have just emerged from a brawl.

The photo was a strong start, but Al needed evidence that hit the mark. She searched again, her coffee having turned cold the next time she sipped it.

She began locating the original Césaire family's "first papers," or their "Depositions of Intent to Become a US Citizen," filed in the New York County Courthouse at City Hall. The years were dated between 1808 and 1829. But the forms listing their births had no country of origin.

"Yes, yes," she muttered, finger-crawling through photos and records, her heart pounding now that she was finally getting somewhere. "Come on."

She came across a document for Maria Josepha Tossou, daughter of Omalara Tossou.

Omalara was the first ancestor, a Dahomean girl originally taken to France as a court servant for a French noble. That's how her children came to be born at Versailles.

Now that Al had found more than enough proof, her shoulders dropped and she relaxed. One day, she'd find time to catalogue Aunt Jeanne's records. Quite a few of them Pépé didn't have. Jeanne's family papers told a bigger story.

Damn. Already, it was nine fifty-one, and she'd been in Aunt Jeanne's attic almost three hours. Fortunately, she had come dressed for church and she brushed off the dust and dirt. Downstairs, Marion and Aunt Jeanne were getting ready to leave.

But Al had just a couple more questions. She couldn't help wondering. Fingers crawling over the corners of old pages, she searched just a bit more.

"Oh!" Found it!

Maria Josepha Tossou's registration as a mixed-race Afro-French woman. Despite Queen Marie Antoinette's love for the children in her court, and her friendship with Omalara Tossou, her husband, King Louis XVI, did not love Black people. His edicts had proven it, such as the Police des Noirs, a requirement that every single Black and mulatto be rounded up and have their names added to a registry so their whereabouts could be tracked at all times.

Confused, Al scanned Maria Josepha's birth papers now. But they stunned her. The space where Josepha's last name belonged had been very neatly cut out.

Al eyed the other spaces in the handwritten document. Josepha's date of birth was listed. The date of the document was also stated. Her weight and description as a "mulâtre" were listed. The statistical information should have listed the commune or city of birth.

Maria Josepha's birth at Versailles would confirm without a doubt that Al's family lineage connected from Africa straight to France.

Instead of finding that, a second space on the page had been neatly cut out. How long ago had the cuts been made? Twenty years ago, or a hundred and twenty?

If Al recalled correctly, Omalara Tossou birthed five children total who had lived—three biracial children with nobles in the French court, and two Afro-Caribbean children with a Saint-Domingue man.

The birth records of Josepha's siblings would clear up where she was born. They would also have a last name. Al finger-crawled to the bottom of the box, *and* the next. No more birth records.

Al's family only rarely interacted with other Césaires whose forefathers had emigrated to New York. They were such distant relatives after a hundred and fifty years, but now, she wondered if their last names and countries of origin had also been cut out of their forms.

"A'Lelia?" Marion called up the steps. "Honey, we're leaving now. We're just saying goodbye."

With Josepha's cut-up birth paper in her hand, Al stepped down the fold-out ladder.

"Oh, my Lord, child. You will have to change those clothes!"

"The morning got away from me. Is Aunt Jeanne still here? I have a question." Her mind burning with curiosity, Al took the paper and kneeled before her great aunt.

"A'Lelia."

The elder Césaire wrapped her aged fingers over Al's shoulders, and Al kissed her delicate cheekbone.

"You have so much history here, Tata," Al said, using the French title for "auntie." "Some of this stuff I've never seen."

"Marion says you've been up in the attic all morning." Her light voice had lost some of its tenor over the years, but it still spoke with conviction. She flashed a big grin of her dentures. She must have been happy to see a different guest other than the Mother Board or the sick-and-shut-in groups at church. Aunt Jeanne squeezed Al again and patted her shoulders. "Take it all with ya. I never knew what to do with it. Nobody wants all this mess. When I die, this lot around here will toss it in the trash."

"Thank you, Tata, if you don't mind, I might take a few things."

The older woman grabbed Al's hand. "Make time for

yourself, young lady. You're too young and pretty to be here at six o'clock on no Sunday morning talkin' about goin' through a near-dead woman's junk."

"It's not junk, Tata, it's identity and legacy. It's who we are."

Her laugh dismissive, she waved Al off with a hand. "All we are in this big ole world is junk, and God lets us know it when it's time for us to leave here. But you're just like that pépé of yours. He'd do the same thing when he was a boy. In the yard for hours, blowing stuff up. He'd get hot if we told him to come eat. So, what have you been up there cooking up, girl?"

Still squatting, Al held up Josepha's French registration papers. "Tata, do you recognize this piece of paper?"

Jeanne lifted her eyebrows to inspect it. "Can't say I do. What is it?"

"Do you remember ever learning about Maria Josepha? The grandmother of your great-grandfather, Joseph, from France?"

Still in a memory fog, Aunt Jeanne scratched her nose. "Wasn't she Omalara's second?" The woman's eyes glazed over as Tata flipped the pages of her memory now.

"Yes, ma'am, I believe so. She was born in France. To a French noble in Marie Antoinette's court at Versailles."

Tata worked to follow Al's reasoning. "Uh-huh. Yes."

Al stuck her fingertip in the holes. "So, Tata, if she was born in France to a French man, why are the spaces for her last name and the commune of birth cut out?"

First Tata's eyes groped to clear eighty years of a mental forest. Their faces mere inches apart, in that moment, Al watched her aunt's pupils widen. Somewhere in that foggy forest, Tata had located the answer.

"No. I told you I've never seen that paper. Whoever did

that, it happened long before I, or your grandfather, were ever born."

Aunt Jeanne's relaxed face stiffened into a stone wall of silence.

"I don't mean to upset you, Tata. I was only wondering if, maybe when you and Pépé were kids, you'd overheard the grownups say something…mention anything about…I don't know," Al explained, hating to ask the full question, so she couched it in a voice as soft as pillow cushioning, "if anybody ever spoke about Germany."

Her aunt snatched her hands away. The woman's glare was a lashing. "No! Stop asking about it. Those folks are dead and gone." Reversing in her wheelchair, she pushed away from Al. "Marion, we're already late for church."

"If you two don't mind, I'll just be a few more minutes with the rest of the boxes," Al said. She might even accept Aunt Jeanne's offer and take two or three boxes with her.

"Leave them." Worked up and breathing in short gasps, Aunt Jeanne pushed her wheelchair through the kitchen. "That's enough."

"Mamman," Marion interjected, "you just said she could have them and they'll go to the trash one day. Let her use them for her research. She's always done a lovely job with our family's history. Teddy's so proud."

"Hmph. Teddy." The ninety-year-old rolled her eyes with the attitude of an older sister who knew him as a little brother and not the famed scientist. "He was always more trouble than he was worth. Come on. I said 'no'. Now let's get to church." Her wheelchair was already headed toward the door. "A'Lelia, baby, you have yourself a good Christmas if we don't see ya." As an afterthought, Aunt Jeanne added over her shoulder, "And leave that paper right there."

A few minutes later, Al drove back over the Harlem River,

attempting to keep her eyes on Interstate 87. Her aunt's visceral reaction had spoken volumes. The pastor wasn't altogether out of his depth. Al still had no proof to shut him down.

"I'VE NEVER BEEN in this place. I've only driven by it." Gloria disappeared behind the ten-foot-tall golden Christmas tree that greeted them the moment they walked into Mount Bethel's foyer. Then, she reemerged again, her gaze dancing around the foyer's lovely, tiled walls and floors and its painted ceiling. They hadn't entered the main sanctuary when she gripped Al's arm. "This church is amazing. I see now why you're in love with it. This could work out very well for them *and* us. We'd have this fantastic venue, and the church will receive a nice payday. A win-win for everybody."

"Amen to that," Jill whispered. "This congregation would be crazy to tell us no. But Al, if they don't have the dates available, or if they can't accommodate us for whatever reason, don't sweat it. We'll find our venue for next year."

Al hadn't told them about the pastor questioning her family's legacy and integrity. If BB knew, she would walk out, no questions asked, especially when this pastor had no real proof. And Al wouldn't point Jill or Gloria to any rumors or gossip about her family.

This event would happen. Though she disagreed with her

longtime friend, she kept her mouth closed. She would not start searching for next Christmas, because *this* Christmas was not over.

"A'Lelia, we're glad you could make it." The pastor's daughter, Nadia, came to escort them inside. In her hand was a small notepad. "There isn't any chance your grandfather might show up here and surprise us, is there?"

Al held her ladylike poise. "Our talented youth are what brought us here today, and we're bursting at the seams to celebrate *their* work."

"There's no harm in trying," Nadia said, not missing a beat. "Still, though, you'll at least ask him, right? I mean, I spoke with my father on your behalf so you could get in here today."

BB started to address her, and Al silenced her with a hand on her little sister's arm. The last thing they needed was haughty BB's mouth to talk them out of a sweet deal.

Al kept her tone even and warm. "We're grateful, but I said yesterday that we do have another venue option. And if our family grants an interview, it will be limited to our history. My grandfather has given enough to New York already. He is entitled to rest."

The president of Mount Bethel's Board of Directors greeted them, and Al, Jill, BB, Gloria, and Miss Clara, all entered the main sanctuary. Gloria's and Miss Clara's mouths dropped.

Al was surprised to see that extra onlookers hung around, more than was typical for a church board meeting. A few choir members, ushers, and church elders sat in rows behind them, as if they'd showed up for a spectacle.

BB muttered, "Why would anybody want to watch some church meeting?"

"No idea, B," Jill replied while they slid into a pew.

"So, everyone, here we have with us today the Annual

Christmas Children's Presents," the First Lady said a while later, opening the floor to Al. "They need a venue to have their historic children's program here. We are so honored for them to come. My entire life, I've heard many wonderful things about this awesome presentation of Black babies to the world—the ballerinas, musicians, performances, speeches, the gorgeous decorations that make it look like a Black Heaven on Earth. The program is now headed by Miss A'Lelia Césaire. Her family is almost as famous as Dr. King's family, or the Roosevelts. They've been around almost since New York laid its first bricks. Honey, would you like to get up and tell the Board why you're here today?"

Al stood to project with her best etiquette-refined, Columbia and Oxford trained poise. "Good after—"

"No need." A middle-aged woman still in her choir robe waved off Al's well-prepared speech. "We know what the Presents is. I'm only wondering why they want to have it here now."

Others nodded, along with a few, *Mm-hm's.*

"How come you don't go to some fancy hotel, like you been doin'?" One of the members threw his elbows behind him over a pew. "What you wanna come over here now for?" he asked flatly. Plainly. His tone devoid of pretense.

Al stared around her to see the up-and-down motions of their heads that dipped deep and rose high in their nodding.

"This church been around longer than that Presents have." A young woman jabbed her finger on top of a beautiful pew. "Why ain't y'all never bring it here in the first place?"

"Yeah," others chimed.

Al stared at a frozen Jill, an irritated BB, an uncertain Gloria, and a petrified Miss Clara.

"Well." She had anticipated there would be skeptics. "I can't speak for the people who started this event in 1866, but I believe I can speak for those who passed it on to me." Al shook from her ankles up to her vocal cords. "American Black people have always been labeled as uncouth, uncultured, and uneducated in this country, and the mission of the Presents has always been to show the world that we are far more than the circumstances forced upon us."

Ancestors, come to me. Al began to teach.

"The greatest way we express our resilience, strength, and intellect, which they hate, is by showing off our highest selves. That's why it's called the Presents. After the 1863 Draft Riots, we wanted them to know we were still here, and they would never make us lesser than them, which is what they wanted."

Racked with nervousness, Al recalled her grandfather's powerful retelling the other night, and she continued as if he were indeed sitting here.

"So we used our elegance and education as weapons. Since then, our lavish displays have always been a stick in the eye of racism. Our achievement is a form of rebellion."

She took a soul-sucking breath.

"We want very much to shine as brightly as we can for all the world to see. Whether it be in *The New York Times* or *Vanity Fair*, or *Vogue* magazine, we continue to show the world that Black people are well-represented on the global stage. From our hair, to our clothes, down to the locations in the finest spaces, it is imperative that we display how we're not going anywhere." Al finished, not realizing her fists were clenched.

The women who had come with Al out of sheer nosiness to see the church had turned into Al's choir, clapping with their chests swelled.

"Yeh, baby, that sounds good and all." One of the choir members clasped his hands atop a pew. "Problem is y'all left a lot of folks out of your li'l mission. What about the rest of us shinin' so bright with y'all?"

"Amen!"

Several more *Amens!* cut into the nostalgia and conviction of Al's speech.

One woman aimed her fan at Al. "You say you about rebellion. Well, where was you and yo' rebellion around here? 'Cuz we ain' seen it. Why don't you keep your rebellion over there with *Vogue* and them?"

"That's right. How come ya never brought your rebellion out of them rich folks' neighborhoods?" a teenage girl piped up. "Don't you think the rebellion would be stronger if it had've been in this community from jump? If y'all spent money over here, then our churches and schools could shine bright. That right there would be a rebellion! And you wouldn't be in this situation!"

Other members clapped their agreement. "Gon' head, li'l sista, *preach!*"

Another choir member scratched his chin. "Don't get me wrong. Y'all seem like good people with good intentions and all. Ya just ain' never been good to us. So I don't really see why we should be good to you now."

"Why don't you go have it at your own church?" somebody else asked.

"Them White folks won't let 'em," another answered. "So they come over here an' throw their money around expectin' us to be impressed."

"Right!" the original choir member stated. "Four thousand dollars is a nice bit o' change, but the integrity of this church ain' for sale. You can't ignore us for over a century and then walk in here with your checkbook tryin' to buy some instant respect."

"*That's* what I'm talkin' 'bout!" Another choir member waved her song book at the last speaker.

An offended BB stood up. Al warned her baby sister through her eyes to be respectful.

"Good afternoon, everybody, I'm Roberta Césaire, A'Lelia's sister. I'm from New York like you. You all are making good points today. A lot of your views we were not aware of, but that's why conversations like these are needed. You've given us a lot to go discuss with our circles. There's so much history here in Black New York, and it won't all get resolved here today. Growing together will take time. Just like anything—the Civil Rights movement, everybody moving north from the South, rebuilding after the Civil War —as a society, coming together against injustice was never clean or easy, but we've always gotten it done."

Al watched her sister deliver a convincing rebuttal and it filled Al's heart. Maybe the kid wasn't totally wasting time at UCLA.

"Bringing the Children's Presents here can be another step forward on this path of unity." BB expressed with her hands. "Maybe God brought us to your church for a reason. Maybe He feels like it's time for you to get the acknowledgment you want. But we'll never know if we lean into frustration and hurt rather than unity and hope."

Astonished, Al stared at her little cannonball of a sister. That appeal was eloquent, in its substance *and* its form. She retook her seat where the others patted her arms proudly.

Of course, BB's doe eyes stared at Al and blinked, gloatingly, as if to brag, *I'm about to save your butt again.*

Miss Clara, the eldest of the women, stood, smoothing out her sweater set. "Hello, brothers and sisters in Christ. I originally come from the Caribbean. I was the last coordinator of the Presents. Been here thirty years, and I must say all these girls have said is true. I've heard a lot of complaints over the years that not everybody could be in the Presents."

Miss Clara's stern eyes scanned the pews.

"Many people complained we're too selective. But like a college or a prestigious award, we have a rigorous process.

Like A'Lelia explained earlier, just because we're Black does not mean we don't have high standards. We do. Some folks don't like how it's run, where it is, or what themes we put on. There will always be disagreement over who can participate, whose child will be on stage where, how long they'll be seen, and what role they'll perform. Those tensions will never go away, no matter how we bend over backward to satisfy folks."

Miss Clara's index finger shot up.

"But there has never been any ill will to any group or neighborhood, nor is there some secret conspiracy to keep anybody out. Our only goal has always been to make sure Blackness shines. And like Roberta just said, we can have conversations about how we do that in the future, but the Presents will always celebrate the best and brightest of us."

Al appreciated that she'd brought the others and did not have to do this alone. Now she and her village all squeezed one another's hands along the hard wood.

"Best and the brightest?" an elderly member shouted. "Or do you mean the *richest* of us?"

"Come on, now!" chimed another.

"The people with money," the first woman continued, wagging her head, "who can *afford* to be our *best* and our *brightest*."

To that, neither Al nor any of her cohorts had a reaction, and were left only to digest those bitter herbs.

The First Lady stood after a few more comments. "All right then, everybody, why don't we conclude discussion and call this matter to a vote? All in favor of accepting the four-thousand-dollar offer for the Annual Christmas Children's Presents to be held here, say 'aye.'"

Al could count the lonely *ayes* on one hand. She swiveled around in her seat, and her jaw could have hit the bench. Behind her, the church was half full now. She hadn't surveyed all of it before, primarily only facing the board that sat in her direct line of sight. Many more observers had showed up, filling pews to listen in on the debate, and eying the granddaughters of Theodore Césaire.

Cornered, unable to get up and walk out, the women exchanged quiet glances in defeat. Jill covered Al's hand, in a consoling reminder there was always next year.

Al wasn't sure what to do. Give up? They had already begun voting. Her legs twitched in the seat, awaiting instructions from her gut.

"Excuse me," a male voice spoke several rows behind them. "I know the votin' already started, and I probably should have spoken earlier."

Al had sung to herself while dancing in his arms last night. Now his presence cued up a new song and her insides began to dance.

How did he know about this meeting? Was he a member of this church?

In his simple black Sunday suit, he cut quite a different figure from his leather jacket the night before, plain but fitting, like it had been tailored just for him.

BB and Jill worked their hardest to keep their expressions on the straight and narrow.

"Sir, who are you?" a member asked.

"Oh, that's right. I apologize. No disrespect intended. I'm Emeric McPherson and I've only been in New Yawk from Memphis about four or five months. Not a member."

Even in this tension, Al bit back a laugh at his pronunciation.

The First Lady piped up. "Brothers and sisters, what this young man isn't saying is he's a surgeon, and yesterday, Dr. McPherson volunteered his valuable time in our health clinic for several hours. He did a wonderful job. We received a ton of compliments from many of you who enjoyed his kindness.

Though he is not a member *yet*, his Aunt Deidre Shipman is, and we don't turn down those who give back, so let's hear what he has to say."

"That's not all I wouldn't turn down," was whispered a little too loud, several pews behind Al.

That statement was followed by a rash of *mm-hm's*.

"Sisters," the First Lady said cajolingly to the women, "remember, we're in the Lord's house."

"And the Lord is good and quite merciful," one of the choir members replied, eying the doctor. "Lord, have mercy."

"His mercy endureth forever, yes it does," an usher added.

"The good docta can bring that mercy on over here and it can endure as long as it wanna," somebody else threw in.

"Yes, Lawd, amen, amen."

More chuckles and snorts. The First Lady cleared her throat and ended the nonsense.

Dr. McPherson graciously pretended not to hear it and gave her a curt nod. "Appreciate that. But I didn't stand up to discuss me. I spoke up to discuss you all. You have every right to put your valid questions to these fine ladies." Rather than remain where he was, he moved outside of his pew to stand in the aisle. "From what I heard, you work just as hard as everybody else and you feel it's not fair how you and your children get swept aside. Nobody with any power or position comes to acknowledge your challenges or your needs until *they* need something. Am I wrong?"

The members shook their heads. "No, sir, you're not."

Al had to wonder where this was going.

Dr. McPherson concluded, "You have every right to tell them to go on."

Those unexpected words got stuck in Al's ears. She sat up straighter, and if her eardrums could turn farther outward, they might have.

"But." Dr. McPherson held up his finger. "Before you send

them on their way, I notice there's something you haven't talked about."

Studying him quizzically, the audience stopped whispering and chuckling.

"Self-interest. Now I could go into forgiveness, brotherly love, how we need to stick together and all that, but this is an issue we don't often think of." Humbly and yet boldly, he walked to stand at the end of Al's pew. "We rarely think strategically for our future. These sisters came here with a goal they needed met. Their self-interest. That's not a bad thing. It's what we should all be doing. Have you thought of doing the same? Rather than considering these women your enemy, have you thought of them as an opportunity? For you. Not just money for the church, but real assistance for you."

Pews creaked with churchgoers shifting in their seats and thinking on what he'd said.

"You're looking at some of the most well-connected women in the city—professionals from top colleges who know top people. They are part of top networks. Who in here has a kid graduating high school this summer?"

Two hands rose in the air.

"Mm-hm." Dr. McPherson flicked his nose. "Maybe one of these sisters can write a college letter of recommendation. Who in here is looking for a job? Has kids in need of tutoring, or you're dealing with a tough teacher? Has a legal problem they've been struggling with? A utility bill or landlord dispute they can't settle? These women have friends who are scientists, accountants, realtors, educators, and bankers. These ladies are not enemies. They are assets. Are you really going to turn them out on the street? Or will you negotiate something in this for yourself? Brothers and sisters, we've got to become better negotiators, more clever strategists, rather than throwing our hands up and walking away."

The doctor rubbed his hands together and aimed is index fingers at his captive audience.

"You might not need anything from them today. But are you so wrapped up in your frustration now that you can't set up an opportunity for tomorrow? If you're not impressed by four thousand dollars they would pay the church, be impressed with the benefits you could get for yourself. For your children. Thank you and good day to all of you."

A few members clapped. Others took pause to give his words thought.

"I do have a rent situation that's been a headache," one woman said.

"My building needs work, and I pay my full amount on time every month."

"You know what?" one man stated, looking at Al, "I've seen you in the paper and I would like to visit that New York Historical Society. I want to see what kind of information they over there telling about Black people, and whether it gives the whole truth. I would like to have a private tour."

These were beginning to sound like demands, cold and indifferent, that raised the hairs on Al's neck.

Several more members called out their needs and requests.

"Family, why don't we invite these sisters back for another meeting to talk about how they'll help us later the way they want us to help them now?" Nadia Freeman rose and addressed them all. She turned to face Al directly. "What do you say, Sister Césaire? Would you and some of your successful friends bring your rebellion a little closer to home, where you might work with us? This meeting would be a requirement for you to hold your event here ,and it would occur *before* your event, of course. In addition to that four thousand dollars you would pay us."

A flummoxed Al cast a quick glare at Emeric McPherson and then glanced at Gloria and Jill, the other working professionals who were now at a loss for these sudden obligations thrown on them.

"We're always glad to engage in our community. But we're talking the timespan of a week during Christmas season. And I can't speak for the other professionals who have varying priorities."

Nadia Freeman placed her hands squarely on the back of the pew. "If this event is important enough to bring you in here three weeks before Christmas, it's important enough for your friends and associates to come speak with us two weeks before Christmas if they want their children to perform here badly enough."

"Badly enough?" BB scoffed under her breath. "We are not desperate. Like you said, Al, we've got another option. We can walk out of here right now and those White folks will be glad to have our money."

"We can't." Jill kept her tone hushed, as the women huddled together quickly. "We're already here."

"Right," Gloria whispered. "If we back out now, there's no coming back from that. All of New York will talk about how we ditched the community and went to the White church."

A final member stood and lifted her chin. "I would like for *my* child to participate in the Children's Presents. He may not come from your money, or attend your fancy schools, but he is the class president of *his* school, he makes straight A's, has ranked high enough to be a national finalist on his standardized tests, and he has proven he is *every* bit as worthy of being presented as any youth in your program."

One of the board members stood and jerked her jacket as if she were loading her ammunition. "I would also like for *my* grandchild to be presented. She is the captain of her dance team, is on honor roll, and vice-president of her student council. Opening up this program for more children to take part would be the only way you'll get my vote."

"Well, my kid isn't an honor student but he is fantastic at building and fixing houses to help disabled people who have a hard time getting around. Why are the only factors for kids to participate money and grades?"

Several other parents stood and stated their wish for their children to be presented.

A nightmare unfolded in front of Al, one she'd caused. What had been a casual stroll through a beautiful church yesterday, and an intention to come here and have an informal discussion, had grown into a hurricane.

But something had to be said now, to calm the storm. Rising again, Al addressed them all. "We hear you, and we understand. This is not a decision I can make alone. Ulti-mately, the people who have overseen the Presents for a long time must decide. But as for talking with you more, I can commit to returning for a meeting next weekend. I'll also check for parents who can join me."

"Sounds right on then," Nadia said. "And by confabbing with the other parents, would you also include your father and grandfather as well? Many in our community have only read about their great accomplishments in the newspapers, or heard of them by word of mouth. Our children here at this church would love to meet scientific men in person."

"I would like to meet the great Dr. Theodore Césaire myself! Can't say I've ever seen him come to these parts from his nice building over in Central Park."

"Me, too! I ain' never met no scientist myself." The person speaking chuckled some. "Well, hold up, not no *legal* scientist anyway. I do know a coupla chemists, though."

Laughs erupted around them.

"Boy, hush! You tellin' on yaself," somebody said while hee-hawing.

"Our children could also be part of that private tour at the Historical Society," the original man who asked now reiterated.

"You know what, Doctor, I like this self-interest stuff. Thank you," one usher said.

Yet again, Al brought down the hairiest eyeball on Dr. McPherson that she could muster.

"It looks like I've started something here." Dr. McPherson's gaze at Al was not exactly a plea but a petition. "Which is a good thing. Maybe this is a relationship that's been a long time comin'." He slipped up and almost blew his professional cover, a hint of Southern twang creeping in. "I don't mean to put an unfair load on Ms. Césaire's shoulders. We are not here to punish anybody but to ensure this arrangement works well for all. Everybody should walk out of here feelin' good about it."

He cast a reassuring glance at Al. "Of course, I will attend this meeting myself, and will be glad to roll my sleeves up and help any way I can. I will also reach out to my colleagues about giving their time. This here unity is what we need."

The First Lady's smile was bigger than the Christmas tree in the foyer. "Excellent!" She clapped her hands, clearly grateful that four thousand dollars wouldn't be walking out the door. "In that case, any objections to starting over with the vote?"

"All in favor of offering our church as a venue for the Presents upon four thousand dollars received and with those conditions? Ayes?"

"Aye!" was a chorus across a near-full congregation.

"Nays?" the First Lady inquired.

Not a one.

"You can bring the check and the contract anytime you'd like."

The moment the meeting concluded, Al at the side corridor she'd walked through yesterday. There Pastor Freeman stood, with disapproval all over him. Once their gazes clashed, he turned and marched out.

As the meeting emptied, Jill pulled Al aside, whispering, "How will you tell your meme this? And when? She told you to skip this church, that these people did not like your family."

Meme. Al had gotten so sidetracked over the past two days that Meme's warning felt like eons ago. And Al did not have just Meme to be concerned about. How would all the Presents parents feel about bringing this event to Harlem for the first time in decades? The families had grown accustomed to a certain elegant ambiance and distinguished luxury. She hadn't discussed this change with them.

Seeming to read Al's mind, Miss Clara tucked in her lips with worry. "The other parents will never agree to opening it up. I know your heart was in the right place, baby, but we should have brought this to them first before we came here."

Al's heart thudded practically off its hinges.

"Al, it's all right. Nothing is binding yet," Gloria counseled quietly. "If the others don't agree, we can find a way to bow out gracefully, and still come back to volunteer sometimes."

Al clenched her pocketbook. "You were right the first time. We can't back out of this now."

After First Lady Freeman finished pumping their arms, Nadia approached.

"I'll be in touch with you tomorrow, A'Lelia, about that write-up on your family history. Where will we be interviewing? The Historical Society? Your home would be spectacular for a more personal feel."

Al swallowed irritation. "The Historical Society has the

right amount of collection items for you to view. That will suffice."

"Awesome, and I look forward to your grandfather's answer of when he might come see the community and perhaps sit for an interview. Good day to you, sis."

Al redirected her attention so she didn't redirect her hands. On the other side of Nadia's satisfied face stood Dr. McPherson.

"Li'l sister, what it is?" His beautiful teeth grabbing his bottom lip, he raised a hand in the air for BB to give him a grip.

BB left it right where it was. She folded her arms and cocked her neck back several degrees. "Doc, what was that about? You discussed us like we're Nazis in here or something. We're not anybody's enemy, and we sure enough don't need this church so badly that we need to serve a prison sentence."

Lost on what he'd done wrong, Emeric took a read of Al and her friends.

"Let's go outside." Al shepherded them all out of the pews. But her discontent matching BB's, she leveled him with it now. "Where we can handle this privately."

Out in the parking lot, Jill and the others read the tea leaves. Jill offered to drop BB off at their apartment, and Gloria and Miss Clara headed to their cars with no small talk.

That left Al to spin on her heels and face Emeric directly.

"I'M IN TROUBLE, HUH?" Em started. "I could tell by how you and your clique were peepin' each other, all quiet, like 'who's goin' to get the switch and clean it off for him'? We haven't even went on our first date yet."

"Who said there would be one?" Al closed in on him.

"I had hoped, the way we were gettin' on last night, you'd show me where to find the fattest, greasiest…" He messed his face all the way up. "Nastiest…"

"Self-interest, Emeric? Self-interest! Like we're thugs out to get them?" Al aimed an index finger at Em's nose. "What makes you think, after you just talked about my community and me that way, we're going on some date? You've committed me to a whole other project I don't have time for. When would I have time to breathe these next few weeks, let alone go out and have fun?" Her attitude tilted aside with her head. "What right did you have?"

He turned serious. "Listen, A'Lelia, you needed help in there. They were voting based on their feelings, even after all those amazing things you said about the meaning of this program. They can't relate to it, because one, it's hard to see outside their own struggle, and two, because none of your work applies to their world or their circumstances. They can't connect. Most people in there have never even bought a *Vogue* magazine."

"But if they had voted against us, we would have walked out of there with our heads held high, knowing that we tried. We wouldn't owe anything to anyone. I have no need to prove my Blackness, Emeric, and my family has *nothing* to prove."

He had touched a sore spot, a tender issue she must've guarded with every ounce of her life. Her chest heaved up and down, and her breaths raced out of her just as fast as they did yesterday. He was beginning to see why her blood pressure reading was high. She may have been experiencing a panic attack.

"A'Lelia, nobody's asking for guilt." He softened his voice. Or maybe, her fiery passion for her cause was softening him. "They're asking for respect. They're wanting this arrangement not to be transactional but dignified. And like you, yes, I do come from a successful family. I know people who come from money are used to transactional relationships, making deals with folks we can't stand just to move upward and onward. But people who don't come from money only have their dignity, and they need to look you in your eye and get respect back. In a world that takes so much of our people's dignity, they're always wanting respect first, money second, and that can't come in a single transaction."

Her lovely eyes left him for a moment to roll to her eyebrow bone and back. "You think I don't know what our people have been through, Emeric? My family is blessed. That doesn't mean we don't understand others' hardships. It also doesn't mean we don't go through things. Our problems are just of a different kind."

He reached out his hand for one of hers, inching it off her

hip. "Knowing about suffering is one thing. Knowing how to talk to people about suffering when theirs is different than yours is another."

He took his time, so his tone didn't sound like condescension.

"It means crossing invisible bridges many of us don't see. I'm a healthy young doctor who attends sick people older than me, so I might know a thing or two about this. A lot of us think because we're all Black that we're supposed to automatically understand one another. But we've got too many invisible bridges between us, built by somebody else, most of them we don't even know about."

Em didn't let go of her hand. It felt too good in his.

"The way I see it, you've got an opportunity here," he continued. "You can bring your event to Harlem, open it up to the *rest* of the community, and build some amazing bridges between two worlds."

Her nose started to run. And she felt it, turning away to hide her face. He slipped out his handkerchief his father taught him to always carry, just in case.

A'Lelia turned her head back toward him to take it, but he held it too high and it wound up on her face anyway, so he just covered her nose and pinched. She stared at Emeric over the cloth, stunned at him wiping her nose, but for these few precious seconds, she wasn't fighting or panicking or asserting her authority. She was surrendering.

"Baby sister BB might have said it best in there," he murmured. "God might have brought you in here yesterday for a reason. This could be the beginning of a conversation long overdue."

Clearly self-conscious that he was wiping her nose, Al took over. "Thanks. I'm not sure my friends and family will see it that way." Some of her fight had drained.

"I've made a bigger mess for you, and I feel bad about that."

"You should." Her gaze shifted. "I appreciate you for trying, though."

"So I suppose that fat, nasty New York hot dog I'm still wanting is out of the question?" He also itched to know if she could eat greasy street food.

Amusement lifted some of her worry, for a moment anyway. "For today it is. I have to go explain to the others what's going on." Her gorgeous eyes widened. "And receive *my* tongue-lashing."

"Let me help you."

"You can't." She squeezed her forehead. "I did this myself. My grandmother told me not to come here, and I…wandered in here anyway. What was I thinking?"

"You were thinking about how much you love this, and that's right on." That level of devotion had attracted Em to her from first contact. He nudged her hands down, the perfect excuse to touch her again. "What can I do?"

"Meme…" It floated out of her subconscious as if it hadn't been intended for him.

Still, "What is a meme?"

Blinking her way out of her thoughts, she replied, "French for grandmother."

A Black French family? Well, that was damn interesting. "So you really are French and you weren't just jive talking yesterday in your delirious state? Like how a lot of Black folks say they've got Creole or Indian and they don't. But if I go to France and look up your people, the French government keeps real records on y'all?"

Her sudden amusement lit up everything on her, and reminded him of why he would stick around and keep working to see more of it.

"I didn't have a delirious state yesterday."

"Psh. You could've fooled me."

"And yes, I really do have French heritage. I can show you my family's French government records, *sir.*" She said that with pride, too. "But right now, I have to go."

That was a shame. He wanted to grab unhealthy New York food and debate her some more, or hit another club and watch her mouth another song to herself. "I got you into this, so I'll roll up my sleeves and give you an assist."

That idea was apparently tossing around her mind.

"All right, we hold rehearsal three evenings out of the week from six-thirty to eight-thirty. Depending on what happens tonight with the others, we'll be here tomorrow. You can come then."

Playfully, Em prodded her. "How will I know what you all decide tonight? How do we contact each other?"

Rolling her eyes at him being slick, Al capitulated and opened her purse, rummaging through it. "I suppose maybe we could exchange numbers."

Em produced a pen from his inside pocket. "I was thinking along those same lines." Since neither of them had a piece of paper, he took off his glove and pointed at his palm. "You can just write your number here."

"You're not slick." A'Lelia still took his hand and wrote on it, though.

"I think I am, but if I agree with you and pretend I'm not, can we go get something to eat?"

"Not while I have to go clean up your mess."

As she held his hand and wrote, he smelled the Royal Crown hair grease she probably hot-combed through her hair to smooth the roots she'd sweated out last night. Greeted by that most familiar scent of Blackness, Em suppressed a grin. Her hair wasn't as kinky as his was. Her kink was a little looser, softer, finer, but it was still a kink, nonetheless. Her eyes may have been blue-green, and she may have been French, but he wondered if the hair on certain other parts of her was just as African as Kunta Kinte.

She passed him the pen and headed off.

"Hold up. Isn't it my turn to write my number on your hand?"

"You're not heading up the event. What information would I call you for?"

Em strolled behind her to her car. "What kind of food I like. What I want for Christmas." *Who* he wanted for Christmas. His favorite positions. He kept that thought to himself. "What kind of movies and shows I'm into. My shoe size."

He was glad to hear her giggling. At least she no longer glared at him, ready to beat him with a stick. When she stopped, he stopped in his tracks.

"Damn. Is that what I think it is?"

"What?" she asked, unlocking it.

Em jumped to grab the door handle before she could. "Don't pretend you don't know what I'm talkin' about." He couldn't help admiring her 1969 Mercedes Benz S-Class, a Christmas cranberry, fully loaded with dark-gray seats and a deep woodgrain panel on the dash, one of the most impressive cars on the market.

Indifferent as somebody casually putting on their shoes, A'Lelia slid her polished tassel-top Etienne Aigner leather loafers inside, distracted with what she needed to say to whomever she needed to say it to.

"Until next time, Doctor." She turned the ignition.

"That'll be soon, Miss Whatever-Your-Career-Title-Is. What exactly do you do at this New York Historical Society they kept mentioning in there?"

He couldn't decide what was the prettiest part of her eyes —the substance buried deep behind them or the intensity of light around the edges.

"I'm a Cleaner-Upper-of-Doctors'-Messes." She reached

to close her door just as he was pushing it toward her and she jabbed her fingers against the door panel, flicking them to assuage the pain.

"Oh, I'm sorry. I should have warned you first." He squatted just inside her doorframe and removed her glove to check.

Two of her fingernails were broken. "I just got these done yesterday."

"I apologize. I'll pay for you to have them fixed." He rubbed her fingertips. "I can't get anything right with you, huh?"

"And I can't stop getting things wrong." Tears welled up on the other side of that statement, and her worry about this situation trembled in her bottom lip.

"Al, you're not… I hope it's okay if I call you that. You haven't gotten anything wrong. You couldn't have predicted what that hotel would do. And God doesn't make mistakes."

"I could have been more careful, and now…my family…" Letting out slow breaths, she set her hands on the steering wheel so she didn't fumble again, and waited on him to close the door this time. "I have to go deal with this. Thank you."

Today, she had been ambushed, and Em hadn't made it any better. He'd expected the people of the church to be more gracious. Back home in the South, he was accustomed to tiny, country churches that would have fallen over themselves for such a lavish affair, with *or without* receiving money for it. Below the Mason-Dixon line, where some families still sharecropped the same land their great-grandparents had worked as slaves, accomplished Southern Blacks who'd made something of themselves were considered heroes.

In those same communities, Em still had cousins and extended relatives who didn't look Whites directly in the eye when crossing them on the sidewalk, dropping their heads or staring away until they'd passed. It broke Em's heart.

So Emeric had understood A'Lelia's "quiet rebellion"—achievement as a sophisticated form of revolution. She'd spoken with fervor that aroused him in more places than his mind.

Yet, Harlem wasn't the South. They weren't impressed. One couldn't simply throw money at them and expect subservience.

Em couldn't blame them. He rarely saw this kind of independence and assertiveness among regular, everyday folks who weren't marching. He'd attended college in Georgia, and the Black intellect and accomplishment there had been off the hook. But it was still the oppressive South, very much still Massah's house. A Black person's biggest challenge was "staying in their place," no matter their education or stature.

Yet, here in New York, the self-worth and resolve Em witnessed today among regular folks had affirmed why he'd moved here. Now he understood why he'd been gasping for air in Tennessee where he was born. He couldn't put his finger on it before. Today, for the first time, he could.

On his drive home, he steered around every corner with renewed life. Graffiti art decorated the buildings. Record stores blasted Marvin Gaye's "What's Going On" along the sidewalk. A Black street preacher stood at the intersection and condemned him. He handed a ten-dollar bill to a homeless man in a Santa hat. Feeling good, he hung a right around Seventh onto Lenox where he caught Dr. King's bust at Esplanade Gardens.

Respect first, money second. Em was in *New York*.

But A'Lelia.

Unsure how much time she'd spent in the South, he guessed it may not have been much. She likely hadn't experienced both worlds so she could respect their crucial differences. A bruised fighter, she'd felt that she and her circle were attacked. How did they mend this bridge separating one another on different sides of a divide?

With this on his mind, he didn't stop for takeout. He would humor his aunt and eat her cooking right on up.

"Hey, Auntie!"

"Hey, baby," she called from her living room where she knitted. "How was the church meeting today?" She'd left after the church service.

"It was interesting." He plopped into a seat on the other couch. "Aunt Dee, let me ask you something."

"Go ahead, honey, what is it?" Focused on her needle-work, her hands kept flipping, hooking, and tugging.

"Have you ever heard of a man named Theodore Césaire?"

Her hands continued their flow, flipping the thread over again, her needle looping nonstop. "A scientist. If I remember correctly, he made some device for World War One. You know I don't know anything about science, but he's a very smart man. Lives right here in this city. My daddy might have even known him. Why do you ask?"

Em pondered how much he wanted to share right now. "His granddaughter, A'Lelia, came to Mount Bethel for that after-church meeting."

"Really now?" she said without looking up. "What for?"

"She's asking to have a program called the Annual Christmas Presents, or something like that. You heard of it?"

Aunt Dee's needle slowed, and she peered up. "Shut your mouth. Have it where?"

"At Mount Bethel."

Her needle stopped. "Folks that rich came to *Mount Bethel?*"

He nodded. "Yes, ma'am." He scooted forward on the couch. "I'm thinking about helping her make this happen."

Santa must have flown his sleigh up Dee's face, the bells and reindeer and Christmas presents flying around all over it.

"Oh, Emeric, you would be the perfect person for that." Needle and thread thrown down in her lap, she slid forward and opened her arms. "This would be awesome for you. With an affair like the Presents, you could make a name for yourself."

She pulled him into her big press n' curl, squeezing him until he could hardly breathe.

"I'm so proud of you. With your good heart and fine manners, that high society crowd will eat you right up. You will surely be accepted into the Swordsmen now. Before you know it, you'll be in all the right rooms, going for trips to Sag Harbor and Martha's Vineyard. You might not have to wait two years to leave Hillside either. It could happen in a few months." She broke the hug to study him, her eyes out-twinkled the lights on the Christmas tree. "Look at God opening doors, just like I've prayed he would."

He hadn't exactly thought of all that. His heart was simply troubled because of what his mouth, normally so slick and smooth, had gotten A'Lelia into.

"GRANDBABY, THAT YOU?" Meme called from the sunroom of her home in Scarsdale. She liked to recline with a friend or two on Sunday evenings and play Pitty Pat, Pinocle, whist, or some other card game. If she wasn't up for entertaining, she'd read *The New Yorker*.

In the foyer, a life-sized wooden Black Santa's elf held up his arm to the sky and welcomed Al in, as he had since she was a kid.

"Is that our darling A'Lelia?" Aunt Sara Ann, one of Meme's sisters, asked.

Today of all days, her grandmother had company. Al's legs were already wobbly, but now, they knocked together like bowling pins.

"Good evening, everybody." Al hung her outerwear in the coat closet. "No need to get up. I'm on my way in."

But Meme's hard-sole Daniel Greene house slippers clopped through the house, making their way toward Al.

"BB told me yesterday that you all found a glorious church, and they're available! A miracle!" A broad smile all over her, Meme did a happy jig with her arms. "Get in here and tell me which church it is."

The phone rang.

"Hold your horses. Let me grab this first." She removed one of her clip-on earrings to take the call.

The Christmas bells of Al's heart swung wildly, clanging over every one of her ribs along the way.

"M-hmm," came Meme's reaction after an uncomfortably long silence. She listened to whoever spoke to her on the other end.

"Oh?" Meme asked. "Well, my goodness…I…have no idea what in God's name. Of course. Of… Yes, she's here. I suppose I'll see all of you shortly then."

By the time Meme hung up the phone, her sister, Aunt Sara Ann, stood on the opposite side of the living room.

"Sue, why do you look like that?" Aunt Sara Ann, who they called Sarann, asked. "Teddy all right?"

Meme's body slowly performed a forty-five-degree turn from where she still held the phone receiver. "Girl. What got into you?"

Al gathered her courage for this rare instance of running afoul of her elders. "Meme, it was an accident. I didn't mean to."

"How do you accidentally wind up where I told you not to go?" Meme's limp body almost fell into a sitting chair.

Al rushed to catch her and ensure she was not having a heart attack or a stroke. "Meme!"

The woman's arm shot out, a clear barrier between them, her eyes laser-focused on her third grandchild. "Answer me."

Two more of Meme's friends emerged from the sunroom.

"Suzanne, honey, what's going on in here?" Meme's clueless friend came to greet Al. "Hey, precious, it's been a while since we've seen you. How've you been?"

"Ida, they might need a minute. Come on," Aunt Sarann said.

Meme shook her head in disbelief. "Don't bother. You'll know soon enough. Everybody's on their way here."

"Who? For what?" Sarann asked.

Al swallowed. "Meme, I stopped by yesterday and saw how beautiful it was. I've always admired it from outside, and I was only curious. I only wanted a tour. They offered a meeting, so I went over again today."

"Girl, you wanted to be in that church, and your mind was made up." The hard bristles of her grandmother's glare scraped Al's conscience. "You did what you wanted to do, and turned your back on your family. Now you've gotten yourself—all of us—into a mess."

The doorbell rang, and so did the phone. While Meme answered one, Al went to face the chattering voices on the other side of the door.

"A'Lelia, tell me Clara doesn't have her facts together." Removing her coat and gloves was Tally Hayes, the wife of Senator Hayes. She grabbed Al's hands and rubbed. "Baby, tell us you misunderstood or something. We can fix it. We'll let them know it's a mix-up and you had the wrong location. You were searching for a different church and wound up at Mount Bethel by accident. Your presentation was intended for a different group." She spun toward the others. "How many churches are in New York? When I'm campaigning for Hayes, I confuse them sometimes myself. They'll understand."

"That's not a bad idea," Meme said, eying Al in a silent warning not to say too much. "We could send them a nice letter with a lovely fruit basket."

Before Al could explain some of the very optimistic points Emeric made earlier, the senator's wife let go of her hands to brainstorm with Meme.

The doorbell rang again, and a miffed Aunt Sarann opened the door for two more parents entering.

"Whose idea was it to open up the Presents to the general public? Suzanne, you told A'Lelia to do that?" one grandparent asked Al's grandmother.

"No, honey, she went over there to see the architecture, just being her sweet, curious self, and those people took advantage of a young girl is all," Meme explained while the two hugged.

Al seethed at how that sounded.

"Well, the way I heard it," Eddy Hadley said, "she stood up in church and begged those people to let our children come there. Like we're beggars who've been turned out everywhere else. And that church gave her hoops to jump through, like *we've* got something to prove to *them*. Like we need to prove ourselves worthy of being in their presence."

The elder women spoke among one another, excluding Al. More parents and grandparents arrived, and Meme took them to the living room where they brought out folding chairs and packed into the room.

"Just so we're clear, no contract was signed committing us to that venue, right?" Attorney Adam Payton finally turned to Al and asked.

"No. Nothing has been signed, but—"

"Good. So we have no obligation to go back there. They can hem and haw all they want. Without a contract, or a deposit placed, there's no skin off our backs."

Eddy Hadley persisted. "The Presents has never been held in the ghetto. Excuse my language, but what drove her to such foolishness? A'Lelia's judgment these past four years has been impeccable. She usually doesn't step a foot wrong."

The others nodded and waited, compelling Al to step forward from her place in a corner.

"A'Lelia was getting anxious," Meme answered for her.

"She's been working so the event isn't put on hold for a year. She has such a big heart, and she didn't know any better."

As much as she loved and appreciated what her grandmother was trying to do, quite frankly, Al didn't appreciate that. They discussed her as if she were a hyper child who had run through the grocery store with an open bag of flour. She questioned if she should allow her grandmother to maneuver them out of going back to Mount Bethel.

"That's it then. We'll simply write to them that it was an honest mistake and she wandered into the wrong location," Mrs. Hayes reiterated.

"And then it's solved," Eddy Hadley added. "There weren't any other options?"

They all stared at Al.

"Yes. One," Al answered. "St. Peter's Methodist, a predominantly White church not far from Greenwich Village. Very nice people. They were willing to have us also."

"Oh, I've heard of that. It's perfect!" Meme clapped her hands, a giant laugh of relief ringing out of her.

"Yes, so have I. Child, you almost gave us all a heart attack. There was no need for any of this," another parent declared. "It's settled then. We should get St. Peter's the check and start moving."

Al nervously counted twenty-four parents and grandparents who'd showed up.

Meme rose from her chair. "I'll contact Druella and arrange for Al to pick it up and take it to them so rehearsals can resume."

"Everyone," Al interrupted.

Her grandmother shot her a tacit warning from across the room, for Al not to defy her again. The wisest move right now would be for Al to zip her lips and let her grandmother fix this.

This could be the beginning of a conversation long overdue. Emeric's words sat at the forefront of her conscience.

"I know it's more preferable to attend St. Peter's." She inhaled resolve and exhaled fear. "But I saw the parents at Mount Bethel and heard their pain." Al recalled their faces, the way they'd stood up, as if they were facing a boogeyman. "They have felt excluded from this wonderful opportunity, and they would like to take part."

"That's fine." Mrs. Hadley bucked her eyes. "They can start their own Children's Presents. Nobody's stopping them. This is ours. It was never meant for them to be invited in the first place, and if you hadn't gone over there, they wouldn't have had the chance to invite themselves."

"Al," Tally said, "you've done a remarkable job until now, and we are so grateful. We're giving you a smooth, gracious way out of this error in judgment you had." Her indirect admonishment was elegant.

Did Al tell the senator's wife she could keep her smooth, gracious way out?

Meme cleared her throat. "A'Lelia, grandbaby, that's enough now."

"Meme," Al insisted. "How will it look if we drop a Black church to attend a White one? Mistake or not?" She finally cut to the chase. "Yes, I acknowledge that I didn't come to you all before taking a meeting there. But maybe it's time for this event to reflect the changing times and what this city is going through."

She didn't speak this part, but perhaps, the pastor's upset about their "convenient kindness" was playing out here now.

"Bless you, baby," another grandparent said. "God is surely going to do big things with your amazing heart. But the Presents has held out against wars, a pandemic, violence and marches, assassinations, the Depression…you name it, the Presents has held up. That is the point of the program. It celebrates our perseverance. It honors how the changing times *can't* change us."

Voices of agreement chimed in.

Al pressed. "The PR for this will be awful. How will all of us—leaders and businesspeople of the community—explain that we're not *in* the community?"

"That's not true," Glencora Kirkland replied. "I'm there all the time. Taught there for thirty-seven years. I've got children teaching there now. I've spent much of my life with other people's children, and it has been my pleasure. But the Presents is *our* time. It's *our* space. Once you open it up to everybody, it becomes another unenjoyable commitment I have to attend. You had no right to take that from us."

"Exactly. If anybody can do it, it's not special anymore!" Mrs. Hadley insisted.

"A'Lelia, your heart is in the right place, but you have to be careful with outsiders who aren't us," Mrs. Kirkland explained.

Her grandmother's hands spread before her, signaling an artfully worded, poised mouthful of nothing was on its way. "She was—"

"Meme."

Al held up a hand, to which her grandmother flashed indignation at even tacit backtalk. Al should have just shut up. Nonetheless, she dug into herself for what she *had been* thinking.

"I didn't think of the politics of all this. Again, for that, I apologize. I was smitten by the beauty in a Black house of worship. This hidden diamond in the rough streets of Harlem has also weathered the storms of time. They have also survived. What a powerful visual that would be, all of us coming together for Christmas after these tough years around the City. It could be visionary, not just in New York, but around the world."

The elders stared at one another, their eyes silently calling her naive.

"Baby, that all sounds real nice. But if we have it there this year, they will expect us to have it there every year."

Tally Hayes twiddled her thumbs, deep in thought. "Al does have a point. Aside from all the pretty imagery, back here in the real world, Winston was just elected state senator representing some of the people in that church, whose votes he asked for. What will they think about their senator not wanting their children to participate alongside his? I'm afraid our hands may be tied now. Even if it's just for this year."

"I agree. David's dentist office is in that area, and some of those church members are his patients," Mrs. Waters added.

Dr. Isaacs said, "I have two medical offices in that part of town, and I can't have my patients thinking I don't want my kids around theirs. It's not true, but they won't understand what the Presents means for us. They'll form their own opinions and go to a new doctor. We might be stuck with this. At least for this year anyway."

Mrs. Waters slowly nodded. "This might actually be good marketing if we do it right. A'Lelia may have been off with the way she handled this. But she's not totally wrong in the vision."

"You all can speak for yourselves." Mrs. Hadley rolled her eyes. "The Children's Presents is a classy event, and it'll stay classy. I will not support having it at Mount Bethel, and especially not bringing in outsiders. A'Lelia, baby, I've known you since you were born. Always loved you, always will. But if you'd like to change it, start your own."

To Al's horror, several others agreed.

"They hate us anyway." Another grandparent stood, decades of emotion blowing in and out of him. "Our help has never been enough. We'll never give enough money, or Thanksgiving turkeys, or afterschool programs. One event won't make them any happier. Let's just sit this year out. We can give our kids a break and pick it up again next Christmas. Let's vote."

The fiery sword of Meme's glare cut straight into Al. Ever the high-performing grandchild whose achievements had always pleased, Al had rarely been on this side of her grandmother's firm hand.

"Fine," Mrs. Kirkland stated.

By now, thirty-seven parents, grandparents, and other family members had crowded into the Césaires' living room, some of them spilling into the hallway. That was out of eighty-two children participating in the event, so many families were still unaware, and thus, not present to have a say.

Tally continued. "All in favor of St. Peter's, raise your hands."

Al performed her own count while both Mrs. Kirkland and Tally did so aloud.

"Eighteen," Tally said. "All in favor of Mount Bethel with new terms, raise your hands," she instructed.

"You must be out of your minds!" Mrs. Kirkland declared. "My grandchildren will *not* participate."

"Neither will mine." Mrs. Hadley snatched up her purse.

Nineteen people voted to go forward at Mount Bethel. The other half stood. Too indignant for pleasantries and pretense, they headed toward Meme's front door.

Meme reached for her old friend, Mrs. Hadley. "Everyone, we've been doing this together in lockstep for more than a hundred years. Don't let one awful thing that happened at the Murray Hill break us apart."

"Your granddaughter's silliness broke us apart. Nothing else," Mrs. Hadley snapped while jerking her coat off a hanger.

Al broke to see her lifelong village split in two.

Mrs. Kirkland plopped on her fur hat. "There is no way

you're going to redo an entire fifty-thousand-dollar event in less than two weeks. I will not stick around to be embarrassed in such a pitiful shellacking. And once you hold this event in the trash can, we might not be back next year either."

On the outside, Al struggled to maintain the poise and decorum on which she was raised. On the inside, she sobbed.

"Oh, my Lord," Tally noted upon their exodus. With half of the families walking out, the Presents was essentially canceled anyway. "We can still make the best of this. It might be on the slim side this year, but it's possible."

Racked with misery, Al managed to move the cinder blocks in her feet across the room to see about her grandmother. "Meme...this wasn't my intention."

What words would suffice?

Suzanne Césaire patted her granddaughter's face, her mind clearly somewhere else. "Of course it wasn't. You didn't know. You're just young and naive."

Though Al's spirit languished, nevertheless, her grandmother's words butted heads with the grown woman Al was becoming.

AT ELEVEN-FIFTEEN THAT NIGHT, Em checked Aunt Dee's refrigerator one more time, squinting in near dark, save for the oven light. The message board sat as empty as it had before he'd gone to sleep earlier that evening. A winter draft blew through him.

"The way you keep checking that refrigerator, you must be expecting a phone call." His aunt came padding in.

Harold had called earlier to go out for drinks and pool with the guys, but with Em having three sixteen-hour late shifts in a row this week, he couldn't risk going out and then being so tired he was subpar on the job. Even Pam had asked around town, learned who Em's people were, found Uncle Ike in the phone book, and she'd called.

Wrapping up, he readied himself for nighttime in New York. "Yes, ma'am. What are you doing up this late, Auntie?"

"Couldn't sleep. Your mama wants a full report tomorrow, so I have to come out here and put my hands on you. This way, I'm not lying when I say I checked for myself before you left and you were still just fine."

Em chuckled. "Tell her I'll call her once I put a few rounds out of the way."

"Listening to that frog in your throat, the rounds might put *you* out of the way. You've been in a funk since you came home from that church meeting, honey. You picked at your food. Twiddled your thumbs during the game with Ike. Feet dragging the floor, and you're so good about picking them up. Just like Bennie McPherson taught ya. Did something else go on?"

He loved her too much for her to know the real reason he'd picked at his food. "The congregation wasn't jazzed about having the Presents there. I spoke and addressed them to help the Césaire lady out. Only, I did everything but help. I hurt what she was trying to do. There's obviously some bad blood between certain groups here, and I didn't realize that when I inserted myself. I may have gotten her in a lot of trouble on her side of this, too. So I was checking the refrigerator for whether anybody had called with news."

Or specifically, if A'Lelia had called.

He and Al were not well acquainted, but anybody would notice that the fighter he'd bumped heads with at the hotel was not the disheartened woman he'd parted ways with that afternoon.

Earlier that day, Em had loved discovering the Black folks of Harlem as a collective. They were adjusted to successful Black people with money already. There was no "wow" factor for them at hosting the Presents, and thus, they could turn it down because it wasn't special here in New York. This was the New York he'd been in search of when he'd left Memphis—empowered Blacks. On the other hand, they'd snubbed a young woman doing something for Black youth, and she had thought enough of Mount Bethel to go to them.

His aunt rubbed his arm. "Emeric, these last few days,

your spirits have been up. You were finally finding your rhythm here in the City—instead of coming home and going to bed, you've been making plans and getting dressed up. You're dancing in that mirror like you did as a boy. It's been good to see my sister's young man back to his silly self. I don't want you getting discouraged. Your time in New York might have started off rough, but things are turning around."

"I'm not sure about that, Auntie." Right now, he was due at Hillside.

He'd moved to New York in pursuit of bigger opportunities, but Em was uncertain if something bigger wanted him.

"Well, baby, I can't do anything about how they're treating you at that hospital, but with this situation at the church, I've got plenty friends. I can make some calls. See if they'll ease up. I have a relationship with Pastor and First Lady. I can ask him to step in and fix things."

Em recalled how Al and the pastor had argued something awful on Saturday. He still wasn't sure what that was about. During the meeting, Emeric had seen Pastor Freeman lingering in the corridor, listening to the arguments. But he never came forward to speak on Al's behalf. Em doubted the man would help her now.

"No, ma'am." He had already ruined A'Lelia's position enough. That's likely why she hadn't called. "I gotta go make bread, Auntie. Love you."

Worry all over her, his mother's youngest sister sent him off. "Have a good shift, baby. We're proud of you."

Hours later, New York's Christmas troubles were in full swing.

"Gimme some skin, young man!" Em held his hand way up in the air.

The injured little boy who'd come in with a broken leg and black bruises all over his body, cracked up into giggles. "You're too tall! I can't reach it!"

"Say *what?*" Em teased. "I thought you said you were a big boy?"

"I *am!*"

"Let me hear it again. You're a what?"

"I'm a big boy!" the cute kid said between chuckles.

"Now do it in your big, brave man voice." Em pulled his fists to his waist like a wrestler. "Say it like a football player! Gimme some growl in there!"

"Rrrrr…I'm a *big* boyyyy!"

"Funkadelic, my man!" Em brought his hand down for the boy to finally reach it and give him five.

Then, Em pulled a domestic violence pamphlet from the wall and handed it to the boy's mother who held her son underneath her sad smile. With a black eye and a non-credible explanation, a broken wrist, and stomach pain, the ER had sent her to surgery to rule out internal bleeding. She seemed too weak to laugh fully.

"Ma'am, here are some numbers you can call when you're ready. Merry Christmas." Em and the little six-year-old growled their goodbyes, and Em moved on to his next patient.

On to more car accident injuries, alcoholics sinking their Christmas woes in the bottle and coming in with bad livers, more women with black eyes and cracked ribs who swore they'd accidentally run into a wall, malnourished kids with unexplained welts on their bodies, and elderly people with the same on theirs. People's sadness and stress multiplied during the holiday season. He was still on bottom-floor duty in emergency.

His stomach was talking to everybody in the building ten hours later; he could finally break for a ten-minute bite to eat. No sooner than he stepped off the elevator in the basement than the intercom system crackled to life.

"Code Triage. Code Triage. Any and all available hands

needed in surgery. I repeat, this is a Code Triage. Any and all available hands, please report to surgery or the ER."

Triage? Em flipped over his badge and pulled out the folded code cheat sheet stuck inside. He'd never heard of that code.

External disaster.

He pivoted and headed to the sixth floor. There must have been a massive accident somewhere, like a building fire, a multiple-car collision, a building collapse, or a concert gone wrong, requiring this many surgeons at one time. Along with all the other doctors now crowded onto the elevator, he and the other two Black doctors exited and headed to scrub in.

He placed one cap over the front of his Afro and another over the back, so it would be minimally disfigured. Tying on a surgical robe, he joined the others in the march to the operating wing where the chief resident stood on a chair calling out surgeries needing hands and giving assignments.

"What happened?" Em asked one of the others.

"Bridge collapse."

"Damn." Em shuddered.

The chief resident yelled, "We've got a broken femur with a cold leg, arterial bleeding, life or limb, major vascular emergency, in D4!"

Em lifted a hand. "I'll take that."

"Jackson and Farr!" the chief resident said and moved down his list. "Severe internal bleeding in D5!"

Em raised his hand again.

The chief resident's eyes scanned past him. "Oliver and Durham!" Looking at his list, he continued. "Abdominal bleed in D6!"

At this point, Em simply left his hand up.

"Frazier and Tillerson!"

Finally, once most of the others had headed off, four surgeons remained and there was one surgery left. Em and the other two Black doctors stared at one another.

"Lyles and Bottoms, you two can take the burns in D1," the chief resident said in conclusion. That took care of the last two Black surgeons. The other remaining doctor was Latina.

"Cleveland, I arrived here for these assignments before half of these folks did, and I've got more surgeries under my belt than most of them. Why wasn't I given anything?" Em asked bluntly.

"Those are the breaks, McPherson. You're not in Memphis anymore. You're in New York. Gotta pay dues." The CR jumped off the chair and headed out.

The Latina doctor didn't bother arguing. Apparently, she was more willing to play by the rules: keep her head down, no complaining, wait it out.

Em stopped by the nurses' station to speak with one of the nurse assistants. "Is Dr. Berger around?"

"Yes. May I tell him what this is about?"

"Assignments."

"He's busy with his rounds, but I'll see if he can manage."

"Can you ask him to make time for me when I finish up at four?"

"I'll ask him."

Sixteen hours in, an exhausted Em was buzzed into the chief surgeon's office at the end of his shift.

"Mr. McPherson, how are ya? What can I do for ya?"

"I've been better, sir. I was wanting to discuss my assignments, because I've waited patiently since August and I still haven't scrubbed into a surgery since I've been here. Not even this morning when there was an 'all hands' catastrophe."

"Well, son, it's—"

"Dr. Emeric McPherson, PGY2."

Not son.

The younger surgeon almost stated that last part, but he absolutely could not be that bold, no matter how his spirit raged to scream it after all these months in purgatory. It would have been career suicide.

The attending's eyes still flared, but the ire inside them dissolved. "Dr. McPherson, assignments around here are pretty competitive as you can see. Everybody's jockeying for a chance at some experience."

"I have actual experience. By myself. No supervisor. So why am I being treated like somebody still in training wheels and made to compete with people only starting out?"

"You've told us what you did in Memphis, but New York is a different ballgame."

"How so?" Em dropped his hands down on his hips. "Are the stomachs different here than the ones down there?"

Again, the senior doctor delivered a warning glare that didn't go away this time. "Careful. We'll look at the schedule and consider where your skills and experience will be best for you and the patients."

"That's what you said when I spoke to you last month."

"And we'll continue giving your request urgent review. Anything else?"

The surgical tools in Em's chest cut him up inside. He'd been a fool to come here. Ignorantly, he'd thought there was no racism in New York, and thus no limits to his advancement. There were more Black professionals, but they still suffered here just as in the South. He didn't know what to do. He liked the culture of the City, but not his situation.

Exhausted from more than his long shift, he lacked the stamina to change into street clothes, putting on his heavy coat and scarf over his scrubs. He still hadn't eaten today.

Ready to put some food in him, he'd crash and sleep before he started his next shift at midnight again tonight.

"Dr. McPherson! Emeric!" The front desk nurse assistant stopped him just as he reached the end of the corridor.

He spun around to see her waving a yellow note over her head.

"You have a phone message here."

A SLEEP-DEPRIVED Al sat at the end of the table in Mount Bethel's conference room.

First Lady Freeman frowned. "What happened to the four thousand dollars? And our children were supposed to participate as well."

Today, Mrs. Waters and Dr. Isaacs led the negotiations.

"The amount has dropped to two, instead of four. We don't have as many children participating now," Dr. Isaacs explained in one fatigued breath. "The event has decreased in number significantly, so our budget will not be as big."

"Quite frankly, why bother?" Pastor Freeman asked. "You're less than two weeks away from the event and don't have any arrangements. Why don't you save everybody the trouble and sit it out until next year?"

The First Lady leaned forward and explained in a softer tone, "What the pastor means is that we were under the impression more money was on the table, and since the amount offered is smaller today, you could make up for that by allowing our children into your program this year."

Dr. Isaacs dropped his head.

Mrs. Waters stiffened through her back. "Ma'am, every participant must qualify for a Presents and be selected, no matter who they are or where they came from. This is why it is called the Presents, and not the Free-for-All."

All over her face, the First Lady dropped her poise.

"Mrs. Waters," Al murmured, placing a hand on her back. That had been harsh.

"In light of that, this conversation is over," Pastor Freeman concluded. "Miss Césaire, we appreciate your group considering Mount Bethel, but our answer is 'no.' First Lady, will you please have Sister Rowe escort them out?"

Just like that, one of New York's longest-running programs had burned to ash in these fires of incivility.

"I'll do it." It flew out of Al's mouth before her brain had time to ponder.

Mrs. Waters and Dr. Isaacs stared at her to zip up.

"You'll do what, child?" First Lady Freeman clarified.

Surrounded by people older and wiser than her, Al scrambled for just what she was proposing, or how exactly she would get it done. Anxious, self-conscious, and a smidge scared, she collected her thoughts. Yet, one state of mind A'Lelia did not feel in that moment was wrong.

"I said I'll do the Presents myself." She gazed up at Pastor Freeman. "If we open it up to any Black child in the City who wishes to participate—no qualifications, no auditions, no school grades or family pedigree, or any of that—will you agree? We can call it a special year of unity where there are no barriers between the families of New York. Please bear in mind, we are not committing to hold the Presents here in future years. It is for this year only. Everybody gets to take part. For two thousand dollars. We'll also handle expenses." A'Lelia stared straight at Pastor Freeman.

Eyes wide as snowballs, Mrs. Waters dressed down Al. "Even if we agreed to it, we don't have the manpower for *every* child in the City to participate. How will they rehearse? Order and pay for outfits, have them delivered on time, have transportation to get here because not every family has a car? Al, baby, you always have the best intentions inside that beautiful heart of yours, but this time, your intentions don't add up to common sense. That's why we're in this pickle in the first place."

"So you're not willing to open it up for all children this one year?" Pastor Freeman clarified.

"That's just not possible, Pastor," Dr. Isaacs answered. "Like Mrs. Waters said, that is not what the Presents is about. But more important, A'Lelia could never pull that off with so few people or resources in place. She's lost most of her help, and she's now operating on a skeleton budget. So A'Lelia can't make offers or promises with no way of seeing this through."

"That's not true," another male voice spoke from outside the conference room, just over the pastor's shoulder, out in the corridor. "She'll have help."

The pastor pivoted to see who was behind him. As did everyone else.

"Excuse me. My apologies that I'm not dressed for the occasion. Just finished a shift, and uh, a church meetin' wasn't on my bingo card for today."

Al's heart might have sleighed around every curve in her body.

"Dr. McPherson, we appreciate your services this past weekend, brother, but I don't believe you were invited this time," Pastor Freeman noted.

"Who is this?" Dr. Isaacs asked. "Is he a former Presents participant? Whose son is he?"

Despite his Afro being slightly akimbo, his eyes some-what fatigued, and a five o' clock shadow peppering his chin, the rugged effect aged him as more mature and distinguished, more handsome than Al had imagined him throughout her sleepless night.

"Am I invited, Pastor?" someone else asked, a few paces behind the doctor. A middle-aged woman entered, her face kindly, her aura unassuming. Al suspected she was one of those people who gave amazing hugs. "Pastor Freeman, First Lady, how is everybody? I'm sure you all remember my nephew, Emeric. Our good sister, Ms. Rowe, informed me of the meeting today. I regret not knowing about yesterday's affair or I would have attended. I hope you don't mind me joining now."

Al smiled to learn Emeric didn't have to survive New York alone. His being surrounded by an aunt's love knitted another thread into the fabric of his character.

Since she already focused in his direction, Al allowed her eyes to take a full-body tour of him. After all, his coat *was* wide open.

Still donning his scrubs from the hospital, his slender frame boasted contours, particularly along the pectorals of his chest, down to the quadriceps of his thighs curving in his pants, right over to his...

They were in church.

She redirected her gaze back up to find his eyes waiting, a knowing side-grin on his face.

"Mrs. Perry, what brings you by?" First Lady Freeman's lighter tone indicated a certain high regard for Emeric's aunt.

Mrs. Perry's round cheeks seemed permanently jolly. "What is this about Mount Bethel having an opportunity to host the Presents? Why are we not chomping at the bit to do so?"

Pastor Freeman reiterated his concern. "It just can't happen this year. Even if Miss Césaire still had the money, she doesn't have enough hands to do all that work."

"That's why my nephew and I are here," Mrs. Perry

replied. "And if the extra two thousand dollars is the final deal-breaker, I'll cover it. What do you say about wrapping it into my upcoming annual donation? Instead of five thousand, we'll make it seven?"

Dr. Isaacs and Mrs. Waters stared at this woman.

"Ma'am, thank you so much for your kindness. But if I might ask, who are you?" Mrs. Waters inquired. "And why do you care about the Presents, seeing as how you are not part of that community?"

"Oh, to the contrary, ma'am." Mrs. Perry removed her hat and gloves. "I was born into the Shipman family. Many decades ago, when I was a girl, before my family fell on hard times, I, too, participated in the Presents. Those were some of the best years of my life."

Dr. Isaacs thought about that. "It's been a long time since I've heard the name Shipman."

Upon hearing this revelation, Al's insides trembled, and she gazed at Emeric again. Now, he had hardened, and avoided eye contact. That must have been a terrible situation to bear. Where were his parents? Al had only heard scant rumors about the Shipmans, with no specifics. That tragedy occurred before she was born, so she'd never met the real people involved.

"It's not so easy getting to Martha's Vineyard when you're working two jobs." Mrs. Perry's voice wavered under the weight of whatever she'd endured, but she pushed her chin up. "So if someone here is suggesting the Presents be made accessible to all children—even if it's just for one year—I will help their dreams come true."

Al's load she'd been carrying for days seemed to lighten on her shoulders.

Stumped, Mrs. Waters cleared her throat. "I also knew of the Shipman family years ago. It's good to see you're doing all right, and I hope your people are as well. At this point, though, Pastor Freeman may be right. The window may be too tight."

"Or is that an excuse for you to avoid opening up the Presents so *every* child can feel they are worthy of being *presented* to the world?" Mrs. Perry replied, not dropping a whiff of her pleasantness.

"I'll make sure she has whatever manpower she needs." Emeric came to sit in the empty seat on the other side of Al. "Every moment I'm not working, I'll be here. I'll make sure Miss Césaire has hands."

While the others continued discussing the terms, he hung his arm atop her chair. "French."

Atoms and electrons. Lighting up just about every cell in her body, brighter than all the Christmas trees in Central Park. "Doc."

Nonchalant, he faced forward, one of his fingers resting on her shoulder through two layers of clothing, every bit as tantalizing a sensation as skin-to-skin.

"It's just Emeric. Em for short."

Underneath his primary scent of an over-bleached hallway lay notes of his outdoorsy cologne, faint but distinctly him.

"Thank you for being here," she murmured.

Answering with a nod, his eyes still facing forward, he said nothing further. Yet, the something else between them was still speaking.

"Dr. McPherson, you're committing to this endeavor along with your aunt and Miss Césaire?" a concerned Mrs. Waters asked.

He didn't bat an eye. "Yes, ma'am."

No sooner than the words left his mouth did an animalistic growl rip out across the room. Everyone stared in the direction it had come from. Al shifted and her head turned with all the others.

Another loud howl erupted across the table. Behind it sat an embarrassed Dr. McPherson hugging his stomach in, as if trying to suppress the hunger pangs. "Like I said, it's been a long day."

People were as sympathetic as they were amused.

"We've got a little meat and bread in the kitchen," the pastor said.

"I'll go make you a sandwich to tide you over, baby." His aunt was already up on her feet.

Pastor Freeman studied Al.

There is no way—and I mean none—I would ever let a family of thieves and murderers walk in these doors and pose like you're good people.

The tacit question hung between Al and him. Who would be the thief now if he robbed his church of this opportunity?

"Very well then," the pastor said. "It appears the young lady has more heart than we thought."

On the spot, Al pulled herself together and restarted her planning, all over again. Having scrapped the entire Presents playbook, she would have to recreate it in a matter of days.

"First, we need a theme. What do you all think of, 'The Stars of New York Are Brightly Shining'?" she asked.

"I love that," Mrs. Waters murmured.

"Beautiful," Mrs. Perry agreed.

The wheels of Al's mind creaked forward. "Then, there's ordering new uniforms, but first, what roles should we have? Will they be angels, wise men, hierophants, trumpeters—"

"Why not let them be whatever they want?" Emeric linked his hands together over the table, where he seemed to lose himself inside them for a moment. "I know we're in a church, but from my understanding, this Presents program is about talent and intellect. If these kids are stars brightly shining, let them show us what brightly shining looks like in *their* minds. Let's empower them to define it for themselves."

His vocal cords thick with emotion hinted at a story there.

"That is precious," Sister Rowe murmured. "Absolutely precious."

Al hadn't extracted herself from the stars Emeric was hanging in her sky, all of them twinkling in her head. A hard cough from Mrs. Waters snatched Al out of the clouds.

Three hours and many faxes, phone calls, discarded ideas, and pieces of paper, lists, and diagrams later, they concluded the meeting.

A tired Al wrangled on her coat. Behind her, firm hands grabbed it and guided her arm into the sleeve, jerking it nice and snug around her shoulders. She reached for her scarf, but he already had it, wrapping it around her neck twice, just as tight as her mother and grandmother once did.

"Thank you."

"You're welcome," he replied in a voice heavy with exhaustion.

Emeric tucked her scarf into her coat collar to filter out the winter wind, and then lifted Al's collar up to her ears, the metal of his silver-and-gold watch brushing her cheek.

"Why are you here?" she finally asked him. "Giving your time when you don't have to, for an event you've never been part of? You're clearly worn out."

"These past few months, I wasn't clear on what led me to New York. I just knew I couldn't stay at home." He now wrapped himself up for the cold. "I had started believin' I'd made a mistake comin' here, that this place wasn't for me. Then, a few days ago, I bumped into a girl with a flame in her, whose candle lit up a city." Not letting go of her gaze, he picked up Al's saddlebag to carry it. "Who wouldn't want a front-row seat to the fire?"

The big Nor'easter of a snowstorm Al had brought down

on her community all settled into perfect peace, the way he'd just described it.

In the parking lot, Al battled herself.

I didn't choose that. I never chose *you. You were pushed on me.*

Luke's words months ago burned rubber on the streets of Al's mind. What if her inner fourteen-year-old was mistaken again this time? What if the good doctor Emeric simply liked to help people and did not share her intrigue?

"Would you like to come over and I'll make you a proper dinner?" A condensation cloud of Al's heat floated out of her.

Whether he shared her interest or not, the man had come here straight from his job and he deserved a hot meal.

His face dropped. Instantly, Al regretted asking.

"I have to start my next shift at midnight. Or I'd love to see if your skillet is just as strong as your spirit."

"Midnight?" He'd spent his entire evening here right after work and had to return to work *again* soon? "That's in three hours, Emeric."

"Every minute of this has been worth it." In the parking lot, the temperature had likely dropped to the teens, but not on Emeric's face.

"Then use my couch. If I remember correctly, I believe the Shipman family was of Sugar Hill, and that's farther Uptown. Our building is closer to Hillside."

His lips glistened, and Al couldn't help watching them while they moved.

"Yes, ma'am, that sounds copacetic. I'll tail you."

A'Lelia had no clue what she was doing, but of all the chaos and uncertainty swirling through her right now, the one sentiment she didn't feel was wrong.

EMERIC HAD VISITED plenty of nice buildings on family trips throughout the South, and particularly in Atlanta with his fraternity brothers. But this one they'd named The Saint-Emilion, situated at the top of Central Park West, was not another nicely designed building.

From the moment the Black doorman threw open the door, greeted them with a massive smile that actually seemed genuine and not tolerant, to the polished floors without a single streak on them, to the Black lift boy heaving the lever to operate the vintage elevator, it was not just another build-ing. This building was a time machine back to Old World New York.

"This is a righteous spot," Em murmured on the jour-ney up.

Al smiled at his reaction. "I'll tell Pépé you think so."

"Pépé? Who is that?"

"My grandpa."

"I thought his name was Theodore."

"It's grandfather in French."

"Oh." Em's surprise rose with the numbers over the door.

He exited the elevator that deposited them directly into the penthouse. "You'll tell him, as in, he lives here? Or you'll tell him—"

"As in, he had it built in 1912."

Oh. Emeric kept that one to himself. He couldn't act like he'd never been anywhere or met anybody. A lot of families he knew were fortunate to afford a tiny one- or two-room shanty while others still resided on their former owners' plantations, let alone commission whole buildings in the heart of one of the biggest cities in the world.

"Why is it called the Saint-Emilion then? Why not The Césaire? Who is Emilio? His brother or something?" He had so many more questions to ask, his astonishment dancing down the long hallway of niches holding awards and honors.

Chuckling, she kicked off her shoes and removed her outerwear like she was relieved to finally be back in her space and have the day behind her. "Saint-Emilion is our ancestral town in Bordeaux, France, where my family returned to after the French Revolution. Some Césaires still live there. Every other year, we go for a visit."

Just as Al said this, she ripped off her hat and instantly froze at the vision of herself in the hall mirror. Her long, smooth locks from the first night at the Murray Hill Hotel had fuzzed up tightly in the winter elements since church yesterday. Self-consciousness combed over her, and blood rushed to her face, maybe as she realized that spontaneously inviting a man to her home meant inviting him to more than just the top layer of her.

"I like it better nappy."

The two stared at each other in her mirror, both of their rock heads testifying to how busy the last few days had been.

"Sorry for the mess. I've been swamped with class and research."

The place was immaculate.

"Class and research?" He removed his things. At the same time, he eyed the framed degrees for A'Lelia Antonia Césaire, a Bachelor of Arts in History and another in French from Columbia University, and a master's from the University of Oxford, England, in French and European History.

"I'm studying for my doctorate up the street. You want to give me those and I'll wash them, so they're fresh when you go in?" Her hand held out toward Em, she wore a hokey grin that brightened her up. "You can put on Papa's warmup while you wait. It might be kind of big, but it should do."

Em could have waited until he'd arrived at work in a while for a fresh pair of scrubs, but he had been wearing these nearly twenty-four hours and probably smelled like one of the stray mutts on the street at this point. "Yeh, appreciate that. So do you call him Papa or Pépé?"

"My father is 'papa' and my grandfather is 'pépé'."

This French lineage was interesting.

"Mind if I shower?" he asked, now that he recalled just how long his day had been.

"No. This way." Again, she turned her head as soon as he noticed blood rushing to her face. As if she was running from close proximity, Al spun around and walked into the doorframe.

"Oh, snap. You all right? That had to hurt." He reached for her head. "Let me look at it."

"It's fine." Her face was scarlet before, and now deepened into an embarrassed beet red. "Really, I'm cool. I'll bring you those warmups as soon as I find them."

Emeric started to bring her to him and calm what must have been nerves, but he let her go on. Even if he found her clumsiness adorable, running into a wall must have been awkward enough without him magnifying it for her.

He helped himself to the liquid soaps and a piping-hot shower in a spacious, old-fashioned bathroom. Once he shut it off, there was a soft knock on the bathroom door. Tying a towel around his waist, without thinking, he swung open the door.

That clumsy student had changed.

In her furry kitten slippers, black leggings glued to her shapely calves and thighs, she was cozy and cute underneath her oversized sweater. An hour glass had nothing on her. Through blue-green eyes, and large, butterfly eyeglasses, she stared back at him. In her natural element, her kinked-up hair now tied back with a silk scarf, A'Lelia was the sexiest he'd seen her.

Her gaze froze at his bare chest and then dropped. She blinked several times at what she saw. Em's chin fell to his chest so he could see what she was seeing. He was also having quite the reaction. There was nowhere to put it, so…

She pushed the warmups toward him. "Found them."

Em hadn't been thinking much today, only acting on impulse. Why start thinking now? Instead of the warmups, he reached for what he really wanted.

Grabbing her waist, he drew Al to him and went in for some sugar. Caught unawares, her arms crushed between them, she still held the clothes. He took them out and dropped them on the floor, removing the next-to-last barrier that kept him from all of her. Soft as the ripest strawberries, her lips were too succulent to stop sucking. Her fingertips skating over his chest hairs didn't help his reaction go down. At full length, it poked into the top of her belly, where she was lush.

They entered one long, never-ending tongue thrust, mouths connected, Al's tongue stroking his, and Em inserting the one organ that he could into her. So caught up in how good she smelled, how passionately she spoke, how fiery and determined she fought, how luscious her hips were that she hid underneath those fancy clothes, Em couldn't bring himself to disconnect, not even to bite, nibble, lick, or breathe. So their faces just stayed attached, one burning Christmas flame.

His hands made a home atop her butt, ample and round, with more than enough meat for them to rest on. Al shuddered when he pressed his manhood against her midsection. He imagined the curves, ridges, and folds of her womanhood closing around his fullness. More than a kiss, Em lost himself in her, and he hadn't yet entered her.

Her fingers crawled up the nape of his neck to play in his Afro. He could have sworn her nails caressed every pore of his scalp, sensations so relaxing he was sure he would bust a nut. Her thumb-stroke along his jawline tickled body parts far past his belly button. Al's whimpers finally lured Em's tongue from her mouth down her chin and along her throat. The pulse over her collarbone clamoring, nipples knocking through her sweater and bra, her breaths quick and excited, Al's body activated his, natural and effortless, like air feeding fire.

Em forced himself out of a blaze, not taking this any further. He had to go to work and if they started up, he'd lose his job. The universe affirmed his decision.

"Sissy!"

The door up front opened and closed suddenly, and the two pulled away from each other. Al spun around and stood in front of his erection.

"Everybody all over town is talking about how you blew up the—"

Baby Sister stopped at the other end of the hallway, a surprised, goofy grin breaking out all over her. She gave Em a nod. "Doc! What it is?"

Standing behind Al in the bathroom door in only a towel around his bottom half, Em threw up a wave. "Baby Sis, what's happenin'?"

Dramatically, the kid swallowed. "Apparently, a lot." She pointed in another direction. "I'm just gonna go mind my Kool-Aid." Backing away, she quickly shot her sister an ecstatic face.

Self-aware yet again, Al pivoted. "I'll be upfront on dinner duty when you're ready. Sit anywhere you want."

"All right then, French. I'll be there in a minute."

She tried to close the door, but he held it open, and Al gazed at him with a question between her eyebrows.

"You can go ahead," he told her.

Regardless of how tired he was, he would watch her walk away. Shaking her head, giggling, she started off down her hall. But he wasn't playing. Twice as developed as her sister, Al's figure needed an entire Presents all by itself. And she was wearing leggings. He dared not miss this.

Once he donned Papa Césaire's oversized running warmups, he took his time in the hallway, peering at various photos and paintings of Césaires dating as far back as the early eighteen hundreds. Some paintings depicted peaceful countryside, what appeared to be vineyards, quaint country chateaus and farmhouses, White men linking arms in grape fields, underground wine caves filled with barrels and well-dressed White men and women toasting with glasses, large smiles on their faces, and depictions of various elaborate buildings and monuments in what was clearly Paris.

Over the decades of the nineteenth century, the people and families in the paintings transitioned, from their skin color as starkly White to having shade ever so slight that one could miss it if they didn't look hard enough. And Em was looking. At some point, *one* of those White men *had* to interface with somebody Black.

The scenery also evolved, from rural countryside porches and fields to unpaved streets running between cramped buildings, as well as horses, carts, and carriages. Sandy-toned men and women stood proudly in shops, over desks, in parlors, and in front of huge steamships, shaking hands, and holding up documents.

In the center of them all, he finally found what he was searching for.

"What's happenin', Doc?" a voice asked behind him.

"Baby Sis," he began, pointing at a photo of a long building. "Why do you all have a photo here of the Palace of Versailles?"

"That's where our Black ancestor, Omalara Tossou, started this family. She was brought from West Africa and given as a bodyguard to a French noblewoman in Queen Marie Antoinette's court," Baby Sister explained.

Em's attention finally whipped away from the photos so he could study her long and hard. "A bodyguard?"

Baby Sis grinned, her pride letting him know she told no falsehoods. "You ever hear of the Dahomey Amazons?"

Em's jaw fell slack.

"Of course, you already know those White men weren't going to let a sista be great," Baby Sis explained. "White men turned her into a concubine, made her start birthing kids. Once the French Revolution started, Mama Omalara disappeared. We don't know much about her after that."

The only dark-skinned person on the wall sat in a cushioned French parlor chair, dressed in a fancy, European gown that seemed to offend her so much she could not bring herself to smile and pretend she enjoyed wearing it. Surrounding her were five children of happier disposition— three clearly of mixed race, and two who were unequivocally Black. It was as if, like most Black people, this ancestor in the photo lived two lives—the one she may have been forced into, and the one she'd tried to enforce for herself.

"Who are those two Black babies? Did you all come from them?" For every answer, at least a hundred more questions popped into Em's mind. The only other Blacks he'd met who could recite non-slave history descended from true Creole heritage, or their forebears had been born to White planters or White businessmen who'd spared them from the whip.

"Those are her younger kids she had with a Haitian man. Either he was Haitian or West African. We descended from this one here. Maria Josepha Tossou.

Baby Sis pointed at a lovely mixed-race girl with long, kinky hair that could not be controlled with lace, pearls, and satin bows. About age thirteen or fourteen, the girl draped one arm protectively over her African mother's shoulders, and her other hand on her youngest Black sibling seated in her mother's lap. No smile adorned her face either. To the contrary, baby girl's expression almost dared anyone to touch a single one of them.

Damn. They were the descendants of a Dahomey Amazon. Now, he saw where Al got it from. He wondered what her PhD dissertation would cover.

Emeric's body finally forced him to search for the nearest couch. His shift started in just over a couple of hours.

The scent of baking bread had filled the halls, along with smoked cheese, cooked ham, baking apples, cinnamon, and nutmeg, all pulling him by the nose. Once he rounded the corner, he faced a large living room on one side, and a kitchen and dining room on the other side. The scenery beyond the panoramic window had to be one of the most gorgeous views to exist and it still didn't compare to the woman in the kitchen.

Expansive New York City at night, all aglow, its surrounding suburbs in the backdrop, beyond barren trees of a quiet Central Park in the foreground, all whispered to the Memphis transplant the promise and potential that had summoned him here.

"I'm almost finished," Al called out.

Em sensed he was standing in a location almost as significant as the Lorraine Motel, and he wanted to explore more of the French Renaissance grandeur. But he couldn't.

"Your family line is…off the hook." He finally fell onto a cozy, elegant sofa near neat piles of open resource books and papers.

An open textbook was stamped, "Property of Columbia University," one of the country's eight Ivy League institutions she'd cavalierly referred to as "up the street."

"I have a lot of questions, but one I need to ask now." Fighting sleep, he struggled with his words.

"Shoot." In the kitchen, she transferred something from the skillet to a plate.

The next time Em opened his eyes, he'd died and woken up in Heaven. Sunken completely in the large couch cushions, a light throw over his legs, the temperature just right, no garbage trucks, carburetors, screaming kids, or surface noise just outside his window, he was immersed in quietude and peace. Over him stood an angel, her hand gentle on his shoulder, reminding him of being awakened for school by his mama in childhood.

"It's eleven twenty-eight." With Al's glasses removed, her eyes invited Em into her home all over again. She murmured, "I tried to let you sleep as long as possible, but I don't want you to be late. You have four Monsieurs all wrapped to take with you so you're not hungry at work today."

"Monsieurs?"

She grinned and shrugged. "A Croque Monsieur is a French version of ham and cheese. Nothing special. I was trying to make something quickly."

"I'm sure it's fine. Thank you." He resented having to go anywhere. Emeric McPherson's only Christmas wish was waking up just like this every day.

His scrubs folded and warm from the dryer, he changed

fast, and in the bathroom, she'd set out Royal Crown, Soft Sheen Care Free Curl Activator, Classy Curl Oil Sheen, and a large pick to shape up his misshapen bob. But tonight, he'd have to skip it and jet. He dared not be late. All the chief resident needed was another excuse to keep sidelining him. Once he exited the bathroom, Al stood at the door with his food in a fancy lunch bag.

"If you can't make rehearsal tomorrow night, I understand," she said. "Go home and sleep."

"I promised you I'd be there, and I will. Even if it's just for a couple hours. I've got these next two shifts to work and then I'll be around most of the weekend to help. Plus, I'll find you more volunteers."

Skeptical, Al leaned her own tired weight against the doorway. "I don't expect that many signups this close to Christmas. A lot of families have already made other holiday plans. They don't have time to prep their kids for an event in ten days, let alone in one week. We won't need many more volunteers when there aren't many kids now." She let out a sad sigh. She'd gone through so much, only to see this fall apart. "I just appreciate you being here to support it."

That statement reminded him of his question, but Em didn't have time. He pressed a simple kiss on her forehead. If he did anything more to her, he wouldn't have been leaving. "I'll see you tomorrow evening, French."

"WE SHOULD DISCUSS THE ITINERARY," Al said to her friends and sorority sisters gathered in her dining room the next morning. She'd fallen asleep after Emeric left, and was back up again at five. For the full day ahead, she had a meeting for her research with a mentor at one-thirty, and before she headed to Mount Bethel, she'd stop by her grand-father's office and apologize to him in person.

Her family deserved more loyalty from Al than her going to a place that disrespected them. She'd embarrassed them with that fiasco on Sunday. Though she was torn on what else she could have done, she would still go address her pépé in person. For now, she worked to clean up this mess as best she could.

"I don't want to talk about scheduling." Gloria sat back in her seat with her non-alcoholic cider. "Does anybody else want to talk about the itinerary?" she asked their Madames sorority sisters who'd signed on to help.

They all shook their heads.

"I want to talk about Emeric McPherson," somebody said bluntly. "Where'd he come from?"

An uproar of hollering, high-fives and hand-clapping broke out around the table.

"That's the only reason I hauled this belly on over here!" Gloria testified.

The others chimed in. "Mm-hm."

Jill laughed. "I don't have a belly to haul, but it's why I'm here."

Al rolled her eyes at bigmouth BB, sitting there all smug, an Afro puff on either side of her head. She'd called up practically everybody in town before the man had left.

"What did you have on?" Jill squared her shoulders, eyes lit up and ready for the skinny.

"Ladies, we need to work," Al reminded them. But in her head danced the memory of Em's appreciation when he'd thrown open the bathroom door and saw her. Under time constraints to cook, wash his scrubs, and construct a plan of action for the next few days, she honestly hadn't thought much of her loungewear. But then came his physically endowed *appreciation*.

"Not with you sitting there smiling like that!" Gloria scratched her belly. "So what *did* you have on? A nightie? Silk jammies?"

"She was wearing raggedy black leggings," BB reported to the congregation.

"They weren't raggedy." Al didn't own anything raggedy.

Jill lifted an eyebrow. "Leggings aren't a bad move, raggedy or not."

"There was no *move*." Despite her denials, she couldn't stop grinning every time she recalled Em's freak face.

Luke had never devoured her that way, had never communicated with his entire body—from his eyes to his manhood to his feet firmly planted—that if all of New York was on fire, he'd die a happy man right there with his mouth on hers.

Last night, for the first time, A'Lelia understood what Luke had been trying to say.

I've only been with you because our parents pushed us at each other when we were too young to say 'no', Al. All the cotillions, banquets, and balls, I had to be your escort and people started putting us together for everything. I didn't choose that. I never chose you. *You were pushed on me. But we don't have to do this anymore. And I want a* real *woman, not a pretty prude too stiff to shag her way out of a book. You're a nice girl and all, but you're better off with a guy who likes being bored.*

Confused these past eleven months since Luke had broken off their ten-year semi-courtship—if she could even call it that—she'd spent the year asking herself what was wrong with her, rejecting invitations in shame and making excuses to avoid the gossip mill.

Though he'd been rude in speaking his truth, Luke was saying they didn't match. Their courtship had never amounted to a true relationship. It had been a performance, and he was pulling the curtain. In freeing himself, Luke had done Al a favor, too. If he hadn't, she'd still be hoping and wishing for a half-ass commitment from a man whose jaw didn't drop, who didn't leave his job to come to her, who didn't encourage her, speak up for her, or see her as a flame lighting a city.

And that was before she even thought of Emeric's tongue, or his erection.

"Who is Emeric McPherson?" somebody else asked, breaking up Al's flashback. "What high school did he attend? Seems I would have remembered the name Emeric. Is he with the McPhersons of Jersey or the ones on Long Island?"

"Neither," Gloria replied. "He's here from Memphis. I think he went to one of the Atlanta schools and then to Meharry. I heard his mother was one of the Shipmans."

A pall fell over the table. Just about everybody had heard

the tragedy of the Shipmans, one of the many Black families who had risen at the turn of the century, clawed their way to the top, even surviving the Great Depression, only to eventually fall.

The elevator dinged again, and another Madames sister stepped off. "He still here?"

As Gloria predicted, they didn't get any work done, but Al was grateful for the silliness after the chaotic last few days.

"So this guy just spoke up for you at the church?" a sorority sister asked.

Jill cleared her throat. "The day *after* he swept her off her feet. You should have been there. She was falling all over herself. He said he'd had to carry her. Since when does Al faint?"

One of the sisters leaned in. "Never. Little Miss Perfect is always in order. I need to see who this is that's got you weak."

"Is he a good kisser?" somebody asked.

"You and him kissed?" Eyes wide, Jill sat up in her chair. "When were you gonna tell that part?"

"None of your business, nosy! I'm not answering that!"

"You don't have to. Those nipples are telling it all," an observant Gloria pointed out.

Al inspected her chest, and they'd hardened. The entire table was at it again, high-fiving and bursting into laughing fits, when the phone rang and BB got up to answer it in the kitchen.

"Al, it's for you." Her sister held out the receiver, but with the others laughing and chatting, Al took it in the living room.

Picking up the phone, she tuned out the noise in the other room. "Good afternoon."

"Hey, A'Lelia, it's Dorothy Haven. I just wanted to let you know my children will skip this year's Presents after all. Since it's wound up on the small side this year, we could just take them to do other activities instead. We wish you luck with it, though, and hope you and your family have the loveliest Christmas."

"But Mrs. Haven, it will be beautiful. The church has agreed, and with the candles and stars and all, it'll be so… Hello? Hello?"

The phone line had gone dead, and the busy signal indicated she was in a conversation by herself. Al faced her sorority sisters and friends on the brink of tears.

"Another parent canceled. Instead of twenty-nine kids, I have twenty-seven now."

"Oh, chile, it's not the end of the world." Gloria held her arms out so Al could come over for a hug. "No matter how this year turns out, you got yourself an Emeric McPherson out of it."

That didn't exactly lift Al's hopes. She'd singlehandedly ruined the Presents.

Later that afternoon, at school, she rehearsed what she'd say on her way from Fayerweather Hall on Amsterdam and around the corner to Pupin Hall on 120th Street. What words sufficed to apologize to one of the greatest Black men alive for sullying his good name?

"Hi, Lydia," she said to the department secretary. "Is Pépé still around?"

"Oh, good afternoon, Al, he's just wrapping up with a student."

Pépé's door swung open, and his pupil came out.

Lydia extended her hand toward his office. "He's all yours. Except for your grandmother, I'll hold his calls."

"Thanks, Lydia."

She didn't fear retribution since her pépé never fussed at

his four children or eleven grandchildren. Patient and thoughtful, he only required them to explain the logic of their decisions. He always swore the shame of their foolishness would convict them harder than he ever could.

"Muguet." Not looking up from the magazine he read, he called her the French name for the Lily of the Valley flower, what he called all of his granddaughters. "Just a moment. Want to finish this paragraph. This old mind might not remember where it's at when I come back to it."

"Take your time." Stepping over piles of papers intertwined with books, she plopped into the stiff seat on the other side of his monstrous desk.

"Ha," he muttered to himself, taking a pen and wrapping a big ink circle around the paragraph. "Kid actually knows what he's talking about." He stuck the pen inside and closed the magazine. Laying his thick glasses atop it, he remained hunched over the desk. "Well? What is it and how much does it cost? And who do you want me to talk to? Your mamman or your papa?"

No amount of rehearsing this had prepared Al to face him and tell him she'd screwed up. Always proud to brag about her achievements, it was strange to sit here in failure.

"Ahh, it's not a money-before-Christmas kind of problem. It's the other kind. You came to tell me something before somebody else tells me."

Sunday, she'd left his house before he'd gotten home, driven to her parents' house and slept there while her mother made calls to try and salvage some relationships.

"I'm sorry, Pépé."

"No, no, there won't be any of that." He was cajoling and reassuring even while he was firm. "There are actions and consequences, and then there's—"

"Facing them," Al finished.

"Yes. So why don't you start there?"

"I'm looking for volunteers to help, and since a lot of people took their children out, we need more families and children to participate at this late stage. I've really made a mess. People are upset, and I hurt Meme."

Confused, he wrinkled his nose. "Volunteers? For what?"

Now the confusion had passed to Al. "The Presents, Pépé."

"The Presents?" He thought for a moment. "You're talking about that thing happened over at Murray Hill?"

"Yes. What did you think I was talking about?"

"I thought you were coming to tell me you'd met some boy and he got you pregnant. That's what Roberta's been telling everybody."

Al could just wring her neck. "Pépé, she's probably joking that it won't be long before he and I are married and I'm pregnant." Not that that was much better.

Pépé's ears didn't always catch the entire conversation, either because of his hearing or because he wasn't interested in hearing.

"Well, then, what are you worried about the Presents for?"

"A lot of your friends took their children and grandchildren out of it." She let out a big sigh.

"And you didn't dance a jig?"

"Pépé!"

"I'm kidding. Sorta. Of course, a couple of them came to me worked up."

Al's head fell into her hands. "Meme told me not to go."

"And you did. You're an adult now, a leader in your own right. You made a decision. We'll stand behind you. Stand behind yourself."

"I've divided our circles and ended a hundred-year tradition."

"How do you know it wasn't high time for tradition to change? I couldn't say this in front of your mother and grandmother, but the Presents has gotten old, stuffy, and uninteresting. When I was a boy, we just wanted to exist. It was not about privilege or excluding others. Whoever wanted to be in the Presents, could. Many kids didn't do it because they had to work and didn't have time. Not because of requirements keeping them out. It just so happened that the youth with a few more resources, of which I was, could take part. In 1900, many kids were helping support their families. Not prancing around on some stage. The Presents has gotten away from its roots—a celebration of everybody's perseverance and survival. Not just a select few."

As always, a trip to see her grandfather never failed. Not one moment with him was ever wasted.

"It's hard to ignore all the people we love, and even harder to only see twenty-nine kids there."

"Do you know probably the top reason seventeen million civilians and soldiers died in the First World War?" he asked.

Al thought a moment. "A lot of the military was slow to use new technology."

"Exactly. Officers still doing what was comfortable and old. Not adapting to radio, airplanes, and searchlights after Edison gave 'em a lightbulb. All of it could have spared blood. When we don't adapt, we die. The rules are no different for Black folks, rich or poor." His eyebrows rose and lifted his aged eyes, indicating he was concluding the lesson. "Do you think it's good adaptation in a financial crisis to hold a pricey party at a White establishment when the city is hurting? Particularly Black New York?"

He had an amazing way of bringing life into sharp focus.

"No," she murmured.

"No. It wasn't a good idea during the Civil Rights marches of the fifties and sixties, either. Not when most people couldn't enter a White hotel. It was tone deaf."

"Pépé, this is just hard."

"True leadership usually is. Now, who is this boy BB is talking about?"

Giddiness rushed through her at the memory of covering Emeric in his sleep last night. He was having an appreciation moment Al didn't want BB to see.

"Oh." Pépé snickered. "That's who he is."

"It's not a big deal. I just met him. He'll be helping with the Presents."

"Who are his people?" He returned to his magazine, which meant he was getting bored.

"Word has it he may have come from the Shipmans. But he recently moved here from Tennessee. He's a doctor."

Pépé's finger slid down the side of his nose. "Mm. Damn shame what happened to that family. Where's he doctoring?"

"Hillside."

His nose wrinkled up again. "So he doesn't know anybody."

Al used this opportunity to put in a small ask. "Maybe at some point, you might help him out and make a call."

His finger returned to the magazine. "I haven't talked to him, yet. What's this about him staying over at the building?" he asked pointedly, his gaze leaving the magazine to point at her.

"It was just for a little while. He'd helped me out of the Presents situation. He was tired, hungry, and had to clock in soon. I fed him and let him sleep on the couch. I'll be careful and look out for myself."

"Thank you. You're a Césaire. Make him earn you."

Emeric had already started. "I will, Grandpa."

She stood to go. Mount Bethel was calling.

Mount Bethel.

Pastor Freeman.

Before leaving her grandfather, Al searched her mind for how she would approach the pastor's loathing for her family.

How would she navigate this once her grandparents appeared for the program?

This certainly must have been the season for miracles. While she organized her thoughts and lined up the question properly, Al's focus landed on Pépé's bookcase near the very end.

"Pépé, what is this?" Al walked toward what may have been the oldest book on the shelf.

Tattered at its seams, delicate pages darker than her hands, hanging threads barely binding it, wooden boards as covers, it had to be two hundred years old, maybe even three.

Her grandfather briefly peered to see what it was, and his eyes flickered with recognition for perhaps a single atom in time.

"Careful," he cautioned as she lifted it, ever so gently. "I believe my cousin might have left that the one time he came over here. I forgot it was there."

Al marveled at this random occurrence. How had she visited his office so many times and never seen this? "Your cousin, Leopold? He came here to the States?"

"Yes. I had planned on giving it back to him on his next visit. Unfortunately, that never happened."

The Great War started, and eventually, France ordered Leopold to go fight. Her grandfather winced with pain, a rare display of involuntary transparency. Questioning whether to tell him about her discovery, Al decided to give him a moment and returned her focus to the book.

Without question, it was the oldest Al had ever held. So old its covers were made of wood, which meant it was printed in the earlier days of the printing press, as far back as the 1600s or 1700s, but she would need to have it authenticated by an antiquarian. How could Pépé forget something like this? And what was Leopold doing with an antique so valuable? Why had he brought it here? Questions sprouted all over Al's brain.

"Take it," he instructed her. "I don't suppose there's anybody else who'll do anything with it."

In disbelief, Al wrapped the antique tightly in several layers of notebook paper, so it would not fall apart, and then tucked it inside her saddlebag.

Taking a breath, she wound herself up for what she'd wanted to know. "Pépé, speaking of your cousin, Leopold, for my family research I went over the dates of the letters you and him exchanged. And I wonder. Did you ever receive any between August 31, 1914, and May 4, 1915, that you may have misplaced? Or maybe a letter slipped into a pile somewhere?"

"No letters arrived between August 31 and May 4." His pen still marked up parts of the article he wanted to return to later, but his voice faltered. "I was awaiting word from him. Nothing came."

Al's knees almost gave out. Should she mention that he had, in fact, received word from Leopold?

Theodore Césaire's gaze shifted up all of a sudden. "Why do you ask?"

What did Al say? He could help her clear all this up. Or just as likely, that mail receipt could throw the lid off a coffin that had been closed for over sixty years.

"I'm still compiling records as part of my work." She couldn't bring herself to outright lie to him, so she danced around the truth.

"Jeanne called your grandmama," he said in reference to his older sister. "Said you came by the house the other day, digging around. Asking questions about France and Josepha. What is the meaning of this business?" His hand circled around over his magazine.

Keeping her nerves in check, Al remembered that sometimes the best answers were no answers. "Pépé, you've never complained about my curiosity before."

"You've never been so specific with your questions. They've always been general. What year did you design this? Why'd you do it? Why did you go there?" he said, imitating Al. "It's never been 'why doesn't the name and date on this piece of paper match the name on this other one'? You must be turning into a historiography detective or something. If you've got something to tell me, I'd appreciate you saying it and not beating around the mulberry bush." He lowered his head to peer at her over the rim of his glasses.

She still didn't have the letter in her hand. There was no proof. Only a mail receipt. Maybe the letter fell into a gutter, or a mud puddle, or he had gotten it and stuck it somewhere. Al needed to nail this before disrupting his world that way.

"I don't have anything right now." It was as far as she could stretch the non-lie before it actually touched the perimeters of lying.

He nodded. "I'll come help with your event when I finish doing things I find more interesting."

On her way up to Harlem, Al was certain of one thing. Pépé knew the story behind Pastor Freeman's resentment. Knowledge had flickered in Pépé's eyes, just as it had his sister's.

First thing in the morning, she would go to the Naturalization Archives and look up Leopold Césaire's "first papers," or his Declaration of Intention for US Residency—why it had been denied.

For now, she wouldn't risk the book Pépé had just given her being seen by an outsider. At a red light, she removed the notebook-paper-swaddled book from her bag. Her heart suspended, she carefully shoved under her seat the *Biblia Sacra Vulgate, Editionis, Sixto-Clementine,* or in layman's terms, the official Bible of the Roman Catholic Church.

She would take it to Dr. Abrams so they could call in an antiquarian to evaluate its authenticity. Al still reeled that Pépé had even let her take it.

With it safely tucked out of sight, she drove on to Mount Bethel, where Al's eyes surely deceived her.

Astonished, she grabbed her boxes and stepped out of the car, unsure of what to do. At the same time, Pastor Freeman came to stand outside the church doors, clearly marveling at the sight.

The church must have been hosting a big event this evening. How could she hold rehearsals with her twenty-four youth in this predicament?

A tired mother approached her, tugging her two children.

"Excuse me, ma'am," the woman said in a tired voice, "is that the right line if we want to sign our children up to be in the Presents?"

Stretching out of Mount Bethel, through the parking lot, down the street, and around the corner was a line of parents and their children, all waiting in the cold for the doors to open and signups to begin.

A flabbergasted Pastor Freeman walked over to her and plopped his hands on his hips. "We're going to need more than one night for this."

"WE'LL ARRIVE on December twenty-third. You *did* take days off work, right?" Em's mother asked when he called home during his work break.

"Mama, I'm a new resident here. I can't take many days off, but I will be with you all every moment I can spare."

Em reached for his last Croque Monsieur. In one work day, he had already eaten the other three, starting with his first while he'd driven to the job. This sandwich had a whole lot more in it than just ham and cheese. Whatever that stretchy cheese was Al had baked on top of it, the stuff dragged all over his chin, and there must have been four or five other types of cheeses in this thing, plus a creamy sauce that gave the bread a moist sponginess while still crisp and brown on the edges. Did he eat it now or reserve it for later?

"Your aunt says your social life has picked up a lot. You're going out more. What's this about you're helping organize the Presents this year? You don't have any children, so why are you?"

Emeric carefully threaded his response through the small needle of his mother's anti-northern bias. "I've met a few folks and picked up a Christmas project. I'm doing some-thing in the community. Aunt Dee had it right when she told me to go to her church. It's been copacetic."

He played down his eagerness to jet in a minute and head to the rehearsal, where Al was probably overwhelmed. Even if he only stayed a little while before going home to sleep, he wouldn't leave her there alone in a mess he'd helped create.

"Maybe you should choose another volunteer project. Did your Aunt Dee tell you about the Presents? How cruel those people are. Have any of those people said anything unkind?"

"Actually, people have been pretty nice."

"I suppose you need a way to pass the time until you can leave there. I saw Dr. Lew at a charity dinner over the weekend, and he'd love to have you back with him. He said he was shocked when he heard you were leaving, and he would have given you your own surgeries and patients. Have you put in those calls yet to Jefferson Memorial or The Med?"

"Um, I haven't had much time for that, Mama. I'm just focusing on things here since this is where I am. Listen, I need to run. Tell Rose, Carmen, and Billie, I said 'hey.'" He was eager to put this last hour of his shift behind him.

"Billie and Rose are coming next week, and Billie's bringing the kids. Carmen can't come since she's six months now. You might call her and say 'hello.'"

"All right, I will," he said.

Last night, the paintings and histories on Al's walls had sucked him into new dimensions of Blackness. Black French people? What was their story? As much respect as he had for his relatives and community back home, Em hungered to learn what else Black people were doing in the world. He longed to see this New York Historical Society the church members kept talking about. To meet this great Theodore Césaire they either loved or loathed.

In front of Al's apartment window, he'd stood on top of the world, and if not the top, then pretty damn close.

"Are you trying to push me off the phone?" his mother asked pointedly.

Heaviness rolled through him.

Laying his head on his forearm against the wall, he replied, "Mama, I'm not trying to *push* you off. I was hoping we would just conclude the conversation so I can get back to work."

That motherly sigh hit him every time. "Your father and I are excited to see you in two weeks."

"It'll be good to see you, too." Mere weeks ago, Emeric's conversations with his mother were keeping him sane in a New York that was often unforgiving. Back then, he'd eagerly anticipated his family coming to check on him over Christmas.

That was before A'Lelia. New York looked a whole lot different having met her, Harold, and Baby Sister.

"Love you," his mother said from the other end.

"Love you, too, Mama."

Sticking his last Monsieur sandwich in the Litton Minutemaster microwave oven, he turned the knob to "Reheat" and pressed down the wide switch for "Push to Cook." He'd relish this last sandwich now and figure out his food situation later.

"Hey, Dr. McPherson."

He peered up. "Pam, hey."

"You going to Sparkle Club this weekend? Grand Master Flash is having a throwdown with Kool Herc and his Herculords. It'll be a groovin' party. You caught on to those breakin' moves quick last weekend." She flashed her wide, gorgeous rows of flawless teeth. "We had us a nice rhythm goin' at Hevalo."

Em probably should have opened himself to more

options and taken out some different women. He had only known A'Lelia a few days, and that was too soon to even think of commitment. Yet, he couldn't lie on how he felt around her either. Pam seemed like a nice lady who deserved more than only half his attention, which honestly, was what she would get if he took her out. Not to mention, they worked together. Having a woman at work as an option already flashed a fire hazard sign in his head.

"Pam, it's righteous how you've been so cool." He took a breath. "But I don't really date at work." That was the best way to put it.

Apparent in her neck rolling back, the news stung. "But you *do* date women from foul families?"

"Foul?" What kind of jive was she talking?

"That girl you were dancing with the other night? The Césaire girl you kept putting me off for? Her family is foul. Hmph. I thought you were better than that."

The bell dinged on the microwave oven that his Monsieur sandwich was warm.

"I don't discuss other folks' business, Pam."

It disgusted him. People gossiped about his family all the time, especially his mother's origins as a Shipman from the North. Mama rarely talked about it, and her silence only invited more rumors. Then, when it came to money, if relatives couldn't get what they wanted out of his father, they resorted to making up lies.

"What? You don't want to hear the truth?" With disappointed tears crowding her eyes, she choked up. "They killed their own. Her granddaddy is a murderer. Square biz. But you have fun with that." Pam took off from the break room with a fierce stomp.

Em hadn't expected the convo to go in that direction. How could Theodore Césaire be guilty of that, as a Black man—even one with skin as light as A'Lelia's— and walk free on the streets? Particularly, interacting with dignitaries, teaching at Columbia University, and sending his grandchildren there.

Al must have heard rumors like this all the time. The way she had stood up that Sunday and gracefully fielded all those questions about her grandfather and family, she was clearly accustomed to her people being discussed.

Once his shift was over, Em put the thought out of his mind and turned the corner onto Seventh Avenue. He drove into Mount Bethel's parking lot mystified. Cars packed the lot, others still roving up and down the aisles for spots. Meanwhile, people were exiting the city bus, leading their children into the church by the hand.

Today, Emeric entered the sanctuary with chattering families whose collective vibe had shifted. Their shoulders didn't sag with sickness or pain this evening. Rather, chatting on the way inside, their chests were open with anticipation.

At the front, near the pulpit, Al and several other women organized the youth, took their information, and gave them sheets of paper. More women served cups of hot drinks and snacks. Another section of women measured children's sizes. They had formed a makeshift processing line.

Em walked down the main aisle to stand at the back of the line of kids and wait his turn.

"Hey, Doc."

"Hey, Dr. McPherson."

"Good evening, Doctor."

Emeric studied the pews. More young women filled them tonight than he'd seen on Sunday. Their eyes big and bright, the ladies offered him their sweetest smiles.

Feeling like one of those rotisserie chickens rotating on a stick, Em offered an awkward wave. "Evenin', everybody. Merry Christmas. Good to see y'all."

At the sound of his voice, Al's head lifted. Over the children's heads, the pretty chairwoman radiated joy, even if she seemed somewhat tired. "Why are you standing way back there?"

"I didn't want to jump the line."

"Do you want to be fitted for a costume?"

He stared down at his scrubs. "I thought I had that part covered."

Past the line of curious and chatty children, Emeric walked toward a purposeful A'Lelia.

"What are you doing here?" she asked. "You should be resting up for this weekend when we really put you to work."

Embarrassed, he admitted, "I ate all my Monsieurs."

Her open-mouth laughter was a Christmas carol. "*All* of them?"

"All of 'em." He scratched his chin. "I was wondering if I could get some more."

She wasn't fretting, or tense, or nervous tonight. With her eyes shining like that, teeth shimmering, who needed a Christmas tree? "It's kind of busy here but we might be able to work something out."

Her flawless press n' curl from last week was long gone. Hardly any makeup stained her face. Instead of dress slacks or some fancy getup, Al had entered hustle mode—jeans, flats, a chunky turtleneck, and unkempt hair that hadn't been touched by a pressing comb in days. Tending to the city, working out her historic event, Al was nothing less than perfect.

To steer his mind from the lascivious direction it was going in church, he surveyed the groups of children. "How many kids you got here?"

Al rubbed her thickened crown of hair. "A hundred and four, and this is just the first night of signups."

She gave her clipboard to someone else and led Emeric away from the others. With worry coming out of her now, she spoke in a low, soft voice. With her in those jeans, her vocals so husky, memories flooding his head of her in leggings last night, Emeric fought to control his thoughts in the Lord's house. He discretely rearranged his equipment inside his coat.

"We'll need a bigger stage," she explained, concern pouring out of her. "More props. And if this is going to be an acceptable Presents, we'll need more men to work with the boys on their enunciation and presentation. Some of them don't know how to project with confidence."

Before he could respond, a pat on his leg shifted his focus to a boy at his side.

"Are you really a doctor?" the boy asked.

Thankful for a diversion from Al, Em lowered himself into a squat so he was eye level with his young visitor. "Yes, sir, I am a doctor. What's your name, man?"

The boy's eyes widened in amazement. "My granny says that job is only for White men. She said the Black boys drive garbage trucks, and trains and buses, and they fix cars."

"Well, you can tell your grandma that tonight you met a Black man who fixes people in a real operating room inside a real hospital. Why don't you tell me what *you* are?"

"I'm just a kid." His gaze plummeted to the floor. "I'm supposed to shut up and listen, and I get in trouble when I don't. So I can't tell my granny nothin'."

"That's strange. I don't see any kids around here." Emeric gazed up at A'Lelia. "Al, do you see any kids around here?"

Her eyes deepening, she played along. "No, Dr. McPherson, I don't see a single kid in here."

The little boy's curiosity shot up again. "But this whole church is full of kids!"

"That's not what I see, man. All I see are smart young men and smart young women who have very important jobs."

"Jobs? What jobs?"

He pointed at the little boy's chest. "It's your job to teach us adults how to be brave and have courage. You see, once we adults get older, we become scared. We're afraid of embarrassing ourselves, or losing our friends, or not being able to pay our bills. But not the younger men and women like you. You're still strong. You're still fearless. You still have good ideas, and you're not letting anybody take them from you. Smart young men and smart young women don't let anything or anybody scare them. Let me see you make a muscle."

The boy started off unsure, not wanting to do it in front of observers in the pews.

"Come on, man," Em pressed. "Forget those folks. Make your muscle."

The boy's arm was limp, still self-conscious.

"You can't do better than that? What's wrong? You're not that strong?"

"I *am* that strong," the boy insisted.

"Show me then."

The boy strengthened his arm. His face toughened, mouth forming a tight "O", eyebrows lifting weights.

"Now are you a kid or are you a strong, brave, very smart young man?" Em asked.

His arm still curled into a muscle, face still straining, the boy answered. "I'm a strong, very smart, brave young man."

"And what's your job, young man?"

"Showing old adults how to be brave."

Em stuck up his fist. "Right on. Come back tomorrow and I'll have a stethoscope for you."

The boy's shock came out in a gasp. "Really?"

"Really."

Behind them, other children's hands shot up. "Can I have one, too?"

"Me, too?"

Em and Al stared at each other, miffed.

"I'll see what I can do," Em told them all and then gazed at the girl who was making all this happen. "I'll do what I can to find you some extra men."

The soft lights bouncing around the church reflected through her eyes and up at him, or maybe all that light was emanating from only A'Lelia.

"You should go home and get sleep."

He hated having to leave, but Al was right. With practically everyone in the pews studying their every move, Em resented not having privacy to give Al the thorough goodbye he'd imagined all day.

Al's gaze danced everywhere, the rush of blood into her cheeks turning them blush pink, a telltale sign she was quite aware of his thoughts.

These self-conscious moments and pregnant silences were becoming their most effective way of communicating.

He offered her a sexually frustrated, church-appropriate, very respectful nod. "Until next time, Miss A'Lelia."

"About those Monsieurs," Al murmured, "next time can be tonight. Stop by before your next shift and I'll see what *I* can do."

"All right then, French."

Seventeen
EMERIC

"MAN, WHERE HAVE YOU BEEN?" Harold asked on the other end of the phone line. "I was thinking you fell off the planet or something."

"Work, man," Em told him, starting on his second Monsieur of the day. "We can't all ride around town pickin' our hair and lookin' pretty. Some of us actually work to pay bills."

Snorting on the other end, Harold made it apparent he was already lining up his next dig. "Space cadet, what bills you need to pay living with your auntie?"

"I got plans, Negro. Listen, don't worry about it. What's been crackin'?"

"Twilight Zone is gonna be off the hook Saturday with this breakin' throwdown, my guy. Plus, Lionel's got a couple of grooves he's having at his pad. One this weekend, and another one for New Year's. We're opening up some investment opportunities. You said you wanted to get into some things. We've got moves for you to expand your horizons, brotha. If you come through, bring your own woman. You can't have none of mine."

Amused at this kid, Em took another bite into warm, toasty parmesan crust with gruyere cheese drizzling over his chin. Al had thrown a few extra ingredients into it like tomatoes and a green fresh herb. The creamy sauce also kicked another spice onto his tongue this time.

"You don't have to worry about me wanting nobody y'all got over there, man. Look, I need you to do me a solid. Over at Mount Bethel, we've got a project going on. You've probably heard of it—the Presents?"

"Yeah, I had to do that back when I was a young pimp. They're having it at Mount Bethel, though? Last I remember, don't they put that on at some hotel downtown? When did they take it over to Harlem?"

Between bites of his sandwich, Em explained, "When the hotel started spazzin'. A whole mess went down, so we're doin' somethin' new. Anyways, we need brothas to show up, build some sets, talk to these Black boys about giving speeches. You think you can make it this Saturday afternoon, and maybe one evenin' out of your busy schedule, Casanova? If I catch a break, I'll come through for New Year's."

"I suppose I could do another charity thing, try to get in good with Santa, see if he'll take off one of my strikes."

"Yeh, and bring your fellas with you, man—Lionel, Brent, Filer, and whoever else you can find. Daddy, granddaddy… we'll need 'em all."

"I'll see who I can round up."

Emeric pulled another business card from his pocket. Before this next phone call, he stuck his head outside the door and checked for bystanders. Quickly, he rotary-dialed the next set of numbers on the card.

"Dr. Franklin's office," a secretary answered.

This must have been Christmas indeed. The man was available.

"Dr. Franklin here."

Em lowered his voice. "Mornin', Doctor, this is Emeric McPherson from Memphis. We met at the Murray Hill Swordsmen intake."

"Yes, I remember. How you doin', son? Hangin' in there?"

Em peeked over both shoulders and down the hall again. He was still in the clear. "You remember when you said you couldn't help me transfer my assignment, but I could call you if I need something else? I took your advice and started volunteering at Mount Bethel's health clinic. Have you ever heard of the Presents? I know this weekend is a big one for Christmas shopping, but Mount Bethel needs help. You think you can get together a few Swordsmen?"

Dr. Franklin gave names of men he could call. His notepad against the wall, Emeric wrote them all down to call on his next break.

"Hey, Emeric," the front desk assistant said. She held up a bag of toy stethoscopes the hospital gave out. "Found 'em for ya!"

A few hours later, he'd completed his third straight sixteen-hour shift and made his way to rehearsals before going home to crash. Seeing Al offered the same gratification as his first sip of Folger's in the morning, or having his eggs exactly the way he liked. Not life or death, but to deprive himself of that small indulgence would leave a hole in the rest of the day.

He drove by Mount Bethel's street, unable to turn onto it. Traffic poured out of the church lot, preventing him from driving any closer than two blocks. Sitting right out front were two vans for television station news crews.

When Emeric entered the doors and walked past the large golden Christmas tree in the foyer, a totally different vibe dominated this place than on Sunday. Those church skeptics who'd questioned A'Lelia's motives days ago now grinned big and proud, their chests out, while speaking with news reporters about how special and unifying this experience was for the community.

Clipboard in hand, Al performed tasks as simple as marking spots with tape or instructing the maintenance crew, but she could have just as easily walked with the vision of Harriet, or Abraham, or Moses, herself being used by a higher power.

Emeric carried his boxes to her and stood aside patiently until Al looked up.

Her chuckle was the greeting. "What is this?"

He set the boxes down and opened one up. "I have two more boxes in the car and can get more if we need them. A donation from Hillside."

Excited at the stethoscopes inside, A'Lelia seeing all this come together was the gift he could open over and over.

"I thought you were going home to sleep before we work you this weekend?"

"I never got to ask my one question." He thought for a moment. "Actually, I have a lot of questions, but I'm pacing myself because we're gonna need a few dates for that. We can handle those later. But right now is the biggest question."

Clipboard pressed to her, her cheeks reddening, she seemed unsure if she was ready for what came next. Next in this moment. Next in how the Presents would play out. Next in the coming new year of 1977. Next in moving on from whoever that guy was at Hevalo the other night.

Quickly, she licked her lips and her clipboard moved up and down against her breathing chest. "I guess you've earned a question this week."

Now it was Emeric tempering his breaths. Was he ready? After pushing off commitment for such a long time, still unsure if he even belonged in New York, should he ask a woman who loved her city so much?

"There's this really big event happening next Saturday." He couldn't understand for the life of him why his nerves jingled in his ears. "Everybody around here says it's important. I wondered if you had somebody to escort you while you're brightly shining."

"THANK YOU SO MUCH. We're so glad you came by." Al passed boxes of fruit donations to Jill so they'd be taken to the kitchen.

Over their heads, technicians stood atop ladders where they hung luminous stars from the al fresco ceilings where angels appeared to fly among the stars. Builders hammered together makeshift stages at the front of the church with more techs installing lights along the edges. Between the stages, more craftsmen erected eight-foot-tall wooden cutouts, sawed down and painted to form a silhouette of New York City.

Al received the next well-wisher, a middle-aged woman who gripped Al's entire arm.

"We just love what you're doing, opening up the Presents. I don't have any children, but when I was a girl, I wanted so badly to be part of it. God bless you, Miss Césaire, and all the incredible work you and your family have done for our city. Here's a check."

Al accepted the fourth thousand-dollar check she'd received that day. Some had given more, and she was moved when these donors gave with no guarantee of public acknowledgment. They'd opened their wallets with no motive or incentive.

"Thank you. Truly, this means everything to the youth." She passed the check to Jill and whispered, "Set that aside for the costumes fund."

The news coverage triggered an outpouring of residents from every borough and the suburbs, who'd come in to applaud "the opening of the Presents."

In her interviews with news reporters, Al tried to correct them that this had not been an intentional move, and that it may not be permanent. She wanted to curb false hopes for next year, not when they'd already agreed this would be a one-time deal. But reporters latched on to the more attractive storyline that the Presents was finally a public event. They blew past Al's corrections that didn't offer the same luster.

With reporters and headlines came the local politicians. The mayor was visiting the next day to address the congregation from the pulpit. State assembly men and women, City Council officials, and candidate hopefuls appeared for photo ops and press interviews. Celebrities who lived in the area had even dropped in to meet the children.

BB and Gloria led the groups of girls in rehearsing their lines and "presenting" their dreams and ideas to the world fearlessly, while Miss Clara and Mrs. Waters organized their fittings and their positions in line.

On the other side of the sanctuary, to Al's relief, the Swordsmen had arrived. Throughout Friday evening and all day Saturday, they worked with the little gentlemen on how to escort a lady and present themselves with proper diction, assertive posture, polished manners, and above all, fearlessness.

"Hey, A'Lelia, how you been?"

Al peered up from the schedule and greeted this unexpected arrival with minimal emotion. She wasn't fourteen anymore. As he'd so aptly reminded her.

"Luke." She knew he was a Swordsman, but Al had been so busy the last few days she was forgetting to remember him. "I didn't know you enjoyed boring charity work."

With a half-laugh, he scrubbed a hand down his face. "I deserve that. I was talking to some of the brothers at the Harvard Club, and they were telling me about you in the news and everything. I only wanted to congratulate you. If anybody deserves these accolades, it's you. I was surprised to see you at the cl…um…out last weekend. You looked good."

"Thanks. Listen, I don't mean to rush you, but we have a lot going on here. Did you want to do some work?" Time was winding down for Al and the children. They had one week to pull all of this together. With three hundred and seven children signed on, and signups still open, they were now spreading performances across three nights.

He seemed caught off guard by her bluntness. "I left messages for you with BB."

Al hadn't known that. Her sister had clearly decided not to pass that on. Any other time, Al would have been annoyed with BB's meddling. Today, she was grateful for her sister's interference. Not being torn over Luke had allowed her to focus on Emeric, akin to knocking down a wall that blocks a prettier view. On the other side of the sanctuary, eagle-eyed BB observed them carefully.

"It's been a packed week. My apologies if I missed your messages."

"I've done some thinking after the summer, and maybe when things slow down for you, I can pick you up. We can talk about the future."

"Luke, we don't have a future. You were mostly right the first time. We didn't choose each other; our circumstances pushed us together. I deserve to be chosen. I didn't know any better. Once I met a man I actually want, not just somebody who's there, I understood completely what you were trying to say."

In that way he tended to do when he felt a conversation was beneath him, Luke scoffed and looked off to the side. "Al, you don't have to be mean."

"I'm not. I'm truly grateful. You saved me from settling for you. I'll always thank you for that. Now that I know better, I can't go back to what I would never choose. If you'll excuse me, I really do need to go. Have a good Christmas, and I mean that." She squeezed his arm, because Al didn't wish him any ill will.

Walking around Luke, she left him where he was.

Gloria, Jill, and BB so happened to be eating during a snack break, all silently standing on eggshells.

"Well?" Jill asked. "What did he say?"

"No, what did *you* say?" BB leaned over a pew in wait for the answer.

"I said this pretty prude has moved on," Al reported calmly, while her giddiness jumped up and down on her face.

In church, they couldn't act up the way they wanted, and instead, held their muted celebration with ecstatic smiles over their non-alcoholic apple cider cups.

From the church's back offices, Emeric emerged leading a group of boys, all wearing stethoscopes around their necks. They carried their scripts for what they would say to introduce themselves, their dreams, and how they would change the world. Since the number of children had grown so big, rehearsals were divided into groups and a professional was assigned to help them memorize and state their lines. Once the stages were up, after church tomorrow, they would begin full rehearsals.

Handsome in slacks and a sweater, giving out high-fives,

Emeric seemed taken aback when some boys locked their arms around him for a hug. He'd even started writing his phone number on their scripts for boys to call him.

Returning somebody's pen, he looked beyond it, and his gaze crossed with Al's.

Every Christmas gift Al had ever opened, every Christmas morning she'd run down her family's staircase, coalesced under the Christmas tree of her heart just then.

Em started toward her, but one of the Swordsmen pulled him aside and several of them fell into a confab.

"Who is the guy in that red jacket?" BB eyed the group of men. "That 'fit is righteous. Haven't we seen him before?"

"That jacket is loud. I can hear the red velvet way over here," Gloria said to a round of chuckles.

Al rolled her eyes. "BB is loud, too, so there ya go."

"It's been a long time, and I'm not sure, but I think he's a Middleton," Jill said. "Isn't that Lionel? Or is it Linus, the older, finer brother?"

Al surveyed the group conversing with Emeric. "I think that's the younger one, Lionel. It's been a few years since I've seen the Middletons, not since we were in high school when his brother asked me out."

That revelation sent Jill backward. "Asked you out? Fine Linus Middleton? You never told me about that."

"There wasn't anything to tell." Hardly even remembering it, Al shrugged now. "Girls were hanging off of him left and right, and he and Luke didn't like each other. It was so obvious he was only asking because he wanted to use me for bragging rights." She sipped her cider. "Aside from that, I don't know too much more about them."

For BB, her inquiry hadn't ended, still eying Lionel, maybe even entertaining possibilities.

Al hoped Emeric wouldn't begin spending too much time with them. The best part of him was his caring, gentlemanly heart, not yet tainted by the egos and politics of New York high society.

"Hello, Al. Good evening, ladies."

From her cross-legged position on the floor, Al looked up and was gobsmacked. Standing there were Mrs. Hadley and Mrs. Kirkland, her grandmother's friends who'd sworn Al would fail. The last time she saw them was the previous Sunday when they'd stormed out.

Al's sister and friends remained quiet in a subtle rebuke to the elder women who'd abandoned the event. Yet, making a decision, Al stood.

"Mrs. Hadley and Mrs. Kirkland, we're so glad to see you. What can we do for you?" She hadn't forgotten how they'd spoken to her, but she also understood their initial shock over a tradition they felt was theirs.

"We were wondering if there's still space for our grandbabies to perform next weekend," Mrs. Kirkland said.

Mrs. Hadley's eyes toured Mount Bethel's heavenly architecture, inspecting the high ceilings, appreciating this rare expression of Blackness. "Hmph. I've never been in here before. I've only driven by it on the street. I had no idea all this was in here."

For Al, that was the point. While Jill directed them to the signups, Al made her way to the group of Swordsmen. One of the brothers tapped Luke and he turned around.

"That sure was quick," he told her. "So you were just faking me out, huh?"

"No. Every word I said, I meant." Inhaling, Al ignored the others and walked up to Emeric. "Got a minute?"

Em's admiration scoped her head to toe and back up again, the way it always did. His attention unnerved Al, the way it always did.

"For you, I've got two minutes." Setting his cup down, he slid his fingers through hers and led her into the back corridor for privacy. Once they were alone, he leaned against the wall. "So I just met your ex."

Al shook her head. "He's not really an ex. More like a 'circumstance.' It's been months since we talked, so I didn't know he was coming. Or I would have set that up better."

"It's chill. Lionel, Harold, and them are sliding through that throwdown at Twilight Zone tonight. They asked me to come, and I wanna see you sing to yourself again. You and Baby Sis goin'?"

How did she tell him? Would she lose her attractiveness in his eyes if she wasn't a stone-cold fox out on the town every weekend? Or worse, did that make her a stiff prude?

"What is it?" he murmured. His eyes were microscopes magnifying her vulnerability.

"I love dancing, and it's cool to go out sometimes, Emeric, but…" She swallowed and owned it. "I'm not a big clubber."

The pupils in Em's eyes deepened, spotlights encircling her, centering her. "Then, who are you?"

Sucking in a big breath, Al readied herself to explain, the way she explained when she gave tours, when she taught the significance of her people, and when she had explained to the congregation last Sunday why New York still needed a Presents.

"Don't tell me." He seemed to fall into her. "I wanna see for myself."

No smiles, jokes, or wisecracks. All transparency.

Hesitant, Al considered what to do, what to share with a man she didn't know beyond this situation. "We can go anywhere?"

"I'll go with you anywhere."

Nineteen

A'LELIA

"I CAN'T WAIT to see what this is you're craving. It'd better be good, too." Em followed Al's driving directions, turning onto Adam Clayton Powell Jr. Boulevard and heading north to 132nd Street. "Don't have my mouth all ready to go, for you to take us to some silly Bozo the Clown hamburger shop that don't even serve liquor."

Al laughed with the jubilation of a woman who had seen a miracle come together in a week. More than ready for her reward, the Presents organizer had earned every drop of greasy sin awaiting her. "Here. Here. This is it!"

Pulling over, Em peeked out of his windshield and read the sign aloud. "Chicken and waffles? I thought I was about to see somethin' special."

"It's not just anybody's, though. It's *Wells* Supper Club. Hurry up! They already look busy." Al's belly growled almost as loud as Em's had the other night. At the rehearsal earlier, she had been too busy and nervous to sit for a full meal.

With the event coming together again, she could finally breathe better. The Presents wasn't totally in the clear, yet, not with nearly four hundred costumes needed in a matter of days, four nights of presentations needing choreography, four big dinners, and a host of other issues that came with such a huge undertaking. But Al was doing it, far bigger and more marvelous than anything they had done at the Murray Hill Hotel. She had earned this chicken n' waffles.

Emeric came around to get her, and when he threw open her door, light snowflakes cascaded from the sky. Swirling around him, they fell into his Afro so his coils glistened under the streetlight. His gloved hand held out to her, he glowed like the guardian angel he'd shown himself to be since they'd first bumped heads.

"You gettin' out, or you want me to get back in and we just look at it?" he asked.

Electrons orbited atoms, all of them electrifying Al's heart, and flowed into a man who was plugged into her. Connection. It was the reciprocity she'd wanted from Luke for years, but he'd left her disconnected.

She trusted Emeric enough to let her guard down and confess, "I wasn't looking at the restaurant."

He knew just what to do with his part of the electricity.

"Well, excusez moi, let me turn on around and model the full package, so you can get a good view, girl." He did a spin on the sidewalk under falling snow. "I've been told I look like Don Marshall on my good side and like James Edwards on my other good side." With a dip in his hip, he finished up, patting his Afro in his window reflection. "What you think?"

What would she have done this week had he not been there? How did a complete stranger show up at a perfect time? The laugh rising up from A'Lelia was more than amusement at his antics. It was a release of several layers of anxiety. Not due to one man, but to a greater hand at work, of which this one man was evidence.

"I think it's time for you to do what you said you would last weekend—take me on a date. Can we go order and grab our food now? You done?"

"Grab our food?" Em pulled her up with a firm hand. "You mean we're not sitting down? So I can stroke your hand and stare in your eyes, drop my tightest lines, have you wondering if I was Shakespeare in my last life?"

Lips tucked between her teeth, Al was lifted. No nervousness. No blood rushing to her face in a sudden flood of uncertainty or self-consciousness.

As natural as snowfall, Emeric threw the restaurant door open, held it, and as easily as the Northeastern winds swept snow around, A'Lelia walked in with the breeze at her back.

Emeric murmured, "You were that little girl, weren't you? Wearin' bows so big they almost swallowed your head?"

Al checked for what he was talking about, and at a table sat a girl in a toddler chair, adorned in a velvet dress, her head topped with a giant bow that competed in size with the dress itself. Recalling her childhood and how her mother heavily dressed her and BB for their portraits to be painted, especially for their cotillions and coming out balls, she suppressed a chuckle. "I plead the Fifth."

"Naw, you ain' gotta plead nothin'." He broke into his relaxed, Southern drawl. "'Cuz I already know. You look like you understand exactly what that life is."

Studying the menu together, their hands intermingled, their aromas of honey and leather flirting in her nostrils, rowing through her brain, it was Christmas.

Was she silly for letting herself relax too much with him? For allowing herself to let go of womanly lessons learned with Luke and simply trust that it was okay to feel giddy?

While Emeric reached around her to hand cash to the cashier, his cheek stroked hers. His maleness caressed her womanness. Their physical and mental proximity stroked parts of her she'd never felt safe entrusting to Luke. Emeric's hand protectively on her waist, they exited. An activity as simple as ordering takeout was the Christmas gift.

"Where to next?" he asked behind his steering wheel. The scent of freshly fried meat and flour straight off the iron filled the car when he started it up.

Al settled in. "Back down Seventh, in the direction we came from."

"Is Seventh also known as Adam Clayton Powell Jr., meaning the street we're on?" he clarified in a moment of confusion.

Giggling at her assumption that everybody on the planet knew her New York as well as she did, she motioned for him to flip the car around. "Oh, that's right, you're new. Yes."

"You're not giving me a hint?" Before he steered away from the curb, he stuck in an 8-track, and fast-forwarded to Diana Ross's "Do You Know Where You're Going To, Theme from Mahogany." He turned the volume down so it didn't take over but remained in the background, just loud enough to become a song on their soundtrack.

"What would be the fun in that?" Staring out the window comfortably, she moved her neck to the mellow sound. "You can drive down to Seventy-Seventh Street."

His finger tapping on his steering wheel, he took it all in, the glare of the city's Christmas lights and trashcan fires reflecting off the windows, crossing his eyes.

"What do you think of it all so far?" she asked.

"Not what I had expected. The way my frat brothers at Morehouse always spoke of New York—Sag Harbor, Westchester, the clubhouses, the private soirees, golf, beaches, and boating—I had this picture in my head like Black people here didn't have the kind of problems we had at home. Yeah, I know there's rough situations everywhere. But

I came here believin' New York was New *Yawk!*" He held his hand up the way Pastor's held up the Bible.

The gesture was cute.

Focusing ahead, he reflected. "I moved here thinking this place was more professionally advanced than what it really is. It's still much more advanced than where I come from, but not as much as I was expecting."

"Why did you come?"

With city lights continuing their journey across his pupils, his expression shifted. "I love my home, my family, and all. Memphis is the joint that never goes out. It stays smoking." He thought a moment. "But it's not always good bud. After I moved back home from Atlanta, it felt like no matter what I ever accomplished, something would always be missing. Memphis has got hella sharp brothers doing their mean green thing, but the South conditions Black people to stay in our place, and most of us go along with it."

The discomfort of saying that was obvious along his tightened jaw. "I wanna change it, but that is lonely. Like I'm one Negro trying to think bigger for everybody within a three-hundred-mile radius. I don't wanna feel like I'm screamin' into a void." His fingers casually spoke, twirling at the top of the steering wheel while he waited for a red light. "I want to look to my left and my right, and see other damn good Black men who share my vision, and they're big and audacious enough to go after it right along with me."

His thoughts were a train driving over his eyebrows.

"Knowing what you know now, if you had to decide all over again, would you still leave your joint and come smoke a new one?" Al asked.

Her play on words impressed him.

"Ha-ha, check you out, doin' a li'l razzle dazzle."

Relaxed, at ease, she replied, "Not a little. A lot."

Their effortless humor was a joint in her that wasn't going out.

He pulled his Cadillac up to Seventy-Seventh Street and peered out, realization hitting him. "Ha. The famous New York Historical Society." Sitting back a moment, he threw his arm over her seat. "So this is where you work."

The mission inside that building was her heart's desire. "That's who I am."

"That's bomb. I'm diggin' it. So you're a…curator? Archaeologist? Bone collector?"

"Historian." She returned her attention to him. "Back to you telling me if you'd come to New York if you could decide over again." Somebody else's perspective of her town was always intriguing. Even if it wasn't positive, akin to the children from Kansas she'd led through the museum the previous week.

He shut off the ignition, one hand on the back of her seat, the other on his steering wheel. Gazing downtown, he still absorbed it all.

"Yes." This question brought up something in him. "I've gotta believe there's a reason home didn't feel like *my* home anymore. Like your favorite pair of Chucks you thought you'd be wearin' forever. But after a while, you notice they're worn down and you've just been wearin' 'em out of habit. Then you notice you actually outgrew them and that shoe doesn't suit you anymore, so it's time to graduate your closet. Time to graduate yourself."

Al couldn't fathom outgrowing New York. Though, there may have been certain aspects of it that needed change, and this may have been the reason she was born. A tiny smile rose inside her as she thought of the Presents.

Emeric's aunt had said she'd participated in the Presents, too, and Al had questions about his family, the Shipmans.

Maybe now wasn't the time to bring it up. She doubted if that was even her place.

He pulled his gaze from the view ahead to the lady at his side. "So am I gonna see some ghosts in here? Dead people? Why you bringin' me over here at night?"

Food in hand a few minutes later, they walked around to the rear entrance where Al whipped out her keys.

"This place must *really* like you. You got your own key and everything." Emeric's attention skiing all over the place, he pointed at the tube camera in a corner angled at them. "You sure they're not gonna see me in those cameras up there and send the pigs after me?"

"Calm down." She punched the security code into the newer model wall panel the museum had convinced the city to purchase, despite the budget crisis, since some of New York's oldest memorabilia was housed here. It fell short of the wide-ranging surveillance setup that was needed, but the cameras and panel served their purpose.

"Who are these cats over here?" Once inside, Emeric walked toward the wall where Native Americans studied him back from their assigned wing of the museum. "New York had Indians way up here? I mean, I suppose it makes sense. They were everywhere, but whenever I think of this state, I think buildings and skyscrapers, not rural camps and villages like the mid-West and the South."

"The name Manhattan comes from Manahatta, originally home to the Lenape tribe. New York has the biggest Indian population in the country," she explained, reactivating the alarm with them inside. "They've been here for well over ten thousand years, since at least the Ice Age."

Al and Dr. Granger had decided the Native American exhibit should be displayed on the museum's first level. Since those natives had come first, it was determined they should have been seen first, just as when Columbus had invaded.

"It's hard to think of New York as anything other than a concrete jungle." He ventured toward the section housing African-American historical pieces. "They let Black folks come up here before 1865?"

"Would you believe me if I told you most Black New Yorkers were slaves?"

"Shut your mouth! New York had slavery?" His eyes bucked, Em stood back and clarified with his hand. "Now you're not just talking about them couple of Black folks who belonged to George Washington and them. Slavery was a regular thing and everybody had 'em? This was supposed to be the north! Negro Heaven! Where all the plantation Blacks escaped to get away!" Engrossed, he inspected more memorabilia. "I feel like all this time I was lied to."

His Southern tongue was taking over the more he relaxed and let himself come out.

"By the American Revolution, New York had the second-highest number of enslaved Africans after Charleston, South Carolina," Al explained while getting blankets. "Let's eat. The food's lukewarm."

"Hold on. You can't drop any information like that and then just say, 'let's eat.' What is this big map? What are all these dots in the downtown area?" He pointed to a map of Central Park, and then to a place n Lower Manhattan and eyed her. "Don't gimme no bad news either. I can't handle it."

Just about to take her first bite, Al peered up to see where he pointed. That question shot her back onto her feet. "This area here around Fresh Water Pond is Little Africa. Back in the 1600s, when New York was still New Amsterdam, Blacks could gain 'half-freedom' from the Dutch. These half-free Blacks received land so they could be a buffer between the White Dutch men and the Indians."

"So the Black men died first if people got to squabbling," he concluded.

"Unfortunately," she said. "The good thing is, Black people back then had their own land, in their independent community, separate from their owners, called Stagg Town. Little Africa was mostly Black until the mid-1800s, when the Irish, Jews, and Germans started coming over."

In her peripheral, she observed his eyes still reading the descriptions. He was still invested. Al kept going.

Reaching across him, she explained, "In this area, we believe that's the Negroes Burial Ground from the 1700s. Thousands of free and enslaved Blacks are likely buried there, though it's never been confirmed."

He rested a hand over the bottom of his face, and Emeric squinted. "Why don't you know for sure where thousands of Black people are buried? Isn't that hard to miss?"

"It's like anything concerning us, especially brutality. They'll hide it or keep it out of sight as long as they can."

"But you're sure about this?" he insisted on knowing. "*Thousands* of Black people are underneath this city, and New York won't acknowledge them? Like they never even existed."

"My grandfather's grandfather, who was alive in the 1800s, told Pépé about Black people being put to rest there. My great-great-pépé attended their burials and even distributed the insurance payments to their families, many times. It was part of our family business back then. It's also documented in some of our family's papers and archives."

Her last piece of information saddening her most, Al pointed higher on the map.

"Here, in this area where we are, Central Park was built on Seneca Village."

"What's Seneca Village?"

A'Lelia inhaled. "A community of mostly Black people who owned property in the 1800s. The city took it from them to build the park."

"Wait." His eyes flickered with lights turning on in his mind. "That's Eighty-Seventh Street. Isn't that where—?" His involuntary gasp escaped.

"Yes. My family's building is in the area now."

In shock, he stared between the map and Al, a silence pregnant enough to gestate either new respect or new resentment.

"Pépé wanted to defy the White men who hurt his father and his grandfather, so he bought some of the land those men had taken from others."

Emeric studied her. "Quiet rebellion."

Al released a tiny sigh of relief. He understood.

"How did a Black man in 1912 buy property if White men didn't want him to have it?"

"He used his connections and friends as straw men. You asked the other night why our building isn't called The Césaire."

Discovery spread over his face. "That would have made it too obvious."

"And put a target on his back." She finished the thought. "So he named it after his family's village in France, Saint-Emilion. Since my pépé was born in America, and so was his father, it's harder to connect, unless one goes way back."

"And most people won't. Genius."

"But some Black people feel anger about that, like we capitalized on the suffering and loss of earlier Blacks, Emeric." She had dealt with these assumptions on occasion, when somebody actually knew about the history of Central Park. "My grandfather built there almost sixty years after Seneca Village was pushed out. He hadn't even been born."

They stood close enough to kiss but just far enough to still turn away.

"Why did you tell me that?"

Why *did* she? "Because all of this is who I am. Not the most exciting stuff."

Unblinking, unmoving, undisturbed, he replied, "Your quiet rebellion is exciting as hell. I'm missing my own life if I miss a minute."

They drew toward each other, another Christmas present opening her. Emeric kissed A'Lelia tenderly, his fingertips warm on her neck, slow with each suck. Curious and promising with his tongue, he promised more to come, in rhythmic motions singing her a Christmas carol, smooth and elegant as Nat King Cole's version.

Still in a daze, A'Lelia missed his lips once they'd pulled away.

Against her forehead, he whispered, "What else about you do I get to know?"

Fingers loosely linked, she led him up the stairs. One of his fingers hanging from the belt loop of her jeans.

She flipped on the lights in one particular wing, and history was illuminated.

"Wait a minute." He wandered off on his own and immediately headed for the Paris section. "Are these the folks I saw on your wall the other night? Your family's got your own wing in the museum?" He rushed from one acrylic display case after another. "Black people in Paris." His finger jabbed the case. "And this is Mama Omalara Tossou, the one your sister told me about? The Dahomey Amazon?"

"Yep, that's her. When she arrived in France, they forced her to change her name to Marie Louise, but we don't call her that."

Hanging back, she leaned against the doorframe, as Emeric floated from one case to the next, reading and absorbing, on his own voyage of discovery.

Em rubbed his chin. "Whewww, man, she looks like she can beat somebody's tail good, too. I can't imagine what she must have gone through during that time. You know how the world comes at Black women that tough."

Recalling the humiliation last week of being kicked out of the Murray Hill Hotel, she murmured, "I do know."

He gazed up at her over a display case, in a silent moment of solidarity, of atoms and electrons. Then, he returned his eyes to one of the last cases.

"So you all started coming to America from France in the 1700s?"

"Yes, America was growing at a fast clip, and Omalara's biracial sons, Jacques and Leopold, had money. They wanted to take advantage of shipping and real estate in Boston and New York."

His finger moved over the glass. "But their names weren't Césaire, yet."

"No, not in that generation. Omalara named them Tossou."

"Habsburg," he finished, reading it off a piece of paper.

A'Lelia's heart nearly stopped. *No, they were named "Tossou."* Emeric must have read it wrong. What paper was he viewing? She waited for him to move on.

Clueless, Emeric continued inspecting family papers and artifacts.

Habsburg was not a name Al had ever seen on their family documents. It had been a long time since she'd placed those documents in the case, but without a doubt, she would have remembered a potent name like Habsburg.

Once Emeric meandered to the later generations of the family tree, Al cavalierly approached the document he'd read aloud.

Her blood, and her DNA, backed up in her veins, forming a traffic jam of two hundred years. Taking out her key, she unlocked the display case. Lying wide open was a family letter carrier, already opened. It displayed naturalization "first papers" of intent. They were for Omalara's two sons to move from France to New York.

Al had never seen these papers before.

Jacques Habsburg-Tossou.
Leopold Habsburg-Tossou.

He'd come to New York in 1789.

"You all right over there?" Emeric asked.

"Y-yes, I just noticed something I might need for my research. I'm almost finished."

How had she missed these? Three of Omalara's children carried this name.

She sifted through them. Within seconds, Al found what she was searching for— a copy of the French registrations of Omalara Tossou's children, including when they were born.

And *where* they were born.

This was the information that had been cut out of the papers in Aunt Jeanne's attic. Too nervous to breathe now, Al flipped to her direct ancestor.

The information required several reads. Even then, she remained in disbelief.

Name: Maria Josepha Habsburg-Tossou

In this collision of her world, Al worked to control herself so Emeric didn't notice. She kept reading Maria Josepha's registration.

Date of Birth: April 6, 1768
Place of Birth: Hofburg Palace, Vienna, Austria

The Hofburg? Austria had never figured into any of their family history. Where had this paper come from?

She moved to Omalara Tossou's second child.

Name: Jacques Habsburg-Tossou
Date of Birth: September 21, 1770
Place of Birth: Paris, France

Finally, Al moved to a *third* Habsburg child.

Leopold Habsburg-Tossou in 1776, Paris, France.

Even after Omalara had been in France several years, she'd given birth to a Habsburg. How?

Something was terribly off.

If Omalara Tossou's first child was not born in France, then either Maria Josepha was not Omalara's birth child, or Omalara's first destination when she left Africa was not France. It would have been Austria, where she gave birth to a daughter, and then *later* she was sent to France.

Oh my God. Oh my God.

Multiple doors unlocked and opened up a portal that had been shut off for centuries.

"What's wrong?" Emeric came over and squeezed her shoulder from behind. "Don't tell me it's just research either, because your vibes are out on Mars or somewhere." Once he saw her face, he grew concerned. "Baby, you good? Which one of these ghosts scared you speechless?"

Mentally, she still groped through ancestral fog, partly in wonder, but mostly confused. Why had this never come up? Did Pépé know? How had these papers popped up out of nowhere? Since Al was the one who helped the museum curate her family's wing, she should have seen these already.

"Emeric, I think I just realized something."

Jokingly, he held up both hands. "Hold on now, girl. Don't be hittin' me with them serious words right now. We're still gettin' to know each other." He chuckled and squeezed her hips. "But, square biz, what'd you find?"

Afraid she was misinterpreting this, or engaging in wishful thinking, Al feared saying it out loud. What were the odds? "I think my family originated from another country besides Africa and France." Careful not to say too much before she'd confirmed it all, she limited her words now.

"How many continents did your people hit?" he joked.

"At this point, your guess is good as mine." Al rushed to the kitchen for Saran wrap and a trash bag, to wrap the old letter carrier and its documents inside.

Anxious, the historian immediately layered these items in a plastic trash bag and a blanket to avoid any chance of them getting wet in the snow outside.

She would take these artifacts, along with Leopold's Bible from Pépé's office, and have their origins appraised and authenticated.

"You think you've protected 'em enough?" Emeric crossed his arms over his chest.

"Quiet." Al was now invested in this truth as more than a historian, but as a descendant of a Black narrative that didn't tell of bondage.

Omalara Tossou hadn't just given birth once either. She'd produced *three* heirs. Whoever the white father was, even if he had taken Omalara's womanhood by force, nevertheless, he'd cared to the point he'd given all three children his name. So his relations with her were not a secret. To the contrary, he'd wanted the world to know he'd been with her. How had she wound up in France?

At some later point, her descendants stopped calling themselves Habsburg.

A'Lelia's family had been living a lie. But why?

"You're still thinking about it," Em said a few minutes

later while they ate their food that had turned cold. "This must be important. You haven't spoken for five minutes."

"I apologize. That's rude."

"Don't." His smile lazy, he shook his head. "It's cute watching you do your thing in real time, talkin' to yourself and all that."

Al almost spit out her chicken while snort-laughing. "I did not!"

"I swear you did. I heard what you said, but I'm not gonna tell you." He smacked on greasy chicken and forked waffles in his mouth.

"What did I say?" Embarrassed, she inwardly chastised herself for getting too comfortable.

Staring directly at her, Emeric repeated, "Didn't I just say I wasn't telling you?"

"Why not?" she asked, slight irritation rising in her cheeks.

"That little snapshot of you is mine, for me to relive and enjoy."

"But I'm the one who spoke them. They're *my* words."

His eyes fixed, he confirmed, "You can have that perception of you for yourself. But over on this side, I'm the one who witnessed it through these eyes and ears the way it's meant for me. You can't have *my* perception of you right now."

Half of Al creamed in her jeans at his mental armor he hadn't allowed her to penetrate. The other half of her was still calculating a way to reclaim her moment from his head. How had she been postured? Was it awkward?

"So, you're going to replay in your mind how I was talking to myself, but I don't get to know what words I said that you'll be thinking about?"

"Correct." Suppressing a laugh, he took his final bites and

cleaned his plate. "So, are you finished, or do you wanna keep goin' round and round about it?"

A'Lelia Antonia Césaire could only give him her hairiest eyeball while finishing her food.

"So, what other country did you just find?" he asked.

Right now, Al would be careful with what she shared. Her suspicions were still just that. But if these documents were real, and her timeline and lineage were correct, this would be huge. Her family was far more significant than she'd previously known, and they had deliberately buried it.

"Austria."

"YEAH, HEY, MAMA, WHAT'S SHAKIN'?"

"Excuse me, *Dr.* McPherson?"

In his bedroom, he sandwiched the phone between his ear and his shoulder while he kept packing. "Yes, Mother, how do you do on this fine day?"

Emeric packed up an extra pair of clothes in his duffle bag to take with him. Unfortunately, he had to work tonight, but before that, he would spend a couple of hours helping with the Presents setup. It was an all-hands kind of day, the last full day of preparation before rehearsals and then, the event next Saturday.

Other than the main church service today, Pastor Freeman had canceled all other church activities for continuous construction, building, cooking, and decoration. Everything needed to be in place by Thursday afternoon for the first dress rehearsals set to begin that evening. Emeric was working the next four nights, so he could be there for both dress rehearsals and the first night of the Presents.

"You sound sleepy. What are you doing with yourself?"

He and Al had stayed at the museum talking into the wee

hours about everything and nothing—the north versus the South, career choices, colleges, upbringing, parents, places they had traveled and where they still wanted to go, television shows, books, among so many other things.

Their conversation didn't require effort, especially not with all the teasing and jiving, and that's how he felt before he reflected on the *rest* of her.

"Workin' and volunteerin', Mama. There's a lot goin' on this week."

"So Dee tells me. I hope by the time we get there, you'll have caught up on rest. We haven't seen you in months. The kids are excited."

The air sacs in his lungs could have been brittle trees, branching out and scraping at his insides. This feeling was coming up more in his calls with his mother lately.

"I'm really excited to see those jive turkeys, too." The realization set over him that he hadn't bought Christmas gifts for his nephews, his sisters, or his parents.

Between work, and helping A'Lelia with the Presents, his family's visit had slid to the back burner. Now, with the Presents so close, and a ton of work still required, he would not have time for Christmas shopping. Plus, Harold and Lionel were planning to introduce Em around at some holiday soirees, and they wanted him to bring Al. Then, in January, the Swordsmen would receive applications and select new members. His life in New York was taking off.

"Emeric?" his mother asked from the other end of the phone.

"Yeah, Mama?"

"Your father bought a one-way ticket to New York, just in case you needed him to ride back home with you in your car."

Emeric deciphered what she was really saying. His assignment at Hillside was still crap. He still hadn't performed a single surgery since he had arrived. How much longer would he allow his career to stall?

Before he answered, his Aunt Dee appeared in his doorway, as if she'd sensed he could use an emotional support.

"Cool. I appreciate that." No longer packing, he wrapped the coiled phone cord around his finger.

"Well? Emeric, are you coming back home with us or not?"

With sharp, bare tree branches scraping his lungs now, he remembered two moments in which he'd felt anything was possible.

The first had been at the Presents rehearsal when he'd stood in a circle of many prominent, wealthy Black men who weren't hiding or cowering. Rather, they laughed and confabbed in the presence of young Black boys who'd stared at them like they were gods.

The second had been last night, watching an awestruck A'Lelia stand over two hundred years of her family history that had *nothing* to do with slavery, and reconstruct everything she thought she knew. Emeric longed to learn where her discovery took her.

New York's backbone was audacity, in every rib, up and down its spine of hardscrabble citizens. In this town, nobody thrived without audaciously pursuing their highest selves. There was no greater example of this that he'd personally seen than A'Lelia.

"I don't know, Mama."

On the other end, he heard shuffling, as if the phone was being passed.

"Son, how've you been?"

They rarely spoke, and despite that, his father's voice was still the giant tree trunk planted in the center of Emeric, spreading its branches across every limb he had.

"Pop, hey, I'm good." He deepened his voice, and even

though his dad couldn't see him, Em straightened his shoulders and stopped fidgeting. "Busy. How've you been?"

"Well, I'm confused, Emeric. What is this you mean that 'you don't know'? Your job situation still hasn't changed. How long will you keep letting all your talent and knowledge sit on ice? We went along with this idea about you testing something different. It didn't work. I could have told you that going way up there with sinister people too smart for their own good would not get you anywhere, but I held my tongue. You had to see it for yourself. Now that you do, how many more lessons do you need to learn? How much more time will you waste, son?"

In Em's mind, he couldn't decide which version of A'Lelia struck him most—the first time he'd met her, marching through the Murray Hill Hotel, or last Sunday when she'd faced Mount Bethel's attacks on her family and still defended what she believed in with grace, or last Saturday when she was singing Diana Ross to herself in the club, or when she'd awakened him on the couch with hot French sandwiches ready, or her excitement last night when she was ordering chicken and waffles, or her illuminated face when she stood mesmerized over a display case and whispered.

Was he staying here in the scary, exhilarating unfamiliar, or was he going back to what he already knew? If Al could bravely defy her naysayers and change a hundred-year event, what was Em's excuse?

"Pop, you said when I was ready, that I could get grandma's ring. When you come, I'd like to have it." That would mean removing it from his mother's hand.

Emeric stared at his aunt, still in the doorway. Floored, Aunt Dee raised a hand to cover her open mouth.

"Now just you wait one minute." On the other end, now it was his father's voice that shook from the roots. "Who is this? The girl your Aunt Dee's been telling your mama about? Her grandfather is Theodore Césaire, a war profiteer?"

Suddenly, Em's mother was back on the phone, as if she had been standing right there listening. "So you'll marry into a family of killers, Emeric? You've only known these people for a short time."

Emeric squeezed his head. "They're good people, Mama. Did you know they bought back some of the land that was taken from Blacks, and they hire Black men to work their building, plus rent it out to Black people? Do you know last night was the first time I learned about Seneca Village? Why didn't you ever tell me about that? Why wasn't I taught about Black people having their own land here way back in the 1600s? The 1600s! New York is not bleeding with evil every-where I go, Mama, not the way you always said. Why did I have to come find out for myself?"

She'd never wanted him to see New York for its opportunity.

Aunt Dee entered his bedroom and placed a supportive hand on his chest, also a subtle reminder that he was still talking to his mother.

"Don't get caught up in all of that, Emeric Orenthal Shipman McPherson. All those fancy parties, clothes, big houses, they don't mean a thing. The moment you fall on hard times and you can't keep up, they will leave you! They are not your friends. *We* are your family. *Tennessee* is your home, and I will not let what happened to me happen to you."

There it was, the winter tree branches, barren and deso-late, scraping him at his core.

"Mama, I'm not you. I'm neither one of you. Al didn't kill Granddaddy and Grandmama, and she didn't hurt anybody else in your family. She is beautiful and admirable and an angel. I want to introduce her to you. I'm not saying I'll ask her for her hand right now, but if things keep flowing for her and me, then yes, down the road, I may. Since you two are coming up here anyway, if you leave the ring, we won't have to worry with shipping it later."

"Let's say you do reach that point, son. Is this northern girl from such a longstanding background going to leave behind her life and family to follow you down here?" Mr. McPherson asked.

I'll go with you anywhere.

At the time he'd said it, he hadn't thought about it that deeply, only meaning it on the small-scale sense of going to a theater show, or the top of the Statue of Liberty, or trying a new foreign food. He'd only known Al just over a week. Yet, he'd bumped more than her head on that first encounter. Beyond physicality, her *purpose* had beckoned, its call faint but undeniable. Far beyond intimacy at this point, the gifts Al possessed *inside* her benefited the world, and whether he wound up in a personal relationship with her or not, the essence of her was worth knowing.

"Pop, I'm not ready to say that. I only want the ring for whenever I am ready. If we reach that point and she says yes, she and I will decide our future for ourselves." Speaking those words took a hell of a lot of guts.

Drained of nearly all his energy, he set the phone back in the cradle with the little Em had remaining.

"You did good, baby." Aunt Dee's own tears brewed from the relived loss she shared with her sister. "She might be denying it, but maybe you being here is the start of your mama making her way back home."

He turned to his aunt. "Auntie, I'm a grown man. Why can't you just tell me?"

Her blanked-out expression told him she was revisiting a place where he couldn't follow her. A hand loosely rubbed her own throat for comfort.

"It's not my place if your mother has said she doesn't want me to."

"I was fifteen when she said that, Aunt Dee. I'm twenty-seven now. Why do I have to go to a library and get more information on my own grandfather than I can from my mother and aunt?"

"We never wanted our suffering to be yours."

"And by keeping us ignorant, all of you gave our generation a whole new cross to bear." Emeric dropped his chin.

She reached to squeeze his arm, but he drew back. Her shock filled the void, joined by his own surprise at himself. Deidre was his favorite aunt, and aside from that, Em was rarely disrespectful to his elders.

"I'll be back after work tomorrow, Auntie."

The front wheels of his car left the street curb a few seconds later. He was due to head to Mount Bethel for a while, but a disturbed spirit kept his foot on the gas, and he drove right past it. Grateful to pass an open flower shop, he stopped for a small bouquet.

A few blocks up the road, he shut off his car at the hollowed out, low-income housing complex. For a while, he remained behind his steering wheel.

As a nine-year-old boy hiding from one of his cousins in the attic, he'd accidentally found his mother's teenage journal. With his limited reading skills, and not knowing what he held, he read the parts of her cursive he could decipher.

Back then, he'd wondered why she didn't have any parents, and the explanation they were in "Heaven" had never been enough for him. Why were they in Heaven? What happened? That day, nine-year-old Emeric learned she'd indeed had a mother and father who she'd loved dearly. The things he read those few precious minutes—how she wished her daddy was around to stop evil, abusive relatives, how she no longer wanted to be a doctor since her parents wouldn't be there to see her cross the stage—had inspired Emeric to become a doctor *for* his mother.

Since then, he created his grandfather's laugh in his mind. It would have been boisterous and full of life, barreling down the dinner table, hearty and reassuring, in a promise his children or grandchildren would never have to fear or want for anything.

If Orenthal Shipman had lived to see old age, what kind of grandfather would he have been? Would he have defended Emeric with his parents? A man that successful must have wielded a strong sense of self and purpose. If she'd had a father, would his mother have pursued *her* purpose? How different would her life have been?

Their tight-knit family loved each other and had a good time, but life had always been safe. Emeric's father never made waves or put a foot wrong, and that was likely the reason Grace Ann Shipman had married him. Her husband was totally opposite of her father. Quiet Emory McPherson took the beaten, assured path, instructing and rearing his children rather than loving and nurturing them. No daylight entered the McPherson household for chance, risk, rebellion, or independent thought. Emeric had needed light.

Two hours later, he hadn't realized how much time had passed.

Getting out of the car, as always, he pictured the property the way it may have been in 1936, as he'd seen it in a couple of pictures and a newspaper article, the manifestation of a Black man on the move and making his mark. Walking to the curb, Emeric set down his flowers as he had countless times he'd arrived in New York. Kissing three fingers, he pressed them on the cleanest spot he saw, in front of what once was the grand O.R. Shipman & Daughters Furniture Store.

Twenty-One

A'LELIA

AL SURVEYED the one hundred and sixty-one children in Sunday's section rehearsal. The bright eyes of children from every corner of the city, regardless of background or lineage, stared back.

Six days before the Presents was set to kick off, with just over six hundred participants total from all over the city, they'd had to break up the rehearsals into different nights and sections with assigned leaders.

"This is unbelievable," Jill whispered. "You pulled all this together in less than a week."

"The city pulled all this together," Al corrected her.

BB squeezed Al's arm. "Accept your accolades, sissy. You nailed what they said you couldn't."

"We aren't out of the woods yet."

Overnight, art shop guys had built out the wooden set of New York's skyline, complete with illuminated cutouts, so they modeled dark skyscrapers with lit windows. Someone had even placed a miniature Rockefeller Center Christmas tree in the midst of them. Technicians had placed colored stage lights beneath the buildings and hung glimmering stars above to depict "Stars Brightly Shining."

Miss Clara, Sister Rowe, the First Lady, and several other women were organizing dinner, tables, guests, and parking for four performance nights.

In her hand, Al held the scissors. Right in front of her stood boxes containing the first sets of costumes that had been ordered and delivered quickly for the new participants. Now, wide-eyed girls and boys from all over New York sat on the edges of their seats, stretching their bodies in anticipation.

She peered around the sanctuary and then at her watch, hesitant. Where was he?

"We should get started. Who wants to help me open this box?" Al asked her captive audience.

Hands shot up everywhere and, as always, Al searched for the two smallest children.

However, several boys squirmed, restless in the pews. One of them got up and approached Al, the "strong, brave, very smart young man" from a few days ago, whom Emeric had instructed to make a muscle.

"Miss Al, is Dr. E coming?"

He was thirty minutes late.

"He must have had something come up, but don't worry. We'll have somebody to help you rehearse," Al said.

The boy wrinkled his nose like she'd just offered him rotten food. "We don't want anybody else. We want Dr. E."

They weren't the only ones. Al had also been stalling in wait for him to stroll through the door with his swagger. He hadn't mentioned missing rehearsal last night. Emeric was just as much a part of the Presents now as Al and the others. This moment belonged to him, too.

"Let's see if we can find out." Heading to the back of the church, Al searched for his aunt.

Despite being here all week, the two women hadn't interacted much, not since she'd surprised Al, appearing at the meeting and announcing herself as a former Presents participant.

"Miss Shipman?" Al popped her head into the church conference room, where she and the other women pored over charts and lists.

"My married name is Perry now." The woman waved Al in. "Come on in, baby, what do ya need?"

"Emeric. His young men are asking for him. I wondered if you'd gotten word from him so I'll know what to tell them." And because she'd also come to expect him to just be there.

His aunt's clenched hands answered honestly, and then, she must have remembered to fix her face. "I think he mentioned he had to handle errands today and he would get over here if he could. He may have had too much on his plate, though."

"Too much on his plate?" Yesterday evening, he'd mentioned none of it. How would so many commitments arise in only twenty-four hours? Additionally, it was only three-thirty in the afternoon now. Emeric wasn't due to start his shift until much later. He had no time to stop through and greet the boys at all before then? This didn't add up. "I hope he accomplishes everything he needs to. Will you let him know we missed him?"

"Of course, sweetheart." His aunt's face seemed more tense now than a few days ago. "Don't worry yourself. He'll be just fine. I know he surely cares for you a great deal."

Al stopped before exiting and thought a moment. She never said anything about worrying. Was there something to worry about?

"Thank you for that. These children care for him a great deal."

Back in the sanctuary, she faced disappointed boys, as well as a few teenage girls who had been crushing.

"Unfortunately, we'll have to start without Dr. Emeric." Her spirits matched their faces. "Young man over there, you, what's your name? Why don't you come help me with this box?" She called over several more.

The flaps opened, and out came the organza, satin, sequins, and bow ties, to the applause of children and parents from all over the city. Holding dresses and tuxes under their chests, they spun around for each other, pretending to be princesses and imagining themselves as kings and presidents. Some of the outfits had been paid for by anonymous benefactors who had chipped in after watching a news broadcast or reading about the situation in the paper. For a few families, this was the first time they were seeing their children in formal attire. Opening up on parents' faces were worlds of possibilities for their children.

A few of them wandered up to her during the rehearsals to shake Al's hand or throw their arms around her.

"Miss Césaire, I just wanted to say 'thank ya' for doing this," one parent said.

"Yes, ma'am, me, too. We'll never forget this. Sonya hasn't stopped talking about it with her cousins in Boston who wish they could be here to do it. God bless you, miss."

Another family associate approached whom Al recognized from last Sunday's meeting, one of the parents who had harshly criticized Al's family and her motives for coming here. Al skated over a thin-ice puddle of anxiety, concerned for how the woman would attack her today.

"You know, Miss A'Lelia, when you showed up last weekend, I didn't see the vision, and I might have been hard on ya. For that, I apologize. God sure does work in mysterious ways. We never know who He'll use, and if it wasn't for Him bringing you in here, we wouldn't be having our first

Presents. So thank you. We hope you won't be a stranger once this ends."

Behind the woman, a line formed of other parents and relatives patiently waiting to speak with Al. These interactions were not what she had expected last Sunday when she'd simply walked into a pretty church. An ugly situation that began at the Murray Hill Hotel, along with being abandoned by quite a few people she'd long admired and adored, had brought this entirely new outpouring she hadn't expected, now circling around her.

The love and gratitude they showered on her might have flooded her heart too much. Al looked away for a moment to recollect herself.

Beyond their heads, she could have sworn she noticed a familiar figure in the back of the church, an elder's leisurely stroll, his shoulders hunched over, a tweed newsboy cap topping his head.

"Pépé?" Her grandfather had come!

Al stood on her toes to see through the line of people and call out to him, but just as quickly as it appeared, the newsboy cap was gone. She spun toward BB to ask if she'd noticed him, but she and Jill were helping the girls with costumes. Maybe it had only been wishful thinking.

She wasn't the only one wishing. At the end of rehearsal, Emeric still had not arrived, and his absence put a damper on the Christmas excitement, particularly among the boys reentering the sanctuary with their heads down.

AT ONLY TEN o'clock in the morning, Em still had six more hours before his shift ended. That conversation with his mother had thrown him off course. Then, coming in here today, only to be shuffled around to every assignment other than doing what he had trained to do, and excelled at, was like being asked to work with thorns shoved into his sides. Needless to say, he'd been struggling all day, from one patient to the next.

The situation affirmed his mother's warnings. Her accuracy was vinegar on his bruised ego. Coming here in search of something more, maybe even in search of his grandfather's fearless footprint, had been a mistake.

Paying for a breakfast sandwich in the cafeteria, he couldn't help overhearing the conversation between two other doctors in line.

"Yeah, can you believe that? What on Earth is he doing here? Of all the hospitals he could go anywhere in the city, why would he come to Hillside?" one of the doctors asked another.

"I hear Dr. Berger is deciding today who'll be operating with him," the second said.

"Who do you think he'll choose to operate on somebody that important? Whew. Talk about pressure. I'd probably pee in my pants from being so nervous."

The second made a face. "Either that or puke."

Em had learned to tune out these eager conversations that held no opportunity for him, too. They were a tease. With fifteen minutes left on his break, he exited the elevators and headed for the break room.

"Dr. McPherson!" Essie stood up from the nurses' station. "You're wanted in OR."

The other two doctors stopped and, flummoxed, they listened in.

"I didn't have anything for pre-op or a new patient."

Essie shook her head. "It's a last-minute call. And you should hurry. They've been waiting for a while."

Emeric tossed his breakfast. Was he due to be somewhere? Had he accidentally missed something on the schedule?

At the same time that he stepped onto the elevator for the ninth floor, his curious colleagues reentered the elevator with him and followed him up.

At the next nurses' station, several doctors were already waiting and pointed in the direction Em should take. Today, the operating floor buzzed with more excitement than normal. Several doctors lingered in the corridor, what they all did at times, hoping to catch the attending's eye and win an emergency operation under tight time constraints.

"Well, gag me with a spoon," another doctor commented at seeing Emeric approach down the hall.

"Holy smokes, no way," yet another doctor groaned at the sight of Emeric.

Before he reached the assigned room, he heard voices inside.

"Now, sir, I understand you want who you want, but this is still my department," Dr. Berger spoke, albeit more gently than Emeric had ever heard him. "And I must decide this as responsibly as I can. This procedure should be performed by surgery-oncology, and certainly not by some general surgery resident."

"Well, son, I appreciate your responsibility, but it was my prerogative to come here and I only came for one doctor. The only way I'll have this surgery at Hillside is with Emeric McPherson. Now, we've been doing this for some time. Is he here, or isn't he?"

Blown away, Emeric entered the room. Facing him was a well-dressed elderly man, remotely familiar, whom Em couldn't quite place. This elder cut a fine figure, as if he'd missed a street and wandered into the wrong neighborhood. Yet, his aura emanated wisdom, a sureness in his advanced years that Em didn't usually feel in this chaotic hospital.

"Good afternoon, gentlemen," was all Em could offer. "How may I help you?"

A flustered Dr. Berger also turned toward him. "Dr. McPherson, this here is—"

The elder pointed his wooden cane straight at Emeric. "You Orenthal's grandson? Your mother is Grace Ann Shipman?"

Floored, Emeric wondered how this man knew that. Had Al been talking to him? But how did she know the name of Emeric's mother? Unsure of what was happening, Emeric swallowed his questions for the time being. "Y-yessir."

The elder turned back to Dr. Berger. "Him. I want him to do it. That'll be all."

Dr. Berger's hands rose. "Now, Dr. Césaire, I'll be the lead surgeon, and my best resident should be assisting me. That's

Merrill Cleveland. I highly recommend that he be with me, especially since you are not having this procedure at your own hospital among staff familiar with your chart. Dr. McPherson can be in the room observing."

"Dr. Césaire?" Emeric asked. "*Theodore* Césaire?" A'Lelia's Theodore Césaire?

The self-assured gentleman stared at him with penetrating clarity. "You know any other ones?" He directed his clarity at Dr. Berger. "He'll be the lead, and he'll choose his own team. Solely him."

"Now, Dr. Césaire, I have admired you since I was a boy myself and hold you in great regard. But you choosing a resident to lead a surgery this consequential would be akin to me committing medical malpractice, and you know it. I'm afraid I can't go along with that."

Feeling out what was happening, Emeric decided to make his pitch. "I've performed three hundred and twenty-six surgeries already, two hundred and five that I led, and—"

"I don't need you to sell me, son," Dr. Césaire said. "If I didn't know already, I wouldn't be here." He folded his hands on top of his cane. "Dr. Berger, whether you go along with it or not, it's my health to commit malpractice on. I'll pick whoever I damn well please, and those are my terms for this operation being here in your department, instead of across town."

"Dr. Césaire, again, if you're making such a consequential decision, you'll have to sign a release of liability. We will not accept fault should any mistakes or errors occur."

At that abject disrespect, Emeric almost lost it. "Mistakes or errors?"

"You may be a doctor technically, son, but we don't know you around here."

"Technically?" an irate Emeric repeated. "I've got more

surgeries than all of your residents and most of the attendings, and you won't let me *touch* the knife!"

"I'll sign your papers." Dr. Césaire addressed the attending surgeon. "And Dr. McPherson will have full authority, *son.*"

Dr. Berger continued, "We'll need to operate quickly, within a few days. In the event the news isn't good, we'll need to develop a treatment plan to send back to your primary medical team."

Dr. Césaire was standing to his feet. "Very well. Dr. McPherson, you'll stop by my office tomorrow after your shift for a chat."

"What exactly am I operating on?"

"A colon mass at the splenic flexure," the eldest doctor in the room replied. "And not *one* word to my granddaughter."

Em's thoughts immediately veered to Al and Baby Sis. Why didn't his family know he was here?

A roller coaster couldn't have jerked Emeric harder than this conversation. "No, sir."

Dr. Berger stared at Emeric on his way out. "You'd better not screw this up."

Still in disbelief, Em stumbled into the corridor. Droves of other doctors were waiting, many who'd never spoken to him.

"So, McPherson, who are you picking to be on your team?"

He'd removed colon masses at least two dozen times, but out of an abundance of caution, he'd locate an attending from surgery-oncology, one who controlled the schedule and could mentor him, plus help Em snag better assignments while he remained at Hillside.

On top of preparing for the surgery, a whole other set of nerves came undone inside him. The upcoming meeting in Dr. Césaire's office scared him more than the surgery. What could this man want to talk with him about? He was still ruminating about it fifteen minutes before his shift ended.

"Dr. McPherson, you must be Mr. Popularity today. You have visitors," Essie said, back at the downstairs nurses' station. "In the waiting room."

In the waiting area, he didn't see anybody he knew.

"Dr. E."

Behind him, three smart, brave, very strong young men, lingered in the corridor, hands shoved in their pockets. In the halls of a Lower Manhattan hospital, full of New York City's most vulnerable, the boys being here brought *his* being here full circle.

"Fellas, what's crackin'?" Emeric gripped each of them.

"Where were you yesterday?" Daryl asked. "Why weren't you at rehearsal?"

"I had a personal issue to attend to. My apologies, gentlemen, but you men were in good company with the other guys there, right?"

"No." Marvin wagged his head. "Dr. Franklin is all right, but he's not cool. He tries to make us laugh, but he ain' that funny. When you comin' back?"

Em muffled his laugh behind his hand. "He's good people, man."

"It's not funny, Dr. E," Raphael complained. "Why you leave like that?"

"I didn't realize I needed a sign-out sheet, but now that I know I've got higher-ups to answer to, I won't take anymore personal days without permission."

"Yeh, that's what's happenin'," Daryl said.

"So, how come you gentlemen aren't in school?" Em asked. "How do you plan to become doctors when you're skipping classes, huh?"

Marvin cocked his neck. "We didn't skip. Our ride picked us up after school and brought us."

"And who would that be?" Emeric asked.

They all aimed their thumbs over their shoulders, gesturing farther down the corridor, where Emeric hadn't looked far enough. He scanned the people strolling through the walkway for a recognizable face. Em's inner eye saw her.

A vision leaning on the wall, eyes every bit as intense as the night they'd met, her gravitational pull was talking and she hadn't said a word.

"Fellas." He slid some cash out of his wallet, too distracted to count it. "Head to the cafeteria in the basement and get yourselves some drinks. Juice only, no pop. It's bad for you. Give me twenty minutes."

"Can I have a candy bar?" Daryl asked.

"Fruit," Emeric answered, his mouth watering at the fruit ahead.

"Aw, man," they groaned on the way to the elevator.

"Potato chips?" Marvin asked.

"Nuts." Em was coming pretty close to one himself.

"Jesus *Christ*." Raphael rolled his eyes.

"Imma be countin' my change, too."

Meeting her grandfather today, finally, had been an unspeakable honor. But it didn't come anywhere close to falling for what had to be Dr. Césaire's greatest achievement.

"Am I in trouble a little? Or in trouble a lot?" he asked her.

Her pillowed lips parted, tiny breaths flowing in and out. "Neither. We're the ones in trouble when Dr. E's not there."

Magnetic energies excited, their hands engaged before he laced his fingers through hers. He was already heading toward a free checkup room with an open door, tugging her behind him. Smooth and indiscreet, he ushered her inside and shut the door with a quiet tap, locking it. He pressed her against the wall.

Up close, over her brow, her worry mixed with nervousness and questions.

"I'm sorry. I needed some alone time," he started.

Her eyes turned chastising. "We can talk about why you needed that when you're ready, but it's Christmas. We're in the middle of a major event. You can be alone any other time of the year, just not now."

"You've got a lot of good people helping at this point, so I assumed things would be all right."

"You assumed wrong. The boys were expecting you, and your absence was distracting. So the next time you need to be alone, inform somebody, please."

He stroked her hairline with his thumb. "Were *you* expectin' me?"

Her half-grin disappeared as fast as it appeared. "Just don't miss any more rehearsals. Now do you want to move forward or just keep going round and round about it?"

All she hadn't explicitly said hid between the words she had. Her concern lay kisses inside him before they touched.

He kissed the same mouth that painted a portrait of stars brightly shining, the same mouth that opened a pathway to a quiet rebellion. Deeper than physicality, Emeric kissed A'Lelia's mind.

Flooded with attraction and hope and exhilaration, nowhere else to release it and not wanting to kiss her so deeply he choked her, Emeric reached inside her coat and around her waist, pressing his feelings into her flesh. The rhythm of her heavy breaths became a sensual Christmas carol.

Sliding his hands under her butt, he hoisted her up, shocking her on their way to the examination bed where he set her down.

He lowered to his knees. Easing his hands under her skirt, he felt for the top band of her winter tights around her hips. In Emeric's eyes connecting with hers, he asked for a different kind of permission. A'Lelia raising her butt from the bed for him to jerk down her tights was her answer. Once he'd gotten them to her ankles, he stuck his head underneath so her bundle of shoes and tights rested on his back. Scooting her toward him until her butt hung off the edge, he smelled her attraction before he fully pushed up her skirt. Nudging the seat of her panties aside, he removed the final barrier between him and *all* of her, vulnerable in her fertileness, her desire for him slick and inviting.

Hating they were pressed for time, he approached the edge of her womanhood. The windows of her eyes open to him, her breasts rising and falling between them, ebbs and flows of blood from her heart through her womb into the flesh forming her entrance at his mouth, the portals of A'Lelia were spreading for Emeric. He took his first taste, her jaw dropped and head thrust back, and they both ventured in.

A'LELIA

She couldn't scream out. Afraid a hospital staffer would hear somewhere in the main corridor, Al shoved her scarf in her mouth and bit her ecstasy into it. Legs wide open, his head tucked between her thighs, her ankles bound with her tights, she was restricted in how much she could writhe. Which was a shame while Emeric bobbed and thrust his head like he was licking away the top coats of her until he could reach the tender core of her soul.

The smack of his tongue in a pool of wetness intermingled with sounds of his throat opening and closing, her cream sliding down it.

They weren't married, had only gone on one date, and she had no idea what Emeric's intentions were. This level of intimacy was sin. She'd fallen into her desert of carnality and lust that hadn't been satiated in nearly two long years, since Luke last did this when she'd returned from her studies in England.

And despite her brain flipping through objections about respecting herself and what came next, she simply allowed herself to enjoy Christmas. He pried her legs wider, stretched his arm over her abdomen and opened his hand.

Al slid hers inside. More than carnality was gazing back at her, holding her hand, while his head dipped and his tongue stroked away every rational thought. Her womanhood thoroughly and rightly being loved on dismantled any doubts and questions of how she should conduct herself for others. Captive to uninhibited ecstasy, A'Lelia was free to bask only in the gift of her own pleasure.

Their fingers intertwined, Emeric stroked her higher, where she met her highest self, screaming out her elation before she remembered their location and cut it off.

"Dr. E?" one of the boys called from the hallway. "Miss C?"

Their time was up.

Already laughing in his eyes, Emeric licked off the remaining juices of her orgasm.

Her legs weak and shivering, her body recuperating from his skills, her mind from the delirium, and her heart from the possibilities, she lay still for a moment to recover.

"I see now, I'm not gonna be able to take you nowhere." Standing to his feet, he found a couple of clean towels and passed them to her.

She cleaned herself as best as she could, and wrestled up her panties and tights, while he wiped off his mouth and chin.

"I didn't mean to. It just…came out," she explained in reference to that shriek. "But I hope you take me lots of places." Where had that come from? What did she even mean? Why hadn't she thought about it first before she blurted stuff?

As if he heard her internal conversation, he stopped what he was doing and pivoted toward her. Al's chin in his fingers, Em sucked her lips, and she tasted herself on his tongue.

"I intend to take you lots of places if you let me." His breath carried her essence.

"I'll go with you anywhere," she whispered, repeating his words from days ago.

His eyes didn't blink. "Does that mean you'll be my girl if I ask?"

He was asking. Not assuming. And waiting, like he was hoping.

So this was how it felt. The physics of atoms and electrons, their attraction so undeniable there was no need to choose. It just was.

"It means I'll think about it. If you ask."

Every woman who wanted it deserved this. To look in a man's eyes and see her hopes and dreams projected back to her.

"What if I'm asking?"

Al grinned. "Then I suppose I'm thinking."

"Dr. E?" a voice spoke outside.

With all the euphoria of a man who'd just claimed the biggest prize at the fair, Em sucked her lips a final time and flung the door open before Al could stop him. He cleared his throat.

"I'll see you guys at rehearsal in a couple of hours. I need to stop by the house first and change."

"Emeric." Al covered her mouth, unable to suppress her laugh.

Marvin looked up and wrinkled his nose. "Dr. E, what happened to your head?"

Daryl sniffed. "What's that smell?"

FOR SOME REASON, Emeric knocked on the door softly, even though the secretary had told him Dr. Césaire was ready for him to come in. Maybe it was because the man was old, and going back to the long summer days when Emeric had to stay quiet during his grandmother's "stories," it had become habit to do that for older people.

"Come in."

Emeric entered a nice-sized corner office that could never have enough space for all the piles of books crammed inside it, with gadgets plopped on top. Most of them were old, many half open, hanging off a chair or shelf, as if the scientist and professor had been in the middle of a thought when he'd abandoned it and switched to another thought. On top of a few lay folded notepads underneath telltale layers of dust.

"Have a seat."

The professor sat behind a regal Georgian-style, mahogany desk that could have belonged to Woodrow Wilson. Atop it, the scientist's vintage, red fountain pen kept its frantic pace, dragging red ink across some poor student's typed labor.

Emeric certainly didn't miss those days. Still standing, he stared at the books in both chairs.

"Either one will do," Dr. Césaire added without looking up, his focus following his pen that scrutinized the lines.

Once Emeric moved a pile of books from one chair to the other, he sat and appreciated the view outside the window for the next couple of minutes. The day was cloudy, winter had browned the grass and thinned the trees. Still, Columbia's sidewalks that filtered into New York's bustling streets all held their own allure aside from the weather. Everybody out there walked through the brisk cold with purpose and intentionality. He was finally starting to feel like one of them.

Shuffling in his seat, Emeric sat in wait and twiddled his thumbs. After too much unnerving silence, he spoke. "So, I was wondering. Were you asking me here to discuss your pre-op away from everybody else?"

"No." The punishing red fountain pen continued its scrutiny. "Was my colleague, Dr. Lewis, in Tennessee, lying to me when he told me you were more than capable of doing this?"

He had spoken to Emeric's attending and mentor back home, Dr. Lew?

"No, sir."

"He said you were his best. That you had heart, and he was quite disappointed when you announced right before your Meharry graduation you were leaving."

Memories of Dr. Lew's disappointment snowed inside Em now. He hadn't wanted to let people down. But he'd needed to stay true to his disturbed spirit. He loved medicine, and he loved Tennessee. But he didn't love the limited opportunities or the general complacency with that.

"Thank you. I appreciate that."

"So? Why did ya?"

"Why did I what?"

"Leave."

Emeric shifted, thrust in an impromptu interview he hadn't expected to be about him. "I needed...something different... I wasn't sure what, though. There's this slowness to the South that'll have you feeling like, even though you're putting out your best, you're still not going anywhere. Either that, or like the world around you is not moving." In thought, the budding surgeon scratched his cheek. "Similar to being an astronaut floating around in space. No matter how much you move or which way you turn, the absence of gravity is a constant. You can't do anything about it. It's not changing. You have to move within those laws. That's the South. A beautiful place full of powerful souls, and seeing so much power suppressed can be suffocating."

"Once you get your feet on the ground, what are your plans?"

He hadn't thought of the specifics, only a few vague goals—chief surgeon one day, contributing to a school-to-medical school pipeline, teaching some. "I don't know exactly, but I'd like to host young men and women from back home here in the city, so they can see something different. Occasionally, go home and be a visiting professor at Meharry or TSU, and do my part. I'm not turning my back on home altogether. I just want a situation where I can be fed, too."

"Do you intend to take my granddaughter with you?"

The Memphis native thought carefully. "We're not there yet. If we get to that point, though, that's up to her. But I'd love it if she was interested in visiting with me." Why were they entertaining a conversation he and Al hadn't even had?

Dr. Césaire's vintage fingers flipped a page of the paper, and red ink resumed flowing.

"Hm. Do you know about this desk?" the scientist asked.

"No, sir," Em answered, curious as to why this was important. He wanted to grab food before heading uptown for rehearsal in a while. "I don't. But the designs on it are right o…lovely."

"It was custom-designed and made by your grandfather."

Emeric focused in on it again, this time with new eyes, through the lens of a boy in search of a hero. The intricate carvings and ornate detail in the wood spoke of a cabinetmaker's love for what he gave the world. "You knew him?"

"I did. How much do *you* know about him?" The pen finally stopped. Behind the eyes he shared with A'Lelia, Dr. Césaire's vault held multiple gems.

"Not much more than a short retelling here or there. Something funny he said or did."

"He was indeed a funny man. He made this desk for me the year I was nominated for the Nobel Prize. He wasn't yet known at that point. Still fairly new on the scene. He was a kid from the Five Points. His mother sold toys from a mule-drawn cart over on Canal Street. I would know since my mother bought them from her for my siblings and me."

Out the window, Emeric directed his rising emotions. His ancestors had walked those streets, *worked* those streets, budding businesspeople fulfilling New York's promise, contributing to its rise. Unanswered questions became living, breathing people hugging his heart.

"Orenthal outgrew toys and started making bigger things. I gave him some business, commissioned him for this desk and a few items at the house—bookcases, my children's cribs and whatnot. Word got around about his eye for detail. By the mid-twenties, his name took off. He started running circles around the big boys. His quality separated his work from the rest, and the rest weren't too happy about it."

With this information, Orenthal's grandson could finally

take a candle into the cave, lighting up cracks and skeletons of a tomb where the best part of his mother was buried.

"He loved to have a good time. That's for sure." Dr. Césaire laced his fingers together over the desk, and this time, the scientist's gesture was significant enough to be life-giving. "He loved his Scotch and his women. Don't ever tell your mother I said it." He held up his hands in front of one another and shook them. "He had this laugh that…" His eyes disappeared in a forest of memories, his mouth opening in joy, like he was missing good ole days that were better than heaven. "A giant laugh that bounced everywhere. When he was in the room, you definitely knew it. I had about ten years on him, but we became friends. Once he was making respectable money, bought himself a house, he asked me to be the executor of his estate."

Upon recalling this, he winced. "It almost seemed Ory had a premonition his success might do him in, or either he was catching some heat he hadn't told us about. Anyway, I wasn't interested in getting into anybody's personal affairs, but he wouldn't stop nagging me. Said he didn't trust anybody else in his family to use it the right way."

"The executor of his estate?" This was the first Emeric was hearing of it. His mother had always complained they had nothing. The several relatives who divided her and her sisters and took them in spent whatever money they might have received.

"Yes." Dr. Césaire eyed him from the other side of the desk. "It wasn't a whole lot, but we made it work."

"We?"

"Me and a few guys around town who'd liked him. A couple of 'em had come up with him. We felt awful about what befell him, despite how we'd warned him."

"Warned?"

A'Lelia's grandfather shared her intensity. "Yes. Warned

him. More on that in a bit. Nobody could take in his children. When Ory died, we were still in the Depression. A lot of friends had lost jobs, businesses, investments. Not to mention, people kept moving in here from other places, hoping for better than in the South. We were trying to help a lot of souls in a rough time, while we kept our own heads above water."

"Executor of an estate." Emeric waded through his mother's stoic silences when he'd asked about her city. "Mama always said she was alone, her relatives took the little she got, and nobody around here stepped in to help."

The scientist's expression was solemn. "I'm sure in many ways she was. I cannot imagine a worse loneliness than going to sleep in a beautiful home and waking up the next day an orphan, split up from your siblings, losing your valuables, sent to relatives who may not have had your blessings and will now punish you with their resentments. I hope you've shown her some grace."

Tears rolling down Emeric's nose fell onto his slacks. This was more story than he'd gotten his entire life.

The oracle of information reached inside his desk and sat a box of tissues on top of the table, pushing it toward his late friend's grandson. Emeric took a tissue to wipe his eyes and nose.

"How is she?"

"Mama? She's a good lady. Real good. She loves her some jazz. Every now and then, she talks about Granddaddy taking her to hear Louis Armstrong and the greats. Sometimes she'll put on some old records and play a game," Emeric recalled between his sniffs.

"Pinocle?" Dr. Césaire guessed.

The involuntary guffaw breaking out of Em sent him spitting everywhere. "How did you know?"

"Her daddy loved that damn game. You wouldn't find

anybody more fun with a bigger, more giving heart. Or a larger personality."

The older man's yellow brick road of memories dissolved, and his eyes shifted somewhere else.

"That laugh of his got him through a lot. Those Depression days were also Harlem's heyday. Famous Black people who made money off White audiences could afford Orenthal's pieces. He was shipping custom designs as far away as Hollywood and even London. With his prominent clientele, he was making out all right. And he should have left it there. But that giant ego of his always needed stroking. Ory's electric personality was also his curse. His competitors took notice, offered to buy him out. He said 'no.'"

Those words wound up an emotional Emeric. "What would you have done?"

"Sold. Let them have it and gotten them off my tail. And started something else run by a White middleman that didn't have my name on it. That's why The Saint-Emilion isn't called The Césaire." The older man's moment of pause delivered a tacit rebuke. "Yes, the elevator lift told me you inquired."

The eighty-six-year-old's iron blade of wisdom sharpened Emeric's surface-level understanding. Though Em knew the principle, he still felt sympathy for any man having to abandon what he'd built.

"He had a right to keep what he worked hard for, and he shouldn't have had to run."

"No, he shouldn't have, but as long as we're Black, run we will. I don't mean to dishonor your grandfather's memory, and I say this as somebody who cared. I told him to quiet down. He didn't listen. Then, one night, at closing hour, Harlem was watching a great fire. A man, his wife, and their toddler son were locked inside, nobody able to free them. As it turned out, on a school night, his daughters were asleep at home."

Both men's heads fell toward what remained of Orenthal Shipman, his desk.

Emeric's heart was full with this new knowledge, and yet fullness weighed down on him. It was a lot to process in one afternoon, particularly when he'd come here expecting to discuss either A'Lelia or Friday's surgery. "I can't thank you enough for this."

"I'm sorry we're not meeting under more fortuitous circumstances."

The elder man gave him a minute.

"Now, about this pickle you're in at Hillside. You sure I'm trusting the right person with my life?"

The young surgeon recollected his wits. "Yes, sir, without a doubt."

"Very well. I'll leave the particulars to those of you who know better than me. And I trust you'll use your opportunity to choose your team prudently."

Understanding what that meant, Emeric nodded. "Yes, sir."

"Good. Once I'm out of surgery and we go over what you find, I'll call Franklin to make a place for you over at Harlem as soon as he's able. Clearly, if I don't wake up, I won't be making the call."

Though such a consequential situation was not funny, Emeric couldn't stop his small grin. "You'll be waking up, sir."

"That's helpful to know."

"You don't want support from anybody in your family at all?" Emeric asked. A'Lelia would be sick if she found out.

"My wife. She stayed through everything else. I don't see why she shouldn't suffer this one, too. *Only* her. Nobody else."

Emeric nodded. The life of A'Lelia's grandfather would be

in his hands, and not telling her felt wrong, but he took patient-doctor privilege seriously.

"As far as my granddaughter is concerned," the man said, seeming to read Em's mind, "should you ever hurt her, just as I can make this call, I can make another. Should I be dead and you put a foot wrong, the call will still be made. Do we understand one another?"

In that warning, Emeric learned today's second lesson. Not to take Theodore Césaire's warnings lightly.

"Yes, sir."

"Good. Oh. There's one more thing. I don't have it here with me now, but I have something I meant to return to your grandfather and I never got the chance. I'll try and remember to bring it Friday."

The contents of this conversation still settled over an unsettled Emeric—a man, son, grandson, transplant, and doctor, confused as to which one should take the lead in this moment.

"Sir, you're showing real faith in me, somebody you don't know, for a procedure that has a lot weighing on it. May I ask why you would do that? Not that I'm incapable, but how would you know? And why did you invite me here?"

"My granddaughter asked me to help. I needed to know who I was helping. If you're anything like your grandfather, you care about what you do. Dr. Lewis confirmed that. Second, I wanted to meet Orenthal's legacy, see how it panned out in his absence, and perhaps offer you some perspective your folks wouldn't have."

He picked up his fountain pen, toying with it, seeming to use it to scroll his mind for anything he'd forgotten.

"You're in New York now, Dr. McPherson. Your money and success will increase in direct proportion to the tough choices you cannot avoid. Some of those choices might be the difference between literal life and death. Let your grandfather's life be your lesson. Choosing wrong could mean the downfall of your house."

At this point, Emeric's head was almost too heavy to nod.

"When I retire, this desk and anything else I have that your grandfather made is yours. Should I make it out alive this Friday, I'll write that down somewhere." The scrutinizing red ink resumed its course. "That'll be all."

"Thanks again. I really appreciate it," Emeric said on his way out, but the man had already become absorbed in his work.

Once Emeric hit the stairs, tears in his eyes, sobs choking him up, he sorted his hurt for his mother alongside the joy of finally having answers. A litany of questions left him confused on the sidewalk.

His mother had had it all wrong. People *did* help them, even if it had been from afar. She had been too caught up in her pain and struggles to realize it. Add to that how Emeric did not walk this road alone. A'Lelia had convinced her grandfather to assist and massive floodgates had cracked open.

Em would be performing one of the highest-profile surgeries in the city! His risk coming here to New York had paid off! Dr. Césaire had advised him better than his own father.

A little leap and a spin on the sidewalk, and he almost crashed into a passerby. "Sorry."

Coming back down to Earth, he headed for his car and Mount Bethel. Once he successfully removed this colon mass and did what he did best, Em would be leaving Hillside. On to Harlem Hospital. And upward with his dreams.

Lighter, hopeful, Em strolled into church, sure as a man who'd been shown the road to the pearly gates. A stranger no more, with the right connections, the right girl, and the right opportunities, Emeric Orenthal Shipman McPherson was arriving.

FROM AL'S OPEN SATCHEL, her letter carrier jutted out, a reminder of her overdue investigation into her family's French registration documents. Her heart picked up new vigor when she remembered the new information awaiting her in Saran wrap and a trash bag. Swamped with pulling together the Presents this week, she hadn't had time to return to her fascinating historical discovery last weekend—the Habsburgs.

How had one of the most powerful houses on the planet never come up in the Césaire household? Especially if that name belonged to their ancestor.

"Christmas gifts," Miss Clara blurted, and bumped A'Lelia from her daydream.

Seated in the first pew, the woman continued, "Now I know that's not our problem, but some of these participating families can't enjoy this experience because they're worried. They wanted their kids to take part, but they can't afford to put gifts under the tree. I've overheard some of them talking while their kids rehearse. They're having to choose between meals, rent, and presents. What's the point of all this if those babies don't have anything to open on Christmas day?"

Concern sobered Al's circle that had gotten her through this. They only had three more days until the first of the four nights began.

"Let's pass out a questionnaire to the youth and see what they would want." Al folded her arms and paced the floor. "We can get their ages, so if we can't grant their request, we can find something close and age-appropriate. I may have an idea."

"Al to the rescue." Jill dangled a foot up and down over her leg.

Al scratched her scalp through her kinky hair she'd been taming with a silk scarf since she had little time for a hairdresser. "We're all rescuing each other right now."

"What I want to know is who's rescuing *you*?" With a slick grin, Gloria switched subjects.

Jill joined in the distraction, bucking her eyes at her friend. "You see that face? You're over there smiling like there've been new developments. We haven't gotten an update in a minute."

"And you don't need one now." Butterflies fluttered in Al's belly the moment Emeric resurfaced in her head, his Afro bobbing between her thighs.

She bit her bottom lip to control her giddiness, but it didn't work. That was catnip for the others.

"You catch that?" Jill asked.

"Yep, I caught it." Gloria snickered. "He's been updating her."

They started high-fiving and acting up.

"I'm going to leave you young'uns to your business," Miss Clara said, getting up.

Al motioned for her to sit back down. "Don't mind them. You don't have to go away, Miss Clara."

Gloria rubbed her belly. "No, ma'am, you don't have to go, but me and this baby might go into labor early if we don't get the scoop now."

Al rolled her eyes. "Just gag me with a spoon. We are in a church."

"The Lord is our Shepherd, we shall not want," Jill chimed in.

"And you're looking like you don't want for *nothing* anymore." Gloria's hairy eyeball was good and suspicious. "Spill."

"There's nothing to say. We've been…planning this event."

"Don't lie now." Jill sipped her hot chocolate. "We've seen you and him in here making eyes, holding hands, sneaking off—"

"We do not sneak!"

"What do you and him do when you two go around that corner?" Gloria teased.

Al laughed. "Talk!"

Gloria turned to Jill. "Did you see how he wasn't here two days ago, and you could read it on her face? Girl, she left outta here real fast and in a hurry. Our good doctor marched that tail on in here yesterday, though, didn't he? Right after baby girl walked in, he was like 'yes, ma'am, I won't be absent again, ma'am.' She's already got him trained."

"How'd that happen?" Jill inspected Al.

Their silliness was welcome relief from all the work they'd been putting in.

"You two are seriously jiving right now."

"No, you're the one. We've got eyes," Gloria replied. "You telling us, or do you want us to keep reading it on you?"

Like they'd summoned him, Emeric filtered into the sanctuary with some of the youth, joking around and teasing with them. Today, the boys were stoked on their way in the door, jumping in the air and flicking their wrists to shoot make-believe jump shots, apparently debating basketball players.

Without bothering to look over her shoulder, Gloria grinned. "Her body is talking. He must've just walked in."

Jill snorted. "How much you want to bet he leaves those boys where they're at and comes over here before he goes anywhere else?"

Al's hormones clashed with her neurons in millions of tiny explosions from the deepest parts of her brain to the most sensitive tips of her, the closer he came.

When Emeric meandered to the circle to speak and a flurry of giggles broke out, he froze.

Al tried, ever so slightly, to give him a heads-up that he was entering a trap.

Gloria snorted. "Dr. McPherson, who've you been operating on lately?"

Jill's voice imitated an intercom announcement. "Dr. Emeric wanted in Gynecology."

Caught completely off guard, he stared at Al. With tiny shakes of her head, she signaled again for him not to engage.

Emeric backed away and eyed them all knowingly. "I see what's goin' on over here. I'm just gonna head to the back and grab coffee."

"You two are awful," Al said to the laughs.

After rehearsal, once the vans took off to transport children home, parents and volunteers were clearing out, and the area was safe from Al's friends, the good doctor reappeared at her side.

"So this is you thinkin' about it? Tellin' everybody in here?"

Giggling, she put on her coat. "I didn't say anything."

"But you didn't shut 'em up either." He pushed her other arm in her sleeve. "Did you at least tell 'em I was good?"

Al shot him a glance. "How do you know you were good?"

"That's how I understood your little scream you couldn't keep to yourself." He lowered his voice next to her ear. "And everything else that came out of ya."

"Are we talking about this in church? You're just as bad as they are."

He held open the door for Al, and even their brush against one another in the door generated magnetic reactions, from the tingling sensations of skin underneath their coats to the coils on their heads reaching out with static. Their glance, an instance of warm atoms and electrons, nearly brought their heads together. Squeaky brakes in the not-too-far distance snapped them out of it. They pivoted from that near-kiss, hearts still thudding.

"It's late, but you wanna stop through Sylvia's and tell me how bad I am over a plate?"

It was late. Nine-thirty at night, and Al was about to drop.

"They close in thirty minutes. We should move if we want to make it."

"I'll tail you."

"Goodnight, Dr. Emeric and Miss A'Lelia!" Jill yelled just before he closed Al's door.

Fortunately, Sylvia's soul food restaurant was only a few blocks away on Lenox Avenue and One Hundred and Twenty-Fourth. Since it was a late night in the middle of the week, not many patrons were there.

Over ox tails, smothered chicken, and short ribs from the "Wednesday" section of the menu, they were receiving their plates when the door was locked.

"You asked me the questions last time." Emeric slid an oxtail bone out of his mouth. "My turn. I've got a good burning one to ask, too. Why did you have to do this with just a few of your friends? For the Presents to be so prestigious, where were all the other families from the Murray Hill

I saw that first night? Was it really so hard for them to let strangers into the event?"

"Yes." Al's tired answer gave no jive. "They view these events as sacred, a reprieve from the rest of the world. The way they see it, I took that from them and changed it single-handedly. It's not my private event to change."

"But look at how it turned out, how inspiring it's become, how many lives you've lifted."

"We." She corrected him. "We all lifted hearts. Not just me. And I lost quite a few good mentors and neighbors that I grew up with."

"For them to walk out on you, maybe they weren't the good neighbors and friends you thought. That's what my mama always says anyway."

Al thought of the humiliation and lost relationships to her grandparents and parents. Her family had been gracious and nurturing with her, but seeing their friends at the holiday parties had to be difficult. Since Al had been so busy the past few weeks, she hadn't faced much of their blowback directly, yet.

"That's not how I see it. Who would want an entire city crashing their party? Aside from that, don't give me too much credit. I didn't plan all this. I walked into Mount Bethel on a whim, not taking it seriously."

Quizzically, he smiled. "You talking about that afternoon you almost fainted?"

"I did not almost faint."

His eyes danced around. "You and Pastor Freeman were going at it pretty hard out in the hallway. What was that about? And, yeah, you did."

Al remembered literally reeling from that exchange and the pastor's words about her family. "I didn't realize people could see us. It was a personal matter."

"For a minute, I thought you and him had a little thang

going on, but then, First Lady Freeman almost broke her neck to keep you there, so I figured that couldn't be it."

"Pastor Freeman is like a lot of people who have opinions about the Presents, the Great War, and men like my grandfather who had a part in it."

Emeric scraped his plate, seeming to choose his next words. "What's your opinion on his part in it?" His gaze left the plate and forked into her.

Every time Al confronted this question, it cut her apart. The way she understood it, at the turn of the twentieth century, the Césaire wealth was diminishing. It had been over a hundred years since their family had fled the French Revolution with jewels, coin, and dinnerware from the courts of Marie Antoinette. But throughout the 1800s, the Césaires struggled in a fast-growing Industrial America. Decade by decade, their status fell, from Afro-French Americans out of France's royal courts in the late 1700s to "high yella" Negroes acting above their station by the late 1800s. As droves of enterprising Irish, Germans, Jews, and other Blacks had flooded New York, the Césaires went from insuring ships and voyages on the high seas to treading water in everyday life.

Then came World War One. It offered a chance for a young scientist to put his family's name back on the map.

"He's a hero. How many people's lives have been saved because of my grandfather? He didn't start the Great War, but his device protected a lot of men fighting in it." Of that, she would never be ashamed. "Yes, like many corporations and inventors that made out nicely, he got paid for what he contributed."

Somber, Emeric and A'Lelia were no longer eating, each of them having explored each other's vulnerableness at this point. Yet, he wore a weird expression, neither judgmental nor angry, but perhaps ruminative, as if he were deciding an internal conflict.

Did Emeric, a medical doctor whose job was saving lives, have a problem with her grandfather or her family? By now, he'd met other guys among the Black elite, and he'd probably been talking to them and getting their opinions on Al's family. If Em was now second-guessing what he'd asked her the day before, Al would just have to accept that. But never again would she stretch herself to try and prove she was Black enough, or try to make amends for her lighter skin tone or her looks, or be treated as if her grandfather had singlehandedly dropped an atomic bomb, or try and earn a man's affections.

With the silence now too empty, she picked up her fork to resume eating.

Em placed his hand over hers.

"After the Presents this Saturday, can we go somewhere besides another Presents rehearsal?"

The laugh of relief burst out of her. "Yes."

She turned her hand over, and he laid his atop it. His thumb stroking her inner palm stroked the insides of her.

"Where do you wanna go?" he asked.

"Have you ever been to Studio 54? We'll already be dressed up and won't have to change. I feel like dancing."

"Right on then." Taking out his wallet to pay, he seemed to remember something. "Oh, by the way, I can't make the dress rehearsals tomorrow or Friday."

"So you're leaving your boys for me to manage? You know they'll be disappointed." She sucked her teeth. "And I might be, too, a little. I thought you didn't work on Thursdays and Fridays. Everything okay?"

A big sigh preceded his next words. "My first surgery is Friday afternoon, and even though I've done it before, I just want to spend Thursday going over a few things with my surgical team, and Friday hanging around to make sure this particular patient makes out with no problems."

"Oh, sweet Heavens, Emeric! That is righteous. How wonderful!"

Oddly, the joy in his smile was muted, as if pinned down by a double-edged sword. "Thank you."

"You're not happy? I mean, you shouldn't have to celebrate just being allowed to do your job. But the fact that your admin are finally getting out of your way is good, right?" Confused, Al waited.

He finished his Coke. "They're actually not getting out of my way. The patient requested me. If it weren't for that, I'd still be in purgatory. Since my first shot here in New York could be my last if I don't get it right, I must be flawless. The story of Black folks' lives, right?"

Now Al understood his reticence. This opportunity was being used, not to mold him into a better doctor, but as a means of elimination.

Intrigued, she leaned over the table. "You were *requested?*" Her jaw dropped, and she excitedly shook his arm. "Emeric, that is awesome. Who?"

He shook his head. "I can't. Doctor-patient privilege." He sucked in a big breath. "I have you to thank, though."

"Me? You were a doctor before you met me."

"I was having a rough time when you and I bumped heads that first night. I would probably be packing to go back home right now if it wasn't for you, the Presents, how hard I saw you fighting so the Black community didn't lose it. Watching you, interacting with those kids, I was reminded I also needed to stand up and be a strong, very smart, very brave man. Helping you helped me. You're the star brightly shining for the rest of us to see in the night, baby girl. Your circles are mad about losing the little privilege they had, but you don't owe them anything."

Lifting her hand to his lips, Emeric lifted their connection to the sky. "You have new people around you now," he said with a side grin. "Your blessings and name around the city have increased tenfold. If God wasn't in this, that wouldn't be the case."

"I came up at their expense."

"You didn't plan that, though. God just decided it was your time, and He bestowed it on you, and we all watched it happen. They could have come up, too, if they were willing to grow. But here you are, shining harder without them than you were when they had you on the back bench. So stop worrying about who's criticizing. Just soak up all this love from who's lovin' you."

EMERIC'S CONSCIENCE lay wide open on the operating table of his guilt. A'Lelia's endless sea-green eyes were knives slicing him open down the middle.

He took his doctor-patient privilege seriously, but two nights ago, he had been on the verge of telling A'Lelia her hero was going under the knife.

An adenoma indicated colon cancer, and that was nothing to play with. In Emeric's eyes, Al and her parents had a right to know that their family patriarch might not make it out of this, regardless of which doctor did the procedure. But Em had made Dr. Césaire a promise, and Emeric was a man of his word.

If her grandfather didn't survive, and Al ever found out that Em did the operation *and* he kept it from her, how would that play out for them? The possibility of him losing her trust almost pushed him to tell it. Almost.

Had he told her and she'd gone running to confront her grandfather, then, Emeric would have violated an equally important trust as a doctor and as a man, aside from risking his opportunity to finally leave Hillside.

Finishing an early breakfast Aunt Dee had made him, he took his plate to the sink. Somewhere outside his state of focus and calm, the phone rang. Totally immersed in today's procedure, he put on his coat and was layering up for the cold.

"Emeric?" Aunt Dee called. "Your mother wants to speak before you head out." Before passing the phone, she covered the receiver. "Be patient with her. She hasn't been back in New York for thirty-five years since she left. She may be getting nervous about the trip, so you and her take it easy."

He nearly stopped his aunt from passing it. The last thing he needed today was to go into surgery with conflicts on his mind.

"Hey, Mama." He would have been just as disturbed had he not taken it.

"Not yet, young fella, it's the big boss on here. I heard they put you in charge of the hospital, and now all of New York is sick," his oldest sister, Belinda, teased him from the other end.

"Girl, when they put me in charge, they'll never have to worry about being sick again. Healthcare'll be off the hook."

"Now that you're big time up there, you can't call anymore?" Billie asked.

"No, now that I'm up here, I'm too scared to call and say how it's really goin'."

He missed their jokes and their family's easy way with each other.

"You're a Casanova with that knife, and everything you've ever done, li'l brotha. This ain' any different. It's just taking its time, testing how bad you want it, is all."

Those words felt almost as good in his belly as her hot water cornbread. "Thanks, baby girl."

"Carmen says she's sorry she can't come with us to see you next week, but I'll be there to see your big ole rock head.

Until then, you keep your chin up, space cadet. Mama says you're having your first surgery today. Don't kill nobody, all right?"

"If you see a headline on the evenin' news for 'doctor on the run,' just leave me some cash and a getaway car in the backyard. I'll handle the rest."

"I love you, baby."

"Love you, too, sweetheart."

"Emeric?" Mama's familiarness was an instant comfort, even if annoying at times.

"Mornin', Mama, I was just on my way out the door."

"Dee tells me you're going into surgery today. They finally gave you one, huh? If you were here at home, how many surgeries would you have already done by now?" she asked.

Pinching the bridge of his nose, he held his peace. "I'll be glad to see everybody next week."

"We really miss you around here, son. If you were coming back home, we could have all kinds of things planned for ya. We could cut that New York trip short, you'd follow your daddy back here, and we'd spend the holidays cooking, eating, playing with the kids, and having us a real good time."

"Mama, there are good things happening around here, too. Would you believe me if I told you I know where your grandmother used to sell toys?" he asked in an effort to redirect the conversation.

"How do you know that? Somebody older had to tell you. Nobody young knows that."

"It doesn't matter how I know. When you get here, let's take a drive around the city with Rose, Billie, and the kids. You show us your favorite spots."

"I don't have any favorite spots there. I only have one son I want to bring back home where he belongs. Now who have you been talking to?"

Carefully, Emeric pieced together his response. "A good friend of Granddaddy's."

"Daddy didn't have any friends who were good, only fools he shouldn't have trusted. What's the name of this one who's in your ear?"

"You really believe there was nobody good in yours or Granddaddy's lives?"

"It certainly wasn't the case when my sisters and I were bouncing from house to house."

"And if I told you people saw to it that your college was paid for?"

"It's a load of crap. I squeaked by on scholarships."

"Scholarships sent to you only? No other students?"

A pause on the other end ferreted out the memories. "I went to the financial aid office, and my counselor handed me applications for the ones I qualified for. What kind of lies have you been told?"

"Did you ever hear other students discussing those same scholarships?"

Another silence, another answer. "Emeric, do you think I'm lying that I had to make my own way? My life was deplorable, and the people we called friends back in New York were not worth returning to after college. Are you believing somebody else over your own mother?"

"No, ma'am, I just wonder if your pain blinded you to the kindness you were getting and didn't see."

"So this is how it'll be for us? You second-guessing me every time you meet somebody new up there? Questioning my common sense like I don't really know what I went through? You're so desperate for them to accept ya, you'll believe anybody who'll talk to ya. Why should I come way up to New York for you and me to do this?"

Emeric's heart dipped into his stomach. "Because, Ma, maybe it's time for you and me to do *exactly* this. From what I keep hearing about Granddaddy and Grandmama, they both loved life. They loved havin' a good time, and you got it from them honest. The way I see it, they would not have wanted their children growing up filled with so much animosity and misery. So yes, maybe you should come way up here so we can deal with this. I've gotta run. I love you."

He handed the phone to Aunt Dee for her to talk, grabbed his lunch Al had made him, and walked out.

In the car, he cued up his O'Jays 8-track, forwarding it to "For the Love of Money" and rode through the city.

Once he arrived at the hospital, a gaggle of doctors hung out around the doctors' lounge.

"Hey, Emeric," one of them called to him for the first time in his five months being here.

"What it is, Emeric? Got any free spots in your OR today?"

"Emeric, buddy! How's it going? Need any help in there?"

Changing clothes at his locker, he greeted his team and then made his way toward the waiting lounge.

"Mrs. Césaire?" He offered his hand. "I'm—"

"Orenthal Shipman's grandson."

"Yes, ma'am, Dr. Emeric McPherson."

"Well, if you're half as good at your job as your grandfather was at his, I shouldn't have anything to worry about. Just you make sure my husband comes out of there today, and I can take him back home to his family."

"Yes, ma'am. We have every intention of you doing just that."

Inside the OR, someone had already cued up an 8-track tape in the overhead player. He glanced at a sleeping Dr. Césaire to confirm he was properly anesthetized.

With all of them in regular latex gloves, Emeric monitored as another Black resident painted the patient with the orange betadine sanitation solution in the areas where Emeric would cut.

Once he'd supervised that process, at long last, Emeric headed to the sink to scrub in for several minutes. His hands in the air, touching nothing, so they remained germ-free, he moved to the circulating nurse who waited with towels to dry them. She opened the gloves to slide them on his hands in the sterile technique. After all the surgeons danced from one nurse to the next, maintaining a clean environment, the scrub tech finally brought the kits of sterilized medical tools.

The last person to enter the room was an attending surgeon from surgery-oncology that Emeric had strategically sought out, and who controlled one of the schedules, to be in Emeric's corner in the future.

In exchange for a high-profile, career-defining surgery such as Dr. Césaire, this attending would help Emeric secure better assignments until he could leave Hillside. Dr. Césaire coming here had given him leverage.

"Everybody, ready for action?" he asked the others.

Lyles and Bottoms joined him in the dance, and they all approached the table.

"Since the beginning of time, feels like."

"Well then, let's get this brotha home for Christmas," Emeric said to his majority-Black surgical team.

With the O'Jays' "A Prayer" playing over the sound system, Emeric picked up his scalpel and made his first incision.

"SISSY, YOU LOOK SO MAGICAL." BB stuck one of the family's heirloom, Parisian diamond-encrusted hair clips in Al's press n' curl, swept over to one side. Little Sister wrinkled her nose. "Well, as magical as we can manage. You're going to a church."

Cackling, Jill snorted her soda.

"She looks absolutely perfect," Mamman said. "Roberta, get into your dress. It's almost time to leave."

Behind their mother's back, BB made a gagging motion at Al's more demure Ruben Panis floor-length gown and matching long-sleeve jacket, all of which left no trace of sex appeal. Al had had to ditch her more risqué Halston strapless liquid satin she would have worn at the hotel. She'd had their private costumer find her pieces that were more church-appropriate for those four nights.

"Where are Meme and Pépé?" Al maneuvered her earrings in her ear holes. "I haven't talked to them in days. How are they getting there?" She referenced one of her father's younger brothers.

"Mamman said yesterday Pépé came down with a bad bug and he'll have to miss it, baby. They don't want to chance it turning into pneumonia. He wants you to stop by and give a full report once you've gotten some rest."

Meme wouldn't be there? Al, Jill, and BB all swapped silent concern in the mirror.

Al's father entered the room, along with her sixteen-year-old brother, Fernand, whom they called Nandy, home from boarding school ahead of Christmas.

"Look at my oldest baby, trying to be a stone fox and I'm not ready. Why are you in this grown-up woman's gown? What happened to the barrettes and ruffles and bows in your hair?" Papa kissed her forehead.

"Wow, Ally Cat." Nandy tugged one of her curls. "You look like a real grownup."

Al rolled her eyes.

"She's got a boyfriend now, and I don't think he wants to see her in little girl clothes," Mamman said with a side snicker.

"Boyfriend?" Papa repeated.

"Mamman, he's not my boyfriend."

"Yet," Jill added.

"Yes, he is. He's been over here and even spent the night," BB tattled.

Papa held Al away from him, to inspect her and deliver a silent diatribe. "I was only in London a few days."

"She's exaggerating, Papa. He was only here for a couple of hours before he had to go to work."

Papa popped foie gras and fig jam on gingerbread in his mouth. "And what is he exactly? A gravedigger? Undertaker? What does he do that he's working at night?"

"A doctor," BB answered as if he'd asked her.

"At Hillside," Jill added.

Papa's mouth flatlined. "My Lord, that's almost as bad."

"And guess what else? He's a Shipman."

Papa dug into his memory. "Shipman? You mean…?"

"Yep." BB kept going. "*Those* Shipmans. And guess what else? Al blew up the entire Presents, and now our family doesn't have any more friends. You really missed a lot, Pop."

Papa stood confused. "Where are my mamman and papa at?"

Al's mother handed him his tie and cuff links, also from the Césaire family vault. "He's under the weather, and to make sure he's in good shape for Christmas, they're taking it easy. They tell me he's been seen by a doctor, and as long as he stays inside and drinks plenty of fluids, it should pass. Nothing to worry about. His next doctor visit is Monday, and they'll update us then. Erwin, get your cuff links and tie on. Everybody, we will not be off schedule! We are walking out that door on time!" Mamman clapped behind her crew.

"I'll give him a call first thing in the morning then. See if he needs anything. We haven't talked to them about where Christmas will be."

"Our house." Mamman fixed Nandy's tie. "They shouldn't be hosting any big gatherings while she's taking care of him."

Papa studied Al in the mirror. "Ally Cat, this is a big night for you. Why's your face dragging the floor?"

"Are Meme and Pépé mad at me, Mamman, and the real reason they're not coming is because of what happened?" Al studied her mother for any signs of hedging.

"He really is under the weather, baby, and they are not mad." Mamman started wrapping up the appetizers to put away. "He might be a bit disappointed that you disregarded your meme's wish for you not to go to Mount Bethel, but you know she would never skip something major of yours in anger. Especially not when it's turning out so well. You know how your meme is. She would show up with her newspaper friends, just so they can put you and her in the papers, and she could have her revenge on all her naysayers."

That was somewhat reassuring. Jill rubbed her back.

"I should probably call them and just make sure, and tell Pépé I love him and tell Meme I'm sorry."

Mamman came and guided Al by the shoulders toward her lists on the dining room table. "No, you should be over there making sure you haven't forgotten any of those lists, or the itinerary, or anything else you should have."

The elevator to her suite buzzed that someone was coming up.

"Dr. Emeric McPherson is on his way up, Ms. Césaire," the doorman called up from downstairs.

"Oh, God." Al fanned herself. "When did this dress get so hot and heavy?"

Though this was her fifth year hosting the Presents, it was her first going on a man's arm. Luke had always taken the position it was a kiddie event, and as such, hadn't attended since he was a kid.

Her best friend came toward Al, arms open, and drew her into a bear hug. "I'm so excited for you," Jill whispered. "Good luck tonight. I'll be at my post lining up the kids, but just throw one of your heels or something if you need me."

"You know I'm not throwing anything at you."

"Love you, foxy."

"Love you, too."

Al started for the door, but her father stepped in front of her, stopping her in her tracks. Judging by his non-smile, he still wasn't over the news.

"Won't be anymore Lucases mistreating my baby again," he said in reference to Luke.

The elevator opened, and patent leather shoes stepped off of it, underneath a perfectly tailored, velvet-lined tuxedo with a velvet bow tie, diamond cuff links, a solid, twenty-four-karat gold watch, and an Afro trimmed into a neat bob. In his hand, he carried a single flower. "Hello."

Al could only catch a glimpse of him since her father was in the way.

"So, I understand you're Doctor McPherson?" her papa asked.

"Yes, sir, I am. How are you doing?"

Papa's arm moved forward. "I'm *Doctor* Césaire. Number two. My father is a doctor also."

Al scoffed at her papa's antics.

"So I heard. Right on. Pleasure to meet you."

"I'll be the judge of that. One flower is all you brought with ya? On your salary? Even for Hillside? What's your reputation and character? Where'd you come from? I've never heard of any Emeric McPherson. Why should we trust you are who you say you are?"

"Papa!"

"Erwin," Mamman snapped.

Al, BB, Jill, *and* Mamman all exchanged their horror behind him.

"Well, sir, I actually had something else a little more personal that I wanted to put on A'Lelia…in private."

"Excuse me? *Put on her?*" Papa cocked his neck as he repeated. "Well, what is it? Give it here. I should have a look at it first."

"*Daddy!*"

"Erwin!"

"What? I need to know he's not pulling any fast ones on my daughter."

Still behind him, Al hit his back, and finally, he stepped aside.

"Hi." She moved toward Emeric, who was breathtaking despite beads of sweat forming around his temples. "He's not always like this. He's really nice once you get to know him.

He's still jet-lagged from an overseas trip. Emeric, this is my mom and younger brother."

During the introductions, the young man working as the elevator lift suppressed a chuckle while collecting Al's things for downstairs.

"I suppose I can go ahead and do this here." Em began digging inside his inner jacket.

"No, honey, you wanted to do it in private. Follow your first mind," Mrs. Césaire said. "Ignore my husband."

"Since my character and intentions have been called into question, I don't want to give the impression that I feel anything toward her other than respect." He produced a long box and opened it.

Every neck in the room craned.

Taken by the beauty of it, Al touched a hand to her neck. "Emeric."

He lifted a vintage diamond necklace and passed the box to Jill while he unclasped it. "I was told this belonged to my grandmother. I'm also told she used to wear it a lot, and you sound very much like her—kind, big-hearted, gracious to everybody who came in, nurturing, and s-sweet." His voice faltered from emotions the longer he talked, making apparent why he'd wanted to do this in private. "Since my mother isn't here yet, will you wear this small part of her these four nights?"

Mrs. Césaire practically broke her wrist fanning her eyes to stop the tears from ruining her makeup. Jill grabbed a napkin. Her tears had already arrived. BB's open-mouthed smile accompanied her fist-pump in front of her chest.

Light and airy, Al nodded. "M-hmm. I-I'd be honored to."

She circled for Em to place it on her neck, and everyone else in the room turned toward Dr. Césaire.

Hands in his pockets, he sucked his teeth. "Want some kind of drink there, Doctor?"

"No, sir, I'm driving. Where's your coat?" he asked Al.

"Good answer." Al's father sniffed. "Just checking. You wanna tail us over there?"

"She has to arrive early, Erwin," Mamman said.

"I probably drive too slow for you anyway, sir. I might lose you."

Al's mother grinned, impressed at how quick he was on his feet, while she handed him Al's Lilli Ann mohair swing coat trimmed with fox fur. After throwing it over Al's shoulders and tucking her in it, he guided her onto the elevator.

"A lot happened while you were gone, Pop," BB said.

Right before the doors closed, Al's anticipation air-kissed her father's wistfulness. The air between them had shifted.

The moment they were both in the car, Em opened his palm over the center console, she slid hers inside it, and they closed the last three days of separation. They hadn't seen one another since their Wednesday date. Their chemistry was growing beyond a simple attraction. It was apparent in the rhythmic pulse of their tongues swirling and foreheads hugged up.

Emeric's other hand holding the back of her head, his thumb sweeping up the sensitive nerves along her neck, reciprocating, answering, returning her feelings in multiples. Emeric's kiss held nothing back. Having missed him the past seventy-two hours, A'Lelia acted on her longing. Curious and enamored, she removed her hand from his and trailed her growing emotions over his thigh. Uninhibited by doubts or suspicions of his motives or whether he felt the same, in this new confidence with a man, a first for her, Al took a risk up to his swollen manhood that responded to her touch.

Apparently jarred, Emeric jumped, grabbing her hand to stop her.

"I'm sorry!" Al snatched her hand back. "I'm sorry. You didn't like it?"

A pretty prude who can't shag her way out of a book.

"No! I—"

"You didn't?" Oh God. Tears crowded her eyes, and she looked away so he wouldn't see.

"Yeah. I mean, yes, I love it." He turned her face back toward him and cupped it, holding her gaze reassuringly. "Baby, I loved it. Trust me. But if we start that, you won't be going anywhere. Just…we can't do this while me and my life are parked right in front of your building. Your daddy is obviously planning to take me through the ropes, so I wouldn't live to feel you do it again." He tasted her lips a final time. "And I really wanna feel you do that again." His eyes didn't break from pouring into hers while he kissed her fingers. "You're stunning, by the way."

"You're funny. You look amazing. And you handled Papa well. Sorry about him."

He started up the car, and she used a handkerchief to wipe her lipstick off his mouth.

"He's not doing anything my daddy didn't do with my sisters. He's hilarious himself. We should make out all right once he chills."

"How was your surgery yesterday?"

A Rockefeller Center Christmas-tree-sized smile broadcasted his excitement, magnified by the multicolored street lights of Seventh Avenue flickering over him on their way farther Uptown. "It went well. My patient is doing pretty well. Once I ace this exam we have to take, I'm hoping in a few weeks that I'll transfer up to Harlem."

"That's righteous, Emeric."

"That *is* righteous. Now I'm about to escort the woman of

the hour, who happens to be the foxiest, stone-coldest woman in New York, into *her* operating room for her big moment. It doesn't get any better than that." He inserted an 8-track into the player, and Bill Withers's "The Gift of Giving" came on the stereo.

Once Al situated herself in his passenger seat, their hands interlaced, the night was heavenly. All that would be missing were her grandparents, and though her mother had told her it was all fine, the guilt still bothered Al. Her meme had been a part of this process in the beginning, as she was every year, but these past two weeks, she hadn't visited Mount Bethel a single time. Al would go see her in the next couple of days, apologize again, and find a way to make this up to her. Even if Pépé were sick and Meme had needed to attend him, Meme would have called several times to hassle Al about this seating chart or that guest or some other minutiae Al wouldn't have thought of. Suzanne Césaire, the consummate hostess and socialite, had perfected the art of relationships and community to neutralize her husband's controversial part in two international wars. The battle-tested wife, mother, and philanthropist now had socializing down to a science. Yet, this week, she had not called at all. Though Meme wasn't saying it, the hurt still had to be festering.

Arriving at Mount Bethel, they were still early, but the church staff, hired stage team, and volunteers were already present and going over logistics for the night. One of the parking guys threw open her door.

"Dr. McPherson, Ms. Césaire, good evening."

Sprays of soft ground spotlights bathed the church in ethereal vibes, inviting them into a safe haven from the city's hardship.

Taking her pile of lists and leather bag in one arm, Emeric took her in his other, and they headed through the big doorway that, just two weeks ago, seemed insurmountable.

Once inside, Al's breaths failed her. Emeric's astonishment danced everywhere. Though Al had been coming here everyday, immersed in the daily rigors and stresses, she now surveyed what they'd all united to build.

Stars had been lowered from the sky to Earth, now burning over her head, just above a replica of her beloved city's skyline, a symbol of strength and perseverance around the world, but especially tonight here in Harlem. Beneath the larger scene, three stages of differing heights had replaced the pastor's pulpit. They were built inside four smaller, model Black historic communities—Stagg Town from the 1600s, Seneca Village from the 1700s, Little Africa from the 1800s, and Harlem from the 1900s—so the past fittingly ascended into future, present-day New York. Interspersed among them all were miniature Christmas trees, and Kwanzaa's kinara, Kikombe Cha Umoja, and mazao. And all of that was before the church's natural Gothic architecture shined through to bless them.

When she turned for where Emeric was, he had taken a step back to let her take it all in. Hands in his pockets, he was now studying her.

"You did this."

"We."

"There wouldn't have been a 'we' without a 'you.'"

Behind him, reporters and news writers entered and made their way to the back corner of the church where they set up cameras, cued tape recorders, and flipped open notepads. In walked Jill, BB, and Gloria, shoulders hugging their ears, hands balled under their chins, and entered a collective embrace.

"Who are all those new people over there? Where did they come from?" Al asked.

As if the universe answered, a smartly dressed woman approached and offered a manicured hand. "Hello, Miss

Césaire, I'm Sasha Montague with *Vogue* magazine, and we're here to take some pictures tonight, but I was also hoping we could set a time to interview you for a spread in the magazine?"

Floored, Al stared at the others emphatically wagging their heads for her to say 'yes.'

But she tamped down her amazement and collected herself. "Actually, I'd love to, as long as all the other women who helped me organize this are interviewed and their pictures are included as well."

"Al, no," Gloria insisted. "You staked your reputation, relationships, family, and everything on keeping this party alive when a lot of us were peeling out. Don't hide your light behind other people. Stand fully in the fact that this risk you took *and* the payoff—is yours—lock, stock, and barrel."

"She's right," Emeric said. "Take a bow and own it."

Checking in with herself one more time, Al turned to Sasha. "What I said before remains. I wouldn't have been able to stand without the people you see here holding me up. I'll do the interview if they're in the spread also, as well as the city's children if you can manage a group photo that size."

Sasha smiled through her eyes. "Copacetic. I see why your gr...why people speak so highly of you. We'll be in touch to set it all up. The appointment might take a couple of days."

Al had caught that. Overwhelmed, she clutched her chest to keep it from bursting.

"Meme," BB murmured.

"Without a doubt," Al agreed.

Her grandmother had sent the cavalry to report on how this turned out, so all the Black elites who'd turned their backs couldn't miss Al's victory, whether they were here to see it or not. The move was classic Suzanne Césaire.

Sister Rowe, Miss Clara, and Emeric's Aunt Dee approached from the back, arms outstretched.

"Oh!" The moment Dee laid her eyes on Al's neck, the woman stumbled, as if stricken by a storm of emotions. "Mama's necklace! I haven't seen that in forty years."

Unsure what to do, Al stared at Em. "I can take it off. I didn't know it would be a problem."

Em covered his mouth, as if realizing something. "Auntie, I'm sorry. I just got it yesterday evening. I've been running around for today. I never had a chance to show it to you and ask if it was all right. She's only borrowing it, wearing it because I asked her to."

Al started looking for the clasp. "You know what? Don't be troubled. This should be a happy night. Here. You wear it. If you haven't seen it in that long, you absolutely should. I can see how much it means, and it's only right."

"No, no." The woman ran her fingers along the treble clef musical note encrusted with emeralds and pearls. "If my mama was still here, from the little I remember about her, she would love how an angel such as yourself is wearing it. Seeing it again, out of nowhere, just shocked me, is all."

Al drew the woman into her arms. "I promise to take good care of it until this is over. I'll give it right back. I'm so glad you're here. Thank you for showing up."

Over his aunt's shoulder, Emeric mouthed, *I'm really sorry. I'll take care of it.*

The woman squeezed Al, slowly releasing her. "I'm so thankful for *you*, sweetheart, and all you've done, bringing the Presents back into my life. Reminds me of when my folks were still alive and they would get my sisters and me all dolled up before Christmas. I'm reliving some of my best years."

"All right, everybody, the children have started arriving," Miss Clara interrupted softly. "It's time to move into our positions."

Together, they all joined hands and prayed in a circle

before breaking up for their posts. Emeric gave Al a wink and headed to round up his boys.

"Dr. E! Where you been?" one of them asked. "You've been gone all week!"

"Jive turkey, chill out. It was just two days."

Al started off toward the big door to join Pastor and First Lady Freeman in greeting the public.

"A'Lelia."

She stopped in her tracks. Behind her stood, "Luke."

"You look incredible, girl." He walked over and kissed her cheek, crowding her space that she squirmed to reclaim.

Puzzled, she had to ask, "You've never come to this."

"Hey, Al!" a guest interrupted. "Congratulations, baby, this is your best Presents yet!"

Luke explained, "I've been calling you for days, and either there's no answer, or your sister says you're busy. Besides that, the Swordsmen are one of the sponsors. We donated a lot of toys and tuxedos for the boys who can't afford Christmas. So, I decided to swing through, wish you luck."

"This is definitely not your taste."

"Congratulations, Al," another guest said.

Hands in his pockets, Luke eyed her from her curls to her shoes. "Tastes change. Just like people do, as you seem to be showing everybody. There's something different going on with you. More makeup or something? Can we chat in private for a minute?"

"I have responsibilities here, Luke."

"It's not for long, Al. We were together for ten years. I can't at least have that?"

She laughed. "We weren't together, Luke. We just happened to occupy the same spaces at the same time. We spent, what, a few weeks together at a time? When I wasn't away at school or you weren't away at school. And for most of those weeks, during the summers or the holidays, we were with our friends. You were right about that. Why are you second-guessing all you said back in January?"

"I might have been wrong for not being more patient with you, and not giving you more time to come out of your shell."

Al considered that. "Mm, no. It happened the way it needed to. And there was no shell, Luke. You don't talk that way, so where did you get that from? Your mother? I simply don't trust you."

Though, at the time, she hadn't understood, and could not articulate it. She'd thought her hesitation, panic, and uncertainty meant she was flawed. But those signs had always been her heart telling her he wasn't the one. Her head had been trying to convince her to chase the popular "it" guy women wanted.

"Give me a chance to earn your trust then." For a flash of a moment, the lines on his forehead may have offered a sincere apology. "I'm saying I'm sorry. I'm becoming a different man who *wants* a good girl. I want you. We can try this again."

She reached for his hand so he wouldn't take her words the wrong way. "I do believe you're sorry, and it'll make you wiser for when your real girlfriend shows up. You and I can always be friends."

Dipping his head toward her, he lowered his voice. "Our friends are talking about you and this country bumpkin, Al, how he's bringing you down. You've upset a lot of people by tossing the Presents and coming here. And I've seen how you look at that cat. He's taking you to clubs and to the 'hood? Since when do you go to those places? That's what you're letting him turn you into? Now you're doing the Presents at Mount Bethel when there were a million other places you could have gone?"

"Congratulations, Al, all of this is amazing!"

Al did not bother lowering her voice or concealing their exchange. "Make up your mind, Luke. Exactly which version of me do you want? A pretty prude, or a *real* woman? And who are you to chastise me on where I go when Hevalo is exactly where I found *you*. But it's all right for so-called gentlemen to have a side life, so long as I stay in my place and be at your disposal like a 'proper girl' should?"

Wide-eyed, he seemed floored to be seeing this side of her. "Can we just go somewhere and talk about this?"

"Al." Emeric stepped to her side. "Pastor Freeman and First Lady are waiting for you up front. We should probably get you up there."

"Aye, man, can't you see we're having a conversation?" Luke glared at him.

Emeric didn't blink. "*You're* trying to have a conversation. She's trying to come with me."

"Aren't *you* trying to become a Swordsman in a few weeks, man? You sure this is how you want to act with a Swordsman?"

Unmoved, Emeric leaned in. "Are *you* sure that's how you wanna act with somebody already accepted as a Swordsman at a private dinner last night you weren't invited to…*man?*"

Emeric excused himself and took A'Lelia with him.

"You really already got into the Swordsmen? How?" she whispered.

"That operation yesterday was on somebody with a lot of leverage in this city," he answered.

"Somebody important went to *Hillside* for medical care? No offense."

Emeric led her to the front of the church. "Somebody that important came to Hillside and helped me out, because somebody else important asked him to."

"And you still won't tell me who?"

He kissed Al's cheek and brushed his lips on her ear. "I guess now I should tell you, I'm possessive to a fault."

Back to playing around, A'Lelia cupped her hand over his ear. "I'll keep that in mind if another ex tries to hijack me."

He pulled back, his eyes quarter-sized. "How many exes you got?"

She shrugged and pivoted to the greeting line. "I don't know. I lost count."

Twenty-Seven
A'LELIA & EMERIC

A'LELIA

"Everyone, bow your heads in a moment of silence for the ancestors, known and unknown, *especially* those whose names we'll never know, who came here to the shores of New York either by free will or by force, to lay their blood, bones, and dreams into the foundations of this great city, that their sacrifices might fertilize and strengthen future generations who would blossom. Let us now honor those original seeds without which we, the dream, would not have flowered." Pastor Freeman bowed his head, and all the one hundred and sixty-eight families in one of the most heavenly churches in the city followed in prayer.

Jumpstarting the event's tempo with joy, the children's choir began with Mahalia Jackson's "Come On Children, Let's Sing," as the youngest child and the oldest participating teenager both lit the Kwanzaa kinara together.

Handsome as ever, Emeric showed up at Al's side, playfully gripping his bottom lip in his teeth and looking her up and down.

"You'd better be glad we're in church," he murmured.

"*You'd* better be glad Papa is in church."

"Oh, you're a comedian now?"

They could have hassled each other all night, but too many cameras snapped photos and recorded, and they had a job to do. She slipped her arm in his, and they kept ribbing one another with their eyes on their way to the stage. After one last squeeze of her arm, he escorted her up and winked before stepping back down to wait.

As if the night couldn't have ascended higher, the entire church stunned her, rising to its feet. No matter how many times Al urged them to sit, motioning her hands downward, the standing ovation and cat calls lasted over a minute, led by BB. Her parents, aunts and uncles, and lifelong colleagues who had stayed, united with the people around the city for whom this night wasn't even imaginable a month ago.

"Thank you, old friends, new friends, and loved ones, but we really must stay on schedule. As you well know, due to these special circumstances this year, we have a big itinerary. We ask that you kindly respect the presentations, and how nervous they may be, by remaining quiet, and reserving your applause for the end of this first segment. Please stay for the entire program. Our presentations at the end of this ceremony deserve the same love and deference as those who present at the beginning." After thanking the organizations and businesses who had sponsored toys, clothing, or services, she pulled out her first list. "Let us begin."

Emeric came up the stairs and held out his arm to get her, his admiration blending with his humor.

The first presentation took his position. "Good evening, world, you will honor and respect me as Saul Woodson, of Queens, eleven years old, son of Veronica and Bruce Woodson. I now train for my future wealth and greatness in fifth grade at Long Island Sunrise Elementary School, where I am preparing to be a nuclear physicist. My favorite book is *Song of the Trees* by Mildred Taylor. My favorite song is 'Dancing Machine' by the Jackson Five. My favorite quote is, '*The strongest house you can ever build is your integrity, because no one can ever tear that down,*' by my uncle, also the person I admire most in the world, Horace Woodson, a construction worker. I will attend Massachusetts Institute of Technology for my studies in Physics."

The very second presentation was illuminated on the second stage.

"All Hail, Enneas Fennessee, of the foster care system of New York, thirteen years old, son of Rebecca and the late George Fennessee. I am already an activist and a voice against injustice, oppression, and inequality through my graffiti art. I bless *and* curse the world through my uncomfortable portraits and tortured quotes from the amazing other wanderers making their homes wherever they can. My favorite artist is my friend, Jean-Michel Basquiat. The person I look up to most is my mother, Rebecca, an *excellent* mother and a strong foundation for my siblings and me, despite what the government says she's not. But the second person I admire most now is Doctor Emeric McPherson, the first Black doctor—the *only* doctor—I know. For my future, I will gain my master's degree from the college of life, so no society can ever fool me into believing my freedom is secured in a textbook. Peace."

Discomfort was a sound heard around the sanctuary. Bodies shifted, murmurs hummed, gasps flew, and throats cleared in the seconds needed to digest the layers of truth.

Emeric waited for the young man when he came down, offering a handshake and a tight hug, along with the exchange of a few private words.

Before the night was over, Emeric's name came up thirty-one times, out of one hundred and sixty-eight presentations.

At a clip of forty-five presentations per hour and three

ten-minute intermissions, they came in at just over four hours, not including the Christmas feast at the end for those who still had energy. Surprisingly, most of the families stayed. While the catered menu from restaurants all over the city was delicious, they stayed for the shared pride in their children, to gush and fellowship in this rare opportunity to take part in the Presents. Taking a break from survival, they mingled and shared advice over cinnamon-scented candles and Christmas poinsettia arrangements, even if it was just for one night.

Several tables away, instead of eating with his family, Emeric was on his feet in a corner, his jacket off, so some of the boys could teach him a new breaking move. Al couldn't stop giggling while he practiced getting it right.

"My heavens, are they over there street dancing? They are in church." One of the church mothers frowned.

"Better that these young men are here in safety, surrounded by angels tonight, than out on the streets dancing for money, though. Right, Mother Shirley?" The First Lady surprised them all when she spoke from the next table.

As if the jingle bells in her belly subliminally rang him, Emeric looked up from the group to find Al admiring him, and he came over.

"I've got me some new moves cued up. I'm ready for Studio 54."

"I'm ready when you are."

They headed for the dining hall exit.

"Miss Césaire?"

She turned to find Pastor Freeman standing behind them.

"A moment? Got something for ya." In his hand, he held envelopes. Old ones.

"Actually there, Pastor, hold on to that a little longer," Emeric interrupted and grabbed her hand. "I've been waiting on her for the last two weeks. Tonight is my night." Going for their coats, he wrapped her up first and muttered, "Every time that man talks, it's like listening to a funeral director. Not happening tonight. Not after everything you just did for this town."

Al had thought her feelings for him couldn't swell any bigger.

"I don't want to go to Studio 54."

In the middle of putting on his coat, he froze. "Huh?"

A'Lelia froze. Was she wrong? Was this right?

"I want to know who you are tonight, Emeric. Show me."

This was a first. No smart comeback or teasing from him.

Caught off guard, he wandered off in his own mind, scratching his chin, maybe breathing through some uncertainty Al hadn't yet seen in him.

She'd flipped their dynamic on its head. For the first time between them, he wasn't the protector or the defender or the motivator. He was simply a man facing a woman.

"You're the interesting one here, Al. I'm just a doctor, and I'm not taking you to no hospital. I haven't been in New York that long, so I don't have any place cool like a museum to sneak you into with a family history that's been around for hundreds of years."

On their way out of the church doors, his eyes traveled in thought, as if he did possess a portal to himself and was pondering whether to bring her inside.

"I'll go with you anywhere, Emeric." Hugging him from behind, Al nudged her chin into his back. "You've spent so much time in my world, helping me, inspiring these boys, and you've learned so much about all of us. Who are you?"

$\sim$

EMERIC

"So what's special about this?" Emeric rolled down his passenger window, despite winter freeze biting his face.

"These streets border the neighborhood that used to be called the Five Points through the 1800s." Al steered his car to the curb of historic Canal and Center Streets. "Back then, a lot of free Blacks, Jews, Germans, and Irish lived in tenements around here. But even before the other groups migrated here, this area was home to the first free African settlement in North America, dating back to the early 1600s."

"The *1600s?*" Emeric's aunt had driven him through here once, when he'd first arrived in New York, and shown him where Orenthal Shipman and his siblings were born and raised in the early 1900s. But as she was the baby alongside her two siblings, his aunt did not know as much as his mother did.

"Yes."

"This is where the half-free Black people were?"

"Yes. Their area is listed in the covenant deeds alongside White men's properties as 'Land of the Blacks.' Do you know when your family might have come here? Or where they came from?"

Emeric rubbed his chin. He couldn't remember if his mother had ever mentioned her grandmother or grandfather, so he didn't recall their names until the other day, when Theodore Césaire had told him. "I don't know where Harriet and Nathaniel Shipman came from."

"I can take you to the archives and we can do some digging if you'd like. I actually have to stop through there and research records myself soon. We can go together."

"Thank you. That'll be dope."

Al touched his shoulder. "Why did you need to come here to this corner?"

"I've been told my great-grandmother made wooden toys and would come sell them here in this area, on the back of a cart hitched to a mule." He tried to picture it in his mind. "She's where my granddaddy picked up his skill for making things, and he grew it into making larger objects like furniture. So, my ancestors might have lived around here."

"We can definitely confirm it at the archives when we request census records. Lineage is always a beautiful puzzle to put together. A lot of people don't care about the past, since no one can bring it back. Why is learning about it important to you?"

He thought about rich guys like Lionel Middleton, how boldly and confidently Lionel could claim who his family was, and how far their bloodline went back in America. It was rare that a Black man could talk with *that* type of ownership and pride. Then, Em thought about his childhood friends back home, about his cousins still living in Mississippi backwoods.

"I wanna be more than ash in the wind," he finally answered. "After they burn us, we just wonder. That's how some white men want us—ignorant, not connected to our past, not able to claim anything important. Then we don't have value to carry around. White guys can walk with their heads up, chests out, because everything looks like them."

He began acting it out with his hands.

"Their identity is about what their forebears already proved. Take that away from them, and *then,* what do they have left in their account? That's us. Most Black men can't walk that proud because they don't know who or what their daddy was. We try to fill that void with music, money, or liquor and women, but that only works for a little while. By the time America is finished burning us up, we're ash."

"Their white forebears became what *our* people made them. My ancestors didn't come to America in chains,

Emeric, but we still had our cross to bear, jobs and contracts for less pay, charged higher taxes and fees just for breathing, and accepting their abusive business practices just so we could survive. They profit off of us all, in one way or another. No, white men didn't thrive because they're so much better, but because we made them 'better.'"

Lights from business signs splashed into the car, their contrasts harsh and shadowy on her face in the dark, an Andy Warhol painting. A'Lelia's mind, heart, and magnanimity, all a work of art hanging in the world-renowned showroom that was New York, could astound any observer for hours, and indeed, she had. Touched that she was not only listening, but invested, Emeric hooked a hand around her neck and drew a masterpiece to him.

Al matched him, her hand entrenched in his Afro, her tongue insistent. Her kisses were a demand that did not equivocate. For the second time that evening, her fingers tarried in the valley of his thighs. She seemed to be working up her courage. Emeric took her wrist and pushed her hand onto his enlarged evidence that he wasn't playing when he'd said he wanted her to touch him there.

He hadn't been sexed in months, not since a goodbye tryst just before he'd left home. But he wasn't simply longing for sex now. After the last two weeks of witnessing her conquer New York, he was good and ready for as much of A'Lelia as he could get.

The Presents chairwoman had changed from her gown into corduroys at her house, so he lacked access to the ways he could express his need.

Their fingers battled in a race to remove the barriers, pushing aside her coat, freeing her from her scarf. He started at the outermost layer of Al, her skin supple and fragrant as a plum, a reward for his taste buds caressing the softness of her neck. His tongue trailed a path down the priceless heirloom chain he had placed around her neck.

The edge of her sweater peeled down, he took small bites along the slope of Al's breast, where her heart's vibrations telegraphed her response, and his fingers played over the wool fabric. He bit through it, through the satin on her bra, latching his teeth on to her nipple, which he could already envision nourishing his children, now ripe and inviting him to start that journey. Her ampleness in his palms had Em reassessing how much of a gentleman he wanted to remain. Al's labored breaths in his ear, and the thrum of her pulsating skin, didn't help. Despite the softness of her breasts, Emeric reminded himself not to disrespect *Doctor* Erwin Césaire's daughter on the street.

"Aye!" Rapid taps on Emeric's driver's window yanked them from their trance.

"Oh!" A terrified Al panicked and instantly jerked away from the window.

Emeric threw his upper body over the center console to grab his pistol from under the seat, and he knew its precise location so that no fumbling or feeling around was required. He whipped it out and aimed. "Get the hell outta here!"

But Emeric paused once he saw the familiar face.

The street hustler had opened his coat to display his jewelry but dropped it to hold up his hands. "Say, mane, I don't want no trouble! I'm sorry, mane, don't kill a working man!" The stranger eyed Em's gun that Em now held over the steering wheel. "Y'all need a necklace? A watch? Rang? Issa 'bout ta be Christmas. Y'all sure y'all got everythang?" The street dealer opened up his flap to display his neat rows of jewelry.

"Dude, no!" Emeric snapped. "Don't you see we're in here trying to talk?"

"Looked to me like y'all in there neckin'. I'm runnin' a

two-for-one special tonight. I'll give y'all a deal since you a new customer."

Al peeked around to see what was happening, and her eyes grew at the sight of Emeric's weapon. Then, she stared at the man on the street.

"Miss Al?" the hustler inquired through the window.

"Jimmy?" Al shared the recognition.

"You know this cat?" Em asked her.

Relieved, and obviously embarrassed, she rubbed her face. "His mother is a security guard at the museum, and sometimes he comes by. Jimmy, what are you doing out here?"

"I'm trying to make a dolla. What *you* doin' out here at these late hours?" The man bucked his eyes at Al in clear judgment.

"Didn't I ask you already to leave us alone?" Em returned to his hard-edged street tone.

"All right then, mane, I was just sayin' 'hi.' I'm gone. You don't have to be unreasonable. Y'all change ya mind, I'll be over at the next corner. Miss Al, if you don't tell my mama I'm out here sellin', I won't tell your granddaddy you out here neckin'. Y'all have yaselves a good night!" With that, he took off.

Dropping her head on his chest, Al started giggling uncontrollably.

But Em was still on edge. That could have gone the other way and ended in tragedy. Because he had been playing around and not paying attention, like some damn boy. And on the lethal New York streets of all places. Not only had he been irresponsible, he'd been reckless. He couldn't have lived with himself if anything had happened to Al.

"I shouldn't have even had you out here. Let's switch sides. I'm taking you home."

Irritated with himself for being so dumb, he threw open

his door and got out. Gun still in hand in case a real criminal might have been watching, he walked around his car to the driver's side.

But Al remained right where she was and stunned him when she clicked the locks.

"Move over," he said to her through the window.

She stared at him from the driver's seat. "I'm not going home."

"Yes, you are. Now open the door. It's cold out here."

"I'm going wherever you're going. We agreed."

His father had taught him to never let a woman run him. Growing up in a houseful of women would naturally make him more understanding, but Bennie McPherson instilled in him that being the baby boy to a line of girls was not to render him silly, spoiled, or soft.

"A'Lelia, it's not safe out here. You just saw that. You're going home. And you're sitting in *my* seat in *my* car. *Move.*"

"I'm only leaving this seat to go call a ride or to *walk* home." The turquoise rocks of her eyes remained impenetrable to him *and* his gun. And did she just roll them? The nerve!

Step two.

"It's twenty degrees out here. Will you *please* scoot over?"

"I didn't tell you to get out." While she talked, her side-swept hair swung along her face. "You can freeze for all I care."

From the street, he stared at her through the window. "A'Lelia."

"Emeric. You asked me to drive. Now *I'm* driving. When you're finished having your tantrum, you can tell me where we're going next." Her hair whipping over her shoulder, she turned back around and faced the street, as lovely as a heart attack.

Three sisters had taught him that this would only get

worse if he kept it up. On his way back around the car, he thought about whether he really wanted to take her to where he was going. After strapping back in and sliding the gun under the seat, he sat back and pinched the bridge of his nose. If he wasn't so irritated with himself, seething about the danger he'd put them in, her feistiness would be a turn-on.

"Head to Queens."

Twenty-Eight

EMERIC

"THIS ONE?" Al asked on their way down Linden Boulevard in Addisleigh Park.

"The next one after." Em pointed to the correct driveway. "Are you fine with parking this car?"

In silence, Al maneuvered his long Cadillac, switching the gears from 'reverse' to 'drive' repeatedly while inching it into the driveway. Once she'd demonstrated that she could park his car, she finally shut it off and handed him his keys.

Sitting in the driver's seat, she waited for him to come around and open her door. Emeric deprived her of that, exiting the car and going to the side door of the house to unlock it.

"Since you're making all the decisions, are you getting out, or will you stay in there all night?" he asked her from outside the car, clearly indicating he wasn't coming to get her.

They hadn't spoken the entire ride from Manhattan to Queens, other than for him to give her directions.

In apparent disbelief, she got out and marched inside,

after which Emeric went back to his car, locked it, and went in the house. They both kicked off their shoes in silence.

"What is this place? Where is your aunt?" Her gaze journeying everywhere, Al explored on her way to some destination she sought. "Why is it so bare? It hardly looks like anybody lives here."

He went to the refrigerator and grabbed himself a beer. "Do you want anything to drink? I only have water and orange juice."

Popping off the top of his beer with a bottle opener, he was still unsure how he would navigate Al wedging herself into a part of him he wasn't ready to open. He lifted his bottle to sip.

His beer was removed.

Al turned up the bottle and took a long swig while staring at him, her lovely throat swallowing for several seconds. After sliding the back of her hand across her mouth, she gave Em his bottle back. "Stop running from me."

"Who's running? I'm right here. Aren't you standing in my house?"

"Where you didn't want to bring me," she said. "You weren't taking me home out of concern for my safety. You were taking me home because you didn't want me here. In this private part of you that no one else sees. You only want me to see the fun, friendly, public-facing Emeric. Not this. It's your house?"

"It was my grandfather's." He took a sip from the beer bottle, the same brand his grandfather drank.

He watched her read between the lines, putting together fragments of him. "This is where your grandfather lived when..."

In silence, Em turned the bottle up again.

Her gaze danced all over the kitchen now with new focus. Placing one socked foot in front of the other, Al walked along the counters, sliding her hand over the cabinet doors, opening them and looking inside, running her fingers along the wooden panels on her journey through the part of his family—the part of his mother—he'd never known, through the questions he still had, piercing the veil in which Em's mother often enclosed herself.

Al's graceful fingers left the cabinet doors open.

Every one of them.

Somehow, such a small and insignificant move was the catalyst. All the open cabinet doors across the kitchen had reframed it in his perspective, creating the potential for openness and possibilities he didn't envision when they were closed. The possibility of an opening for him and his parents, instead of closed woodenness he'd inherited from them.

He squeezed burgeoning tears before they could fall and make him out a sissy, because he wasn't. He was a man.

Al faced him from the other side of the kitchen. "No closed doors between us. You saw me at my worst. Now it's your turn."

That's not what men did. Men needed to be formidable, in charge of their emotions, not whimpering or pouting about what they didn't get as kids. They maintained, and handled life's commitments in spite of their emotions. Tonight, he had failed at handling his commitment to protect the woman with him. His father and mother were right. He wasn't cut out for New—

"Emeric."

Al's voice snapped him out of his head and back to her.

"This is personal family stuff you're asking about. It doesn't concern you. Why do you care?"

"The same reason you cared to help me with the Presents that didn't concern you."

"This is not a public event. This is my *private* domain. Do you see me all up in your house, going through your things?"

"You did, in fact, come into my home, look at the photos on all my walls, and see my 'white-passing' ancestors dating back to 1700s France. Did you not? Do you think I allow just anybody to have access to the private details of my family's mixed-race lineage? I have money, and worse than that, I have light skin. I must be thoughtful and careful about how I carry myself, and stay conscious of my position in society and opportunities compared to others. It's like walking on eggshells because, no matter how considerate, giving, or careful I am, I will be hated by some Black *and* White people, anyway. You've seen that for yourself."

She studied him from her side of the kitchen.

"But I trusted you with the intimate side of my family that we don't share," Al said. "Trust me."

He took another swig of beer and considered it. "Or you'll lock me out of my house next time?"

"If that's necessary to bring us back to where we are now."

"And where are we now?"

"Open doors. The truth. No taking me home when your real feelings are coming up." Al walked to the center of the kitchen, surrounded by open doors, and offered her hand. "I'm not pretending with you. You won't do it either."

His aunt couldn't be the only person who understood him. Setting the beer bottle down, he walked to meet her at the center. "I'm a man, Al. It's my job to be alert so I can keep you safe." Instead of taking her hand, he slipped it under her chin. "So I can't be breaking down emotionally or letting myself be weak, but I will be real with you. Seeing somebody get that close to hurting you scared me. I was mad at myself for slacking and not paying attention. It placed you in harm's way."

His eyes drifted, and Al's touch brought him back.

He continued, "For a second, I remembered how disappointed my pop would be."

"And you wanted to be rid of me, so you could come here and stew about it, to fuss at yourself *for* your papa. There are times we disappoint our parents. It happens."

"That's not how you saw it two weeks ago when you thought you'd embarrassed your own family at Mount Bethel. You were toting worry all over your whole body. In my family, I'm the only boy. On top of that, my mother lost the most important man in her life at a young age, so they really put a premium on me being solid as a man. A few minutes ago, I was anything but that. Now, I spent all those years resenting them for being so strict and demanding, but they were right. The first time I was tested here in New York, I failed."

"God didn't fail, Emeric."

"I don't wanna test God again, A'Lelia. In the future, if there's ever a situation where you're at risk and I ask you to move, please do that. And I promise you, I won't run from you."

His little historian leaned toward him and laid a hand on his chest. "Deal. I'll give you your moment, but I'm a woman, Em. It's my job to be alert to you mentally and emotionally, so that while you see to my physical safety, I take care of your heart. In the future, I'll only lock you out if you try taking me home again instead of opening up and giving me your real heart. Deal?"

He was kissing her forehead before she'd finished talking. "What am I gonna do with you?"

"I have some ideas. But you didn't shake."

Taking her hand was as natural as flipping on a light switch and showing her just how much she illuminated him. Their tongues brought the electrons, orbiting and buzzing around the core of their electric connection. Al slipped her fingers from his hand and feathered them down his stomach, past his navel, over his abdomen.

She was back at his manhood again. Every stroke over his tuxedo slacks stretched his need. She cupped part of Em's length and massaged him, with slow, deliberate motions so tantalizing they called out his future children he already ached to put inside her.

Under her spell, Em was brought to the point of climax, and he stopped her. He didn't want his first orgasm with a work of art to happen so cheaply, outside her body. Em snatched up her sweater. She followed his lead and raised her arms for him to yank it over her head. They unbuttoned the other's pants at the same time, but she struggled with the zipper of his slacks. Her lips swollen and wet, Al stared at how badly he wanted her. She shocked him. While he helped her with the zipper, she lowered to her knees. Once Emeric freed himself from the zipper and his briefs, his size knocked her in the face. Staring at him, Al closed her gorgeously fluffy lips around the head and sucked slow.

He reveled in her tongue shimmering with saliva. It began at his sacs. A paintbrush of her affection, she swiped it up his shaft for the first stroke. Her face underneath his length, bobbing right between her eyes, drove him nuts. Em's head fell back at the feel of moist softness, devastating in the sucks and tugs. The twist of her head one way, and then the other, shoving his length between her tonsils, where he thrust softly, was paradise. He closed his hand over hers and guided her in how much pressure he liked. His other hand he placed under her chin, tilting it to open her throat more. She gagged some while adjusting but held her focus on him. Not rushed, or insistent, nor rough. His artwork displayed *her* real heart to Emeric, her gorgeousness on his manhood a portrait he'd never forget.

He was lost in every deliberate, heartfelt stroke, with his ejaculation on the rise.

"Get up, baby." He guided Al up.

"You didn't like it?"

The concern in A'Lelia's eyes about satisfying him intensified Emeric's attraction.

"I don't want my first time with you like this." Wiggling off her corduroys and picking her up by the butt, he carried her through the dining room and up the stairs.

"Emeric, it's really cold in here." Goose bumps rose on her arms, and she started shivering on their way up the drafty stairs.

Since he wasn't living here full time, not all the utilities were turned on yet. However, there was a fireplace in the main bedroom with stray logs of wood, and he had a box of matches in the kitchen drawer for lighting the stove pilot. Once he'd taken several minutes to fire up some random paper kindling and cold logs, blowing on it to get it going, the way he did when his father would take him on hunts in the woods, he reassured her, "It shouldn't be long before it heats up."

Grabbing a condom he'd placed in his tuxedo jacket just in case, he wrapped up with her in bed, tucking them inside the lone comforter he'd bought so far. Al nestled her leg between his and rubbed her socked foot on his calf for heat.

"Don't put them cold hooves on me."

"Imma put 'em on you and you'll like it." Playful, Al sucked his bottom lip and let it go.

He more than liked it. He returned the affection and tenderness with which she'd sucked on his manhood, kissing the stone-coldest woman in all of New York. Immersed, hot, they generated half the room's heat. Emeric took his time and savored her. Detailed in the attention he gave her, he applied her nuanced historian's way of doing every damn thing. Emeric felt he was sexually space-traveling in slow motion. He couldn't imagine the command Al would have once she was on top of him.

Reaching around her, he unhooked her bra and slipped down a strap so he could finish what he'd started in the car. He mimicked her unhurried rhythm on her nipple, tugging it between his teeth and slowly massaging the tip with his tongue. Dazed in her half-open eyes reflecting the flames, she'd entered a space portal of her own. With her nipple still between his teeth, he eased down her panties and she lifted to help him. Like her body was tethered to his instincts, Al's legs spread wider, her back arching with expectation, mouth ajar and moist, her tongue half out.

Himself trembling now, Em touched the entrance to her. Just as Al shivered and whined, his head fell limp on her chest. He had touched her and she was ready. The proof covered his fingers. He slipped his fingers in his mouth and tasted her salty sweetness because his appetite demanded it. Then, he slid his fingers in her open mouth for Al to sample what was pushing him to the edge.

Emeric was ready to ejaculate, his erection so intense he feared squirting prematurely outside of her if he waited any longer.

He had been fantasizing about his manhood disappearing between her thighs since he'd met her. Eager, nervous, he moved atop her. The ocean water in Al's turquoise eyes stared up at him, stirring his insides.

If that Negro who'd tried to call Em out tonight was the man he was competing against, Em needed to show out and make her think twice about ever going back.

Naked, they lay, nothing more between them, save the condom. Her hands anchored to his back, Al wrapped her legs around him.

All right, Emeric Orenthal Shipman McPherson, time to do your job.

"HAAAA...HM...HM...HM...HMMM..." A drill had penetrated straight into her undisturbed garden. Al balled up her toes and clawed Em's back, the torture sending her forehead into his shoulder for refuge. "Hmm." Tears of pain pierced her strength of will and slid down her temples.

On top of her, Al felt Emeric's back stiffen as he entered *her* truth. Pushing up, in shock, he stared down.

"Baby, you're a...you mean you...you and that dude never..."

Emeric's physique was melded with A'Lelia's now. The most vulnerable part of him throbbed inside the most vulnerable part of her.

"You just sucked me, though?" Confused, waiting for an answer, he stared. "How'd you lick me so good? Did you do all that to...?"

"No! No. That was my first time doing everything I've been imagining." She and Luke had never gone this far. The most she'd given him was a hand job. Though he'd given her oral a few times, she'd never returned it.

"You're serious." In disbelief, Emeric waited again. "You

kind of did it like you knew how." Astounded, laughing nervously, now Emeric started easing out of her. "Why didn't you *say* something, sweetheart?"

"Emeric, no! Keep going. I'll be fine."

They had already started! How embarrassing would it be if *this* man—one who'd seemed so sensitive and compassionate—didn't want to show Al the tenderness and patience she knew Luke would never be capable of? Em had even asked her to be his girl!

"We could have planned this better. We could have smoked a joint and shared a bottle of something first, and set this up for you to take baby steps."

"I don't need you to baby me. I want you to make love to me like you would any other woman."

"Baby, it doesn't work like that. First, we need you to get used to having a foreign object inside you. Plus, you deserve to do this some place nicer than my grandparents' dusty old house. This is not special."

"Yes, it is, because the man *in* it is special."

Emeric paused in the firelight. The only movement between them was their diaphragms breathing, as if he were inhaling A'Lelia's words that were oxygen.

"What's special for me, 'baby,'" Al continued, "is not the physical location. I thought I already spent the last two weeks showing you that. What's special isn't *where* you're being loved, but *who's* loving you."

Al craved passion and intensity, but didn't want to wait until marriage. Still, she refused to give herself to just any man, not even if he was the one all the other girls wanted. It was the reason she'd always been unsure with Luke. Naively, she had wanted it to be him and hoped for the day his eyes lit up while she shared some historical deep-dive or described some unsolved mystery. Al kept waiting for him to mature into someone more sincere, who would cherish her.

Finally, after pressuring her since they were sixteen, he'd ended it and called her a pretty prude, incapable of shagging her way out of a book. In previous years, Al had remained steadfast about the thorough loving she longed for, but this year of aloneness—not just from Luke, but from many of their circles—had left her stuck in her own head. She'd had plenty of time to second-guess her decision and whether her expectations were too high. If maybe she was being a prima donna and wanting too much.

Now, she closed her eyes and let the hot tears fall.

On her forehead, Em's lips touch her skin, his breath entering her pores. He kissed the path down her tearstained temples, and then, her cheeks and her nose. When Al opened her eyes again, the man she had chosen gazed down at the woman who was choosing him.

His bronzed face reflected back to her that he understood. "I'm honored." He thumbed away her tears. "Stop all this."

He covered her mouth with his and sucked Al's lips, holding her lips between his so long she started giggling her relief. The man was goofy even in bed. Em finally released them.

"But I *am* going to get you some liquor."

"I don't want any. I can handle it."

"I can't feel like I'm torturing you. Not like this anyway. That's not enjoyable for me either. You need to relax your mind, so your body can adjust, and we can find our rhythm. We won't get you drunk, but let's chuck some of these nerves. Okay?"

He waited for confirmation they were on the same page.

Al hadn't made a mistake. The Empire State Building of doubt and worry crumbled off of her. She nodded. "Okay."

Once he got back with a bottle of Cognac, he twisted off

the cap and took a couple of swallows himself before passing it. "Drink that."

"How much?"

Rarely was Emeric McPherson's smile sheepish. "Until I say 'stop.'"

After she'd chugged about a sixth, he took it and tossed his head back for a few more swigs. After he put on another condom, they settled into the sheets again. This time, her worries, insecurities, and fear had begun dissolving. The brick walls of gossip, other people's opinions, and what was expected for "such a pretty girl like you" were dissipating. Al began to relax. Not just because the alcohol was melting her on the outside. But she was with Emeric, and she had chosen wisely, which reassured her on the inside.

With her head lying between his arms, the scent of his cologne floating off his neck and into her nostrils, his heart thumping rapidly against her bare breast, A'Lelia was cocooned underneath him.

Covering her hand with his, he placed it around his manhood, heavy and thick in her palm. Emeric's breathing slowed, deepening in her ears, shooting sparks across her body down to the atoms and electrons of her cells.

"You feel that?" His voice changed.

In her hand, his erectness ignited a lust beyond girlish fantasy, his nearness, this new and unexplored maleness from him—from any man—so intense it excited Al down to the nerves in her labia that quivered. Exhilarated and scared, her hand still intertwined with his around his girth, Al journeyed with Emeric along the valley to her womanhood.

Of all the trips A'Lelia had ever taken around the world, that first stroke of his manhood up her folds had to be the sweetest, most heavenly ride she would ever know. The pressure of his thickness, sliding through her moist folds and valleys, up and down, stroke by tormenting stroke, elevated her from imagining to realizing.

At the thresholds of their bodies—tender, vulnerable, stimulated, ready— A'Lelia Antonia Césaire and Emeric Orenthal Shipman McPherson introduced themselves all over again. His breaths, her whimpers, his shifting Adam's apple, her teeth clutching her bottom lip.

He hadn't entered her yet, but her body was running amok.

His goatee scratched her forehead, his breath warm in her hair. "Did you know you got a pretty pussy?"

Low and sensual, his voice licked the central nerves of Al's womb. Her body answered. The syllables of his words fluttered into her ear, inscribing themselves in the chambers of her heart, and chiseling their way across her body's crevices, sacs, and folds, down her vagina, and exiting her body in the form of womanly cream.

Pools of her essence, evidence of Emeric's effect on her, drizzled onto her fingers and wet up his tip. His manhood, still stroking the outside of her, smacked her wet flesh, and the sounds competed with the crackling flames.

"You want me to tell you what your pussy tastes like?"

Al's jaw dropped. Her lower abdomen shuddered in anticipation, contracting her vaginal walls, open and closed, gushing more evidence of her attraction to him.

"A'Lelia, I'm talkin' to you."

His erect manhood still stroked, still slipping up and down, heavy in her fingers. Al was somewhere between the clouds, so high it was hard to breathe.

"Your pussy is sweet like a plum with a li'l salt on it. The minute I first set my eyes on you I knew I was gon' chew on this pussy."

"Emeric!" She couldn't take it.

"I knew you tasted sweet. A nigga couldn't wait to get

your juice all over my chin, and drown in this shit. I can suck on you forever, put you in my mouth and let my tongue play all in your meat." Splashing sounds of her cream accompanied his taunts. His hand over hers, the torture didn't end. "Suck up all that good pussy wine and spit it in your—"

"Emeric!" Closer to the edge of nirvana, Al was drunk and not on liquor.

"I'm not finished."

Al needed deep breaths. On her next major inhale, at the precipice of orgasm and gasping for the breath to survive, Emeric entered her.

This time, he pushed his length fully into Al's depths, forcing out her involuntary shriek.

"Breathe," he murmured, his hand stroking her hair to comfort her. "No, don't hold it. Let it out."

Al listened, doing as he said and exhaling.

He slid back. "Breathe."

Al inhaled, and he pushed into her again, introduced her to this physical manifestation of her womanhood, acclimated her to the presence of a man, the needs of a man, the pathway of life, the journey of her future babies, the domain of her fertility and her power.

Emeric introduced her to his feelings for her. With his open mouth on her forehead, Al smelled notes of his leather, shoe polish, woodsy cologne, and hospital corridors.

His hardness introduced Al to more than ten thousand nerve endings lining her clitoris, all of them excitedly sparking up and down her vulva, with his every stroke. Her lust oozed from her canal, sloshing as he dipped into it, separating A'Lelia the woman from the girl.

One hand atop her head, his other under her butt cheek, he held her steady.

"Breathe."

Inhale. Pressure. Repeat. In her belly, he met her at the

physical intersection of pain and pleasure. In and out, his every stroke penetrating, reversing. She breathed while they established their rhythm. While she made room not just in her body, but in her world for Emeric.

"Baby, your pussy is lockin' around a nigga. You feel so gatdamn good and tight, you got me wantin' to come in you right now."

With his next push, Emeric McPherson remained, circling his hips, rhythmically gyrating, searching.

Along her ten thousand-plus nerves, the sensations lifted her higher, where she touched her love for herself. Where she was sexy, sexed, sensual, where she *was* lusted after, lustful. Emeric's physicality hurt her virgin body, but the heat of his skin on hers, his tripped-up breaths from his throat, sounds of spit on his tongue when he swallowed, his excited drilling and digging for more of her, ignited Al's craving for nirvana.

A'Lelia opened.

A fountainhead emerged somewhere inside her, tender and responsive.

"Aah!" Ecstasy rocketed through her, infusing Al with pleasure she wasn't sure it was right to feel.

Synchronized with A'Lelia, Emeric's back trembled under her fingers, as if he'd found what he'd been seeking. Next to her head, his arm shook, his breaths labored, like the weight of bliss may have been too much.

Pressure emanated from within her womanhood now, in call and response to Emeric's thrust, the bliss curling into her toes. "Emeric!"

"I felt it."

Al couldn't handle the rise, even while lost in it, her eyelids heavy and half-open. How was this possible? "Emeric."

"I feel you, baby."

He'd discovered *her*.

This was…

In his stroke, he communicated how he felt Al, craved Al, needed Al, truly saw and worshipped A'Lelia.

"Aaaahhh!" Hurting and soaring at once, Al grabbed his butt and held on, clinging, breathing through it, higher…

Now, *he* shrieked. Beat the mattress with his fist.

In her first vaginal orgasm, its intensity Al could hardly bear, Emeric locked in, and trembled on his last thrust.

The climax was too much. Al's vocal cords betrayed her, so that all she could do was ugly-squeal. Emeric's face in the pillow muffled his scream he released for them both.

Nestled underneath him, weak, Al's legs and arms plopped around his as he lay down and settled over her.

"You cool, sweetheart?" he mumbled, his voice hoarse.

In the throes of sex and disbelief and physical and mental depletion, she couldn't manage even a hoarse response, so Al nodded. He eased himself out of her, but didn't get up, instead, tucking his face in the crook of her neck. He rested his arm across her naked breasts, his hand next to his grand-mother's necklace around her throat.

"You'll be sore. You want aspirin?"

That would require him to leave bed, and Al wanted them to remain just this way, for as long as the outside world would allow. She shook her head.

"This is mine now. Don't even think about takin' it nowhere else."

Thirty

A'LELIA

"SO YOU AND him *did* do it." BB squinted for laser focus on her sister, and scanned for a single sign that would give away the answer.

"I didn't say that." After the past year of giving tours to White children at the museum, Al was a master at holding her poker face. She brushed on her mascara. Privy to her sister's tactics, she didn't blink. Eying BB through the mirror, Al finished applying her makeup. "Don't you have anything better to do than dip in my potato chips?"

Thankfully, the intercom announced that Emeric was on his way up, and BB rushed to meet him and to try tripping him up.

Jill laughed and held up Al's gown for her to slip into. "Was it good, though?"

Al scoffed, and whispered, "How did you guess?"

"You told on yourself at Mount Bethel the next day. First, you said you'd come from your grandparents' house in Scarsdale, but later, you slipped up and said Queens. None of your family is in Queens, ma'am." Jill cackled while zipping

Al's gown. "I let it ride. Figured I'd let you have that for a minute." Jill's eyes met Al's in the mirror. "So? Was it?"

Her face turning scarlet, Al's chuckle resonated from a place deeper than her belly. "Good is not the word, Jill. There is no word for this, and I've got plenty words. Do you know he told me I can't take it 'nowhere' else?"

Tongues out, they hi-fived, and Al's heart hi-fived her lungs.

Jill placed Emeric's grandmother's necklace around Al, and they swapped giddiness in the mirror. "I don't think this will be the only jewelry he puts on you, lady. I'll give it less than a year before he asks you to—"

"No, no, don't," Al pled. She wasn't ready for expectations or other people's opinions of what the two of them would become or should be.

This most magical night before Christmas, she simply wanted to enjoy the stars brightly shining in every cell of her body, all the way down the thousands of nerves in her womanhood, and straight to the tips of her toes. Whatever happened later, Al would savor this for what it was tonight. No labels, or projections, or outside intrusions. Just magic.

"What about you?" Al asked her friend. "We'll have to get you hooked up now." She started searching her mind for which of the men she'd seen around the church that might sync with Jill.

"How do you know I'm not already?" Jill raised an eyebrow. "Madam Chairwoman's been busy."

Al's mouth dropped. "Spill."

"Later."

"Oh, no, you don't get off that easy after you just hustled me."

Out in the living room, Emeric laughed with BB. "You can't shake me down, li'l mama. You didn't know I'm Shaft? Don't even try it. Ya sister already told me about you."

Al patted her fresh updo a final time. "I suppose I should get out there and save him."

"I suppose you should."

Al cut her eyes at Jill. "But we'll come back to you later." Before she forgot, she removed Jill's Christmas gift from her purse. "I've been busy, but not too busy to snag your present."

"What could be a better gift than these last three weeks of working nonstop?" Jill joked.

"And I'm really grateful for you." Al handed her a slender box, and fanned her face to fight off coming tears. "I haven't been a good friend this year."

"Honey, no, you will not do this."

"Yes, I will. You let me have my space to just live on the couch, and you didn't shame me or force me to go do what I didn't want to for the sake of appearances. Thanks. I took a hike from life this year. That'll change for the next."

Jill untied the ribbon, unwrapped the box, and cracked open the envelope inside. Al had inserted a gift certificate to the luxury spa at the new Ritz-Carlton Westchester.

"Honestly, my Christmas gift from you was watching you give that putz his walking papers last weekend." Jill pulled her in for one more hug.

"We were young."

"Don't make excuses for him. He was playing the field, keeping you on hold while he did whatever else he wanted."

Al put on her earrings. "What man hasn't?"

"You might have a point. Damn shame. I can still loathe him, though, for doing it to *you*. Like I said, I was so glad he had to watch you with Emeric."

Al slipped on her shoes. "I should have said it at fourteen." Once her life settled down again, Al would spend more time with that question—of "courting." Why she'd allowed ten years to pass of sitting in limbo while waiting for a guy to mature and become a proper boyfriend. Though she'd gone on other dates, Al had still made herself too accessible for Luke, available whenever he'd called.

In expectation of him "settling down," she had played the "good girl" and allowed herself to be put on hold. That's what "future wives" did. This was no less the case in "proper society," where a girl's social status was dictated just as much by her "intended" as her last name, starting at cotillion age. Girls and boys were steered toward each other long before they knew themselves, what type of person they liked, or who they wanted to be in the world. Let alone how they should support somebody else who didn't know themselves either.

Al could not be upset with Luke. He'd owned his truth, but apparently had woken up to Al's value once Emeric showed up.

"You said it exactly when it was meant for you to," Jill said. "You didn't have to give me a spa day, but I'm going to love it."

"I love you, honey. Merry Christmas."

"Merry Christmas, foxy, I'll see you over there." Jill followed her out of the bedroom.

Emeric pivoted from the window to check her out. With one glance, him rubbing his hands around each other, teeth gripping his bottom lip, he returned to his Queens kitchen all over again, undressing her in his head. His gaze was one of her Christmas gifts.

"Ready?" she asked.

"Always."

Al tucked her hand in his and tugged him toward the elevator, depriving nosy BB of the kiss she wanted to inspect.

"Aw, come on!" her little sister complained.

"See you there, Roberta, don't be late."

The guy who worked as the elevator lift was off today and tomorrow for Christmas, so it was just the two of them once the elevator doors closed.

Emeric slid his hands inside her coat and claimed her waist. "What are we doin' our first night together with no Presents to think about?"

"I'll be reading dusty history books. I swear I'm boring."

"If a book is all you're gonna be wearin' when I come home, that's about to be my favorite kind of entertainment."

Al thought about that. "What if a book is all *I* want *you* to be wearing when *I* come home?"

"Sh...where do I sign up?" He hugged her close to him and placed Al's hand inside his coat, where she felt his erection. His lips against hers, he murmured, "Did you know you got your own buh-*lack* cherry wood bookrack right here? You can hang any history book off that you want to."

Al wondered how she would survive him through the night when they hadn't even left the building. "I walked right into that, didn't I?"

"I'm 'bout to buy me a bookstore so every time you walk in the door, I'll have a brand new book for you to grab off my di-" The elevator doors opened suddenly and a neighbor waited on the other side. Em waved. "Hello. Merry Christmas." He escorted a giggly Al out to his car, and let his gaze drop to her hips while he opened the passenger door. "Baby girl, with all that you got...you want me to put on an apron and a chef hat, too? Buck neked."

The next several hours, the final ones of this year's Presents, were bittersweet. With no idea what the future held for next year's event, or if she would even be organizing it, Al soaked up the love. It came in every form as they showered her with spontaneous hugs, Christmas cards, drawings, homemade necklaces with her name made out of beads and block letters, yarn bracelets, containers of cookies and cakes, and a range of other gifts she hadn't received in all her previous years combined. The next morning, Al, BB, and

Nandy, would drive the food and flowers to Hillside Hospital and local shelters to donate it.

"Speech! Speech!" the audience demanded at the end of the night. They refused to close out until she'd delivered final remarks, which she never did. Pastor Freeman always closed out the evening with his prayer.

Tonight, she was astonished. He stepped back from the microphone, and stretched out his hand in an invitation to address the sanctuary from his pulpit.

Al moved to the podium. The people who'd criticized and questioned her only two weeks ago now stood up. A rapturous ovation followed.

For all the lifelong associates from her social circles she'd lost, who had walked out on her, there were scores of parents now whistling and cheering with grateful tears for their children having the opportunity they never did.

After a full minute, Al finally raised her hands to bring the applause down. "My heart is clapping just as hard for all of you as you are for me. We may have saved each other this Christmas. We met each other two weeks ago as strangers from separate worlds and divided social circles. Now, look at us. We're a city united. And not just any town, either. We're the world's greatest city. New York."

Over the cheers and whistles, she continued, her heart swelling with their sentiments.

"It's been the honor of a lifetime to fight for you. I had no idea that's what I would be doing when I walked in here to see the architecture," she said to a round of laughs, "but thank you for letting me in. I promise not to return to my comfort zone and silos, and don't you do it either. For the love of this city, let's keep listening to each other and helping whenever we can. If you're ever around the New York Historical Society, drop by and say 'hi', okay?"

"Tour!" Many of the audience members called out.

"A history lesson!" others demanded.

"Deal," Al promised. "Let me catch up on sleep first, and then, yes, we'll visit three hundred years of Black New York. Merry Christmas, everyone."

Leaving the stage, she wished her grandparents could be here to see this. Pépé had been right, but of course, no one ever had to tell him that.

She looked for Emeric, who normally came to escort her down the steps, but he was nowhere to be seen. That was unlike him. Yet again, she was taken aback when Pastor Freeman filled in and held out his hand for her to take it on her way down.

"Thank you."

"You're welcome."

During the final meal, while Al talked with parents about setting their children up to apply for Columbia or NYU, there was a light tap on her shoulder.

"Miss Césaire?" Standing over her was Pastor Freeman. "A moment?"

She was unsure if she wanted to hear whatever was coming. As much as she hated admitting it, she hadn't managed to disprove a single thing he'd said two weeks ago as far as her heritage was concerned. In fact, the more digging she had done in her effort, the more evidence she'd uncovered that proved he was right.

"Sure." Her gaze fell to what he held in his hands.

He'd been holding them the first night of the Presents, but Emeric had stolen her away.

Three small, yellowing envelopes carried dirt smudges and grease tracks indicative of a long journey, through space *and* time. It reached its audience at long last.

Her lungs sank to the floor of her diaphragm. The handwriting was unmistakable. It matched all the others she'd seen.

A'Lelia said her goodbyes to the others and excused herself from the table to follow him to his office.

What began as her innocent, well-meaning inquiry into her family history two weeks ago, for some reason, now felt like she was exhuming her ancestors' dead bodies. She wasn't prepared.

"You're welcome to sit."

"I'm afraid I can't stay long. With it being the final night, I have to be available for cleanup crew, tech wrap-up, and any incidentals, per our agreement in the contract." The truth was she didn't think she could bear more than a minute or two of whatever would unfold.

"Of course." He nodded. "In 1914, my grandfather was the mailman for Theodore and Suzanne Césaire. Grandpa was around when Dr. Césaire's cousin, Leopold, came over from France and stayed several months."

Pépé had mentioned that in his office when she'd found his Bible. "Right."

"According to what my granddaddy told my grandmama, sometimes, your grandfather would invite Granddaddy to take a break from his mail route and join a poker game."

That sounded par for the course with Pépé. He never limited his socializing only to the well-heeled, often enjoying the company of everyday men, he'd said, who weren't too high on themselves.

The pastor continued, "This Leopold man was present for poker games, and that's how my grandfather met him. Leopold met a few of your grandfather's friends, and he decided he wanted to move here to New York with his family. Based on what Granddaddy told Grandmama, Leopold was telling everybody he would go to France to collect his wife and two small children and would bring them back here. But while he was there, Austria and Germany started the Great War."

He pushed three envelopes across his desk toward Al.

"Granddaddy was interested in this Afro-French man and whether Leopold would make it back here, so he looked out for Leopold's letters to make sure Theodore got them. Grandpa delivered several letters to that building you stay in."

Confusion strained his features. "But later on, Theodore asked Granddaddy if he had anything from France. It was like he'd never received those letters. Granddaddy started to suspect Theodore wasn't getting his mail from France, so Granddaddy confronted the only other person who had access to it—your grandmother, Suzanne. The next two letters that came, Theodore was traveling, and Grandpa refused to give anymore to Suzanne, so he held them for Theodore to return." His index finger hammered down on the two letters. "These."

"Meme would not have been the only one with access to those letters. We have service staff and housekeepers," Al interjected.

"Not sixty years ago, when Theodore was in his twenties and just starting out. Back then, my father told me the Césaires had one housekeeper, and she didn't have access to his private effects, documents, and mail. Grandmama said Granddaddy delivered valuable things like that into a box he locked, and only the Césaires had the key."

Al folded her arms and studied him. "You certainly do recall a lot."

"My Grandmama admired Suzanne Césaire—rich, pretty, educated. Granddaddy would come home with stories of the Césaires and my grandmama thought the world of them." He scratched his chin, his eyes drifting again. "While Granddaddy waited for Theodore to come back, Suzanne went to the post office and complained about him. She had clout around the city, and he was terrified he would lose his job."

"No disrespect to your grandfather, but if he withheld my husband's mail, I might have done the same."

The Pastor took a breath, and continued, "They didn't fire him, but they reassigned him to some route faraway on Long Island that would have been hell on him and Grandmama. They would have had to move for him to keep his job. While he waited for transfer, one more letter arrived." Again, his finger drilled down on the third letter. "This."

He sank back into his seat, seemingly not lighter to have that weight off of him. "While he was working his route, Granddaddy was so stressed out he died of a heart attack. The paramedics took him away with this here bag of mail. He never delivered Leopold's letters. And it's my understanding Leopold Césaire never made it back to the United States."

"He was drafted into the war."

"On whose orders?" The pastor didn't flinch.

"*What?*" Every muscle in her asked that.

"Miss Césaire, the rumors over at the post office back then, and across the city government, were that your grandmother didn't want your grandfather's cousin to come back."

"Now, just you wait a minute!"

"The mail-checkers at the post office during the war had to—"

"Yes, I know," Al snapped. She had hoped after these last two amazing weeks, they could move on. "They read foreign mail to prevent espionage. What does that have to do with my grandmother and grandfather?"

"People at the post office talked." He stared at her. "Leopold's mail was checked especially carefully because of the last name he wrote on his first papers that he filed for citizenship before he left—Césaire-*Habsburg*. Austrian." He put emphasis on that last word. "And Austrians are…"

German.

She peered down at the return address on the letters. "His name only says Césaire on that."

"Think, Miss Césaire. In a war started by *Austria*, why would he write his *Austrian* name on foreign correspondence other people would read? But government workers talk. Rumors over at the city were that, on his official documents, he had to give his actual birth name—Césaire-Habsburg."

None of this made sense. No. Just, no. This pastor was trying to turn her against her own family. There was no way an outsider would sow discord between her and her grandparents, *especially* not when Meme had forewarned Al these people had something against them.

"I need to go."

"I've come to respect and admire you a great deal these three weeks, Miss Césaire."

"Then, why dump this on my shoulders? Why didn't you ever give these letters to the person for whom they were intended—my grandfather?"

"I tried. I called your granddaddy's office. He came. Two weeks ago. He told me to give them to you. He said you would know what to do with them."

Two weeks ago? She thought she'd seen Pépé out in Mount Bethel's foyer two Sundays ago, but he never surfaced. Her eyes hadn't deceived her that day. He *had* come here. Why wouldn't he have greeted her?

A soft knock at the door jarred them both.

"A'Lelia?" Emeric called from the other side. "You in there? I've got somebody I want you to meet."

The Pastor eyed the letters still on the desk. "You can come in, doctor." The pastor delivered his last point in silence. "We're done."

Al picked up the weight of the letters, and it did feel as though the sands of time shifted from the pastor's side of the room to hers.

"Come on now, Pastor Freeman, all these women you've got around here, you can't be taking mine." Em checked her. "You all right?"

"I've only had one date for twenty-four years there, doctor, and most of the time, she is more than I can handle."

"I'm ready when you are," Al said. She left his office ruminating over all he'd said.

"Hold on. I need to put these away." She searched for a safe, closed space to put the letters where no one would spill anything on them. The storage!

"Baby, hurry up!" Em called excitedly from the storage room door.

She quickly tucked the letters in a box of Christmas decorations.

With an excited Em guiding her to the front of the church, Al pushed aside her most pressing question for now.

The 1890s would have been during her grandfather's time. If Leopold Césaire was actually born Leopold Césaire-Habsburg, of France and Austria, what did that make his distant cousin, Theodore Césaire?

"WHAT'S GOING ON?" She nearly ran to keep up with Em.

He threw an arm around Al and ushered her in front of him. His wide, proud grin may as well have stretched down to his toes.

"Mama, Pop, this is A'Lelia. Al, this is everybody."

"Oh!" Wide-eyed, Al gazed at the people who were very clearly Emeric's family. "You didn't tell me they were coming to the Presents. You could have warned me, so I'd have myself together." She pushed up her falling curls and moistened her lips since the color had worn off.

"Sweetheart, you stay together. They surprised me and just showed up. Aunt Dee didn't tell me."

"Hi, it's just Al for short." With a hand out, she tried to make out who was who.

His two sisters were certainly related to him. Same slender faces, bony noses, medium height, complete with folksy accents, welcoming expressions, and quick-witted humor at the ready.

Only one brought a spouse, and both sisters, Billie and

Rose, had children. Clearly, they were all about family. Al and Em had only discussed family over the past few days in their blink-and-miss-it time together, between his work shifts and her putting out any fires from the Presents. But Emeric's rapport with his nieces and nephews clearly affirmed what he'd already demonstrated as far as the young men who looked up to him, that he wanted a family of his own one day.

Al tried not to think about it, but truth be told, his affinity for kids enhanced his sex appeal. Her attraction easily slid into thoughts of a future with him.

"A'Lelia," a stern older man held out his hand. "It's nice to meet you. I've heard a lotta good thangs about all you're doin'. Emeric and Dee can't speak enough 'bout how smart and well-read ya are. You and I will have ta dive into some history at some point when things calm down for ya." With a clear aura of authority, this had to be Emeric's father, even more deeply southern than his son. Unsmiling, but not in a mean way, he spoke slowly as he sized Al up every bit as much as she was doing to him.

"I'd like that, and thank you so much, but this wouldn't have been possible without Miss Deidre and Emeric pitching in. I hope you enjoyed the presentations. Your son helped these boys tremendously, and they love him. We're really glad to have him here in New York. I'm sure Tennessee is missing somebody special."

Al took a quick breath for the biggest introduction. She came forward, a very lovely woman who did not appear much older than Al.

"A'Lelia, what a beautiful name for such a stunning girl. You are far prettier than Emeric could have described you. And he says you're quite educated. A historian."

Mrs. McPherson extended her hand, but Al threw her

arms around the woman responsible for bringing Emeric into the world.

Oddly, the woman went stiff. Al did not feel his mother's arms return her embrace, and Al drew back.

"I apologize. You're not the touchy-feely kind?"

The woman stood transfixed. The barrels of her eyes aimed straight at Al's neck.

"Where did you…?"

Emeric suddenly jumped in. "Mama, I met one of Granddaddy's friends who gave it to me, and since you weren't here, I let Al wear it until you came. I didn't know you'd be here tonight. You'll never believe the story I heard. Granddaddy lost this necklace when he put it up for a bet in a card game." Emeric talked fast to explain away this awkwardness.

Al had spent enough time with him at this point to know when he was relaxed and playful, and when he wasn't. Right now, he was talking to cover up his discomfort.

The only other time Al had seen him this worked up, and out of his fun-loving element, was last Saturday when she'd taken him to the Lower East Side. His mood had soured when he felt he'd screwed up and fallen short of his parents' expectations.

"I know *exactly* how Daddy lost it. I was there. What is it doing on *her*?" His mother burned with anger until her eyes were brimming with tears.

The sharp blade of Mrs. McPherson's tone compelled Al to grope at her neck for the clasp.

Al mumbled, "I'm so sorry."

"Mama, we weren't expecting you to pop up. I loaned it to her."

"Mama, take a chill pill, all right?" his older sister, Billie, asked. "It's a necklace."

"It's not *just* a necklace. It's my dead mama's, and my first time seeing it in forty years. It's around the neck of a murderer's granddaughter."

The woman fired at Al as if Al had stolen her mother's life.

Filling up with venom of her own, Al finally located the clasp for herself, because Emeric was emotionally absent, having been infected with whatever virus moved between him and his mother.

Al took it off and passed it, whereby his sister, Rose, accepted.

"It's okay," Rose explained. "It's her first time back in New York and this is a lot."

Mrs. McPherson glared at Al as if still deciding whether to demolish Al here on the spot.

"I'm going to go. I have a lot of cleanup. Excuse me." What could Al possibly have done to this woman?

"Sissy!" BB called a few rows away. "I want you to meet my classmate from…"

"Miss Césaire! Can we get a quote from you for the news?"

"Miss Césaire!"

Tripping over her own feet, Al rushed back to the storage room. Nobody—not even her grandfather's worst critics— had spoken to her like she was *less* than a bug. Before she closed the door completely, it was stopped.

"Al!" Emeric squeezed in and closed it behind him.

"You need to go back to your mother."

"I need to be right where I am. Al, she went through a lot as a foster kid, shuttled from relative to relative in New York, with no parents. She was living in a stable home with a happy family one night and the next night, her parents were burned alive. After that, she was sleeping with family members she hated."

"*What* does that have to do with *my* family?" Al snapped.

"Your granddaddy and mine were friends," he blurted.

"Come again?"

"Your grandfather knew mine. They played poker together, and my grandfather designed some of your family's furniture." He talked fast, and dropped his voice. "Al, the first surgery I performed last week was on your granddaddy. He did it as a favor to help the grandson of his friend, Orenthal Shipman. And because you asked him to. I'm thankful to you for that. They were friends. The person who won that necklace in a poker game was your granddaddy. He gave it back to me, and I was planning on giving it to Mama, but I loaned it to you until she got here. I did not expect her to pop up and surprise me tonight, or I would not have put you in a bind like that."

Al processed the truckloads of information he was dropping. "Surgery? My pepe? He was fine the last time I saw him." Was it really two weeks ago? Is that why he hadn't wanted to see her? "Is he okay?"

"Of course, he is, baby. I handled it. But you can't ever mention this to him. That's my medical license on the line. He didn't want any of you to know. I'm only telling you, and *only* you, so you can understand my mama's feelings aren't about you."

He gripped her face and brought it to his, so their eyes didn't lose the pathway of atoms and electrons.

"She feels betrayed by anybody here in New York who knew her mama and daddy. She feels like she and her sisters were left out in the cold by all the people Granddaddy and Grandmama called friends. And since your granddaddy is one of those people, she's got resentment. I swear it's not personal to you."

"It felt that way when she called me what she did." Al didn't dare repeat it.

"She saw the necklace and a lot came up for her. I'm

sorry. I'll make sure she says it, too. If she doesn't, you don't have to worry. You'll never see her again, because I know who I'm gettin' down with and that's you, baby. Just let me take care of this. Okay?"

"What's wrong with Pépé? Why wouldn't he want us to know?"

He dropped his head and shook it. "Al, don't do that to me. I can't. I shouldn't have even told you this much, but I need you to understand what's happening here. I can't disclose anything else. Dr. Césaire was my grandfather's friend, and for that, my mother hates him."

"Emeric, how will I date a man whose mother hates *any* member of my family?"

"Because that man—*this* man—loves you." His hands cupping Al's face again, he sucked her lips. "I'm asking you to date *me*. Not my mama. But if this man's mama can't respect the family of the woman he loves, and she keeps choosing her pain over healing, this man will leave his mama. Which he has already proven he's capable of because he's here in New York and not in Tennessee. He'll do that again for you." He kissed her forehead.

Al was touched at the sincerity pouring out of him. In a different set of circumstances, she might have been ready to make love.

"Em, if this man has to forsake his mother, he should do it for himself. Don't put that on me. My heart goes out to your mother and the Shipmans, but my family doesn't do this. We don't…"

"What?" He stared directly at her. "Your family doesn't do what, Al? Be Black? You don't have generational baggage to work through? Way up in the penthouse overlooking Central Park, y'all don't have problems?"

Al thought about that, particularly of Pépé's sister, Jeanne, and her clear animus toward him.

Hmph. Teddy. He was always more trouble than he was worth.

Whatever their sibling rivalry was about, the two of them were clearly hiding a secret when it came to Austria, France, and Maria Josepha Habsburg-Tossou. They may have also hidden something as it concerned their cousin, Leopold Césaire-Habsburg. The Césaire's problems may have been different, but they had their issues.

"Don't throw my family's stability in my face like it disqualifies us from being Black, Emeric. Strife is not a qualifier for Blackness. But yes, we have our own concerns."

"Fair enough. You said you wanted me to trust you with my heart, French." He leveled his gaze with hers. "You said you wanted open doors. Well, this is what open doors look like. Dead grandparents, off-the-wall mamas, and surgeries you can't discuss with your pepe. Okay? *Okay?*"

Heavy-hearted that she couldn't even ask her grandfather, Al wagged her head. "Okay."

"I mean it. Not a word to anybody. Promise me."

She really would have to trust that Emeric knew what he was doing. "I promise."

"All right, I gotta skitty. Merry Christmas. I'll call you from my shift." He kissed her again. "So you're gonna make a man wait for you to tell me you love me back?"

"You do realize we're hiding from your mother in a storage closet, right? This scenario isn't screaming 'Casablanca'."

Her unintended humor brought him a chuckle. "Point taken."

More important than that, Al needed to check in with herself, and make sure what she felt was love and not infatuation, or overeagerness for this new fling. Al had given herself to him, and their attraction and connection were beautiful. That was a strong start. But she would give this a while, and see what sprouted up from those seeds, rather than forcing them into a flower.

"Those are powerful words to say. If you're trusting me with this here, Emeric," she said, rubbing his chest where his heart tapped her fingers, "let me get it right. So I don't hurt either of us. I'll say it in my season."

Squeezing her butt over her gown, he sucked her lips in a final kiss. Al welcomed his tongue and licked it back, confirming what they were growing and that she had absolutely no regrets so far. She just wanted this to grow naturally and not by force.

"Take your time. I'll call you tomorrow. Merry Christmas."

"Merry Christmas."

"IS BABY GIRL ALL RIGHT, EM?" Billie asked on their way out of Mount Bethel. "I'm sure you told her if she's gonna be in this family, she'll need a solid backbone. Especially if you're thinkin' of bringin' her home to Memphis."

"Al is always good. She's stood up to a whole lot more than that."

"She seems nice," Rose added. "A little on the light-skinned side. How'd you meet her?"

"Uncle Em, are we goin' to see the Statue of Liberty while we're here?" one of his nephews asked.

"Forget that. What about Madison Square Garden and seein' the Knicks play?" another asked.

Fortunately, Emeric had told the Swordsmen—or specifically, Lionel Middleton—that his family was coming. The man had delivered.

"Just call over there and tell them I sent you."

Emeric wouldn't need passes for some spots, only to state Lionel's name. From VIP, "no line" entrance to scenic-view restaurants, private tours, and even a couple of exclusive, invite-only dinners at celebrity homes not open to the public, Lionel had established why his big ego and bigger wardrobe may have been justified. He was more than connected. He *was* the connection.

"I might have some Christmas surprises lined up for you guys," Emeric told his nephews outside the church. "I can't join you for everything with my new schedule at the job, but we'll have a whole day for the game and to hit a ball court somewhere so I can tear y'all up."

"Yay!"

It was good to see them all again. He missed his sisters, their children, and even his parents. But one of the reasons he'd left them in the first place now needed to be addressed.

"Mama, why don't you ride back to Aunt Dee's with me?" He was already pivoting toward his car.

Rose came over. Two years older, she was the next sibling before him, making her the baby of his three sisters. "Take it easy on her, Em. She wasn't trying to disrespect your girl. You know it's a big deal for Ma to even be in New York, and she came because she loves you."

Emeric recalled the horror on A'Lelia who was innocently giving a hug, only to witness Grace Shipman McPherson having a psychotic episode. He kissed Rose on her cheek.

"Ma, you ready?"

Once they drove out of Mount Bethel's gates, their family's caravan turned left in the direction of Dee's house. Emeric hung a right and broke away.

"What are you doing?" Mama asked. "The others are going that way. Where are we going?"

"We need to talk, Mama." Over the top of the steering wheel, he hung his generational fatigue. "You know I love you. And I'm glad you came. I realize your life was not easy, and all you went through just to move on, find some kind of peace, and have a family. I can't say how proud your strength makes me. But you had no right at all to say those things about A'Lelia or her family."

She must have been tired herself, and let it out in a large, diaphragm-emptying sigh. "I don't want to do this now, Em. Tomorrow is Christmas. We haven't seen each other in months. Just about everybody is together, save for Carmen. I didn't intend to do it. You said *you* were shocked to see me there. What about me? I was just as shocked as anybody else to see my mama's necklace. The last time I saw her in that, she was feeding my baby brother and dancing to a song on the radio before I left for school. The next time I saw it, Daddy was betting it in a poker game because he didn't have any cash on him."

Choking up, she fixed her eyes on the passing city streets she hadn't seen in decades, and opened her pocketbook in search of tissues. He took his handkerchief out of his inner suit pocket and passed it.

"Twenty-four hours after I hit New York, that's my first 'welcome home' sign? Seeing that on some stranger? Are you out of your mind, Emeric Orenthal? Putting it on somebody else before I had even touched it? And Dee said you didn't ask her, either."

"I'm sorry. Rushing around for the Presents, there was never time for me to do it right."

"Or you just wanted her to wear it and you weren't about to hear the word 'no'."

In silence, they rode across the Queensboro Bridge.

Had he known his mother was in town already, and might see it, he honestly wouldn't have hurt her that way.

"Probably. I want her to know how much I care about her. If I'd known you'd surprise me at the Presents, she wouldn't have worn it tonight."

"I wish you wouldn't have put it on her at all until you discussed it with me first."

"Again, Mama, I'm sorry."

"So you've been spending time with her family, and her granddaddy gave you this?" His mother stared at the necklace, in her hand now. "Why didn't he ever give it to me?"

"Why don't you ask him?"

"I have nothing to say to that man. I only want my son to think."

She gazed out the window at her old flame, the city she clearly still felt something for, and the city he was falling for. Or rather, he was enamored with the city that had produced a girl who illuminated it for him.

"Your son is doin' a whole lot more than thinking, Mama." He turned into Addisleigh Park.

"What are you…?"

He heard the recognition in her lungs that swelled with her bewilderment.

"Don't do this."

He turned onto the street. "Mama, you can't keep—"

"Oooh, Emeric, take me back to Dee's!"

"I will once we do this first. Look at it." He pulled up to the house where she'd only lived a short time as a teenager.

In an avalanche of emotion, Gracie Shipman broke down.

He hadn't wanted to. In a sense, this was cruel. There should have been some mental and emotional preparation first, as in counseling, but she always refused.

"I'll come around and get you." This was the next best thing.

"I'm not getting out of this car!"

"Well, I am, and as cold as it is out here, you're gonna start freezin' real fast."

He gave her another few minutes for the hurt to rip out of her. This was more grief in the last five minutes than he'd seen his entire life, so it was a start. When her convulsions slowed, he got out, walked around and held open her door.

This time, he made sure he had his keys, in case she tried to pull one of A'Lelia's moves.

Inside the house, he started up the fireplace while she took her first reentrance alone. He found her again at one of the bedrooms, where she brushed her thumb over tick marks in the doorframe. Only one other set of marks had been ticked mere centimeters above the first set.

"I remember the day… my sis… these marks, so we… track how… we grew in our new hou…" Quiet sobs rendered her speech difficult to understand, but he understood some of it.

The girls hadn't lived here long enough to keep marking their growth.

His mother kept walking, and he followed, from room to room, for her to claim the few memories they'd left behind.

"How did you know about this house? We lived mostly in Sugar Hill."

"Talking to your relatives and Granddaddy's old friends. Plus, I met a guy who's into real estate investments and he had his people look up Granddaddy's deeds. I also plan to buy Granddaddy's Lennox Avenue property where the store was."

It wouldn't be an abandoned housing complex for long. Along with Lionel and the other guys, they would purchase it as part of their investment portfolio and remodel it into a coop. They'd sell the apartments to young Black families and professionals just starting out.

"And who would this real estate 'guy' be?"

"Lionel Middleton. He wasn't born when you were here so you wouldn't know him."

"But I do know the Middleton name. They're one of the old families, just like the Césaires. So those are the kinds of people you're surrounding yourself with." His mother ventured into the main bedroom where her parents had slept, and stared down at his bed. "You brought her here."

The bed was made up, but on the pillows were traces of Al's makeup.

"I did."

His mother glared. "You had sex with her in my mama's and daddy's house."

"It bothers you that I had sex with her?"

"It bothers me that you're so disrespectful."

"By disrespect, you mean touching a woman besides you?"

"Boy, *shut* your mouth."

"Tell me something, Mama. Were you hurt because Al was wearing your mama's necklace, or because I love another woman enough now to put that necklace on her?"

Her face formed a fist, and if it could have punched him, it would have. "What craziness are you talking?"

"You know what I mean. I've never taken up a serious relationship for long. You always clung to me so hard I couldn't breathe. I was constantly in your grip. Over protecting, loving me too hard, like you needed somebody to make up for all those lost years of not having your daddy, and you couldn't do it with Pop, so you overdid it with me."

"Fool, do you know how many kids out there would *love* to have a mother to come home to? I sure didn't!"

"To make up for what you didn't have, you suffocated me. Being too strict, keeping me at your side too much, not letting me spend the night with my friends, or go to the speeches and marches, like you just knew something would happen to me if you let me out of your sight. I felt bad for you. You're my mama and I couldn't hurt you, so I went along. I didn't have the freedom psychologically to stand up and be my own man. Carrying your grief for you was heavy. I can't keep doing it."

"Is this what Theodore Césaire put in your head? Hm? Is this what that girl's been telling you? If I was so psycho, how come I didn't act like that with any of the other three children I had *before* you? Why aren't they complaining?"

"Billie attaches to Pop. Carmen ignores you. And Rose hides with her friends. That leaves me." Em scrubbed his face. "I'm willing to bet you kept having girls until you finally got your boy. I'm also willing to bet you didn't really love Pop. You only married him so you wouldn't have to come back to New York, and because he was boring and predictable, the complete opposite of your daddy who was the life of the party. With a boring man, nothing bad would happen and you would always be safe."

His mother stalked across the room, and he knew what was coming. He didn't dodge it. That slap toted more emotion than he'd expected.

Hands in his pockets, he didn't bother rubbing out the sting. Already, he'd decided to accept whatever she did to him if it meant the beginning of growth for her.

"Hitting me doesn't make me wrong. You've got some kind of Freudian daddy complex, Mama, and I can't keep playing the part of your father. And at times, even your man."

It pained Emeric to speak his next words, but if they didn't do this now, they stood no chance.

"Mama, sometimes, when you and me are on the phone and you're beggin' me to move back home, you whine like a little girl, and it almost sounds like a child beggin' her daddy. For a few seconds, one version of you—"

"*Shut* up!"

"...disappears and is replaced by a seven-year-old, before the grownup version of you—"

"*Shut! Up!*"

"...comes back on again." Tears refused to stay in Emeric's eyes, no matter how hard he mashed them. He didn't want to say these things. He'd hated to live them. But what else was left to do?

"Boy, *stop* your lyin'! Tell me you haven't taken this trash to anybody else."

"I'm too ashamed. I could never tell Al this."

"You think her family is so perfect? Hm? You think you're gonna marry her and give her babies and she'll give you the perfect life over in Central Park. I didn't lie back there at Mount Bethel. They're killers. Lowdown and cold-blooded."

He shook his head. "I'm glad you asked, because, yes. When Al is ready, I am marrying her. And I pray she wants to have a family with me."

"You pray. Ha! You have no idea what you would be getting into. Theodore Césaire killed my daddy, and you marrying one of them is a betrayal to us."

Emeric listened. "I know you feel like they weren't there for you, but what happened to Granddaddy wasn't their—"

"Theodore Césaire was responsible for that fire! In 1936, Daddy was subpoenaed as a witness to testify at a congressional hearing about Theodore's invention during the Great War. Daddy had booked his train to D.C., and had talked to my mama about what he would say. A week before he was supposed to leave, Daddy and Theodore fell out about something from twenty years before. It involved that invention and a man named…I think his name was Leo…Leonard… Leonardo, I can't remember. It was around the time of the Great War. I can't think of it all. I was only fourteen."

Passionate in her retelling, she leaned so far into her words she almost fell.

"Two days before Daddy was supposed to get on the train to testify against Theodore, he died in that fire! Leonard might have been related to Theodore. I never met him. It was before I was born, so I don't remember. But Daddy was around with them in the early 1900s, when this Leonard guy and Theodore had a big fight. Theodore did not want Daddy to bring any of that up in the hearing. Daddy didn't survive to *testify* in the hearing! Because he knew things about Theodore that Theodore did not want coming out. There is a lot going on in that family nobody knows. But I believe Daddy knew things, and he paid with his *life!*"

Emeric listened, and then took a breath. "Mama, I talked to people who knew Granddaddy—barbers, restaurant owners, and neighbors. I even went and found newspaper articles. The men who set fire to that store were lily White. One of them ran away and was arrested. The other one never made it further than a block before the community beat him down so badly he was hospitalized. They both stood trial and were convicted, though they didn't do any time."

He gazed at her with as much love and sympathy as he could. "The neighbors who owned businesses in the area at that time confirmed that White men had come to see Granddaddy several times about selling, and he refused."

Before meeting Al, when he'd first arrived in New York, Emeric had spent some of his free time just trying to understand the mother who was a mystery to him.

Everything Dr. Césaire said about his grandfather lined up with what Emeric had already learned from others.

His mother shook where she stood. "You're so blinded by your ambition you won't even listen to me. You want so badly to be part of this set, to be rich and important and fake, *just* like your *granddaddy.*"

"Name one family from your past in New York that's still good."

"None of them ever were."

"How can I give any credence to what you're saying when you've been weaving stories about these people for forty years, and everybody is the enemy? When will you finally turn to the victim in the mirror?"

She patted her own chest to soothe herself. "I was just fine until my son decided to move here and open up this Pandora's box."

Emeric walked up to her, and ensured they stood face to face, where she could look in his eyes.

"Mama, I don't *know* you. Do you realize that? Of all the places I could have gone in the world, why do you think I came here? To New York City? Yeah, I was gettin' bored at home. Yeah, I wanted bigger opportunities. But I could have gone anywhere—Chicago, Atlanta, Detroit, L.A. But I came to your hometown, backtracked through your life, and bought this house as soon as it opened up, so I could learn who that fourteen-year-old girl was *before* that night child services took her out of here."

As long as he'd been alive, his mother had always patted her own chest, as if she'd adapted to doing so in her mother's absence. "I'm the woman who brought you into the world."

"Whose dreams I don't know. Your *real* dreams. Not the ones you lie about in front of Pop. The *real* Grace, who probably loves jazz, dancing, clubs, and liquor, the way her father did. Not this zombie who rocks on the pew in church, quotes the Bible all the time, and knits to calm her busy mind."

Her lips twitching, her body stricken to the point she may have been paralyzed, he didn't expect her to lash out at him again.

So he continued, "What would that fourteen-year-old girl have achieved? Where would she have gone had her life not been knocked off course? What plays and TV shows brought her joy? Did you know that part of the reason I became a doctor, and not a pharmacist like Pop, is because I accidentally found your childhood diary as a kid? In it, I read how you wanted to be one."

Her jaw fell. "You had *no* right."

"I was young, maybe eight or nine. I didn't know what it

was when I picked it up. But that day, I decided I would become a doctor to make up for how you couldn't. I would get it done *for* you."

"Well, now that you've done what you set out to, it's time for you to come home, Emeric."

"It's time for me to start livin' for maself." At ease with just the two of them, he felt no need to mask his natural southern accent he hid to blend in with New Yorkers.

"I will not have you becoming one of these coldhearted, bloodsucking men that are all about money, showboating, and stabbing each other in the back. I don't want my good, sweet son turning into one of these people."

He laughed to himself, recalling Al, her clumsiness and the look she got when she was pissed or determined. "Al is good and sweet, Mama. She's as pure as they come. Kind, beautiful inside and out, tough and still soft. You would love her if her last name wasn't Césaire."

"I'm sure she may be nice. That's what New York high society girls are trained to be—deceptively nice, so they can marry properly. It's unfortunate that she comes from where she does, but there are plenty of girls with hearts of gold right where *you* came from."

Emeric was smitten with this city now. He missed his family, friends, and some aspects of home, but his heart was finally finding its radio frequency in this town.

"I like New York and the opportunities here for me. And I think deep in your heart, you miss it. I think you stayed away to cope, and sometimes, you wish you were still here. I love you, and I want you to be in my life. You're always welcome in my home, so long as you never *ever* say anything like what you said to Al tonight *ever* again."

She held up her hand and started twisting off her engagement ring she'd received from Emeric's father on the McPherson side, as was tradition. "Well, then, I suppose your mind is made up." It was the engagement ring Emeric had requested weeks before. His mama now held it out. "You're choosing this ugly, evil, coldhearted city over your family."

"Keep it. Al and I will start traditions of our own." He shoved his hands in his pockets and kissed her jaw on his way out. "I'll give you a minute while I go make some calls for my shift tomorrow. There's a Lemon Yogurt Cake in the kitchen if you're interested. That 'deceptively nice, New York high society girl' made it for you. She didn't want you to be sad coming back here for the first time."

"HOW LONG DO we have to be here again?" Al asked on their ride down to Lower Manhattan.

"Only long enough for him to see our faces. I have to go to work in three hours, so we'll be there just a little while." Emeric raised her hand to his lips and held it there, kissing it repeatedly. "I haven't seen you all week anyway." Between his family being in town and his new schedule, he hadn't had time for Al even when she'd come to the hospital to drop off lunch. "Don't forget, Lionel *did* come support your Presents, and he set up my family very nicely while they were here. I can't be antisocial. Neither can you."

Al made a face. "He's just so 'worship me. Look at how rich I am.' And that's before we even discuss those paisley jacquard curtains he wears as jackets. I can always hear his pants coming. From way across the sanctuary." She slipped her hand out of Em's and rubbed them together, imitating somebody walking while she made sounds with her mouth. "Swish. Swish. Shh. Shh."

Emeric cracked up while driving. "Stop it, silly. The guy is okay once you start talkin' to him. He's got big ideas, and the balls to carry 'em out. *And* the bank statement to pay for it. Where I come from, I don't know too many boys like that. So it's hard not to pay attention to him."

"Just promise me you won't turn into them. More concerned about money than character." Al gazed at him from her side of the seat, her features serious and not joking any longer, as if she had been giving this extended thought.

"Damn, if you don't sound just like Mama. I wish you and her had hit it off better."

"You mean you wish she hadn't nearly jumped me in a house of the Lord and accused me of killing her family?"

"Baby, her mouth said that. But I swear, what was really goin' on is she took one look at how fine you are and she knew she wasn't gon' see her boy again. She might have had a little jealous reaction *on top of* you wearin' her mama's neck-lace." He pointed at the Rand McNally map in her lap. "Gimme the address again."

She picked it up and read it aloud. "Three nineteen Lex—"

"Lexington?"

Blinking a lot, she seemed to be figuring something out. "Al?"

"That's the Murray Hill Hotel. Why is Lionel having an event there and giving them business after what happened to us?"

In a shrug, Em steered. "I'm pretty sure he planned this affair months ago, before the incident with the Presents ever went down."

Al's sudden tension started filling up the car. "Then, why didn't *he* get kicked out and *his* event canceled? All this time, Lionel knew he was receiving better treatment than us. He might have even been able to help us while we were going around, begging for a venue, and he never breathed a word?"

They approached a stop light, still several blocks away.

"Baby, I'm sure there's an explanation. But this is New

Year's. The Presents is over and it's time for you to celebrate how you're closing out 1976 on top."

She was visibly hurt, furling and unfurling her fists. At a stoplight, Em reached over and turned her face toward him.

"Look at me. Over here."

Al shifted her sea-green eyes from the obvious playbacks in her head to the man next to her.

"A'Lelia, you're rolling into 1977 after snatching victory from the jaws of defeat. Are you really mad about that?"

She let out a breath. "No. Not mad, just confused. We're all Black."

With a big grin, he pointed at her. "*You* light, though."

A thunderbolt couldn't have sent her away from him faster.

"I'm playin'! Baby, I'm playin' with you!" He dodged, throwing his arm up to shield himself from her slapping it.

"And *what* are you? You're literally one shade darker than me, country Negro."

"Country as hell and damn proud. I'm just tryin' to take your mind off of it, so you can chillax for this party." Still chuckling, he leaned over the center console and pushed his lips out. "Come here and gimme some sugar."

Sucking her teeth, she ignored him. The silent treatment was her specialty. But her shoulders fell again, so he continued.

"This is business, Al. You have no idea what Lionel did or did not know about your situation, which ultimately worked out for your *good*. You're the winner here. That hotel guy couldn't have missed you in all the papers and on the news, and their stupidity is what made it happen. So don't walk in there angry like you've been wronged. Put a dip in your hip like this is your victory lap. The only person you're hurting if you carry these vibes into the new year is yourself. Ten-four?"

His baby's eyes softened. She rolled them at him, still stewing on that skin shade joke. But just as the traffic light changed, Al nodded. "Right. Ten-four."

"*Now*, may I *please* have some sugar?"

She delayed, clearly to make a point.

"You ain' right, A'Lelia. I'm not the one who took your hotel, but I am the one who helped you secure somethin' else."

Her side grin teasing him, he tugged her to him and kissed her open-mouth smile, teeth displayed, and all.

Inside the Murray Hill, Em grabbed a full flute of champagne and passed one to Al. Lionel, Harold, and Brent were working the ballroom with all their longtime friends and hadn't noticed him, yet.

"Congratulations, Al!" someone called from the bar. "My niece was in the Presents. So beautiful! We can't wait to see what you do next year!"

Emeric gave Al his *"I told you"* stare.

"Thank you!"

"So what's your New Year's wish?" he asked Al over the rim of his glass, genuinely interested in where her head was.

She still hadn't said the words. He was giving her the space he would want a man to give any of his sisters. But that didn't stop him from flying around the airport runway to see if the words might be landing within the foreseeable future.

"I'm not sharing." But that tiny side-grin of hers, underneath those scheming eyes, were daring him to escort her to the front desk so they could grab a room.

"You *know* what you over there doin'. Just tell me."

"If I tell you, it won't come true."

Em played with her gown at her hip, bringing her to him, and spoke under his breath. "Gimme a hint."

She pointed. "Lionel wants you."

Indeed, Lionel was damn near breaking his arm for Em's attention. Emeric placed his hand at Al's back.

"You're comin', too. Be nice."

"Everybody, come on up! We have a big announcement to make before New Year's, finally. There's a lot for us to celebrate." Lionel held a microphone and took the stage. "I want all of you to meet my business partners. Without them, we would not be the brand new owners of this here Murray Hill Hotel!"

A collective gasp flew around the room, followed by shocked applause. But none moreso than Emeric and Al.

Lionel continued, "My buddies and I are on top of the world, and this is only the beginning. Brent, Filer, Harold, Ramsey, Cooley, Drake, Marius…" He kept going down the list of what must have been fifty-some-odd men that formed a Black men's investment group. "And also, let's not forget the new guy around here, Emeric, but we like to call him 'Memphis'. When you see him, pay respect. He'll be another Black Founding Father of the *new* New York that's coming! Black owned and operated!"

At Em's side, Al blew a gasket.

"Like I said, we're only just getting started!" Lionel hopped up and down, too ecstatic to stand still. "The only way from here is up. Stay tuned, baby!"

"You were part of this?" Al asked.

"Just hold your horses. Let's find out what's crackin'." He took her hand, and made his way to Lionel, where he still had to wait behind all the people congratulating him. "Lionel!"

"Memphis! Get over here for some pictures of the group!"

"Before we do that, let's have a word."

Frowning, Lionel stared. "Now?"

"Yeh, man, now." In a corner, Em turned to face him. "Why didn't I know this is what you did with my money I gave you? When you talked about me joining your group, I thought we were buying into Black communities like Harlem, Bronx, Queens. What about those night clubs where you go listen to that 'breakin' stuff and the damn buildings are on fire? Not some WASP-y, racist hotel where the only color in here is the janitor."

Al huffed next to him. "You gave him money? How much?"

"Baby, gimme a minute, please."

His hands together as if in a prayer, Lionel replied. "Brotha, I said we would be majority Black-owned. Yes, we are buying some of those clubs, and some housing complexes like the one at Lennox, but if I invested cash only in damaged neighborhoods requiring a ton of renovation, we would never turn a profit. See, Memphis, you haven't attended any investment lunches, yet. You're always either working or with her. If you had, you would know the mission is to buy up properties that were once Black in the 1800s, but were taken away by White owners. We're making them Black-owned again. Once we own hotels like this and business offices, we can hire Black workers, put money in Black pockets, and create more Black business opportunities. That won't happen if we're wasting too much cash on struggling joints in the 'hood."

"Lionel, did you tell the manager to kick out the Presents?" Al asked flatly.

Em turned to her. "Al, will you please let me do it?" Emeric shifted back to Lionel and thumbed his nose. "Man, did you tell your manager to cancel their contract and put them out with no advance warning?"

Wide-eyed, Lionel seemed stunned. "What? The Presents? It was at Mount Bethel last week."

"It was at Mount Bethel, because they were removed from

here. By your hotel manager, who said the new owners didn't want them here."

Lionel scrubbed his face. "Dude, my lawyers worked it out during the sale that any event contracts worth less than a certain amount—a hundred thousand dollars—had to be revisited. And if any fell short, then *next* year, as in after January 1st, those events could not come back. I did not authorize current events already on the schedule to be canceled. If that dude put you out of here, he was doing his own thing. I've never met him. I don't deal with day-to-day managers directly. There's a management company for that. But I apologize, and I will take care of it. I haven't attended a Presents in over ten years, so I have no idea what goes on with that. My man Emeric said he needed help, so I came and helped out. I didn't connect one event with the other, Al."

"Lionel, we went to court over this for an injunction. Your lawyers had to know." Al pressed.

"Do you know how many of my properties my lawyers go to court for per week? Evictions, slip n' falls, wrongful terminations, theft, you name it. He calls me with weekly updates, and runs down a list of issues. He only mentioned an injunction in passing. He called it a nothing-burger. I took him at his word. Some weeks, we don't even have the call if it's business as usual. My lawyer has good relationships with judges who rule in his favor. I pay him a premium for that. Again, I had no idea this was the issue you've been talking about."

Hands in his pockets, Emeric gazed at Al.

"Do better, Lionel," she said. "It's not an excuse that you never get your hands dirty and look the other way, so somebody else can always be the scapegoat."

"You know what, man?" Emeric rubbed his chin in thought. "You can make amends by letting Al be a partner in your investment group."

"*What?*" Al and Lionel asked at the same time.

"Amends? I don't owe her anything. This was a mishap. I didn't kick her out on purpose. Besides, there are no women in this group," Lionel stated.

"Nor am I interested."

"Precisely why it might be time." Emeric smiled at both of them. "Al loves history projects, and that's essentially what you're describing, Lionel, right? You're restoring Black properties that were lost in the 1800s? And as a partner, Al, you'd have the right to use properties on our portfolio for community events, teaching, talks and forums on the historic places Lionel is investing in. That's also good press for the investment group. The way I see it, this is a win-win."

The two stared at one another like they were being asked to mud wrestle.

"No offense, Al, it's not personal, but this is a men's group." He was saying it as if he spoke to a kindergartner. "New York has lots of women's investment groups out there."

"What a discriminatory statement." Al seethed. "I have investments already, and I don't trust you enough to give you my money."

A wide-eyed Lionel glared at Emeric. "See? There ya go! Why would I do business with somebody who doesn't trust me?"

"Al, Lionel, the two of you might not have a taste for each other, but you're from the most prestigious families around here. And you're both working to restore your vision of Black New York. Y'all are actin' like putzes. Baby, with the museum closing soon, this could be a new way of you doing your history thing. And Lionel." Emeric took a deep breath. "Having a woman in your group could soften your image some."

"I like my shark reputation just fine," Lionel insisted.

"I wasn't thinkin' shark exactly. I was thinkin' more like one of those angry little Siamese fighting fish that's real colorful. I used to keep one in a fish bowl on my desk. What are they called? You can buy 'em at K-mart in the goldfish section."

"Betta fish," Al replied.

Emeric snapped his fingers. "Thank you! That's it!"

"Ya mama, dude. Al, fine. You can join the investment group if you want, but it has to be under your initials only. Nobody can know you're a woman."

"I beg your pardon!"

Lionel help up his hands. "There's a certain male testosterone profile I have to maintain. Once you put in your investment, I'll even let you fire that manager yourself. Now, if you two lovebirds will excuse me, damn."

Once Lionel returned to his party and guests, Emeric was left with the object of his desire, who glared at him.

"My initials? Nobody can know you all have a woman? I bet he wants people to know when he's got a woman in the bedroom, though! Just not the boardroom. What kind of hateful rule is that?"

"Al, I know you don't like it for now, but this way, you can out-hustle him. Sneak into the party, and then go to the backdoor and let in your friends. Start thinkin' like a hustla, baby."

"It was him the entire time," she said, her eyes squinted.

"No, it was that manager you've been dealing with for years. That's how they are—smile in your face, and the whole time, they don't want you there. He tried to get rid of you the first chance he got, and didn't know you'd be connected to the new owners."

"He probably thought they'd be White, too, and that he could get away with it."

"And he would have in most circumstances. But look at what happened by you being here tonight. One door closed a month ago, and several more doors have opened. And as the first woman investor in this group, you'll be in a position to keep opening doors for other women."

In that instance, his mother crossed his mind. Though he knew other people had given Mama opportunities and helped her on her path, a part of him still mourned for the unfulfilled part of her. The part of her that would never be so happy that she could turn around and pass it to somebody else.

Al laid a hand on his chest. Even that move reminded him of Mama patting her own chest, because she had no one to lay a hand there, and comfort her. That wasn't Pop's thing.

"Where did you just go?" Al whispered.

He grinned, and leaned in her ear. "Nowhere yet, but let's go downstairs so the newest owner can gimme a tour of this place."

Suspicious, French eyed him. "It's almost time for the countdown, and that would be rude."

"You think Lionel will notice we're not in here? Show me around."

Making sure Lionel and the others were preoccupied, they quietly snuck onto the elevator.

Al began pointing out separate areas of the place. "Every year when we have the Presents here, it's always held in this ballroom over—"

"Before we go there, what's over here in this area?" Emeric steered her in another direction.

"Where?" she asked. "Oh, no, there's nothing down there."

"You sure?" Emeric kept walking, ensuring her fingers were entangled in his so she had to trail him.

"Yes, there are only offices down here. Nothing interesting. All the good stuff is down the other corridor. Ballrooms, conference rooms, shops, spa facility, a couple of sweet restaurants." She pulled on him. "Emeric, you're going in the wrong direction. We can't be down here."

"Why not?"

Vexed, Al stared between him and the door. "This is the manager's office."

Emeric fished out a set of keys.

Al gasped.

Mocking her, Em gasped.

"What are those?" she whispered.

He whispered back, "What do they look like?" He flipped to the key he wanted and unlocked the door, opening it.

Al covered her mouth. Looking both ways, he snatched her through the door and shut them inside.

"How did you get keys to this office?" Fumbling around, she switched on the light. Al inspected him. "You knew you were an owner of this hotel? That whole thing you just did with Lionel was a—"

"Surprise. That's all. I figured it out a few days ago, after I had already put money into the pot. It was irritating. After I discussed it with Lionel, I figured the best way to resolve it was for you to hear from him yourself. You deserved for this hotel thing to be made right."

Her gaze shifted around the manager's office, while she put two and two together. "So me firing this manager guy was *your* idea that you gave to Lionel?"

Em shoved the hotel manager's papers and file folders off the desk. Then, he slipped a hand around Al's booty, and pelvis-bumped her to the desk edge.

"If it was, do I get a prize or somethin'?" He inched up her sequin gown, and was tasting the champagne on her tongue before she could laugh.

"Maybe," she managed, though the word was lost in the sucking.

"What kinda prize?" As always, her neck was softer than warm caramel. "Does it invollllve…panties?"

Awestruck, she stared at him. "In here?" With intimacy

still new to her, she seemed to consider the act and weigh it out. "Emeric, we're at a formal function. This is improper behavior. My parents will kill me if they find out."

"You plan on tellin' 'em what we do?"

He returned his hands to the bottom half of her gown, maneuvering it up her thighs high enough to access his third-favorite part of her. She didn't stop him from pushing aside the seat of her panties, where Em assessed for himself what Al was too "proper" to say. Upon his fingers caressing her fleshy folds, in sync, they both trembled.

A stimulated Al closed her eyes in pleasured torment and chuckled, allowing for this new act he was introducing her to. She spread her legs wider, her eyelids already heavy.

Her swollen sexual lips *continued* quaking on his fingertips, aftereffects of her anticipation. Em almost came. Forcing himself to stay focused, he wrangled down her panties.

Before reaching to switch off the light, he took another look at her. Ready, mouth open and wet, Al was his. He wanted to witness every moment of him in her.

He dragged her panties until they dangled off one ankle. Once he helped her get the zipper over his bulge, he tore open the condom and they strapped it on.

Al circled her delicate hands around his face and brought their heads together.

The best feeling he'd felt his entire life was entering A'Lelia. The next best was hearing the sounds she made while he discovered her all over again. With the lights on, he didn't dare close his eyes. Didn't dare miss her sex-drunk, half-open, fluttering eyelids, or her tongue barely visible at the top of her teeth.

Moist and fat, her canal was so enveloping, the squishing sounds almost sat him down. Emeric could hardly move. Unable to pull back from her warmth, he just barely managed to rock inside her. Between Al's womanhood closing around his shaft, contracting and heating up, and his drenched manhood needing relief, Emeric would not last.

Somewhere outside, in other areas of the hotel, the New Year's countdown had begun.

Eight...

With Al leaned backward, one hand on the desk, the other gripped his butt. But the rising bliss muted the pain. He knew the way to her most sensitive pleasure point, and pressed it now. Her canal responded, burning hotter, gushing all over his length. Her mouth widened.

Six...

He felt her inner muscles expand and contract around him. Em held out just long enough for Al to peak first while he watched.

Three...

The worlds in her eyes rolling upward, Al stiffened, shaking. The warm rain of her juices flooding his manhood, her essence drizzled out and onto the desk. She disappeared for a moment, her head all the way back.

Rocking harder, deeper, as far as he could go, Emeric chased the ends of the Earth, and since the world was round and she was limitless, the end wasn't possible.

One...

Al's eyes opened. Emeric saw the words explode in her pupils before they came out of her mouth. She hadn't gone anywhere.

"I love you."

Emeric brought her head back to his, her heart back to his, their mouths back together, and rocked a final time.

Though this was only their third time together, she was learning how to feel him, and sensing what to do. Al squeezed her womanly muscles tighter, clung harder to bring more of him into her, where love surrounded and held him.

His love for her erupted, bolting from his manhood throughout his body.

"Mmph..."

Spent, Emeric needed to rest his head on her shoulder for a minute. Her fingers buried in his Afro, her skin hot against his, artery thumping in a frenzy inside her neck, Al was transmuting herself into his eternity.

"I love you, too, A'Lelia."

"YOU'RE SAYING you believe those dead bodies are *still* buried under Broadway?" one of the teenagers asked Al.

These were the kind of crowds Al missed, the youth who resembled her, in shade *and* mind.

"Yes." It was good to be back at the Historical Society again, even if it was only occasionally for these one-off private tours over the summer. "That's what I'm saying."

Seeing how immersed the youth were, their hands covering their mouths in fascination, their attention glued to the diagrams and drawings of New Amsterdam behind her, Al hated to conclude the lesson.

She pointed at the map of New York's first independent Black community. "How else can this be explained? Stagg Town was here in this area, to the Northeast, where the eleven Black men were granted their own land in 1644. And down here, was the African Burial Ground where enslaved *and* free Blacks buried their loved ones. The Burial Grounds are clearly referenced on these land surveys and in deeds throughout the 1600s and 1700s." Al held up her hands in a silent question. "What did the city ever do with all those

Black bodies when it started paving streets and putting up buildings over those burial sites?"

"Why doesn't the city people just go dig 'em up and see?" one of the students asked.

"Who's going to pay those pricey archaeologists to dig and find out?" Al challenged. "Are you all willing to contribute money for such an expensive project?"

Perplexed, they remained silent.

"We didn't put 'em in there, though," another student challenged.

Al slid her hands in her pockets, and comfortably strolled among them. "That's how a lot of people feel. Out of sight, out of mind. Like so many issues our community faces, right?"

"Black people really built Wall Street? I can't believe that," another kid said. "I thought it was a bunch of White men in suits."

"And they sold slaves there?" Another teenager sank her face in her hands and took a moment to process that fact. "Just like where we come from?"

Gazing across all of them, she gave them a moment before she replied, "Black bodies were one of the biggest commodities to kick off American capitalism, if not the biggest commodity."

"Dang. I thought New York was friendly to us. It was supposed to be better than Tennessee."

Al nodded and thought about that. "New York was just as guilty as the southern states, but it began addressing its sins faster. Over the last hundred years, without a doubt, New York has worked to remedy some injustices, whereas the southern states are still kicking and screaming. We still have a long way to go, but we're doing a better job than our southern neighbors. I'm afraid that's all we have time for today." Al spoke her next words with genuine appreciation.

"Thank you all so much for visiting us in New York. It has been my pleasure to finally meet the students Emeric always talks about. I mean *Dr. McPherson.*"

Emeric's high school-to-medical school youth group was visiting from Tennessee for a week. Standing up now, they gave her a standing ovation.

"Good job, Emeric's girl." Some of the guys chuckled.

"Her name is A'Lelia." One of the girls corrected him.

Al winked. "Thank you. I appreciate that."

Right then, the lights went out around them.

"Stay calm, everybody, I'll find out what's going on with the electricity," she cautioned them.

But ascending the museum stairs was a tower of candles.

"HAPpppyy birthday tooo yaa!" They broke out in giddy, off-key song.

Al just stood still and let the waves of their joy wash over her. She did not revel in this kind of attention the way BB did. But she would no longer hide from what she deserved.

BB and Jill carried the cake. Al wasn't surprised to see Pépé since he was due to go after her for his brief talk on inventions and science. After that, the two of them would give Nadia Freeman a very brief family interview for her newspaper.

Helping Pépé along was Meme, as well as her father, mother, and several of her aunts, uncles, and cousins who followed up the stairs. A few longtime friends, who'd stuck by Al through the Presents crisis a few months ago, now crowded in and joined the singing.

"Time to blow out the candles!" BB grinned. "Close your eyes and make sure the wish is good."

Al looked over all their heads and saw that Emeric was missing. With his increased surgeries these days, his absence didn't surprise her and she was thrilled for his new responsibilities. But naturally, she longed for the man who lit her up, always had her back, and made time when she needed him. They would celebrate later with an away trip, and she anticipated that. Still, the moment wasn't

Closing her eyes for a few seconds, she took it all in—the love, blessings, growth, journey, fun, family, friends and strength—and made her wish.

When she opened them again, a book she'd never seen was sitting next to the cake.

The History of A'Lelia Antonia and Emeric Orenthal.

The words blurred until they disappeared in her tears, and she flipped open the scrapbook. Its first pages were complete with photos of them from the Presents over Christmas, the one flower he'd brought her that first night of the Presents, dried flowers from Valentine's Day, a copy of the termination letter she'd given to the hotel manager, the receipt for the first ever chicken n' waffles they'd eaten, a flyer for a DJ battle between Kool Herc and Grandmaster Flash, the handkerchief he'd used to wipe her nose (washed, thankfully), and playbills for the concerts and plays they'd attended over the last few months. The remaining pages of their history book were blank, waiting to be filled from the future.

On the very first blank page, wrapped in organza and tied with a tiny bow, was a ring.

"What it is, French?" He stood right behind her now, and looped his arms around her waist.

At a loss, she hadn't yet blown out the candles, unable to look away from the man who seemed tailor-made just for her.

"Doc."

He glanced at the small organza bag. "You gonna open it up, or just let it sit there while you make a Negro sweat?"

"We like the sweat option!" her father called a few heads away. The corridor broke into amusement and jokes.

After blowing out her candles, she took the ring out of the bag, an elegant sparkler that almost stopped her heart. One diamond in the center, and several diamonds and sapphires surrounding it, the ring was a quaint, pristine version of her. "Wow."

"Yeah, that's how it felt when I was payin'."

More amusement overtook their well-wishers.

He kissed Al's temple, and stirred her belly. "But you're worth countless rings, French."

Taking this ring from her fingers, Doc lowered to his knee.

"Aww." BB came closer with a video recorder.

"A'Lelia, baby, meetin' you has been the best thing that's ever happened to me. If I hadn't bumped into you last Christmas, I don't think I would have survived New York, but more than that, I probably would not have survived life. What would the world be without Al's candle lightin' our way? Will you do this man the honor of bein' his flame and lightin' up his home and his heart for eternity?"

"Oh, my God, that is so beautiful," one of the teenage girls said, and turned to one of the boys, apparently her boyfriend. "You better propose to me just like that, or the answer is 'no.'"

The poor guy, who couldn't have been older than fifteen, stared at her. "We ain' even been to the movies by ourselves yet."

Al's mother cleared her throat, and delivered a silent chastisement.

"Oh, sorry."

Stifling a laugh, Al refocused on her beloved, the man who stretched her as a person, cheered for her, and nurtured her fire so it blazed. But there was just one thing.

"What about your mother, Emeric? And your family? They're important to you, and you know I'm all about family, so I would never ask you to forsake yours." But she stood by what she'd told him at the final Presents. The idea of strife with a mother-in-law for a lifetime was not desirable for her, despite how much she adored and breathed Emeric. "Is your mother going to accept a marriage between our families?" They had talked about it many times over the past months.

"Ask her yourself." He gestured over his shoulder.

At the back of the group, there his mother stood, Grace Shipman McPherson.

"Ya see, baby, three of these sapphires come from the McPherson side of the family, and that was approved by both my parents, and my grandparents. Plus, three of those stones are from the Césaire side. This way, my mother can hold onto her memories from her Shipman bloodline, and we still have both of our families in our union. But if you want something different, the jeweler is spectacular. He'll rework it."

She didn't just marvel at the ring because it was gorgeous and he was proposing, but because what he'd just described represented her wish come true. A man she felt right to trust with her true self. He'd not once shown her any less than love and support, once again, evident with how much thought he'd put into the ring.

With a final glance between Emeric's mother and Pépé, Al checked in to be sure. Emeric's mother gave a small nod, and Pépé rolled his eyes as if to say, *'Get on with it already.'*

"Al, I know I'm young, but I won't be by the time you gimme an answer, sweetheart." Emeric wobbled on his knee.

"I thought you said you could do an eternity?"

"I can, but I would prefer not to do it down here. I thought I'd be standing up or seated."

Al grabbed his face and poured her thanks and joy into lips. "Yes, yes, yes."

His illuminated face was the wish come true. All the admiration and attraction sparking her her chest was reflected back to her all over Emeric. They fed off of each other, and for the rest of their lives, she hoped it kept them full.

A couple of hours later, after the celebration and festivities, Al was double-checking the museum to ensure BB had cleaned up everything. More than that, she stuck around for Pépé's interview with Nadia Freeman, so the ambitious journalist didn't get too intrusive.

"Thank you so much, Dr. Césaire," Nadia concluded as she saw Al approach. "Your contributions to global security have been amazing. We're glad for your service."

"Pépé, you feel okay?"

Al tried to help him up, but being who he is, he pushed out of the seat on his own.

"Of course. Why wouldn't I?"

She'd never shared with anyone what Emeric had disclosed regarding his colon cancer, and Em had refused to shed anymore light on it. She would not betray Em's trust, so if her grandfather insisted that he was fine, she'd have to take him at his word.

"Hey, A'Lelia, happy birthday! Congratulations on your engagement and being the lucky lady who snagged her handsome doctor prince." Nadia smiled across her teeth, but above that, the rest of her features performed a different act.

"Thank you." Al remained pleasant, but was unable to shake her ongoing sense the journalist had an angle.

"I actually had a question for you, too, because I was confused about something."

"Nadia, you got the interview with my grandfather that you'd been wanting. I really do have to jet."

BB wouldn't be in New York for the entire summer, with auditions, TV bit parts, and commercials waiting for her back in California. Al wanted to spend as much time with her sister as she could before the kid returned to the West

Coast next week. Now with a wedding to plan, dresses to look for, a date and venue to select, the schedule would definitely change. They would no longer likely head to a ranch retreat, but zip through wedding boutiques for BB to give her brutally honest opinion while she was still here. Al didn't agree with much her sister did, but BB's eye for high fashion out of the houses of Paris and Milan was unmatched.

Her hands fanning out in front of her, she pled. "This is a quick one. I promise. It's just over here. In your family's wing."

With an eye on Pépé, who'd rejoined the teenagers peppering him with questions, she moved to the Césaire family wing.

Nadia reached into the display case they'd opened only for today, so these youth and their parents could touch and feel the documents that reminded them Blacks had owned businesses in the 1800s, and were more than slaves. In the vintage leather messenger pouch lay some of her family's shipping insurance documents.

"I was looking at some of the manifests from the boats your family insured a long time ago. That is so fascinating to see an African-American family—I mean Afro-French family—insuring these gigantic ships."

"And, Nadia?"

Al peered around the corner to make sure the kids weren't overwhelming Pépé. Emeric had left to return to his shift. The families were chatting, and BB was off doing only God knew what.

"I think you mentioned this already, but you organized all the items here, right?"

"Yes, I did." A hesitant Al sniffed a setup.

"Looking over the insurance documents, there's one receipt here from 1847 that you all—I apologize, I mean your ancestors—has showing the purchase of ten thousand dollars worth of sugar, and then over here, that sugar is reflected on the shipping manifest for transport to West Africa. Specifically, Dahomey, which is now Benin."

"If that's what it says." Antsy and eager to go celebrate her new birthday engagement with the girls, Al wasn't sure where this was going. In her pocket, she twisted her new ring around her finger, still nursing the giddiness in her chest every time she felt it.

"Well, I'm confused." Nadia slid her finger under the page and flipped it.

"Careful. Those records are old, and we're only exposing them to light and air for today."

"Of course. But over here, the cargo manifest at the Dahomey Port of Ouidah shows that only three thousand dollars of sugar was unloaded." She carefully flipped the document over once more. "Yet, a bank statement here reflects a forty-one-thousand-dollar insured deposit once that boat returned to New York shores, for whatever goods came back on that boat. If your ancestors shipped ten thousand dollars in goods, but only sold three thousand, what happened to the extra seven thousand dollars in sugar? And how did they turn it into thirty-eight thousand before the boat came back to New York?"

Al couldn't stay tolerant any longer, irritated that Nadia was going through her family records in search of some crime or evil, when whatever lapse she'd found was likely attributable to a misplaced document.

"Nadia, we have been more than kind in granting you access to our things, and you're here looking for information to use against us? You should go."

"Oh!" a yelp struck her from the balcony area.

"Pépé!" Al took off to the area where her grandfather was. "Are you all right? Everybody, give him space. Back up some, please."

Somewhat relieved, but stunned, she found that Emeric's mother, Mrs. McPherson, had already reached him where he had stumbled. He'd teetered aside, but saved himself from going all the way down by grabbing a column that was fortunately right at the corner.

"I'm all right. My shoe was untied."

Grabbing Pépé under his arm, Mrs. McPherson helped him up and steadied him.

"That's enough for today." Meme came to take over. "You're getting too old for these crowds."

"I am not, woman. And you can forget it as far as locking me up in the house where I can't go anywhere. Not a snowball's chance."

Al's papa assisted. "Mamman is right, Pa, you're not in the shape anymore to be hanging with these kids. Let's get you to the building for now. We'll drive you back to Scarsdale in the morning."

"Thank you," Al said to her future mother-in-law.

"You're welcome." Her sadness seemed a permanent, invisible scar between her eyes, as it did not fade even when she offered a polite smile. "I should go. I'm making dinner at Dee's tonight. Happy Birthday again and congratulations."

"Also, thank you for what you did today. I can't imagine how hard things must have been…your situation and all. I wasn't born yet, but I'm terribly sorry."

She shook her head, not as if telling Al she didn't mind Al bringing it up, but to outright reject the subject altogether. "God works in mysterious ways. As far as me giving my blessing, he's the only son I have. I don't want to lose him."

"You could never," Al replied instantly. "He worries about you. And no matter how things go for you and me, I'll always make sure he calls."

A nod was all the woman could muster. Al could have sworn she was on the brink of a breakdown.

"My mother, aunts, the girls and I, are all going to lunch this week, if you want to come meet us. You're not obligated, though. I'm sure you have your own plans for getting to know the city again, but you are welcome."

"I appreciate that." Without a yay or a nay, his mother excused herself.

Al wouldn't push. She'd done the best she could, and the burden Grace Shipman had to carry Al could not fathom in order to fix her mouth and judge.

When she arrived back in the Césaire wing, Nadia was gone. *Thank the Lord.* Al closed the old messenger pouch, covered it again with the protective cloth, and replaced the acrylic top back on the display case. After locking it, she peeled out to find her friends and celebrate.

AUTUMN WINDS BLEW against Al's face, so powerful they disassembled her hair. Crisp and chilly, they forced her to hug herself while she held open the door with no coat. In many ways, the seasons around Al were changing.

"Nervous about next weekend?" Michelle, the new Presents organizer, reentered Al's building to grab more boxes for the event.

"Oddly enough, no. I'm excited, but I'm also ready for it to be over, so Emeric and I can move on with life." Now that Em had completed a year at Hillside, Dr. Franklin was bringing him to Harlem, and closer to Al and his aunt. His family's Queens home was already rented out to a newer doctor starting at Hillside. She was especially happy they wouldn't have to drive across town so much now, and she could see him more for breaks and meals. They were looking for a house in Westchester, and to leave the noisy city. Once his residency ended in a couple of years, they could move to the suburbs full time.

"Planning a wedding in four months, working on my dissertation, and teaching high school history *and* college history have been crazy town. I'm ready to cross one of those duties off my list."

"You'll make such a beautiful bride."

"Thank you. And you will be an amazing organizer."

Closing up another box of Christmas items for the Presents, she handed it to Michelle who took it outside to her car. Then, she opened the next box to remove any of her personal ornaments and decorations she'd substituted over the years when she'd been in a pinch.

Nestled in the corner of the box were the three letters from Leopold Césaire.

Ten months ago, she'd been so intrigued with what they would say. After the Presents ended and life returned to normal, Al had needed to catch up on her dissertation work, and then, reached out to her friends and revived her social life. On top of that, there was the extra seasoning of doing things she loved with Em now, when he could manage to get away.

She'd lost the desire to go chasing whatever Pastor Freeman had been talking about. What difference did it make now? Like her Aunt Jeanne had said, life was too short for worrying about dead people's problems.

At this point, the family history was no longer a fun pastime to satisfy her intrigue. Those letters stared at her, waiting to tell Al what even her grandparents hadn't wanted to know.

Monday morning, her first stop was the museum where Dr. Abrams met her, and she carried in the Bible from Pépé's office.

"What do we have here?" His eyes lit up while she unwrapped it. "Oh, my. What, pray tell, are you doing with such a lovely treasure?"

"Can you read this writing here?" She'd been too afraid to take it to an antiquarian just yet, not the way word got around in New York. She first needed to find a trustworthy one who wouldn't sell her family business to the papers for a quick buck.

"I can try." Slipping on his glasses, he scrunched his whole face to see the writing. "This could very well be the real deal. From 1780. Not a fake."

"How do you know?"

"The ink is brown. No blurring. That's the color primarily used before the 1800s. No blue or black. And it doesn't bleed on the page, a big sign of a forger who adds brown ink to old paper to pass off a document as old." He bent down closer and sniffed. "Rust. Brown ink back then was made from iron and some of it rusted. I'm no authenticator, but so far, this has all the makings of a Catholic Bible signed by…" His eyebrows shot up. "Gio?"

He scratched the side of his nose.

"This here is Italian. I'll see if I can dust mine off. It seems to have passed through several sets of hands." He read aloud:

27 December 1780

Your Imperial Majesty,

The See expresses its grief and deep condolences upon the departure of your mother. Rome stands a ready partner to address our shared interests. Our government anticipates your invitation to perform our duty overseeing the clergy as soon as is feasible.

Gio

"The See?" He stared at Al.

"1780? The Holy See? That's the formal government of the Roman Catholic Church, headed by the pope," Al noted.

Without another word, Dr. Abrams walked away, leaving

an uptight Al with her growing worry, and minutes later, returned with a book on all the popes to ever rule in the Vatican.

He kept searching. "Gio. Gio. Ah. The pope during that time was Pope Pius the Sixth. His born name was Giovanni Braschi. In this note, he didn't use his formal title, but rather his birth name, and a nickname at that. He didn't ask somebody else to write this; he wrote it himself, making this here a very personal note that didn't pass through administrative hands." Dr. Abram's hands began to shake. "A'Lelia, this is spectacular. If you can confirm it, this note may have been written by the Pope himself, to the Holy Roman Emperor."

"That would have been Joseph II, upon the death of his mother, Empress Maria Theresa, on November 29, 1780."

The Habsburgs.

"A'Lelia, why would you have this Bible?"

Al went and grabbed the blanket where she'd wrapped the French registrations of her ancestors.

"Which one of those is your ancestor?" He peered at the document for Al's direct ancestor. "Maria Josepha…"

"Habsburg Tossou." His mouth shook. "No father is listed." The words barely made it out of his mouth.

He returned to the Bible. "There is a second note located in the back of this book. It reads:

> Darling daughter,
> Your mother chooses otherwise, yet you are ever welcome to assume your rightful place in your rightful home, and to claim your birthright. Your mother took my heart, but what remains is my deep longing for all of you.
> Papa

"It's not dated." Dr. Abrams stared at Al. "Who is this 'darling daughter' being addressed? And who is the 'Papa' that wrote this? Of what birthright does he write?"

They studied the French registration paper again.

"Who is Maria Josepha Habsburg-Tossou that has no father listed on her French registration? This here is your direct ancestor, A'Lelia?" He tapped the paper repeatedly as if he expected the document to answer. "You are absolutely certain you can trace your bloodline all the way to *this* woman?"

Al nodded, too petrified to speak.

His gaze dropped to the paper and read off Maria Josepha's place of birth several times. "Born in the Hofburg? That's the capitol of Austria, A'Lelia. But this document is French. I thought you said your family was fathered by French nobles in the courts of…"

"Marie Antoinette," Al finished. "That's what I was always told."

"Maria Antoinette was originally from Austria. Joseph II was her…"

"Brother. Empress Maria Theresa was her mother."

Excitement kicking him into high gear, Dr. Abrams connected the historical dots.

"The first note from the pope addresses 'Your Imperial Majesty' on the death of his mother. This Bible was likely given by the pope to the Holy Roman Emperor Joseph II, and then Joseph II could have given it to his daughter."

Al attempted to find another explanation. "Even if the Pope sent this to the emperor, he could have regifted it to somebody else who wrote the note to their child."

Dr. Abrams shook his finger at Al. "It wouldn't make sense. Who else would need to hide a *birthright*? This girl, Maria Josepha, was hiding her true lineage. That's why her name and place of birth are listed, but her father is not.

French authorities probably forced her to disclose her legal name, and if her father was the emperor, they kept that part off. If the second part of her last name was Tossou, of African origin, it's quite clear why she would have been hiding."

In a daze, he let out a deep sigh, the effort exhausting him. "My dear God. When your grandfather brought these papers in last December, I intended to mentioned it to you, but he asked me not to."

"What do you mean, when my grandfather brought them?"

Dr. Abrams, wagged a shaky finger over the French registration documents again. "These haven't always been here. Your grandfather came in last December. It had to be a couple of weeks before Christmas, while you were busy with the Presents. He asked me to open the display case in you all's family wing. So I did. I told him I would have you go through these documents. He said you were busy and not to bother you, that you would get to them in due time. I forgot all about it."

It seemed so long ago, but Al retraced her steps now. She had dug around in Aunt Jeanne's attic in search of proof they were fully Afro-French, and found Maria Josepha's French registration, with her birth place and last name cut out. Aunt Jeanne had snapped in anger when Al inquired about it, even refusing to let Al take the document. Jeanne had initially reacted as if she knew the answer, but immediately played dumb.

When Al visited Pépé's office at Columbia, she just so happened to see that Bible on his shelf. In all her many visits to his office, Al had perused his shelves and asked questions countless times. She would not have overlooked this Bible.

"You're absolutely sure it was December that he came here? Not before then?" she asked Dr. Abrams.

"I'm positive. We chatted some about what you would do

once the museum closed, and I didn't tell you that news until after Thanksgiving."

Questions sprang up faster than Al could think of answers. Where had Pépé gotten these good, undisturbed papers? The family tradition was that the oldest sibling in every generation received the most antiques and artifacts. So how did Pépé possess documents better than Jeanne's, with no cutouts? Why didn't Pépé tell her he'd put these here? Why didn't Pépé accept Leopold's letters from Pastor Freeman himself?

Her mind racing, Al scraped for any possible alternate explanation. None came. All of this could only conclude one thing.

"My good God." Dr. Abrams nearly fell into the chair, but held himself up and remained on his feet. "Once you authenticate these items are real—and I have a damn dead-on feeling you will—do you know what this means?"

"Dr. Abrams, please, not one word of this to anybody." Al needed time to check one more lead, go back through the records, ensure she'd turned over every stone, and process the true magnitude of this.

Dr. Abrams studied Al, his expression changing, like he was being introduced to an entirely new person.

"I shouldn't do this, because I'm Jewish, and Maria Theresa hated Jews with a passion. However, her son, Joseph, was more tolerant of religion after she died. And I hold *you* in high regard. With that said..."

Dr. Abrams stood at full attention, and dropped his head in a deep bow, the appropriate greeting in the presence of royalty.

"THANK YOU." At the courthouse on Centre Street, Al received the microfiche and went to a projector to load it up.

After rotating the wheel on the reader for several minutes, she found Leopold Césaire's Declaration of Intention to become a U.S. citizen, filed in May of 1914.

Al's heart rate fell to a slow, tormented trot.

Name: Leopold Césaire-Habsburg

Al strained her eyes.

Occupation: Scientist and Inventor
I was born in: Saint-Emilion, Bordeaux, France

He was a scientist also, like Pépé.

With shaking hands, Al opened the first letter, dated September 8, 1914, the one for which there had been a receipt last year and no letter.

Dearest Cousin,

Word is slow to travel now since the fighting began, but I have yet to hear from you. There are fears across the country that our family will continue to march through France and mistake me for an enemy. I fear more that France may send me to fight our own kin. I have appealed to authorities here, to no avail.

Teddy, the clock ticks longer with each day, as we await your efforts to secure our permissions and transport back to New York. We are eager to depart, and Georgina is deathly fearful. Please advise us of how much longer it shall be.

We send our well wishes to you and Suzanne, and pray our families will celebrate together for Christmas.

Leo

The first World War had already begun. Austria was battling with Germany's help, against France. America hadn't yet entered the fighting.

Al read parts of it again.

"Our *family will continue to march through France...*" Germany had invaded France. Leopold couldn't have been referring to anyone other than German relatives. And he didn't say "my" family. He used the word "our" as if those Germans were Pépé's relatives also.

The next letter was dated January 19, 1914.

Teddy,

Months have passed. What word of your efforts?

I pray you have not forgotten your family's promise to ours, what your grandfather swore to Josepha, that he would make right all injustice and debts.

My father told this to me, of your grandfather's betrayal.

The American Césaires' complicity in the commoditization of our African cousins is documented, Theodore. Your line thrives only because of your treachery. You sleep and eat on blood money.

Remember there is proof. If you have betrayed me, I shall produce it. Should any ill ever befall me, I have ensured my wife and children have the proof.

Please, I beseech you.

Send word.

Leo

Al must have read and reread that phrase a hundred times right at the microfiche reader. *"The American Césaires' complicity in the commoditization of our African cousins..."*

She lost track of time, unaware of how long she'd been sitting there. Yet, the final, third letter awaited, and on this one, the handwriting had changed completely.

June 6, 1915

Theodore,

I curse you and your children. Should God not

strike you now, I pray He never forgets this insult, that one day his finger finds your sons and daugh-ters to lay them out, as lifeless as you have left me.

I remain faithful for my husband's return. But should he not, there will be no corner or crevice where you or your kin can hide from the truth of what you have done.

If you do not love Leo, at the very least, love Leo's children.

Send for them. I am begging for there to be a heart somewhere in you.

Georgina

Dropping those words on the desk, Al returned from the tunnel of the past and mentally stepped into the light of present day. She rubbed her eyes several times to readjust them. But no matter how many times she tried, she would never see her world the same. Her innocent eyes were gone.

On her drive across town in a zombie-like state, she arrived at the four-way intersection of past and present, memories and revelations.

Georgina Césaire-Habsburg's prayer had finally been answered. God's finger had dragged the buried corpses of the past to the sunny, springtime flower fields of 'now', where the stench of rotten bones' choked perfumed petals of muguets.

"Why did you send him to die?"

"He made his choice. I did not send him to do anything."

"You and Meme knew. That's why you stopped

responding to his letters. It's why she stopped giving you your mail. Leopold thought you were helping him when you weren't. You took Leopold's invention for yourself, accepted the credit, and let him go to the front lines to die at the hands of his own Austrian cousins."

Her grandfather studied her. "It's not as simple as that. The sonar system belonged to both of us. We'd worked on it together for years."

"Yet, his name is nowhere on it. You received all the honors, distinction, and defense contracts."

The scopes of her grandfather's eyes narrowed. "Why do you think that is? What defense contractor would have accepted us with the name 'Habsburg' attached? Particularly, at the start of the war Austria had begun? Habsburgs were hated around the world, and Leo refused to drop that name. There was especially no place in America for a Habsburg. Do you know of any? Go on. Name one."

Pépé's piercing wisdom penetrated her through the needle of his eye, and Al scrambled for a fact to thread through the hole of his premise. America had Vanderbilts, Roosevelts, Carnegies, Morgans, Kennedys…

His eyebrows lifted, and he continued. "America has no problem with wealth, dynasties, or royalty. But two things that are anathema to the American construct: Germans and rich Blacks. They've got no problem with a Black person in servitude, you see. They'll let him be their best friend. But ah, let that servant find money. He is instantly a threat that must be eliminated."

"It was wrong. Leopold was your blood."

"Sad and unfortunate, yes. Wrong, no. We didn't do anything different than the British Windsors, who changed their name from the German Saxe-Coburg-Gotha. In doing so, they saved themselves and avoided their cousin's fate, Tsar Nikolas of Russia. The Windsors never sent a boat for

Nikolas and his family, though they had been imprisoned. As a result, the Windsors still rule Britain. Every great house must sacrifice to survive. As Black royals in hiding, nobody understood this better than we did. In the 1700s, we were ahead of our time."

He lit his pipe, at the same time setting on fire Al's innocence, or perhaps her ignorance.

"That was always the problem between the American Césaires and the French Césaires. They clung to the royal titles. We could not. We had to let them go. Omalara Tossou understood that to be true long ago. Her daughter, Maria Josepha, understood it. You are now coming to understand it as well."

Al tested her new understanding in the fining pot of her morality. "Pépé, one family was destroyed so another could rise."

"No. Leo *chose* to keep his Habsburg identity. He could have dropped it. I told him to. He did not."

"So what does this mean?"

"It means there are vaults, underground bunkers, lands, store rooms, and castles across Europe where you own enormous wealth, the value of which you could never fathom. And there are covert rooms and clubs in many parts of that continent where people will bow to you once you enter their presence, and they will call you by your birthright, Archduchess A'Lelia Antonia Césaire-Habsburg, direct descendant of Joseph II, Holy Roman Emperor, and before him, of Maria Theresa, Queen of Austria, Hungary, and Holy Roman Empress, and their forebears."

A part of Al had walked in here hoping this was all a big mistake, and he would correct her. That he would give her some arcane fact she'd missed and they'd laugh over the ludicrousness of this.

"What about Leopold's family?"

"They have been paid handsomely, in addition to their portion of the Habsburg possessions to which they are still entitled."

"He references African slaves in one of his letters."

"I was not yet born. I only heard whispers here and there as a boy that some of our family members did betray our African kin. I'm not aware of the details."

Al suspected he wasn't telling the truth. "But if your grandfather made a promise, Pépé—"

"I took care of it. Our side of the Césaires owed a debt. Once the invention was patented and sold, I sent his wife and children the checks myself. The Great War came at just the right time for that device. We all needed the money."

Frustrated, Al squeezed her head, as if that would stop her mind from spinning. "I don't understand. How were you so broke if you were so rich?"

Through the clouds of smoke, he diverted his focus out the window.

Yet, Al put the pieces together in the maze of her mind. So heavy was the truth that it sat her down.

"They wouldn't give you your inheritance. The Habsburgs never acknowledged Omalara, Joseph's maligned lover, or his illegitimate children—"

"Wrong." His voice bulldozed hers. "She was his wife. His queen. The empress. And that made his children *very* legitimate."

Al was bulldozed. She took a few moments, not just with what he'd relayed, but the emotion with which he'd relayed it.

"Pépé."

The trains of past, present, and future sped toward one another from separate tracks, steamrolling toward a collision at the intersection of A'Lelia. She couldn't believe she would utter her next question out loud.

"Did you start World War One?"

In a world of smoke, he puffed on his pipe, as if inhaling the drug of whatever peace he'd made with himself.

"Did you avenge Omalara's bloodline? And pursue your own profit and gain? Did you take part in the murder of your cousin, Archduke Franz Ferdinand, your *White* cousin, who was next in line to the Austrian throne? Did you celebrate the destruction of the Habsburgs in 1918? Did you help orchestrate the downfall of your White royal relatives who never acknowledged you, Omalara, Maria Josepha, or any of their Black kin?"

He finally acknowledged his granddaughter through the smoke. "That's all for today, muguet."

"No, it isn't! Why did you put this on my shoulders? You could have destroyed the papers and letters, and no one would have ever known." Al clawed through these revelations in search of a way to extricate herself from them. "You thought you were going to die. Last year, you went into surgery. You could have chosen anybody in New York. You had the best doctors, but you chose a man I was dating."

"I chose Orenthal's grandson."

"You chose someone you knew would tell me eventually. For the same reason you planted the Bible, the French registration papers, and told Pastor Freeman to give me the letters. You wanted me to have them. You didn't know if you would live. And somebody has to carry the burden of the last two-hundred years."

"Correct."

That word torpedoed Al. He wasn't denying it. There was no chance of a misunderstanding, of them laughing at this as a joke, so she could go back to comfortable ignorance.

His eyes she'd inherited leveled squarely at her from his side of the smoke, from his edge of the world where he stood almost at the end, and gazed at Al, who was only at the beginning.

"When you lack knowledge of who you truly are, and others know more about you than you know about yourself, you will always be a target for attack. When that attack happens—and as long as you're worth something in this world, it most certainly will—you won't have a conniving grandfather here to protect you."

EMERIC

"BABY!" An exhausted Emeric exited the elevator and instantly kicked off his sneakers after working a double-shift on only a three-hour nap. He sniffed to try and guess what Al had made him tonight. Duck? Cod? But he walked straight into the surprising scent of nothing. No food aroma greeted him at the entry.

"Baby!" he called again, ready for a hot bath, hopefully with her. Only, he couldn't remember if she was attending a talk, giving a talk, spending extra time on campus, or doing one of her social activities tonight. "We got any Monsieurs? Some duck? Somethin'? A Negro hungry as hell."

Em strolled into the kitchen, and paused. All the cabinet doors were open.

"Al?"

He walked toward the silence, save the unsettling crackle of flames in the fireplace. Somebody must have been present. There she sat on the end of the sofa. In front of her lay old, browning papers that seemed to stare her down.

"Sweetheart, what are you doin' in here all quiet like you got Vito Corleone hidin' in the back?"

His girl shifted her focus from what lay in front of her to Emeric. Though she opened her mouth, nothing came out. His feet turning to lead, he walked closer. Al's tear-stained agony sunk him to his knees.

"A'Lelia, what is it? Who did it?" He would kill 'em. With his bare hands. "Baby, what did they do?" He couldn't breathe while he waited. Until he saw her inhale, his lungs were arrested.

Al's face red, she confronted the papers on the coffee table like it was a tomb.

Emeric reached for what appeared to be history too old for them to worry about. Why did some of it look familiar? The envelopes. "Are those the letters Pastor Freeman kept trying to give you?"

He picked up one of the aged sheets and skimmed.

American Césaires' complicity in the commoditization of our African cousins is documented, Theodore. Your line thrives only because of yours and your predecessors' treachery. You sleep and eat on blood money.

Emeric rubbed his eyes and held it up again to confirm he'd read that correctly. The words hadn't changed by his fourth read. He picked up another letter.

"...there will be no corner or crevice where you or your kin can hide from the truth of what you have done."

Such a damning statement opened a window of Emeric's mind, one he had closed. Through it floated his mother's heartache last December at her childhood home in Queens.

Daddy didn't survive to testify *in the hearing! He knew things about Theodore that Theodore did not want coming out. There is a lot going on in that family nobody knows. But I believe Daddy knew, and he paid with his life!*

Emeric had read the newspapers from that time. He'd seen police reports and photos of what happened at his grandfather's store. Not a single person he'd asked brought up Dr. Césaire's name, even though they all criticized him in other areas, such as making money while men died in the war, or not coming to Black neighborhoods to help enough. If those people had wanted to add actual murder to the list of things they didn't like about him, nothing was stopping them. Instead, the elders who'd been alive at that time, had all felt Orenthal Shipman was a good, fun guy, but had also incurred his own problems as a show-off who attracted the wrong kind of attention.

This letter confirmed that Dr. Césaire had indeed made some questionable moves. But what had he done concerning Em's grandfather?

Had Dr. Césaire been so nice to Emeric out of guilt? He'd given Em a career-changing surgery, arranged Em's reassignment from Hillside to Harlem, and gotten Em into the Swordsmen. Were these actions a sort of restitution for a wrong? Or had the man just been positioning the grandson of his old friend for influence and power at the side of his granddaughter?

Em's eyes met Al's, and she seemed to read Em's mind, or part of it.

"Are you still going to marry me?"

"What the hell kinda question is that?" It flew out of him

without any thought. Em took her into his arms, and couldn't imagine doing anything else. "*Stop* cryin'."

"The city is going to hate me when they find out. I'll never be able to work anywhere or show my face."

While he was assessing the relationship between their grandfathers, she panicked over what was in the letters. Every time she dragged air into her lungs, Emeric felt Al sucking it from his ribs.

How would they ever know what happened forty years ago, or at the turn of the century? The uncertainty was torture, but Emeric was certain of one thing. He was not leaving what he had with A'Lelia over a suspicion.

There was simply nothing to support Dr. Césaire being a full on murderer. Or at least, not as it concerned Em's grandfather. Em had followed up on what his mama said and checked, and he would always continue to pay attention and be watchful for whether those facts ever changed.

Right then, he bunched up the letters and stood.

That snatched her out of her stupor. "What are you doing?" Al finally managed.

Emeric flung it all into the fire. "Do you know if there's any other proof of this slavery stuff, or this invention thing? That man, Leopold, wrote that he had proof. What is it? Where do you think it's been the last sixty years?"

Al's red eyes flitted from one possibility to the next.

"Come on, baby, think."

Her hands shaking, she pressed her face. "I-I don't know about the invention, but for the slavery, the m-manifests… the shipping manifests, the cargo my ancestors insured, they're not consistent with bank deposits and withdrawals back then."

"So where are these manifests?"

In a panic, she rubbed her hands. "Some of…some of them are at the museum."

"So we can just take out the ones that look funny."

She stared at him, her face confessing that solution wouldn't be enough. "They're gone."

"What do you mean?"

"The day you proposed, Nadia Freeman was… interview Pépé, and she… my family made larger bank deposits than… goods we claimed we had insured."

Since she was somewhat hoarse, he could hardly understand parts of it.

"She was asking where the extra money came from." Al cleared her throat from sobbing, and composed herself. "I didn't think much of it at the time; I figured it was a discrepancy, or could be explained by another document somewhere. Until all this. So I went back to the museum to get the manifests, just in case, and they were gone. She must have taken them when Pépé almost fell and I ran to see about him. I came back distracted and locked the case without checking first."

In a sign of her state of mind, Al's head plummeted into her palms.

Emeric recalled what her grandfather had told him almost a year before.

Your money and success will increase in direct proportion to the tough choices you cannot avoid. Some of those choices might be the difference between literal life and death. Let your grandfather's life be your lesson. Choosing wrong could mean the downfall of your house.

Em had discussed some things with her grandfather over the past few months, but not on this level of the Cesaire ancestors' checkered past, or potentially even Theodore Césaire's own actions. Now, the man's warning made more sense.

Em brought Al to him and squeezed her. "Baby, stop."

"Emeric, getting rid of some papers is not going to shut

Nadia down," she wailed. "The Freemans have it in for our family, and they won't quit until we're on our knees and begging for mercy in the streets. They're going to destroy everything we've worked hard for. They hate us."

He thumbed away her tears. "I'm not gonna let that happen. I'll take care of it. Quit cryin'. You know I can't take that. What's this chick's name? Nadia? Pastor Freeman's daughter?"

"You can't do anything. I don't know why she hasn't written it yet. It's been four months. She'll probably black-mail us."

His mouth on her forehead, Em rejected that possibility.

"No, she won't. You don't worry about that part."

"Don't tell me not to worry. This is my life. *Our* lives. Do you understand how bad this is? There's no fixing it. My ancestors did terrible things, and at some point, it's coming out. I need to prepare for whatever Nadia does."

She was right, and Emeric would need time to think on how to deal with this, even if that meant going straight to Dr. Césaire for a sit-down. Whatever they wound up doing under the table, Em didn't want Al's hands getting dirty.

Along with possible plans entering his head, so too did his mama's voice.

I will not have you becoming one of these coldhearted, blood-sucking men that are all about money, showboating, and stabbing each other in the back. I don't want my good, sweet son turning into one of these people.

Not all of her concern had been rooted in paranoia. While comforting the woman he loved, he had to decide how much that comfort could eventually cost, for them both.

"It's my job to protect you, and that's what I'll do," he said to Al. "You won't be handling this alone."

"You're starting to sound like Pépé. What has he told you? What have you and him talked about?"

With Al's chin in his hand, he tipped her face. Kind, precious, smart, and good, she was worth any risk.

"He told me what my job is. And I accepted."

"So you're still going to marry into my family? Even after I told you I wasn't marrying you with your mother's issues against us. If this gets out, it could affect you and your career, too."

In front of the fire, Emeric gazed at his flame. "Me facing the what your dead ancestors did a hundred years ago is not the same as you facing my mother who is very much alive and in your face right now."

He held her face with both his hands now.

"But the only two people in this room are me and you, Al. Us against the world. Ancestors, mothers, grandfathers, dead or alive. What we do, from here on out, is about protecting you and me. Do you understand me?"

Sniffing back tears, Al nodded. The steely woman who'd locked him out of his car and wouldn't let him leave her behind was returning to herself. "Yes. You and me. Against everything and everybody."

"Right. Now I told you I would go with you anywhere, French. And that's what I meant. So don't ever ask me that shit again. I said I'll deal with this and I will."

Their heads glued together in a firm kiss, he felt Al relax her head against his.

"I love you, Emeric."

"I love you, too, baby girl, more than my own life."

~

"So, this woman's name is Nadia?" Lionel whispered at the altar. "Freeman? Her daddy is the one with the church?"

"Yeah." A jittery Emeric paused a moment to shake hands from attendees at his and Al's wedding and accept congratulations. "Apparently, this chick is some kind of reporter. I have no idea what she knows, or what she intends to do with it. I can't have her embarrassing Al, or hanging that over her head. She's finishing her PhD in the spring and then has to teach. My baby has never done a damn thing to anybody. She doesn't have time for this chick's BS. Just gimme a name. I'll handle the rest."

"Well, slow your strut there, good buddy. Let's put our heads together. I'll see what kind of dirt I can get you so you're ready. That way, your nose stays clean." Lionel slapped a nervous Emeric on the back. "Take a chill pill. This is your baby-making weekend, man. Put that first, and we'll figure out the rest in short order."

Like Lionel had summoned the moment, the bridal music cued up, and the attendees rose. Standing at the altar with Emeric were some of his Memphis crew, his brother-in-laws, friend from Morehouse, Lionel, and Harold.

At the other end of the church stood the most exquisite sight he would ever behold. Every bit as regal and sharp as the day he met her, he couldn't believe he woke up again this morning, to discover God still found him worthy of having this.

"Hi, baby," he murmured, and shook her father's hand.

Grateful, he finally lifted her veil over her head to behold all that was right and perfect in the world.

I love you, she mouthed.

I love you, too, he mouthed, terrified.

She was his now. Whatever threats they faced, Emeric would do any and everything in his power to keep Archduchess A'Lelia Antonia Cesaire-Habsburg McPherson safe. He hoped with his whole heart he got it right.

~

A'LELIA

"Are you kidding?" Jill whispered after the ceremony while they powdered up in the dressing room. Jill's jaw practically hung on the floor. "*Austria*? So you're not just the descendant of some random guy in Versailles—which was still righteous in itself—but you're the great-great granddaughter of an emperor, several times removed. You're related to Marie Antoinette?"

"You can't say a word." Al couldn't bear this alone.

"Of course not. So what does this mean? What will you do?"

"Apparently, there are legal matters Pépé wants taken care of. Emeric and I are going to France, and later this year, we'll head to Austria with lawyers to see what Pepe is talking about."

Jill squeezed Al's arm. "Oh, my God. Should I bow or curtsy or what?"

"Woman, get out of here." Al chuckled.

"Can I have a castle?"

"If you don't stop it." Al made her way out of the dressing room, and Jill carried her train for them to return to the dining hall.

"Have you mentioned it to BB?"

"Later, when she gets a little older. Knowing that child, she would run all around L.A., not speaking to people unless they bowed to her."

Al hadn't mentioned the other, more damaging information about her ancestors, how the Cesaires had stayed afloat in America and around the world. She told herself they had endured, and as a result, now they could help others.

She didn't want to think how their help would be received were it ever to come out what her forebears did to their own kin. It could destroy them. She hoped it would never come up again.

"Doctor and Mrs. McPherson, will you come over for photos, please?"

She would never grow tired of how Emeric lit up when he had her walk in front of him, or how his hand instinctively reached out for hers, or how her heart's flutter lifted her from her feet whenever he did.

"Everybody, say hello to Doctor and Mrs. McPherson. Community leaders and philanthropists already, they are stars brightly shining, the future of New York."

The END

After you leave your review at (CLICK THIS LINK HERE) on my web site, get your preview of one of the messiest marriages of the 80s. Roberta and Lionel kick off the Middleton saga in *Circa 1979*.)

Bibliography
LULA'S RESEARCH & SOURCE MATERIALS
FOR THOSE INTERESTED

CHAPTER 1

New York Draft Riots

New York Draft Riots- History.com Article

"Massacre of a Negro On Clarkson Street," referencing "The Riots at New York," *Harper's Weekly*, 1 August 1863.

"On This Day: New York City Draft Riots," in "Off the Grid," by Village Preservation Blog - Article

CHAPTER 2

Lenox Lounge History - "Sites of the Green Book: The Lenox Lounge." Article by Candacy Taylor.

"**The Historic Lenox Avenue,** Langston Hughes Called It 'Harlem's Heartbeat,'" 1887. Article by *Harlem World* Magazine.

CHAPTER 4

Black-owned Newspaper *Amsterdam News* - *Our Kind of People,* "Black Elite in New York City," Ch. 11, pp. 246. Graham, Lawrence. 1st ed. 1999. amsterdamnews.com

Croque Madam - "8 French Sandwiches to Eat Before You Die." Article by Pagoda, Maria. Apr. 1, 2024. (*Croque Monsieur listed under Chapter 14)

Resources for Dr. Cesaire's challenges in late 1800s

Black Gotham: A Family History of African Americans in Nineteenth Century New York City. Peterson, Carla. 2011

"Black Nativism: The European Immigrant in Negro Thought, 1830-1860." by Rubin, Jay. *Phylon (1960-),* vol. 39, no. 3, 1978, pp. 193–202. *JSTOR,* https://doi.org/10.2307/274515.

"The German Invasion," by James McCune Smith. *The Anglo-African Magazine* v.1. 1859, pp. 44.

CHAPTER 6

House's Barbershop- "Harlem's Rich History, Inside House's Barbershop." By Scales, Jeffrey H. Oct. 27, 2016.

Adele's Kitchen- "Around Harlem, A Long Winter Short on Work," by Serrin, William. Dec. 16, 1982.

Bronx is burning.

"The Bronx Is Burning" - Article & Podcast by Shoe Leather in Partnership With Columbia University Libraries

"Who Burned the Bronx"- Youtube video

"Decade of Fire" © 2020 - Documentary Homepage

DJ Kool Herc as the father of Hip Hop & "Breakin" Music

"'Come as you are': DJ Kool Herc and the birth of hip-hop." Article by Christie's. July 6, 2022.

"The History of Hip Hop." Article by Soc!ety Dance Academy.

"'How It All Got Started': DJ Kool Herc Talks Auction of Vintage Hip-Hop Memorabilia." Article by Browne, David. July 29, 2022.

CHAPTER 8

Police des Noirs and oppressive French laws against Blacks during reign of Louis XVI and Marie Antoinette-

African Europeans: An Untold History, Ch. 3, pp. 84. "The Transatlantic Slave Trade and the Invention of Race." Otele, Olivette. 2021. (****First Black Woman History Professor in Britain****)

Black Count: Glory, Revolution, Betrayal, and the Real Count of Monte Cristo," pp. 68. Reiss, Tom. 2012.

CHAPTER 9

On classism, elitism, and class division among Blacks

Our Kind of People, "Black Elite in New York City," Ch. 11, pp. 246. Graham, Lawrence. 1st ed. 1999.

Aristocrats of Color: The Black Elite, 1880-1920. Gatewood, Willard. 1990

The Original Black Elite: Daniel Murray and the Story of a Forgotten Era. Taylor, Elizabeth. 2017

CHAPTER 14

Croque Monsieur - "Croque Monsieur - the ultimate ham & cheese sandwich!"

CHAPTER 19

History of Well's Supper Club

"Well's Restaurant in Harlem, The Best Chicken and Waffles in the World 1938-1982." Aug. 10, 2020. Article by *Harlem World Magazine*

"The Layered Legacy of Roscoe's House of Chicken & Waffles." Sep. 8, 2020. Article by Adrian Miller. *Resy* Los Angeles. (Owner of Roscoe's Chicken & Waffles in Los Angeles acknowledges that he was inspired by Wells in Harlem. "People in the U.S. have been eating fried chicken and waffles since the 1700s…")

On the History of Africans, Blacks, & Wealth in Early New York

"African Burial Ground," Article by The New York Preservation Archive Project. Accessed February 7, 2025.

"Reflection and Remembrance: The African Burial Ground, 30 Years After Discovery," nypl.org, New York Public Library, Article by Herndon, Lisa. Oct. 4, 2021. Accessed February 7, 2025.

Black Manhattan. Johnson, James. 1930

"Before Central Park: The Story of Seneca Village," Centralparknyc.org, Article by Central Park Conservancy. Jan. 18, 2018. Accessed February 6, 2025.

"Inside Seneca Village: The Lost African-American Community in Central Park," Article by Scotto, Michael. Feb 5, 2020. Ny1.com

"NYC's Early African American Settlements: New Amsterdam's 'Little Africa': Maps, books, and images documenting the city's 17th-19th century Black settlements," libguides.nypl.org, Article by New York Public Library. Last Updated: Dec. 17, 2024. Accessed February 7, 2025. (*Also provides other articles on early slavery in early Black New York.)

"The End of the African American Welcome in Harlem, 1904." Excerpt from *Race and Real Estate: Conflict and Cooperation in Harlem, 1890-1920.* By McGruder, Kevin. Sep. 22, 2015

"The Encyclopedia of New York City" - Article in Virtual New York.

"The Very Different But Connected Economies of the Northeast and the South Before the Civil War," westga.edu, Article by Scott, Carole. Accessed February 7, 2025 (**Extensive list of major U.S. companies involved in slavery.**)

"Wealthy Black Landowners in Early Manhattan — how did they lose Greenwich Village and Brooklyn?" Feb. 12, 2019. Article by Grillet, Sophie.

"When Powerful White New Yorkers Demolished Seneca Village to Build Central Park," AllThatsInteresting.com, Article by Serena, Kate. Nov. 7, 2017. Accessed February 6, 2025.

CHAPTER 24

Sylvia's Restaurant —History of celebrities, i.e., Nina Simone, Ruby Dee, Ossie Davis, Cicely Tyson, Adam Clayton Powell. "Finding Soul Food, and Comfort, at Sylvia's," "Unpublished Black History," by Rachel L. Swains, Darcy Eveleigh, & Damien Cave, *New York Times Article*

Menu at Sylvia's — Schomburg Center for Research in Black Culture, Manuscripts, Archives and Rare Books Division, The New York Public Library. "Sylvia's Restaurant" *The New York Public Library Digital Collections*. 1900 - 2014. https://digitalcollections.nypl.org/items/3e100c60-6220-0132-531f-58d385a7bbd0

CHAPTER 29

More than 10,000 nerve endings in clitoris - Uloko M, Isabey EP, Peters BR. "How many nerve fibers innervate the human glans clitoris: a histo-morphometric evaluation of the dorsal nerve of the clitoris." J Sex Med. 2023 Feb 27;20(3):247-252. doi: 10.1093/jsxmed/qdac027. PMID: 36763957.

CHAPTER 32

French Grandmother's Lemon Yogurt Cake — https://thecafesucrefarine.com/french-grandmothers-lemon-yogurt-cake/

CHAPTER 34

Wall Street's Involvement in Slavery

"'Cargo' was delivered to the southern states and the West Indies, but much of the shipping originated in New York City—in the abolitionist North." Article by Harris, John. (The Atlantic Slave Trade Continued Illegally in America Until the Civil War)

"Munipal Bonds: How Slavery Built Wall Street," Article by Miles, Tiya. pulitzercenter.org. Accessed February 7, 2025.

"New York City's Long and Shameful History of Slavery," Scenawolf, Harry. Article in revolutionarywarjournal.com

"People Not Property: Exploring the Legacy of Slavery in New York's Hudson Valley," Article by Bradley, Elizabeth; Lord, Michael, in Humanities New York. humanitiesny.org. ("Slavery's legacy in New York was hidden, almost invisible.") Accessed February 7, 2025.

CHAPTER 36

British Windsors Not Helping the Russian Romanovs

"Did King George V Betray the Romanovs? The Truth Behind the Russian Massacre, as shown in *The Crown*." Article by Bridger-Linning, Stephanie. Nov. 15, 2022.

"The Kaiser, The Tsar, and King George V - Cousins At War in WWI." Article in history.co.uk

Assassination of Austrian Archduke

"The Assassination of Archduke Franz Ferdinand." Article by Greenspan, Jessse. June 26, 2014.

Leave a review and let's stay connected!

If these characters found a home in your heart, or you made your home among these families of New York, or you valued the depth of research and history, let's be friends! Use the QR code below and choose your social platform of choice. You have no shortage of options for where to go read now. Thank you for trusting me with your time and emotions.

If you bought this directly from me, I press a lot of heart, thought, and study into the craft. If you would kindly take a moment to leave an honest review on my web site, that helps assure other readers that they too will receive more than a fantastic story, but an experience. The link to review this book is HERE.

If you bought this book from a retailer, then please go back to the retailer and write up your honest thoughts!

Again, thank you so much and if you need to reach me, the ways you can do that are below.

Web site: www.lulawhitebooks.com

Email: lula@lulawhitebooks.com

Instagram: https://www.instagram.com/lulawhitebooks/

Tiktok: https://www.tiktok.com/@lulawhitebooks

Youtube: www.youtube.com/@lulawhitebooks

Join Lula's Luxe Suite Reading Group:

www.facebook.com/groups/lulawhite

LULA'S BOOKS - FOR BOOKS ALREADY IN PUBLICATION, CLICK ON THE BOOK TITLE TO VISIT THE PRODUCT PAGE

Books in the *Metamorphosis* series

Who's Lovin' You?

Circa 1979 (Spring 2026)

Of Warriors & Women (2027)

Of Tyrants & Terror (2027)

Books In The *Sag Harbor Black Romances*

Brown Sugar This Christmas - Maddy & Jerrell

Hot Chocolate This Winter - Chrissy & Sheldon Part 1

Flinging All Spring - Adella & Desmond

Overheated for Summer - Chrissy & Sheldon Part 2

Rouse Family Christmas - All Couples

Books in the Sag Harbor spin-off series *Explore Men of the Hamptons*

Christmas Down Under (FREE PREQUEL NOVELLA) - Keenan & Eugenia

Explore You - Kevin & Cher

One Tasty Night (FREE PREQUEL NOVELLA) - Solomon & Chaitra

Taste You - Solomon & Chaitra

Drink You - Lion & Kamila

See Through You - Keenan & Eugenia

Find You - Roland & Neeraja

Books in the *Young & Luxurious* series

Love and Fire - Korienne & Easton

Stand-Alones

The Gift of Us

A New Life for Christmas